Fire
Fury
Freedom

By Amanda Rose

"A veritable saga of a dystopian novel by an author with a genuine flair for detailed originality, and narrative driven storytelling... an extraordinary and truly memorable read from cover to cover."

- The Midwest Book Review

"Powerful and riveting, the characters come to life immediately and tell and engrossing tale...10/10."

- Jeremy Spire, Author of Shadow of Serenity

"Nothing makes science fiction more palatable than great world-building, and Fire Fury Freedom has world-building in spades. The lore is deep enough to get lost in, and you'll be having fun every minute of it."

- Andrew Fantasia, Author of SideScroller

Amanda Rose

© 2018 Amanda Rose

amanda@amandarosefitness.com

Cover by Daniel McCutcheon

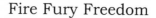

Dedication

I dedicate this book to all the big dreamers; imagination is our greatest strength.

Chapter 1: Boom

"There's no time, just grab and go!" a tall woman with short spiked auburn hair called out as she slung a black backpack over her right shoulder and sprinted away. It was a dark office, with little light shining in from the waning moon. Looking back she called once more as she opened the door, "The one surprise we left will be enough to cause a huge fuss, and if you don't watch it you might wind up part of the 'big bang'! Suako get a move on!" she insisted.

After a few more keystrokes on the control panel Suako looked up, brushing her long brown hair off of her sweat drenched face to reveal an enormous grin, "I thought they might have problems sharing." Throwing her tools into a bag, and shoving her pistol into her belt, she quickly stood up and began to dash toward the tall redheaded woman. Suako glanced at her watch, "Mei you ready?" She asked as they sprinted down the corridor of a large building. "Do I have a choice?" Mei asked light heartily, as she panted, exhausted from running.

The girls stopped dead in their tracks at the end of the hall. Both looked puzzled and panicked. "Shit, which way?" Mei asked aloud. As Suako was about to speak the door to their left flung open. Suako drew her pistol, and Mei pulled out a knife from a holster around her ankle. Two young men, at opposite ends of the twenties age spectrum, and one older man in his late thirties, all dressed in combat clothing which matched that of the girls, came hurtling through the doors. "Whoa!

It's Kato, don't shoot!" the young black male gasped when he saw the women. Mei and Suako breathed a sigh of relief. "A little on edge?" the older man asked as he slammed the door shut behind him, locking it. Mei shook her head with disbelief and put her knife away. "I thought you guys got out already?"

"We can't stay long, *they* know we're 'ere, talk 'n walk, but keep your voices down," Kato said as he marched on forward and kicked open the door to his right. "Vince, how close are we to the exit?" asked Mei. "I have no idea, Mack?" Vince asked, looking over to the older man. "The exits will have been blocked off by this point; we need to get down to the storm drains. We can't use the elevators, or they'll know, but we can use the shafts. The stairs are too risky at this point. Sub level is where we need to get. That's seven stories down. We've got..." he looked to his watch, "just under twenty minutes, let's move!"

They all nodded, and turning a corner, they saw the elevator doors. Kato and Mei went to work on pinning them open. Suako looked over to Vince and noticed blood dripping from his arm. "They got you. Here, wrap this around the wound," She said handing him some cotton wrap. He nodded. "Thanks. The bullet just skimmed me. I'm alright," He said stoically, as he began to wrap his arm. Suako tied it off when he was finished.

Mei and Kato managed to pry the doors open. Suako pulled off her jacket and began ripping it into strips. "Everyone tie this around your hands so we can shimmy down the wire cables. We don't have time to stop for splinter injuries," she threw a piece to everyone and they covered their hands. "Everyone quiet!" Mack suddenly ordered in a harsh whisper. An echo of heavy combat boots rang up through the nearby stairwell. Their hearts began racing, Mei looked to Mack and nodded, "Let's get a move on, we can't get caught before the fireworks! Suako you first, grab a wire and start moving down."

Suako wiped the sweat from her brow with her forearm. Briefly closing her eyes, she deeply inhaled, then stepped forward to the empty elevator shaft. It seemingly stretched down forever into an abyss of darkness. "Now or never," she told herself under her breath. Reaching forward she caught a death grip on the wire, then hopped her feet off of the floor and quickly clung to the wire with them. Vince was getting onto the wire beside her. Reality quickly hit hard, and she accelerated her pace moving down the line.

Soon everyone but Mei had got onto the wire and started descending. Mack held onto the wire and hadn't moved down yet. Quickly and carefully Mei held onto the edge of the floor, then swung her legs up to Mack, who then attached her feet to his jacket. Adrenaline was pumping at its max through each of their systems. "Don't let me fall Mack," she said, looking over her shoulder to him. His eyes met hers and he gave a slight head tilt of indication.

Taking a tear gas explosive from her pocket, she set and threw it down the hall. She then immediately pulled the pins out from the base of the elevator doors, and allowed her body to drop back. The doors slammed shut, it was suddenly pitch black.

Mei hung upside down from Mack's waist. Holding on with one hand he reached to help pull her upright with the other hand. "Y'all ok?" Mack grunted, his deep voice echoing down. "Yes," came Kato and Suako's replies simultaneously. "Anyone got a light?" Vince chuckled. They snickered and carefully kept pressing forward. Mack managed to help Mei onto the wire next to him. "Good to go Mei?" he asked. "I'm a little disoriented, but otherwise good to go," she said.

"Double time people, before lights out we were at sixteen minutes!" Mack's voice boomed. "Oh shit!" Kato exclaimed as he sped up. The darkness was deceiving, and time pressed over their heads. Not until they were able to see a slight bit of light near the bottom had they known anything of their whereabouts. Each one was relieved to feel firm ground beneath their feet again. They quickly forced open the doors at the bottom of the elevator shaft.

They made haste to look for manhole entrances into the cities sewer system. "Mack, time?" Kato asked as he scanned the floor with his eyes. "Two minutes and counting. Let's make this quick people!" He called ahead to the team. "Found it!" Mei called from the front. The others dashed to her. Suako and Kato helped her lift the metal disk up. Vince tied back his shoulder length brown hair, looking over to Kato he joked, "Hope you don't get anything stuck in your beard down there, bud." After placing down the heavy cover he looked to Vince, "It's a goatee man!" then stood and waited for the girls to finish climbing down into the sewer before swinging his legs down onto the ladder and going in after them. "Vince get your punk ass down there now!" Mack ordered pointing to the hole. Vince and Mack scurried downward.

Abruptly Mack's watch began beeping. "Get ready!" Mack said as he dropped down into the filth below. Everyone threw themselves against the wall for support. The ground began to rumble, and an earth-shattering explosion could be heard from above. The roar of it infiltrated the tunnel and rebounded off of stone walls. The earth shook as if there had been an earthquake, and tiny pieces of stone feel from the walls. The intense vibrations nearly caused them to fall over. The deafening noise surrounded them. "Keep moving!" Mack yelled above the roar of the blast.

Suako tried to yell over the noise "There's more then just that!" and with that she scampered down the cylinder corridor. The others followed, trying their best to maintain balance against the intensely shaking ground beneath them. Finally, after several minutes they came across an opening above them, leading up to the streets of the city. "Over here!" Suako called to the others, "I think we're just in time to see the show!"

They climbed up the ladder and onto the streets near the subway entrance. The five of them looked back to a seemingly far off building, reaching up into the sky with flames bursting out of it. One roaring explosion after another fired its way out of the building like an erupting volcano. The fire blazed in its glory as black smoke billowed up into the night sky.

"It's a beautiful sight, but we should get moving. *The Company* will send out agents after us shortly. Split up and meet back at the grid eight warehouse. Don't use the subways systems either, the stench of the storm drains are a giveaway," Mack walked off. Slowly the others pulled their attention away from the slowly collapsing building. Mei and Kato scurried off toward a vacant truck. The street was vacant. The area was destitute, as were many of the surrounding grids around the Companies headquarters on prestine grid one. The ground had shattered glass and other such garbage littered on it.

Suako looked to Vince, "We need to make sure you're not infected." He looked at his arm, "Kato has disinfectant back at the hideout, he can check it out. Let's get a move on," he turned his attention to her and then signalled her to follow his lead. They started forward and crossed through a junkyard; Suako maintained a hand on his pistol, ready to draw at any time. "See any wheels we can salvage?" she asked scanning the area. "Nothing that wouldn't require a lot of time... look ahead, the sun's gonna' rise soon. We need to get to grid eight quickly. Come over here," he said as he walked over to a flat piece of metal that stretched out from a pile of miscellaneous scraps.

Vince pulled a map from the back pocket of his pants. Rolling it out it over the metal frame he showed Suako the layout of the grid system. Each grid area was in the shape of a square. Grid one, the Company's headquarters location, was four times as large as the other grid squares. Twelve squares lined the outside rim of grid one, coming to a grand total of thirteen grids that combined to form the city, Torusan. The number two grid was located to the north-western most section and then the numbers started their count in a clockwise manner. "Here we are in grid eleven, we just have to cross through grid ten & nine and we're home free. It's too far to walk if we want to get there before too many eyes get a glimpse of us. What do you propose?"

Suako paused a moment looking all around herself. "This discarded metal isn't going to help us any. Mack said no subway, but if we can find a change of clothes we can pull it off. Easier to steal clothing than a vehicle, do you agree?" After a few seconds staring down at the map of Torusan, Vince came back with his reply, "Agreed, where to?"

Suako turned away and started walking off. Vince grabbed his map and shoved it in his pocket, then hurried to catch up to her. "This area may be impoverished but they still sell clothing. The stores won't open for a little while yet," She explained. "We can't leave a trail; the company will catch onto our us in no time flat if they suspect it's us..."

"Halt!" a voice without warning called from behind them. Suako spun around and drew her gun. Vince pulled a short sword from a holster around his back. "Who are you?" Suako demanded. "You're under arrest!" A voice called as a figure came forth from behind a pile of rubble. It was a *Company* guard, his gun drawn and aimed at Suako's head. "Drop your weapons!" he ordered.

"Ready Vince?" Suako whispered. "Yeah," he concurred. With that Suako fired her pistol knocking the guard's gun from his hands. Meanwhile Vince dashed forward, using a leg sweep the guard fell flat on his face. Vince pinned the guard to the ground, using his knee in the small of the man's back to hold him down. Pressing the blade of his sword to the guard's neck, he looked over to see Suako walking up. "Who else is headed this way?" Vince questioned the man.

In slight shock, the guard responded in a cold sweat, "N-no one... I'd been tracking you since the storm drain... I'd thought it was an evacuation drill! I didn't who you were until you emerged above, I swear..." he responded in a slight daze. "Did you call for back up?" The guard was mumbling something beneath his breath. "I said 'did you call for back up?'!" Vince pressed his sword on the man's neck with an increased amount of pressure. "No, my radio broke... It was smashed in the explosion!" he insisted attempting to pull away from the blade. Vince turned his attention back to Suako. She placed her gun away. "He's likely telling the truth," she said. Vince pulled the sword away from the guard's neck and thumped him with the handle on the back of the head rendering him unconscious. "He'll be out long enough for us not to be tracked," Vince said standing up.

Within the outskirts of grid ten, just as the sun peered over the horizon, they stumbled onto a tiny clothing shop. Suako pulled a safety pin off of her pants, pulled it apart and used it to pick the lock. "Nice trick, where'd you pick that one up?" Vince asked as he kept a vigil.

"Hurry, they'll be here any minute! I can't die here, not like this... What's taking so long? Common, common!"
"Just let me work it. I've only ever seen this done before."
"We don't have time! They're gonna get us...."
"Just shut up unless you want to die in this cell!"

Suako stood there, eyes wide open, not moving, gazing at the door in a trance. "Suako? Suako are you alright?" Vince suddenly interrupted and placed his hand on her shoulder. Suako put him into an arm lock and firmly spoke; "You won't get us today!" intensity burned in her eyes, then gradually faded as she came back to realize reality. Heart pulsing and in confusion she let him go "S... Sorry Vince..." She apologized shook her head and went back to picking the lock on the door. Vince pressed the issue no further.

Seconds later there was a click and the door opened. She nodded to Vince and they entered the shop, quickly pulled off their dirty garments and put on clean clothes from the racks. Shoving their old clothing into Suako's backpack, they wished to leave no trace. "The world is starting to wake up out there," Suako stood frozen momentarily as she listened to footsteps outside. She turned her head to see Vince and he tossed her bag back to her and finished pulling a sweater over his head.

Quickly he looked just outside the door. "Good ears, no ones there right now, common before they show up."

They fled from the store and went down the street. "Vince slow down, I want to get the hell out of here just as bad as you do, but we have to avoid detection. Act Normal." Vince lessened his pace and took in one long deep breath. The sun graced the earth and slowly but surely everyone was out about doing their daily chores.

After a mile-long nerve-wracking speed walk they finally approached the subway. The train was jam-packed. Suako and Vince blended in as best they could. Finally sitting down they felt home free as they were carried off to their destination.

Mei had fallen asleep against he truck window with a small smile painted upon her pale face. Kato glanced over at her and saw the sun shine playing off of the colors vibrant in her hair. The streets were bleak. Houses and shops poorly constructed, out of the cheapest materials around, lined the grids gravel streets. Many homeless slept on the street under newspapers and broken streetlights lined the area. Children played with the remnants of ruined items that gave the illusion that the area was a dumping ground, which wasn't far from the truth.

Looking over to his left as he crossed over a slight incline Kato could see the metropolis of grid one. The enormous central building could be seen even from afar. The cobblestone streets were clean, homes were all like palaces, and parks safe for children to play were found on every block. A grand fence separated grid one from the other grids, attempting to keep all other people from entering their 'perfect world'. Turning his attention back to the road Kato clenched his fists around the steering wheel and shook his head in disbelief.

A half hour later they entered grid eight. Reaching over, Kato gently stroked Mei's cheek with his rough calloused finger. "Mei," he said gently, "we're almost there." She slowly came to, yawned and had a big stretch, "Thanks for waking me... How long was I out?" "Nearly since you stepped in the truck, you had at least a good hour of sleep." Sleepily she rubbed her eyes and sat up in the seat.

As they approached the gates of the warehouse they saw Suako and Vince half way to the doors. They drove across the lot and up to their two companions where they offered to drive them the last thirty some odd feet to the entrance. They hopped out of the back of the pickup and opened the doors from Kato to drive in.

The inside of the hideout was covered in old rusted car parts, and useless tools. A fair size table with cheaply knocked together metal stools around it, and there was a large chalkboard on wheels behind the furthest chair back. Running water could faintly be heard, and then dissipated. "Guess Mack was determined to be the first to shower," Vince chuckled. "And I suppose you two were determined to be the first to look good in your snazzy clothes, hmm?" Kato asked with a coy expression on his face. Mei giggled as she sat on a stool leaning up against the table.

Mack strutted out into the room, pulling a white muscle shirt on, barely covering his numerous scars. "Waters good and warm," he said. Mei and Suako both got up and headed towards the back to shower. "We won't be long," Mei called back as they went off. "Vince you got first watch. If the *Company* is on our trail they'll show up within the next hour guaranteed, otherwise we can assume we're in the clear." "I'm on it," Vince replied, and grabbed an automatic rifle as he walked out.

"So now what boss?" Kato asked as he reclined on a wooden chair. "We've cut down on the carbon dioxide emissions somewhat, but we haven't really crippled them. With the power C.D.F.P. Inc. has they'll have the grid eleven generators rebuilt as soon as they can clear away the debris of the building we just blew. After the reactors are back in motion, the company will follow up by creating another monstrosity of a work facility. The citizens of Torusan live naive to the fact, or powerless to stop it. C.D.F.P. Inc. has created an artificial dome of oxygen around the entire city. As you can tell it's depleting around the edges. Stepping outside of the city the air is hard to breathe, but not bad enough to need a portable oxygen tank with you, at least not yet. It would have been one thing to have just started their plan of idiocy and produce all of the carbon dioxide, but they clear cut forests away for miles, using wood as heat energy. It only fuelled the city in such a manner for three years. Forests just as far as your eye could see, destroyed to fill their pockets and add two stories onto their already oversized houses.

The other cities around the continent that don't permit the building of C.D.F.P. generators don't get the benefit of an oxygen dome. Due to that, the cities are more inclined to comply with the Company... How can't they? Without the domes now it's damn near impossible to live. I don't know what we can do to stop them. We've barely even given them a scratch..." Mack looked down at the floor, feeling defeated.

"Boss, we just don't have enough information to go on. These other places around the continent have to have more information. If we draw attention away from Torusan and get them to send employees to fix up some messes in other places we may get to have a reign of fire here. That should give us enough time to attend to the oxygen scare, right?" "Good idea's Kato, but it won't be so simple. You see, they may be put off for some time, but they'll still rebuild. You were onto something though, we don't know enough..." Mack replied.

"Feels good to be clean," Suako announced as she came around the corner drying her hair. Mei came out a moment after, doing up her belt. "Vince on watch?' Mei asked looking to Mack. He looked up at her with eyes pulled out of deep thought and nodded. "I'll go take watch," Mei said and headed toward the doors. "So, Mack..." Suako started as she sat down, "...what's next on the agenda?" she asked putting her feet up on the table. "Kato and I had just been talking about that... we think we're going to have to leave the city." Suako's eyes shot open at the mere suggestion. "Whoa, whoa, whoa!" she exclaimed rising on her feet. "Hold up Mack. It's a barren wasteland out there! Do we even know where the next city is? Could we even survive it?" Suako began hyperventilating.

Vince strutted up to them, and looked around the table at them in slight confusion. "Everything all right?" he pondered, eyes on Suako. "Take a seat," Kato told him. Sitting down, still baffled Vince's eyes circled the members at the table several times over before Mack finally spoke. "Suako, you're young, and I know you've never left the confines of Torusan so I understand all you have to go off of are the stories you've been told. Indeed, the outer world is a place scarce of life. Without food and water with us we would perish very quickly. In the outer world your body weakens and you become quite fatigued from the lack of oxygen. The journey is challenging, but it is not impossible. I know of a traveller who has mapped most of our continent, cities are scarce as not all cities have the artificial oxygen; those without had to evacuate to live elsewhere."

Suako took the news in like an arrow through her heart. Vince's jaw dropped: it looked as if a pile of bricks had hit him. A single tear strolled down Suako's cheek, "C.D.F.P. shouldn't stand for 'Corporate Distribution Fuel Power'; the initials are better suited to describe them as 'Crazy Dumb Foolish People'." Before she could rage on further Kato patted her on the back to console her.

"So, boss, where's this traveler friend of yours?" Kato inquired. "He's in the south-eastern part of grid three," Vince snapped into attention "You've got to be kidding!" The other three looked to him with raised brows. "Don't tell me you haven't heard?" Vince asked. "Heard what?" Kato questioned. "Well you've all seen the security fence that surrounds the first grid right? Well C.D.F.P. decided a few months ago that they'd have each individual grid monitored, probably because of *our jobs*, like the one last night. Word is that they've already completed grid two and have started construction on grid three. Now they have guards watch everyone who comes and goes past the border into each grid system they're fencing in. With last nights 'big boom', I'm pretty sure security will be tight. I can't speak for the rest of you, but I have prior felons of which the C.D.F.P. police have made me serve time for before, all past criminals are likely to be taken in for questioning, wouldn't you agree?" "He's right. Mei!" Suako called. Mei came in and jogged over to them, "Yes?" "You and I, fake I.D. card duty, let's get going," Suako said as she stood up.

"Alright, it's settled then. As soon as the cards have been completed we leave to go to grid three. Let's prepare water canisters, weapons, ammo, clothing, and don't forget your teddy bear's boys, ha-ha!" Mack grinned, lighting his cigar. "Right, Kato and I will take weapons duty," Vince said as he walked toward the back of the warehouse. Kicking the dirt floor away he revealed a handle. Together he and Kato pulled open a colossal steel hatch to reveal a seemingly ultimate collection of artillery. "Shall we?" Vince cheekily suggestively gestured.

Here we go, it's all new territory from here...

Chapter 2: The Map Maker

"The sun's setting, now's as good a time as any," Mei suggested loading the last bit of baggage into the back of the truck. They all climbed into the truck, except Mack. Standing by his building, he looked over the old rusting storehouse facility before leaving it behind. Climbing in, Mack turned the key to ignite the ignition then drove away. Half way down the long winding road leading away from the storehouse they passed several military vehicles; on closer inspection the writing on the side read: 'C.D.F.P. Inc. Military Division'. Along with the land team a helicopter flew overhead.

"Mack, as soon as they can't see us anymore step on it! It won't take them long to figure out it's us, if we're the ones they're going down this road for," Kato said as he watched the cars in the rear-view mirror slowly pass a curve and vanish out of sight. Mack rapidly accelerated, trying to take them as far from the C.D.F.P. as possible. "I wouldn't worry, by the time they figure out it was us we'll be long gone. For a night raid they're idiots; if we'd still been there that helicopter would've been fair warning for us to get the hell out of there," Mack said shaking his head and rolling his eyes. "Praise be to stupidity," Mei added.

Mack drove throughout the night. They passed through one underdeveloped neighbourhood after another, quickly reminded of the bounty of grid one residents by simply looking to the horizon. By grid five the journey had become monotonous. The indigo sky and crescent moon watched over them as they travelled. As they neared the next border, the truck suddenly stalled and then died on them. Mei rolled her eyes as she opened the door, "Guess that's what we get for stealing from an area that can't afford to get their vehicles checked." "Alright everyone, let's take what we can carry and hightail it out of here. Just take the essentials; we've got a few hour hike ahead of us," Mack ordered. Taking the artillery and water, the troop discarded most other items in the truck, then Mack put it into neutral and then they pushed it into a ditch.

After a short stroll, they came upon grid four's entrance. No one patrolled this area; most grids were hard to define as definite sectors. They made there way through the filthy streets. Very few people resided in sector four, it was a dumping ground for the leftovers garbage of the company's fossil fuels. The stagnant air lingered and made them light headed. Taking a detour around the only protected building of the region, the generator, they eyed it down with heavy hearts.

Stopping dead in his tracks, eyes glued forward, Vince muttered, "Oh no... they're ahead of schedule." The others turned their attention to where his focus was. The entire area was sealed off. "We can't get in that way, they'll search our things," Kato spoke their mutual thought. Mack climbed atop a pile of coal. Looking across the horizon he squinted to see that to the south was the only place that the construction of the mass fencing hadn't begun as of yet, and all the attention of the C.D.F.P. military concerned at the immediate area fabrication. "To the far south we'll cross," he called down to them.

When they eventually arrived, the sun was just beginning to poke its head up over the horizon, illuminating the sky behind them. They managed to sneak in undetected. A few moments later they happened upon the house they were searching for. "Here it is," Mack announced as he rapped on the door. Seconds later a rough voice called out from within and harshly spoke to them, "Who is it?" the voice bellowed out to them. "It's Mack!" They heard heavy footsteps approach the door, followed by a long sequence of clicking noises from the door as it was being unlocked. The house was small and falling to pieces. The splintered door swung inward and a tall, muscular man stepped forward to greet them. "Well why didn't you say so?!" the gruff voice of the man said as he cocked his head to the side. Observing the other members of Mack's entourage, the man introduced himself. "Come in! Come in! I'm Jenko."

They walked inside of his home. The couch cushions were torn, only one half of a window had curtain, broken bookshelves lined the walls, stains covered the floor and numerous holes decorated the walls. His home fit the regular status of an outer grid dwelling; and he could even be considered lucky to have a fair amount of furniture, even falling apart as it was, to furnish the place. "How're you holding up old man?" Mack asked leaning against the wall. "Old man? I'm only a few years your senior! Take a seat," he offered, reclining himself on the couch. "What can I do you for Mack?" he asked. Mack lit up a cigar as the others sat. Kato stood watch at the window. "We're leaving the city Jenko. We need some info info and we could also use your map, we need a reference. We can't get lost out there, it'd be the death of us," he explained as he expelled the smoke from his lunges. A sudden shimmer glazed over Jenko's deep blue eyes. "I can do better then that, I'll be your guide. I've been meaning to get out of here… but what're you leaving for?"

"We need to gather more information about C.D.F.P. from outside forces," Mei began. Vince continued, "We're not getting anywhere hitting one generator at a time within the city. Sooner or later they'll catch on if we did them one after another, say within a week, they'd buckle down security and catch us before we could even get three of them. We need a way to take them down for good." "I get it," Jenko heartily agreed stroking his hand threw his short blonde hair. His eyes darted back and forth several times, then crossed over to Mack. "Alright I'm in. I need a little time to prepare. Unfortunately at that point the perimeter gate's construction will be completed before we get out. We'll have to leave using the Torusan sub city." "Sub city?" Vince questioned.

Suako wrinkled her brow, "Yeah, what 'sub city'?" Mack took one long deep inhale of his cigar and then pushed it out as he began to clarify, "Thirty some odd years ago C.D.F.P. evacuated all of Torusan to a temporary facility constructed to house us temporarily while they put into effect their 'two story city' idea. You see, the entire original foundation of the Torusan you know now is all metal, mostly a steel base, that's why we have grid sections you see. Each grid is an individual metal plate of which they have built upon. They extended up the entire city, and began to dig down beneath the earth."

"When they neared the end of the underground construction the supports above began giving out. The plates fell back to the earth. The shock wave of the collapsed city we assumed was an earthquake; the tremors could be felt vibrating for miles. Although the plan they envisioned had failed, because they dug down into the earth to create the second layer of city, it was unharmed by the fall. They were still going to use it, but a few of the grids wound up with random cave ins. Grid four was particularly bad for dropping debris, that's why they all but modified it into a waste site. The head of safety maintenance wouldn't allow its usage. Nevertheless, some people did move down there and the area is completely accessible. You remember in grid eleven, the storm drains? Well they lead down to the sub city beneath the ground, we can enter that way from here," Mack finished.

"Let's rock n' roll. We need to get out of here ASAP; C.D.F.P. has their military patrol checking houses close to the border. I'm guessing it's due to our little explosion at the grid eleven reactor," Kato said turning from the window. Mei looked over to Jenko, "What do you need? We can help." Jenko told them his essentials for land travel requirements. They attended to his things while Kato kept an eye on the relative closeness of the ever-nearing C.D.F.P. employees.

20 minutes later time had run out. "Time's up, we need to leave now," Kato insisted. Jenko finished shoving a map into his bag, tossing it over his shoulder he nodded. "We'll need to go out the back; they'll see us leave if we use the front door," Kato informed them. "Follow me, there's a window to the back," Jenko told them, signalling with his head for them to follow. They promptly went after him, into a bathroom, that they then squeezed through a tiny window from, and dropped onto the dirt ground below. Before leaving, Suako turned to Jenko "Where's the closest entrance to the storm drain?" pondering for a moment he then replied, "Not far, two streets over there's one far enough from the construction sight that we wont be seen," he led them onward.

Succeeding entering the storm drain system unseen they all felt a slight relief to be out of plain view. As they pressed on, Mei surveyed Jenko with her busy eyes and asked, "Are you packing any heat?" "Since I stopped travelling, I sold everything." He replied. Mei passed him a handgun. Jenko put it away, "Can't be too careful with these underground dwellers." Mei smiled at his comment and Jenko laughed rapturously.

After travelling outside for several minutes down the pipes they came across a large metal shaft in the floor. Vince, Mei and Kato quickly went to work lifting it up. They looked down into the darkness below, taking out a flashlight and shinning it around the could see that the Sub City was quite far down. Jenko removed a rope from his bag which they tied onto a pipe running across the ceiling and threw down the rest into the endless darkness below. The end of the rope reached to the top of some sort of structure of which they couldn't yet define with their limited sight. One by one they slid down the rope and onto the large flat surface beneath. While descending, they noticed how immense the space below was. It was like a lost ancient city from ages ago; preserved in a manner just short of perfection. Although it was dark, the spacious feeling was captivating. The secret city lined the floor like a bed of coral reefs in the sea.

Landing on the platform one by one they decided to attach illuminating phosphorescent wristbands to distinguish each other's location. Suako squinted, looking all around in every direction, "Do you suppose the C.D.F.P. actually made this for the people in the outer grids to benefit from and live in?" "I highly would doubt that. I believe their plan was to have the working class stay where they were and then use this second city for rich people from other cities to move to. They'd hemorrhage even more money then. The C.D.F.P. has never cared about anyone but themselves. Always remember that Suako," Vince told her in his own disgust for them.

It soon became apparent that they were standing on top of a ventilation shaft that they assumed must have been meant for a metal works factory. Climbing down a ladder they'd found on the side of the building they finally reached the streets below. Their feet dropped upon hard concrete, flawlessly preserved, unused and what those above have longed for to be their roads. A constant sound of running water echoed through the colossal underground. Suako looked around, on guard, as they marched through the area.

Time passed as they searched the region, stumbling through the dark, heading toward a light indicating the exit far to the north-west. "Mack, I haven't seen the slightest signs of life down here. I thought you said people lived here?" Suako whispered cautiously, staying alert. "I heard there were a few homeless who'd snuck down at first, though C.D.F.P. cleared everyone out of here. Jenko was just pulling your leg. I doubt if anyone was here, there's no abundant food or water source, and to travel all the way to the surface and back on a constant basis... well, you know, it's not logical," he shrugged. Suako breathed a sigh of relief.

The emptiness of such a frozen city was odd and felt quite unnatural to the ways of life above ground. As their eyes adjusted more to the darkness they could better see the city of which they had penetrated. Tall skyscraper like buildings lined the exterior edge of this lower grid frame. Many reactors and factories were in a central location while residences spiralled around them. Many buildings had left shattered glass and the streets after the floating city above crashed down upon them.

"In here," Jenko waved them over. Entering vacant makings of a hotel, they soon found it furnished much to their delight. They filtered into a large room. "Take a seat," Jenko instructed. He took a flare from his pack to assist showing them the map of the outer world, "This is the continent as best as I could depict. We're here in the south-westerly corner. As you can see from above on the horizon directly north of us it looks like a mountain, well there's actually several, but they create a wall vertically, so it only looks like one from our standpoint here. There is a small town buried within the sanctum of the mountainous walls. It's the nearest town, called Yukoton; I thought we'd strike there first. Any objections?" He looked around the room and no one objected. "Great," Jenko rolled his map and put it away. "I suggest we rest while we're here. The next few days will require a lot of strength from each of you. The mountains only allow those whom have the strength and willpower from within to venture their pathways," With that, he extinguished his flare and they soon fell asleep up on the soft plush beds of which they would be missing all too soon.

Though time had passed, the lack of sunlight left them in a slight state of confusion. They were instinctually disoriented by the difference in surrounding. Mack prompted the departure and they soon pulled themselves out of there. The Ghost City of Blackness soon came to an end; a decent opening between the metal grid and the ground allowed them passage. It was a struggle to ascend as they soon felt the air thinning with each breath. "Everyone cover your skin before you come out the top. The sun will scar you with boils if you expose your skin for any good length of time," Jenko warned them as he pulled a large cloaking jacket around himself. The others followed his lead.

"Let me give you a hand," Jenko offered Suako, who the last one to rise out from the sub city, and see the reality of the real world from outside the dome of Torusan. A painfully scorching heat burned their skin. The land was barren, scarce of life, no roaming creatures, trees nor bushes in sight. Suako's eyes began to well up with tears; an ache pulsed in her chest. Stuttering she finally placed a sentence together, "T-they did this?" she asked with a weak voice, her innocence shining through brightly. "They offered the people electricity and convenience; they promised homes and a metropolis city. They gave it to us, but they took from us too. This bleak world is what we get for receiving such a city and energy that *we* don't even get to use... *they* do," Kato angrily said loading his thirty-eight magnum. Then he sighed and said below his breath, "It's even worse than when I first got here..." Mei, standing next to Suako, in just as much dismay and shock between the heightened breaths, reached her hand over and squeezed Suako's. "This can't be real," she whispered, and shed a single tear.

After allowing them all a moment to adjust to the wastelands stretched out before them, Jenko finally took charge, "Try to keep you skin covered, mid day must have just passed so we have the rest of the afternoon and night time to travel, we'll sleep when the sun comes back up again. The heat is brutal, I warn you now." "You heard him, move out," Mack ordered leading the group with Jenko by his side towards the distant mountains.

Not too much was said over the initial day of travel. The words and stories of how much destruction had come upon the earth, and artwork of it in it's natural beauty that everyone posted around the city, lent no repercussion to first sight. The bitter hatred of which they'd held in their hearts for the C.D.F.P. grew and burrowed its way even deeper within their souls. The dry earth bore cracks and scars of the suns infliction. As night drew in, the temperature dramatically changed from scorching to freezing with next to no warning.

Short, fast breaths of the thin air blessed their lungs but ran from them just as quickly. Their hearts beat slowly and tired muscles were forced to keep moving. Minutes seemed to stretch on like hours and hours seemed like days. If not for the mountains growing larger ahead of them, and Torusan shrinking behind them, the endless plains of nothingness would have left them guessing they had not moved at all. The scenery changed in only the most minute ways.

A couple hours before sunrise Suako collapsed onto her hands and knees. "I... I need sleep... can't go further," she said between breaths, shivering. Jenko looked over to Mack "We should've planned shorter sprints, their lungs aren't ready for this. Let's set up tent here. We're almost as far as I'd planned anyway. Help me with this..." he asked Vince and Kato as he pulled out a large sheet and metal pegs. "Are you alright? Try to slow your breathing a little. Hyperventilating ain't gonna help ya'," Mack told Suako as he pulled her onto her feet. She stood bent over holding her torso up with her hands on her knees. "Sorry Mack... I never expected it to be so bad. Damn them," she growled looking back over her shoulder.

Standing upright she looked to Mack with a cute little smirk on her face, "One day I'll make a bomb that'll make a blast that they won't ever forget." "Hah! Girl's got spunk!" Jenko laughed. Mack smiled and lit a cigar before stepping within their primitive tent.

Before long, Mei, Suako, Vince and Kato had all fallen asleep; exhausted from their first excursion out in a land once beautiful called 'Mother Earth'. Mack and Jenko sat by the outer rim of the tent and watched slowly as the sky turned yellow and crimson as the sun began to hail the day. They were silent until they heard all four renegade soldiers soundly asleep. "Have you found him yet?" Jenko asked, finally breaking a strong tension. "Not yet," Mack disappointedly informed. "You're sure he's not just hidden within Torusan?" Jenko inquired. "No, I hacked the Company's files, all the important documents anyways. I found a transfer notice placed on him. It didn't say where." Mack said, shaking his head. "Is this the real reason we're out here?" Jenko pressed, turning his head to look at Mack. "No… but I won't leave any place we go without checking for him. We're out here to take down the *company*... but I can't forget about him." Mack said firmly. "You still blame yourself don't you?" Jenko asked. Mack looked away, "…Yes." "It was them not you." Jenko said. "I know… but they only did it because of me." Mack said with finality. The two were silent for a time. "Do you think he is even still alive?" Jenko asked. "I don't know. So until I've found out one way or another I'm going to keep searching… let's get some sleep." Mack said, and laid back.

They ventured forth once again after the sun had started back down towards the horizon. The day was still a shock to them; they'd all woken up hoping yesterday had just been some bizarre nightmare, but it was real. Still they found themselves pushing past the heat and the fatigue, trying to picture the world as they'd seen it in the artwork Torusan citizens posted about, lush and green. These thoughts gave enough hope for a promising future so they could ignore the present status of the scarred earth that extended around them.

That evening they reached the base of the mountains. Jenko insisted they stopped and would travel up the mountain trail by day. He warned them of monstrous creatures that roamed the mountain pathways, that were especially on the hunt by dark or night. Due to that once they started on the mountain path they wouldn't be able to stop until they made their way all the way to the hidden city within the guardian mounds. The shadows of the enormous peaks would protect them from the sunlight as they travelled he told them. Taking a breather, they found sleep easy to find, as travelling took much energy from their bodies.

As the sun pierced over the horizon and light began to bless and curse the earth, with its warmth and its radiation, Jenko woke them up. The crisp cool chill over the morning seemed to go straight through their bodies and penetrated their bones. They had a quick breakfast and thrived on the oxygen replenishing water that quenched their thirst. They quickly then packed up their items and they were ready to be on their way. Just before starting on the path Jenko told them to have their weapons handy, at all times.

The path they walked up was steep and treacherous; stones and boulders littered the area. A few evergreens, barren and sickly, were just barely alive further along the road. Once they saw them fascination struck and the four youngest mercenaries scampered towards them at first sight. "I've never seen this before, what is it?" Vince asked. "It's called an evergreen, it's a type of tree. My grandmother used to speak of them growing all over the northern areas of this continent. I remember seeing more of them in my early childhood," Mack told them as he observed the little tree. "It's a tree?" Suako asked dumbstruck. "Don't trees have leaves?" she scratched her head. Jenko smiled "You really are new to this world. Those little needles are its leaves. They grow in colder climates and never shed their needles. They symbolise never-ending life." "Oh," Suako blushed feeling rather naive. "Let's keep moving we don't have a ton of time to take break," Jenko reiterated to them.

Dragging themselves away from the tree each once of them drew from it one needle, which occupied each of them as they went onward. Conversation sparked and they peppered Jenko and Mack with questions that they could only answer through recollection of their childhoods. After a while Mack and Jenko could no longer contain their laughter at the exuberance the youngsters had. The four young travellers were rather confused. "You'd think you were just five years old with your intense curiosity," Mack chuckled. "Ha! Ha! Oh, what could we expect? You four just remember we know only little more than you about the earth. We were brought into it at a time where things were already falling to pieces," Kato sighed. "Guess we'd better find a history book," he suggested walking past Mack and Jenko; his words only fueled their laughter.

The trip went relatively smoothly. On a few accounts some small wildcats scrounging for food came at them but retreated with simple threats. Day was merging into night; turning around one final bend Mei saw before her the city that they'd been tirelessly trudging toward. With a huge grin, she tagged Kato with her hand, "I'll race ya," she said and sprinted ahead. A sudden screech echoed between the rock walls from ahead. Quickly everyone ran around the bend to see the trouble.

A large wolf-like mutated creature had pounced on Mei, pinning her down, and was viciously attacking her. The wolf looked to the others as they had stumbled upon around the corner. The one that held Mei down had glossy hazy eyes and looked ghostly with his filthy matted grey fur. Vince charged the beast, a dagger held in each hand. The wolfish animal growled then jumped off of Mei and darted at Vince when he neared. Vince jumped out of the way just in time, and twisting as he jumped in a 360-degree turn, he managed to double slashed the fiend's chest with his blades. The creature fell to the ground and seemed to be finished. Quickly receiving a second wind he arose from the ground, blood gushing from the deep cuts, and went back after Vince. Suako ran toward the beast with her pistol drawn. Having caught her in his eye the beast turned his attention to her and howled as he ran towards her. Just before aligning her shot Suako tripped on a stone sticking up from the ground and her pistol flew from her hand and she tumbled to the ground. Without time to even think she instinctively pulled herself up and, and the wolf came in for a bit, she kicked the wolf in the head with all her strength. A large crackle boomed in the air as Mack fired off a riffle, and the beast ran away in fear.

Kato ran to Mei's aid. She lay on the ground cringing. Upon closer inspection she had a deep bite mark on her left arm and was covering a large claw swipe on her lower abdomen with her right arm. Kato lifted her into his arms, "You'll be alright. You're safe," he told her. Mack took the flank as they jogged the final quarter mile to Yokuton.

Harsh dead world... Don't tell me this isn't a dream...

Chapter 3: Yokuton

A villager spotted the entourage walking up the mountain path towards the town, and noticed Mei injured, being carried in Kato's arms. The friendly mother figure ran out to greet them. "What happened to her?" she asked with a heavy oriental accent. Her eyes were warm and attentive. "Attacked along the path not far from here by some kind of wild animal," Mack said approaching the front. "Do you have a place we can take her?" he asked the woman. She smiled "Yes come, we'll get her help within the city," she said and led them, her bulky clothing over her tiny frame swaying as she walked. Kato kept a heightened pace.

Entering the city limits the oxygen dome revitalised them. Feeling their lungs become replenished with filtered air, they found it easier to concentrate on Mei's wounds. The woman showed them into one of the first homes, a small limestone hut. Presenting a bed for Kato to lay her down on the woman offered them her home as a place to stay until Mei's recovery. The lady then went off to fetch water.

"How are you feeling?" Suako asked as she sat by Mei's bedside. "I'm fine, really... It's just a few scratches. The air is really helping," she smiled. Mei shut her eyes and drifted into sleep. The others found chairs quickly and rested, weary from their travels. The woman returned in haste with a vase filled to the brim with clean well water. "Thank you, ma'am, do you have a cloth we could use to clean her cuts?" Kato asked. The woman dashed around the corner into another room and returned carrying a small white piece of cloth. Presenting it to Suako she then took her leave to fetch some disinfecting herbs. Jenko and Mack left to fetch firewood to heat the small chilly house.

By the time they returned Suako had finished bandaging Mei's arm. Mei came to and saw her bandaged arm, "Thank you. I'm sorry I was careless." Mei glimpsed up at them, and Mack hushed her. Suako pulled back the clothing around her abdominal cuts and revealed a large old scar running across her belly. Suako's eyes leapt up to meet Mei's, her jaw slightly dropped, "Mei what's this from?" she asked running her finger gently along the exterior of the old scar. Mei's eyes watered slightly; there was an extended silence in the room. All eyes focused on Mei.

Taking a deep breath in, she began to tell her tale...

"It's beautiful Jake! I can't believe you and Daddy finished it already!" A younger Mei with long flowing hair exclaimed as she wrapped her arms around a tall man about her age. They stood outside a small home with wood siding and a thatch roof. "I wanted it to be ready in time," he said, with a caring twinkle in his eye as he turned to her. With an affectionate peck on the cheek she bolted forward in front of the new house, and as she spoke she pointed with her hands. "We can have a little rose bush here and a Zen garden here... oh! And the family shrine in the back," Mei's voice rang with excitement.

Day fell to night's grasp. The eventful afternoon of moving furniture into the tiny house left Jake and Mei exhausted. They sat outside their humble abode sipping green tea as they ate a quaint supper of rice and salmon. "Just look at that... the sky is as rich as gold," a passionate Mei declared. "Indeed, it is my love, as is your radiance," he told her kissing her hand.

The stars came out and began to fill the sky. Despite their fatigue they stayed up through the night. A full moon rose high above them and bathed the earth with silvery emanating light. "We'll raise a good family. Our children will prosper and enjoy all the beauty of this world. Nothing at present could possibly make me any more content them I am now," Jake expressed romantically.

A few months passed in the little village. Fish were bountiful this year, as was the harvest crop. The summer was hot from the blazing sun that glazed over the earth. Flowers blossomed all over the house's front, with plenty of roses to go around. The house stood atop a grand hill beside a stream running down into the town below. Trees flourished around the town's boundaries, bamboo and cherry blossoms especially stood out. Mei looked out from her window and watched Jake as he climbed up stone steps to their home.

As he neared she noticed a troubled look was on his face, though he tried to hide it, Mei knew him all too well. Dashing outside to meet him she hugged him, "What is so heavy on your mind?" she asked worriedly. Sighing he responded, "The Mayor is fighting with those people who brought those machines here. He hasn't told me what the argument was about yet, but he's ordering us to remove the equipment they brought in, and those people

are threatening to remove our oxygen shield..." Mei
gasped, "They can't!"

*The following day Mei watched out the window
again for Jake to come back up those steps, home to her
once again. Across town she finally saw him leaving the
mayor's offices, as well as some angry soldiers and
company officials. The company quickly evacuated the
town. Sensing something must be wrong Mei ran from the
house and down the pathway to talk to Jake and the mayor
immediately. Before reaching the bottom step, an
enormous blast deafened her, which sent her flying back.
Tryting to brace herself she twisted around, and when she
smashed into the rock steps the impact on her front side
was brutally hard. With just enough energy she looked
back over her shoulder to see Jake perish, evaporated in
the rumbling blast of the reactor. With one final glance her
body gave out and she faded into unconsciousness.*

Finally, Mei spoke out, "I'm not originally from
Torusan you know... Three years ago, before I joined your
fight against the C.D.F.P., I lived in a small village. Life was
simple and we were all happy there. I hadn't the slightest
idea at that time about the company... I was married too,
you know? I went by Mei Yoshini. We weren't rich, but we
were happy... I had a little house made of wood that my
husband Jake built with my dad. People used to say it was
the nicest place in town. We had a flower garden too. The
town was inside an oxygen dome like most other places
and there was the Corporation's factory there. No one
knew what it did; all we knew was that they gave us the
dome to have it there."

"I was pregnant when it happened..." Mei's voice weakened and trembled "...one day, there was an enormous explosion. The processor in the factory 'malfunctioned', that's I was told. The entire town caught fire. Everyone burned that hadn't died in the explosion. I don't remember anything but being blown back, then feeling the heat of the flames... I heard all the screaming..." Tears streamed down Mei's face.

"I woke up some time later. I remember my body aching from head to toe. The sting of white light in my eyes... and then... and then... they took her out of me... they said she died in the blast..." Mei broke down, hyperventilating, her sorrow eating at her. Suako wrapped her arms around Mei and tried to console her. "Hush now, it's all over now... I'm so sorry," Suako stroked Mei's head; laying her back down once she pulled herself together.

A glaze seemed to have settled across Mei's eyes, "I got away... I wouldn't let them keep me there, not when I found out the truth. I discovered that the explosion wasn't accidental." Everyone's ears perked up. "What do you mean 'wasn't accidental'?" Kato wondered. "I learned from one of the employees that the mayor of my old town learned what the reactors had been doing to the Ozone, and was ordering C.D.F.P. to close down their location there. Rather then do so, the company wanted to kill the mayor, rebuild and continue production... It was cheaper then closing down..."

Vince stood there paralyzed, unable to move, react, or think. Mack had heard this story one time before, though it tugged on his heart to hear her brutal tale once again, he choked back his feelings. Suako shook her head in disgust, squeezing Mei's shoulder reassuringly, she looked her in the eyes, opening her soul to Mei, "We are going to get them. They've brought us all to ruin. They aren't going to be able to do any more to us, because there's nothing left we have that they can take away. I promise you they will get their just deserves." Suako's voice was both bitter and empowering.

Mack subtly cleared the others out of the room. Kato stayed behind to care for Mei. He finished washing her scratches of dirt and patted her tummy gently dry. Mei's eyes stayed numb and distant for the remainder of the night. Finally, after drinking some camomile tea, her nerves finally gave way to allow her to sleep. The villager woman let Kato stay by Mei's side the whole nightlong. No one could budge him from her side. When Mei's dreaming burdened her with bad thoughts causing her to call out in the night, he gently stroked her face and eased her suffering within. Not once did he fall asleep.

"I never knew," Vince finally said coming out of his temporary mute status. He looked to the floor, "I've always known that they've been killing the planet, and slowly bringing us all to an early grave... I also knew that they have killed a few people standing in their way but... an entire village to get rid of one person..." he was astonished.

"They needed it to look like an accident. The mayor wouldn't have left without a fuss, I doubt, and the people would have caught on sooner or later. Why not just make it simple in one easy swipe? Bastards..." Jenko explained.

An eerie quiet loomed over the room, one of thought provoked dwelling. "I really don't feel up for talking. Let's just get some shut eye," sadness clung to every word that came out of Suako's mouth. The others nodded in agreement. Suako waltzed over to the candle by the window of their cabin room and pinched out the flame. Staring up out the window, Suako could see the blue of the city's dome tinting the cloudy night sky above. Lightly, crickets could be heard around them.

The sound of trickling rain brought them back to life the next morning. While the others slept, Mack sat looking out the window. After some time, he got up to put a kettle over the fireplace, and then walked back to look out the window, as he waited for it to boil. Suako and Vince slept soundly; scarcely would anyone have dreamt the content of the discussion prior to their dreams, for their expressions were not of grief. Jenko opened his eyes and squinted at the light coming in the window hit his eyes. Jenko said nothing and just watched as his old friend look out the window. He wondered what thoughts must have been soaring through Mack's mind. The steaming kettle soon whistled, though Mack was too wrapped up within his thoughts to even notice. Jenko quickly got up and took care of pouring tea for them, so as not to awaken the others.

Jenko soon felt a responsibility to break Mack from his intense state of thought, "Your tea is ready."

Mack seemed as if not to have heard him. "…Mack? Your tea is done," he said again firmly. As if his soul suddenly slammed back into his body, Mack came to. "Oh, um, thanks," he said taking, it and then sat on the floor by the fire. "You *are* going today then?" Jenko blurted out.

"I planned to," Mack said solemnly. "You really think he's here?" Jenko questioned. "I have no idea… this place is just as likely as the next for all I know… I suppose it will be easier to leave while the others are inside during the rain… between here and tending to Mei." Mack stared at his back pack and sighed. "They don't know then?" Jenko asked, surprised. "No. I never told them," Mack replied. "You want it secret then, hmm?" Jenko pried.

"No. I'll let 'em know sooner or later. The subject just ain't ever come up is all," he explained sipping his tea. "Yeah, well I'll let you explain it to them…" Jenko looked away from Mack for a moment, then back to him. There was a change in his eyes; they went back to their usual light-hearted mannerism. "Sure is delicious… wonder if that lady makes this green tea herself?" Mack chuckled at his friends random commenting. "I think you should go before they wake up," Jenko recommended looking behind him at the two sleepers. Mack nodded, got up, grabbed his bag, and dodged out the door into the rain.

Mei opened her eyes to see Kato sitting near her, like a guardian angel that wouldn't abandon her. Dark circles enclosed his tired eyes. Pulling herself up into a seated position she reached her hand out a placed it atop of his. They said nothing, but there was an apparent

"Thank you," speaking through her eyes. For a grand span of time they connected, and his "You're welcome," was just as easy to read.

What seemed all too soon an ending came as the villager woman came in to check up on her guests. Mei thanked her graciously for all she'd done, and apologised for the startle when she'd first arrived. Despite telling the woman that she could leave and wished to no longer burden her, the lady insisted she stay another night. Before Mei could argue she'd been handed breakfast and the woman excused herself.

Not one minute later Suako, Vince and Jenko entered the premises. "Mei, how are you today?" Suako asked kneeling by her bed. "Really, it looked bad yesterday, but I'm fine. I was tired. As soon as the air got to me I was ninety percent better. They're minor in comparison to many things I've had happen in the past. I'm alright to do everything... excluding heavy lifting." She giggled pointing to her arm." "That's great!" Suako exclaimed in her highly energetic manner.

Mei pulled herself from the bed. Walking over stiffly to the window sill where her excess clothing had been hung from. It was spotless after the kindly hostess had finished washing it, further insisted upon by her. Looking out the window she saw the rain speckled ground. The clouds were light and allowed blue sky to show itself every so often. "It isn't a heavy rain. I think we should start our investigation," Mei said after examination. The others looked to one another; little shrugs and head tilts of no rejection passed the room.

Kato walked over to Mei and placed his hand on her upper arms and leaned forward. Whispering in her ear, "Are you sure you're well enough?" a tinge of worry in his usually calm cool voice emerged. "Yes, I will be okay," Mei reassured him.

"How about we start by finding out about this town; its history and such? Then we can go on to asking about the reactor and C.D.F.P," Vince suggested. He was about to go on, and then he stepped back, "I didn't even notice. Where's Mack? I thought he was here when I got up so I never asked but, uh... he's not?" he questioned. Jenko stood upright from the wall, "He's already gone off to gather some info; left at sunrise. He knows just as well as you do that time is precious for this planet. ... On that note, shall we?" he took his leave. With little hesitation, the others pursued him, expecting to find him outside, but otherwise found him taking a seat with the woman in the next room. She smiled and tapped a chair beside her. They all took a seat.

"I'm Jenko Ma'am. I want to thank you sincerely for taking Mei in and allowing us to stay in your extra room," he said, standing and bowing to her. The little woman blushed, "You are indeed welcome. I'm Miss Sui Akron, the town healer, after my late mother. You wish to know about our quaint little slice of land here?" An innocent little grin crept across her elder face, "Indeed I must admit I did hear you. So, I suppose I shall let you know all the knowledge that has been passed on to me about this place."

"If the stories of old passed down through the generations hold to be true, our people originally come from the North. Many centuries ago there was a war between the old Empire across the great sea to the west and our own. Our city lay along the coastline where they were entering our continent through the port. At first we tried to fight, but too many came. The villagers fled the grand city we'd worked so hard to establish with no other options available."

"Our ancestors wandered in search of a place to hide from the advancing forces behind them. That's when they gave the name Yokutan to the city, splicing the name from the ancient city whence we came. When the head of the old town viewed these mountains, he saw it as the best place to bide the time while awaiting the Empire to be run out of our continent... Unfortunately, the invading Empire won, so they just decided to reside here permanently, subjugating our citizens. At first sustaining life within the cavernous rock walls was so hard it nearly drove the people to starvation. They began trading with small cities around us for food with valuables. Soon trade items were coming up short."

"Luckily one young man stumbled upon coal within the mountains... as it has been told to me he was just wandering one day and noticed one of the mountains had a slight discoloration to them. From that they dug into the depths of the mountains and mined the coal. It has been our livelihood, though I must say we rarely use it here. Long ago some company... hmm" she paused to think. "I can't remember the name of it. Anyway, they learned of our coal and they wanted it. Thanks to them we've not just survived but have a fair amount of wealth." The intent listeners all knew it'd been the C.D.F.P. who'd harvested their coal away from them. "That company," Suako began, leaning slightly forward, "They're the ones who built the reactor in your town and offered you the dome coverage too, right?" The woman nodded. "Who is your town leader?" Sui turned her attention to Jenko, sweeping her dark hair away from her brown eyes and behind her ear. "Our chief is a native descendent of the chief who originally lead our peoples here. His name is Mu-Kai Hiroshu. He is wise through his many years of experience. If you wish to meet him, his post is the large stone building with the red roof at the very end of the city," she instructed.

The company stood and bowed to her respectfully before leaving. The rain had since ceased; as they ventured forth into the little community they sensed a real feeling of togetherness. Women were working, seeding the ground and hanging clothing to dry. An ox driver passed them, towing harvested vegetable behind him to the market place ahead. Vendors lined the tiny streets and offered many different ornaments, fresh produce and fine trade items from afar. Trinkets from places all around the vast continent could be seen. Vendors sported small corn dolls, antique vases, statues and the sort for buyers.

Suako stopped to look at a burgundy jewel hanging from a woven cord of cotton. Trying to pull herself away she felt and odd connection to it and offered the vendor an ornamental knife from her belt in exchange. The man kindly agreed and made the change. Tying the gem round her neck she felt a strong vibrant sensation pass threw her entire body, but disregarded it as a shiver. Mei found a hatchet that she admired at a weapons dealer. They all seemed to lose themselves in the glamour of fine things about them. After some time Jenko finally reminded them they needed to get a move on and continue their mission.

As the mountain air felt soft but cold on their skin. The cool muddy ground beneath their feet squished as they walked onward, making the road quite slippery. "I could really go for some of Miss Akron's warm herbal tea 'bout now," Vince declared rubbing his shoulders to warm himself. "Boy if you think this is cold you ain't gonna last when we go north. Not a minute," Jenko shook his head as he laughed.

As they approached the authoritative building of the Chief, the street migrated from dirt to cobblestone. They walked the steps, past narrow pillars to the grand entrance of the building. Jenko told a guard, who appeared more as a host, that he'd wished to meet their chief to discuss politics. They were led in past large dark wood doors, engraved with a picture of their landscape and a guardian deity watching them from above.

The official offices were also home to the Hiroshu family. Stairs detoured from the main hall to either side leading upstairs to the living quarters. Down the centre of the structure, through another set of massive doors was the grand hall in which the chief held his office for foreign affairs. The guard slipped beyond the doors and asked the others to wait for him there. "This place is incredible. I can't believe these doors... the dedication that must've been applied to carve them," Suako said in admiration, running her fingers along the carvings.

The doors further inward soon opened and the guard invited them to come forward before Mu-Kai. They entered a wide grand hall; the floor was laid out in limestone and the bamboo walls had tapestries of fine silk brocade hanging from them. Near the back of the room a large rectangular hardwood table was situated, likely for negotiations with foreigners and for celebrations. Before the table lay pillows for casual relaxation while conversing.

Mu-Kai sat in the casual area awaiting his guests, with a long white silken garb covering his body. Upon closer inspection, they saw Mu-Kai as an older man, with long greying hair and beard. His eyes were wise and sharp, peaking from behind his spectacles. He had the appearance of a loving grandfather, as well as a protective warrior. Mu-Kai's weathered face represented a fully and thoroughly lived life. After approaching the sitting area, they all bowed to Mu-Kai, and then they were welcomed to sit.

"Greeting Mu-Kai, we are travellers from the southern city Torusan. My name is Jenko; these are my travelling companions, Suako, Mei, Kato and Vince, we arrived with an older gentleman Mack, whom isn't here at present. We have come seeking knowledge and hoped that you might be of assistance to us in our quest?" Jenko humbly asked. "Welcome, all of you. If I know anything of use I shall share with you my knowledge. Please, ask what you wish to know," Mu-Kai graciously offered.

They were all pleased at how willing the man was; a generous person indeed. Mu-Kai had a sense about people, he knew instantly of their intentions it seemed. High vibrations connected him to some higher power, they could all sense it, and the strengthened energies in the room heightened their own senses. "We wish to know about Yokutan's connections to the C.D.F.P. Company. Anything you know would be helpful. In fact, if you know anything relating to the C.D.F.P. in any way we'd appreciate hearing of it," Jenko asked then respectfully bowed his head to the chief.

Mu-Kai stroked his beard "Hmm, I see. Well the C.D.F.P. and Yokutan started to have connections after they discovered we had coal tucked away in our mountains. They paid us handsomely for it, especially in my grandfather's day. When the company began to expand, and create their mammoth energy producing machines, they insisted on placing one here. Knowing the strength of the company, the chief of the time, my father, agreed to it. With our past standings with them it would have been rude to turn them away."

"As I can see in your eyes, you know of the black heart that is the core within the C.D.F.P. Company." They all chuckled at his accurate insight. "They are the cause of our mother Earth's accelerated disease. I feel her pain, just as we all do." Mu-Kai acknowledged. The guard scuttled into the room carrying a tray and offered them all some matcha tea. "Though it seems a forgotten page in history, I can tell you how the C.D.F.P. came to be." Mu-kai continued. All eyes sparkled intently upon his words, which seemed like gifts. In his own slow relaxed way of being he paused to drink his tea. The suspense nagged them as they waited for his words to fill in the gaps in their own knowledge.

"Long ago this town was situated north of here. When the Western Empire attacked this continent, we fled to these mountains. After the Empire won the war, they sent most of their soldiers back home to their families. Some generals with no families stayed. It did not take long for them to start their new lives in this continent, after all they'd be the wealthiest ones here and could tax us heavily. They decided upon creating an energy plant. The only thing left to figure out was, what would be the source of their energy?"

"The company started with waterwheels. They were a common practice back to the west. Unfortunately, our currents here aren't nearly as strong as theirs and they could only produce a limited amount. They weren't making much money. They had a scout in one of the cities that we traded with. One day when some of our men were carting in a wagonload of coal that for a blacksmith, their scout learned of our coal mines. At first they heavily depended upon us for coal. They soon excavated the land and found that most of it had coal readily available. Since then they have used coal to some degree."

"As you all know the company is primarily an energy generating company for the people, which has also spawned off other job facilities, correct?" There was simultaneous agreement. "Well what they don't have on the surface is the secret S.E.D." Kato wrinkled his brow, "Chief Mu-Kai, what is S.E.D." "S.E.D. is the C.D.F.P.'s scientific exploration department. In the not so distant past they discovered the cheapest way of energy production. I only know what I've heard from my sources, but it supposedly consists of a liquid chemical concoction they can create infinite amounts of; the down fall of this is that it produces several times the amount of carbon dioxide output as burning coal does. The world as you have recently seen with your own eyes not fifteen years ago was an entirely different sight. I suppose a company of that magnitude thinks they can prolong their own lives even with a dead planet to live on." Mu-Kai sighed heavily in disgust.

"Thank you. Your words will be of more help then you could possibly know. We will heal this planet or die trying. You have our word," Mei assured. Mu-Kai nodded, and the party rose and bowed in gratitude once more before leaving. As they turned they heard Mu-Kai behind them, "Before you leave..." he paused as they looked back to him, "There will be some officials here from the C.D.F.P. visiting within the next two days. They will notice any outsiders. I assume they will find you suspicious, as you have a passionate dislike towards them that does show through you. If you wish to be undetected there is a hidden passage that will lead you out to the eastern side of the mountain region. Please return here before you are to leave and I will have you escorted." A smile came over

Suako's high-spirited face from the kindly offering, "Thank you Mu-Kai, we will never forget your kindness." Mu-Kai added, "Be sure to give your thanks to Mack as well, as he is the partial cause to the release of this information I offer you now." A certain dumbfounded expression came over everyone's face except Jenko who threw back his head and cawed with a laugh.

They took leave from the grand hall and out the architecturally astounding doors. "So I suppose we should gather rations for the trip ahead, eh?" Jenko mentioned as they hopped down the steps. "Yeah," Kato agreed. "Uh... phew I'm just feeling... tired. I think I need to rest..." Mei said taking a dizzy spell. Tripping on the last step Kato rushed to catch her. "Her arm is likely infected," Kato said inspecting the blood seepage on the bandaged bite mark. "I'll take her to Sui to get some disinfectant for her wound," he said raising Mei into his arms. "You just rest up Mei!" Vince called behind Kato as he walked away.
"Right, then you two are on rations patrol," Jenko appointed them. Vince and Suako looked to one another and shrugged, "Ok. We need some gold for trade then," Vince told him. Pulling a tiny leather pouch off his belt, Jenko tossed it to Vince as he strolled off, "Take your time." He waved them off. Suako and Vince made their way back into the market.

"So, did that Mu-Kai have any information for you?" Jenko asked Mack as he walked into their stay room. "Mu-kai said that he was never here. The reactor here is strictly a reactor... He said in other cities where the C.D.F.P. is more predominant, they'd have buildings with prison facilities that could hold him. He said once a convict passed through here with a crew from the Company. Supposedly it could've been him but..." Mack sighed in frustration "The man's face was covered, so he can't even describe him for me." Angrily he pulled a cigar from his pack and lit it up. Inhaling deeply, he released the smoke along with some of his pent-up energy.

"You'll find him... anyway, as the chief probably informed ya', the 'murdering bastards' are on their way here, and 'ill be ere pretty damn soon," Jenko vocalised as he strutted over to his pack and started shoving his things away. Mack leaned up against the wall in his usual way and relaxed as he smoked. "Is Mei alright?" Mack timidly asked. "I saw Kato carry her back." Jenko averted from his bag, "She's a tough girl, but she needs to rest. She pushed herself too fast is all. If she stays put and rests the next little while she'll be good to travel. Guess we'd better see if that Akron healer woman needs some help." Jenko said. Mack nodded and took one last sweet breath of smoke in before extinguishing it.

Next door as they entered they found Sui had just finished placing an herbal mixture over the bite wound and was about to begin with wrapping a bandage back around Mei's arm. Kato sat on Mei's other side gently stroking his rough worn fingers along her soft plush face. "Are we too late to offer you any help?" Jenko asked as he walked in the room. Sui looked up at the two men, "Indeed you are not. This young lady needs a good night's sleep. If you could retrieve some vervain and chamomile from the market I can make a tea to help ease her conscience," Sui requested of them. Without sparing a moment they set off to the streets.

That evening five companions sat around a fire. They watched as the embers burned and listened as it crackled. The rain poured down in buckets outside. Lightning flashed in the distance, followed by the boom of thunder. Not much was said that night, no tension hung in the air; it felt peaceful in the village. For that evening they could forget about the long journey ahead, and enjoy the moment.

The fire danced away; it was mesmerising and captivating. It steered their attention straight to it and held to inspire and stir thoughts within them. Night seemed like an endless spiral before them, and time spawned into eternity. Somehow, they found themselves rising the following morning from slumber, without any recollection of going to sleep at all. Kato quickly dressed and tended to Mei at once. Suako and Vince made fruit platters for everyone to eat.

The sky was virtually cloudless, and the ground was moist from the downfall of rain beforehand. Suako and Vince ventured out into a vacant area of land to practice some concentration and focus driven exercises. Mack and Jenko spent the day checking in on Mei, preparing for the next day's trek, and enjoying the sheer serenity of the brief time they had to spend left within the small community. The day was relatively peaceful, a day of rest before the hard journey to follow.

Kindness shows its face despite chaos; the human spirit lives on.

Chapter 4: Departure

As dawn drew near Mack woke up the troop to prepare for an early departure. They double-checked their packs for all their vital necessities for travelling through a land of nothingness. "Kato, do you think Mei is up for this?" Mack asked in a hushed tone as he pulled him aside. "Yes, but she'll need breaks to keep up her strength… but uh, she'd never admit it so, make up some excuses, boss?" Kato asked. Mack nodded "Does the lady healer here think she's good to go?" Kato nodded, "Yes, though she'd said she wanted her to rest more, it ain't like we got a choice now. We just gotta make do." Mack patted Kato on the back and walked off.

Kato went to collect Mei from Sui's care. "Miss Akron?" he called as he entered her home. Peering out of the kitchen she expressed a friendly expression upon recognising Kato in the shadows. "I was just about to fetch you. She's getting dressed in her room. Here…" she produced a bottle and held it out for him to take. Kato took the vial and observed it. It hard a dark brownish green color to it. "It's a medicinal anti-infecting herbal blend. Just place a thin layer of it over her bite a few times a day, and clean the wound frequently," she instructed Kato.

"How is she then?" He asked. Sui compassionately smiled, "Don't fret, I have successfully flushed the entire area of bacteria. She'll be fine. That dizzy spell you reported to me was because a little bit of the beast's saliva had gotten in. I gave her an antitoxin which will have already cleansed her body," the sweet woman said assuring him. Kato breathed a sigh of relief.

Mei emerged from her stay room with her satchel slung over her shoulder. Delightedly she welcomed Kato with warm eyes. Turning to Sui, Mei thankfully bowed to the woman, "Ms. Akron, I want to thank you for all you've done for me and my friends. I will never forget how kind you were to take us in." Sui seemed to blush, "Save your praise. You are welcome back any time," Sui happily offered. Mei thanked her once more then took her leave with Kato.

The sun began to crack above the horizon as they ventured toward the once bustling business area, now a silent city centre. A pastel mauve and crimson sky blessed the earth with light as the day break gave way to stirring life. The few birds living in the area began chirping their songs to greet the new day. A gentle mist covered the ground in the distance behind them. The town asleep would soon rise and commence another day.

They had reached Mu-Kai's home and office. After climbing the stairs once again Mack knocked on the door. Soon a servant opened the door and told them that Mu-Kai had been expecting them and awaited them in the garden behind his political office. The servant showed them threw the house and to the back. "Ah, Mack, you have come at last I see," Mu-Kai heartily welcomed him.

A young man stood beside Mu-Kai. His posture was that of perfection, long black locks surrounded his pale face, whose brown eyes were accentuated and turned into black pools of ink by his kimono. "This is my son, Kairu. He is one day to rule this city... I would like to ask of you to take him with you. He needs to experience this world before he can lead his people properly," Mu-Kai kept his usual composure, but his eyes had a glint of hope glistening within them.

Mack walked up to Kairu, "How old are you?" he asked looking him over. "Nineteen," the boy quietly responded. "Can ye' fight?" Jenko called from behind Mack. "Yes sir," the boy replied. Suako grinned "More the merrier! C'mon Mack!" she pleaded with her usual enthusiasm.

"...Do you want to come?" Mack asked. The seriousness of the boy left a little and was replaced by a look of being misunderstood. His eyes hit the ground then went back to Mack. "Yes, I really do," Mack consented, "Right then... I'm assuming he'll guide us down the path we're going?" Mack questioned Mu-Kai. "I'm afraid no one else can be spared with the arrival of the C.D.F.P., too many absences become an issue. He knows the first bit of the way, I'm sure you'll be able to figure out the rest my old friend. Thank you for this favour." Mu-Kai said. "No need. In the wastelands we are crossing the more we have t' fight the better."

With that the men clasped onto one another and gave each other a hearty pat on the back. "Good luck on your endeavours. Take care of my son," Mu-Kai wished for them. "He's safe with us... Everyone let's get a move on!" Mack instructed them. Kairu hugged his father, "Good luck Kairu... be safe," Mu-Kai told him, for once with a slight weakness within his tone, yet still maintaining a sense of pride. Parading off into the distant brush the travellers began the next part of their journey. Mu-Kai stood watching until they'd past out of the city's dome limits and disappeared from sight.

"Guess this is goodbye Shangri-La," announced Vince turning back atop the hill to view one last time the lively place below. "Hi Kairu, I'm Suako," she introduced brushing back her long thick hair from her face. "Hello," he replied quietly. "So, I guess I should tell you who everyone is, huh?" she asked, but spoke again before his reply came "Let's see... well that's Mack up there at the front, as you probably guessed. He's our leader, so call 'em boss or Mack. Beside him is Jenko; he's an expert travel guide. To our right we have Mei and Kato..." then whispered, "They'd never admit it, but they're in love," she gleefully informed Kairu. "Last but not least there's Vince to our tail end." "Thanks," Kairu replied in his quiet reformed habit.

Suako cocked her head "You don't say much do ya'?" she asked, looking slightly sceptical. No address was returned. "Sorry... you just left home, that's all it is," she said, attempting to make him feel better. "Well, let me help you forget about that, or you'll just be glum all day! Hmm... well, tell me about yourself," she requested.

"I uh... I'm a jujitsu apprentice. My training is nearly complete. I've also been trained to use samurai swords, but only just recently. I'm afraid my fists are a better weapon," he proclaimed with slight embarrassment. Suako sweetly smiled, "That's amazing.

Maybe you could teach me some jujitsu sometime?" she asked with extra enthusiasm. Kairu finally broke his starchy composure with a small grin of content. "Sure," he looked her in the eye and saw deep within her. Suako felt the penetrating stare and nearly fell aback with its simple power.

Vince walked behind Kairu and Suako, feeling unjustified envy towards Kairu that he did not quite understand. He kept in close step, eavesdropping on their conversation as they went along. The day seemed to pass slowly. They rested at midday, in a tiny crevice along the path, where Mack and Suako prepared lunch and Kato attended to changing Mei's bandaging. Though short, the break had seemingly stretched on into eternity with the unmoving sun perched above them. The lack of breath seemed more easily tolerated the second time around.

After the break at noon, evening seemed to roll around quickly. This path was much longer than the previous one they'd taken up the mountain. With no other choice they set up camp inside a minor indentation of a precipice. They rotated shifts, watching for roaming beasts; the night was clear, cool and starlit. Mack and Jenko took a turn together. "So, where'll we be going after we escape the confines of the peaks?" Mack asked in his straight forward militant fashion. "Take a look here," Jenko said spreading out his map over his lap.

They were midway up the mountain border, then off to the east lay a small town, followed by another town northward by a lake. "Now I'm thinking that if we go here, to Atani," Jenko pointed to the southernmost of the two towns, "Then we can work our way north afterwards. There ain't that much south besides Torusan that's worth visiting. My money's on finding valuable stuff to the north," he said showing a path on the map to a coastal harbour city. "Alright then," Mack said, and that was that. A few hours later Vince woke up and took his shift, the last one before sunrise. His eyes were heavy, but his mind was busy. He looked at the expression on Suako's face as she slept, she appeared fearful. It didn't match her personality; her fighting spirit was strong, and she did not have restful sleep. It was mystifying and left Vince feeling baffled. Bringing his focus back to his watch it was not long before Jenko's snoring became distracting. *Surprising not every beast in the land hasn't come at us...* He thought to himself.

As morning drew nearer Vince vividly kept view of the eastern horizon line as the sky slowly lightened to hues of green and yellow. Vince decided to start making breakfast for everyone. After struggling to make a fire with the lack oxygen, he was finally able to cook some eggs that he'd carefully transported from the city for them. Suako woke before the others and quietly crawled out of the den.

"Hey," she quietly said, rubbing the sleep from her eyes. "Hey, mornin' Suako," Vince said with a smile. She yawned and rubbed her arms to warm up from the chill of the dawning day. "You look tired," she said. "Long night," he said in short. Suako attended to helping him. "Can you pass me the water canteen?" Vince asked. "Sure," Suako passed it to him. Suako turned away from him to go for the canteen, Vince opened his mouth to speak but hushed himself once he heard the rustling of the others as they awakened from their slumber.

Mid-afternoon rolled around before they'd even realised it. They'd just come out of the sanctum of the mountains onto the flat plains. There were very few encounters with any fowl beasts; most of them had been scared away without a fight. After the long trek their limbs felt heavy and stiff. They all longed for deep breaths of air once again to fill their lungs and give them new life. Mack stopped them all as they stood at the base of the mountain ridge to go over strategy before they stepped out onto the open plains.

"That's good n' all Mack, but aren't their a few towns to the south? You can't tell me Torusan is it?" Suako inquired. "There's more," Jenko confirmed. "We decided to go straight to domed cities to the east," Mack explained. "Yeah, but how're we supposed to fight if we don't know all aspects of C.D.F.P.'s impacts? I understand that time is precious for this world. Let me go alone, even if it's just to one place. I'll meet up with you later," Suako persisted, her eyes searching for approval. "...Fine Suako, but watch your step. You have your gear?" Mack said reluctantly, Suako nodded to him. "Then go on ahead," he released her.

Vince watched her as she left. He desired to accompany her, but felt an instinctual pull for him to stay with the others he could not quite explain. A slight bit of concern weighed on his heart for his dear Suako. Kato's harsh voice soon broke his concentration, "Mack I think its best we break here. I should change Mei's bandaging again." With a gesture of approval, Kato went to work.

"Tell us more about the city to the east... what was its name again?" Mei asked with a slight stutter from quick breaths. "It's called Atani. It's a nice little place... The people there are rather formal though. They tried to quarrel with the C.D.F.P. not too long ago. Since then the company has kept the town under military supervision to prevent rebellious actions," Jenko explained as he helped with washing her wound. Kairu sat quietly and watched everyone else, just listening.

"Is it such a good idea that we go there? The company's bound to have a search going on after we blew the grid eleven generator," Mei asked. "Yeah but no one knows we did it, Mei," Kato chuckled. Kairu's curiosity peaked, yet he remained silent and listened.

"Are we sure no one knows? I hate t' say it but I don't think we went completely unseen. How bout you?" Mei asked. "Everyone's got their fakes anyway, right?" Kato asked holding up an I.D. card. A murmur of agreement sounded.

"Low profiles people. These people notice everything. Worst of all they want to be trusted so they won't be prisoners in their own homes. Any info they get on you and yer' crime they'll bust ya'. Trust me," A seriousness override Jenko's usual tone. The mood was broken when Kairu, the silent statue came to life with no warning and bolted off around a corner. All attention gravitated immediately to him. An alarming screech cried out and then stopped just as fast as it'd begun. Kairu returned holding a large bird. They all looked at him slightly dazed; it took a moment to compute.

Kairu saw them all staring at him and didn't know exactly what to do or say. "I thought it might be nice to have a bite to eat," he said feeling uneasy with all eyes on him. Their daze wore off. "Uh, great," Jenko smiled. "Lemme help pluck the feathers for ya'. Someone start a fire," Jenko said taking the bird.

The fire was easily ablaze unlike usual, and they roasted the bird. They decided they might stay there the afternoon and wait until nightfall to travel. Furious rays of the sun were intense and scalding on the plains, and the cool shade of the mountains was bliss. After they ate everyone lazily relaxed and napped. As the others were resting Vince pulled a blank book from the rest of his gear. He began to jot down some random thoughts and feelings he couldn't get off of his mind.

Near supper the fowl was finished and they had had a grand feast. The high protein intake gave their energy-starved bodies quite a boost. "...Ha, ha, so there Kato was standing, the C.D.F.P. watchmen sniffed him out, and he's got this enormous rifle in his arms! Heh, a deep voice calls, 'Drop your weapons, and place your hands behind your head!' Well he stood there looking daft! Ha! I tell you he didn't know what to do!" Mack chuckled as he lit his cigar, his face flushed from laughing. Kato continued the anecdote with slight retaliation, "Yeah, boss only knows that cause he stumbled out the same door as me, an' he was frozen as a statue when he did too!" Kato grinned. "Good thing y' boys got me!" Mei boasted, "I came rippin' through that door and busting caps in asses so these two could run their butts out 'a there!" She giggled. Contentedly Kairu, Vince and Jenko listened as they recanted the story.

"So, how did you all meet?" Kairu asked and he took a swig of water from his canister. "Jenko and I go way back in the day," Mack started "... I met Mei a few years ago in a run-down pub in one of the grid sectors of Torusan. We started talking and realised our mutual despise of the company... One day I was walking down the street and saw a young girl in her teens having a spat with a few C.D.F.P. officials. She was protesting the use of generators because of the pollution they cause. I'll never forget Suako that day she was bound and determined to convince them. Vince is a pal of hers," Mack explained. "I see," Kairu said. He was quiet for a moment then asked, "I keep hearing scraps about your past happenings. Could you tell me about what's been going on with your group? Such as with that generator I heard you... uh, destroyed?" The general mood of the conversation shifted; light-hearted banter soon became serious business talk. Kairu listened intently about the history of the group. It became crystal clear who he was travelling with, their motives and their mission. Having been slightly naïve about the C.D.F.P. the mutual despise for the company between his companions soon become clear to him. Now he knew why his father had him join these crusaders.

Once the talk had ceased Kairu looked to the sky above him. Smog coated the earth in an unceasing haze; the heat emitted from the sun was held onto. The smog caused the UV rays to be magnified, which brutally burned the skin of travellers. Fake atmospheres were the only protection for bare skin in daylight, otherwise came the needs for elaborate robes to cover the body. Kairu thought of how different the sky looked in Ryoko compared to the dry cracked red earth before him.

After reflection Kairu finally came to notice, there were no trees. "Where are all of the plants... the trees?" he asked confused. "Clear-cut by the company," Kato bleakly said. Kairu felt a pain within, as his heart sank. Closing his eyes, he envisioned the trees that enclosed his beloved Ryoko. "I now understand you fully. The company... your hatred... I never held them in high esteem, though now I see them for the true nature of which they've become. I pledge to you now, I will not quit this battle until we've brought them down," Kairu vowed.

Chapter 5: Magick

The land before Suako seemed to stretch on and on endlessly in every direction, cracked earth and sand was all that lay to the south. After several days on foot the heat began to impede her vision. Suako was tiresome, and wished she'd taken a nice long break with the others before departure. Her stomach rumbled; she'd forgotten to eat that morning as well, and felt rather parched. *How far is the town?* she wondered. Her usual persona had abandoned her back at the end of the mountain path. No smile, no shimmer of excitement or content, nor showed any sign of ever existing. Grimly she pressed forward.

After hours of travel she finally caught a glimpse of some structures on the horizon, at first she rubbed her eyes and looked again in disbelief, but they were there. Suako pushed forward with new determination, they got closer and closer, and she longed for food and a bed. There were only a few houses, some of them converted into stores. A large apparatus was placed outside the largest home in the city. One building stood out in this tiny area. It was brilliant, an exquisite temple, unlike anything she'd ever seen before. The roof of solid wood, covered with bamboo shoots, and beautiful sandy red shades of brick constructed the walls. Elaborate glass windows with white wood coverings decorated the exterior.

Almost to the town, Suako thought she was hallucinating when she felt the ground beneath her begin to tremble. Her heart raced, *How could the earth move?*

She thought. The unknown event caused her extreme panic and fear. Another tremor sent Suako falling face forward onto the dry earth she scuffed her knees and hit her head rendering her unconscious.

Bright light hurt Suako's eyes as she awoke. She found herself laying on a soft surface, above her she looked up to see the ceiling was of many criss-crossing pillars of dark chestnut brown wood. Blinking, a searing pain in her temple caused a headache.; she tightly she shut her eyes. She groaned as she felt the aching. "Oh!" a startled voice came from the other side of the room. "Uh… where am I?" Suako queried. "You're in a sacred temple, in the town of Kagawa," the voice answered as it drew near. It was the voice of a woman, soft yet powerful.

Opening her eyes once more Suako perched herself up and looked around. Candlelight encircled the room. Shelves with books and herbs filled the temple, along with an altar and a few statues chiselled from stone. It was a dark interior, but filled with light from the windows. Fabric wall hangings of ivory silk with golden embroidered threads draped over the brick walls. The scent of incense danced upon the air. A small fireplace provided heat that infiltrated the nearby air, nullifying the chill.

It was dusk outside, the last brilliant rays of the sun danced through the window as the moonlight from the waxing moon drew up to take its spot in the sky. Suako soon felt the presence of someone standing over her. A woman, some years her senior, she must've been in her late thirties to mid forties Suako thought, was attending to her. She placed a cool cloth atop her head and said to her, "Relax now, the raging earth has calmed, and you are in good hands here. My name is Yu-Lee. I am the priestess of this temple."

"What happened?" Suako asked with traces of fear within her voice. Yu-Lee sat next to her, brushing her lengthy black hair away from her porcelain face. "The earth is dying and she sometimes feels anger towards those causing her early demise." Yu-Lee explained. "Feels?" Suako felt confused.

"I will explain later. Night has come upon us... here, drink this and we will speak in the morning," Yu-Lee handed her a cup of tea. Without question Suako drank it and soon found herself drifting to sleep. Her wonderment lasted all night long, infecting her dreams with curious questions.

Suako awoke at the crack of dawn, the sun's intense morning light infiltrated the room and made it seemingly glow. "Ah, you're awake," Yu-Lee noticed as she finished tying a gold cord around her white robe that matched the tapestries. Gathering her energy Suako raised from her bed. "I placed a robe by the table behind you," Yu-Lee informed her. Suako placed it over herself; It felt smooth on her skin. The rooms all were interconnected, with only an inverted U-shaped opening just barely pulling the wall inward enough to determine separation.

Yu-Lee was sitting at a small oak table with a tiny bowl of fruit before her and another bowl set across from her for Suako. "I'm sorry this is all I can offer you. We do not have an abundant food supply," Yu-Lee informed her. Suako nodded with understanding and took a seat. Sipping a glass of water by her dish she felt refreshed to finally have some fluid after her long trek. "Would you tell me of what you meant last night, about the planet 'feeling'?" Suako asked, no longer able to contain her impatience.

Yu-Lee smiled which made her scarlet eyes look like beautiful saucers, "Indeed my dear. The planet feels the effects of pollution every bit as much as we do. Take a deep breath in... you see, you struggle, so does she. You see, all life is universally connected and is mutually supportive. There are different levels of life, those of conscious beings and those of unconscious beings. The earth is an unconscious being, but still alive all the same. We share energy with her. She provides us with life and food, and we give her company in a way. The earth provides our basic grounds for learning, growing, and our lives. When we die and decompose we nurture the earth to provide for other beings. It is a continuous cycle."

"Those money death-producing machines in Torusan to the west are slowly destroying the delicate balance of the give and take cycle. That is why we refused to have a generator here just for the sake of a dome. Kagawa will endure, as the earth shall. We refuse to make her suffer more," Yu-Lee spoke with a deep passion and wisdom with every word. Suako looked at Yu-Lee and asked, "Is this the temples beliefs?" A little grin once again grew upon Yu-Lee's perfect face, "These are ancient customs of which all humans used to believe. We have very few artifacts to go off. Most of our information is what has been passed down by word of mouth from generation to generation."

"All of humanity? ...What happened?" Suako was taken aback. "Not all people felt the earth gave them their fair share of bounty. They desired oddities of which weren't of necessity to survival. By doing so they were using up more resources then were available per person. When technology suddenly became a huge aspiring thing within this world even more materials were being consumed," Yu-Lee sighed, "It is just how humans progressed. All respect for this planet was lost by most," she sipped on her water.

Suako was coming to understand the deeper embedded problem with the C.D.F.P. Company. It may as well have been hereditary on a global scale. Only these select few just couldn't be content with the already exceeding life styles to their needs. They wanted more and more and therefore greedily continued to ravage the earth; despite the radical impacts they still refuse to stop perpetuating death. Suako welled up with fury and burst out into tears in a release of tension.

Suako spent the next few days by Yu-Lee's side. She learned many things about life patterns and cycles and the old beliefs held my mankind. As well it became clear just how barren the earth had become. In Torusan and other cities inhabited by any C.D.F.P. influence there was a false sense of the world still being plentiful. The masquerade was well carried out; no one on the inside would ever be the wiser.

Only once did anyone come to visit the temple shrine during Suako's few days there. The town was small and only had a few residents. Many had elected to leave and move to a domed area for their own comfort in the little time they and the planet had left. Those who stayed were either too poor to move or would rather die starving or suffocating just to hold true to boycotting the C.D.F.P. The people were self sufficient and content with their decision to help keep what was left of the earth pure. Their resolve to follow ancient customs was admirable, Suako thought.

The earth trembled every so often, and Suako could not get used to it no matter how hard she tried. It always gave her a scare. Although Suako was unable to feel it at first, after she became acquainted with the thought of the earth being alive, she slowly realized that she could sense the earth's pain. With every shake and shiver she sympathized and felt it ringing within her own body.

Yu-Lee grew on Suako very quickly. She was a wise woman, a mysterious beauty, who did not look her age. She had an enigmatic energy that entranced anyone within her presence. Suako never knew anyone to be as together; Yu-Lee carried her head held high with pride. Each step she took she did with grace, and every word she spoke was elegant in pronunciation and rhythmic flow. Yu-Lee embodied the essence of perfection.

Suako persistently asked Yu-Lee questions about life and spirituality. Yu-Lee was all but too happy to accommodate with expansive answers. "I was wondering exactly what did happen with the C.D.F.P. when they came here hoping to build their energy generators?" Suako inquired. "Well it was, and I suppose still is, something they've been wanting to obtain. Our village is in a good location to provide to some minor communities nearby as well as our own people. Financially it's cheaper for them because it costs less for the distance of the energy to flow. The proprietor before me refused to permit them building here. The company has returned on several occasions wishing to build here. Sometimes they come with offers, sometimes with threats. We will not allow them to ever have this territory." Yu-Lee explained.

Suako shook her head in agreement and then found herself momentarily pausing to think. "How? How have you kept them at bay? The C.D.F.P. takes what they want when they want it, by force. How have they not yet found some way to get rid of you?" Yu-Lee had a grin slowly creep across her face from cheek to cheek. "We are the people of ancient way. We are the magick folk," Yu-Lee said.

Suako didn't know what 'magick' meant, and was unable to put it all together. "What's 'Magick'?" she asked, puzzled. "We are all energy, magick is and expression of the intentional use of energy. Thoughts vibrate our intention, so the thought of an outcome makes it so-" Yu-Lee began, but Suako cut her off unable to contain herself, "Well then, what do you mean you are the 'magick folk'?" "We have been blessed with the power to summon up life energy, the universal powers that cycle through all living beings," she illustrated.

"You see, we have mastered the ancient way passed down by our ancestors. The people of Kagawa can tap into the ever-abundant running energy and use it by bending it to our will. Far to the east of this continent there are ancient ruins of the last standing ancestral city. Within the core of the city is one of few earthly power points. This is where students studying of the magickal cycle are taken to be blessed and are from then on permitted to use life energy." Yu-Lee explained.

Suako couldn't quite grasp the things she was being told. Yu-Lee was used to people's disbelief and justification, having the logical side of the brain combating reality of something new and unknown. Yu-Lee was patient and tried to convey their practices as best she could. Suako was overwhelmed and tried to clear her mind, shaking her head as if it would erase the information inside.

"Um, well... ok, but uh... how does this 'magick' protect you?" Suako asked. "Using magick we have been able to create a force field, or protective barrier, around our city. Only those with good earthly intentions are allowed to pass through without our direct permission by a resident here."

Suako hopped up like an intrigued child and rushed over to the window. Squinting and looking all around she searched for this 'barrier', but Suako could see nothing of the 'force field'. Turning back around she scratched her head, very confused, "There's nothing out there," she stated. Unable to contain herself Yu-Lee let out a tiny burst of laughter. "It is not visible to your untrained eyes. You would have to be able to see the shimmering life energy that coats this entire planet, every inch of space surrounding it, and that of other planets."

Suako felt very let down, and doubt crept into her heart. How could she believe in this if she could not see it, she wondered? "So, you can never see this magick?" she said slightly sceptical, as well as let down. "I should say not!" Yu-Lee exclaimed to Suako's surprise. "Let me show you a small bewitching," she smiled. Crossing her hands over her face and keeping them covering her she chanted gently so Suako could not hear her words. Suako's heart rushed, *is she really doing something?* she pondered, her body tingling with excitement from her head to her toes. Suako felt a strange force moving past her body toward Yu-Lee. Suako did not blink; an intense anticipation shunned all other thoughts from her mind. The second before Yu-Lee pulled her hand away from her face Suako swore she saw bright white flecks, like electricity, swarming around Yu-Lee. Yu-Lee revealed her face to Suako with her eyes closed. Nothing appeared to be different. Suako wrinkled her brow; she felt something must've taken place. Had she just been imagining a gathering energy? All was answered when Yu-Lee opened her eyes.

Suako was so surprised she lost her balance and fell onto the floor. Yu-Lee's dark scarlet eyes were no longer; gazing up at Yu-Lee Suako was bewildered to see amber eyes that burned with fiery flames in the gleaming light, they were orbs of energy. With the closing of her eyes and a wave of her hands Yu-Lee restored her eyes back to their natural color.

Taking a moment to grasp what she'd just seen, Suako pulled herself back onto her feet. Stuttering she attempted to speak "H-How… What d-did you… you do?" she panted in the deoxygenized air in sprints, her heart still racing. "I used the universal life flow energy to create magick, enabling me to manipulate my physical appearance," Yu-Lee explained as if she was a teacher showing a student how to do a math equation. "Amazing…" was all Suako could bring herself to say. Suako walked herself back over to the table and sat with Yu-Lee. Nervous of rejection, Suako took a moment to build up the courage to ask, "Yu-Lee, I wonder if you might be willing to take on an apprentice?"

On the outskirts of Atani Mack and the travelling group we're walking away from the town. "I do not believe they just did that to us," Kato said bitterly as he walked out of the city gates of Atani. They all marched out into the morning sun of the real world. "I wouldn't have expected things had got so bad in so few years," Jenko sighed. "It's just ridiculous," Vince shook his head. "No kiddin', 'oh here's a one-night stay at the inn and a day's rations for each of you. Don't mind the boot in the ass on your way out.' Sheesh!" Mei mimicked.

"It just goes to show how fast the C.D.F.P. will take control of everything they can. We were lucky as it was just to have gotten into the city for one night," Mack impressed upon them, "...well let's keep going on up north," he suggested. They began walking on the hard-red earth. A massive gorge swooped down to their left, between them and the northern mountainside. "Did you see all those guards? There must've been one posted every twenty feet. Wonder if somethin' happened?" Suddenly Kato stopped, "Eh... you guys here that?" he asked looking around.

Everyone looked about. "Oh shit!" Mei was the first to spot pursuers. "So that's why they couldn't wait to get us out of Atani," Mack said cocking his rifle. "Maybe they just want to talk..." Jenko was soon cut off as shots fired by their followers blew past them. They ducked for cover and Mack took aim. Jenko pulled out his scimitar as he ran off to the side, out of the line of fire. Kato pulled out his handgun and fired off a few rounds at the oncoming C.D.F.P. military party of five, and one of them fell holding his leg.

Hiding behind large rocks and boulders they occasionally shot off a few rounds in hopes of injuring their enemies. Kairu closed his eyes and heightened his sense of hearing to the best of his capability. As soon as one of the C.D.F.P. came around the side of the boulder Kairu bounced to life, with a spiralling counter-clockwise kick he knocked the rifle from the man's hands disarming and stunning him. *Whack, thud, right hook, high kick, leg sweep* Kairu knocked about the soldier until he fell unconscious.

The booming voice of the C.D.F.P. commander rang in the air and startled them, "Don't stop until they're in our custody or in body bags!" as he shot off machine gun rounds at them. Dust and pieces of stone flung about from their protective walls. With no other choice but to fight to the death each one knew what they must do. Jenko took one quick peek to see where each soldier stood, then with incredible speed he darted from behind the rock and attacked the closest guard. His blade gleamed with red velvet drops in the sunlight.

Mack whipped around and took the man to the right of the commander into view, and with the pulse of the trigger a gaping hole was seemingly all that remained of the man's left shoulder. Pooling blood slowly drained from his limp body. Just as Mack was about to take out their commander he felt a sting followed by a numbness come over his left thigh. Ducking back down he looked down to see three small gunshot wounds; the bullets had gone straight through him. Pulling off his shirt beneath his coat he tied it tightly around his thigh to lessen the bleeding. Mei snuck behind a veil of dust over to Mack and gave him some fresh water to pour over his leg.

With sniper like reflexes Kato shot out both of the commander's knees, sending him crumping to the ground, immobilizing him. The last standing able-bodied guard was still coming on strong. "Throw down your weapon, or we'll have to kill you!" Jenko said brandishing his sword high. The guard did not heed his warning, and took running toward Mei who'd just stepped aback from the rock, thinking it was over. "Mei!" Kato yelled. He jumped to push her out of the way, grabbing her they both hit the ground hard. As the guard took aim once again at the terrorists, Mei and Kato held one another tightly knowing they couldn't escape. Jenko ran up behind him, raising his sword high, but before Jenko could get to him the guard fell dead with the sound of one resounding bullet. They all looked over to see Vince standing there, pistol drawn. Vince looked to Kato, and Kato nodded at him with thanks and Vince nodded back.

Mack held out his hand to help Mei and Kato to their feet. "You all right?" Mack asked. "Yeah boss," Kato said, nodding. "Thanks Mack. I apologize for my carelessness," Mei bowed her head. "Just take a little more caution next time," He patted her on the back. He walked out to the fallen leader. Kicking his weapon out of his reach, Mack was angry at the attack on their lives and ready to interrogate.

Knocking off the commander's helmet he began questioning the man, "Whose orders were you following to come after me and my men?" Mack's eyes flared with a storming rage. Disrespectfully the commander spit in Mack's face. Mack, in no mood for games, pointed his gun an inch west of the man's head and shot. The commander screamed, the sound deafened him instantly. "Next time you're losing more then your hearing!" Mack shouted, taking aim right between the man's eyes.

Reality hit home quickly; The C.D.F.P. leader lost childish pride quickly. Pellets of sweat edged around the man's eyes as fear gripped him. He focused intensely on the barrel shoved in his brutish face, "All right! Ok, I'll talk!" he yelled. Mei rolled her eyes, turning to Kato with a grin, "Till they're in our custody or body bags," she mocked.

"So, who gave you your orders?" Mack demanded. "It was General Yoshida… The order was issued to all surrounding Torusan military bases… with your picture, that's how we knew it was you! I swear!" he said squirming backward like a worm. Mack began ranting for a minute, and everyone kept quiet. Finally, Mack pulled himself back around to questioning, "What if you had caught us?"

"We were to report to the General, then he'd come to collect you… That's all I know! Don't kill me!" he pleaded. Mack was too infuriated to continue asking this snivelling weasel any more questions. Taking the butt of his rifle, he knocked the general out cold. "Let's go," Mack coldly said throwing his rifle over his back and marching off with a bit of a limp.

No one dared to question anything. Jenko was the first to say anything to him, some time later, "General Yoshida… I thought he was under the impression that you'd been murdered?" he said, wiping the perspiration from his brow onto his sleeve. "So did I," Mack replied grimly. "This isn't good news. He knows it was you back at grid eleven then I assume." Jenko said. "He always knew my strategies… after all, he was my master," from the second Mack's words passed his lips everyone was at attention.

"Whoa, whoa, whoa!" Vince ran in front of Mack. "Hold it a second, what are you talking about?" Mei intruded as well, "Yeah boss, spill!" Mack stopped walking, looked around at his companions searching eyes, then sighed and took a seat on a rock. "Guess you guys ain't lettin' us go no further till I tell ya. Well sit down," he said, lighting a cigar to try and relieve some of his built-up anger. With one relaxing exhale he felt a little better. Everyone sat around him anxiously awaiting an explanation.

"I used to work at the top level of the C.D.F.P. military. I was recruited at nineteen, since I had nothing better to do. They gave promises of wonderful things, like a house in grid one, flexible hours, free energy and early retirement. They neglected to mention that was if you happened to do well, or live to see it..." he blew out some smoke and sighed. "Well I was young, like the other men. The dream drove me to be an achiever. I spent a few months in combat training, they showed us how to manoeuvre, and use the provided military guns."

"Following that I was sent out as a soldier into the fields. I was proud in my uniform. Little did I know I was just 'disposable' to them, just like those flunkies back there." He said, pointing over his shoulder. "Hmmp, well after five years of field work and public safety maintenance I moved up in rank. I got to command my own squad in the fields and my pay got better. I was in grid two, which wasn't too shabby compared to the shit hole I'd been livin' in before."

"Two years later I got lucky. My crew took out a bandit group who'd been pirating energy from the C.D.F.P. At that point I was given another leg up, but they had to make me wait for the promotion though. They said that the man who was going to be 'training' me was away on a special covert mission. I was taken out of fieldwork and issued as an assistant ... no, more like a bodyguard. I was naive and had no idea that no one outside of the company knew about the science labs. I believed them to be legit. At that time, they were creating a new energy form, the new 'earth killer' that they use now. 'Cheaper than coal' phht, bastards... at the time I would've never guessed it would be like a plague. I was curious, I wanted to help."

"They finally assigned me to General Yoshida. I was to be his apprentice. He taught me the only useful stuff I actually got to take away from all those wasted years helping the Company. I followed his every move. I was mesmerised by his superficial life. He had the house, and all that other crap that I'd originally been promised. On top a' that he was an amazing soldier to boot, I looked up to him. On the field I mimicked his every move," Mack took a moment to reflect. "I was integrated slowly into ancient techniques. I was slowly molded into a secret agent. I did all the backdoor missions that Yoshida had previous done alone."

Everyone absorbed all of this quite well. They'd never known about Mack's history with the company, "What happened?" the usually quiet Kairu blurted out as the words came to his mind, he was mesmerised by the tale. Mack looked up with eyes that reached back in depths of recollection. "One day... There was no work to be done outside. I was asked to do some disposal work for one of the labs in the C.D.F.P. headquarters building. It was the same lab I'd worked in before. Some figures caught my eyes before I shredded the documents..." Mack went quiet. A shaking hand lifted his cigar to his lips.

Jenko had heard this story before, he stood up and walked a few steps away keeping his back to the crowd. "What were they?" Vince finally broke the silent tension. "They were... estimates for how long they could subject the planet to... to severe levels of carbon dioxide emissions before anywhere outside the domes would no longer provide any oxygen or protection from the UV rays, until the natural planet was unsustainable for life..." Mack could barely speak. Jenko's voice came in assistance, "Basically an estimate of human extinction. As I remember the story they were disposed of because they didn't want the public to find out, and the leaders didn't believe it, or didn't care. The scientist who calculated the dates, 'mysteriously died' in a chemical fire."

Mack's voice, a bitter rage, took up again with strength, "I confronted Yoshida with the documents. I told him we should go to the company council heads and present this to them. He was expecting a promotion from the secret services division to the highest-ranking military official, 'General'. His predecessor was retiring shortly, so he told me to get rid of the documents. He said, 'Hey as long as we live our lives out before things implode who cares?'"

"After that I faked my own death on a mission that came up. I took it, alone. Everyone bought the cover... everyone but Yoshida. He knows me through and through. Caught by bandits and burned to death wasn't good enough for him. He knew I couldn't be taken out so easy."

"Ever since then I've been tryin' to stop the company and, well, here we are now," he concluded. Jaws dropped and everyone stared dumbfounded. "Well…" Mei blinked several times to snap herself out of trance, "You sure are one for secrets Mack," she said and gave a nervous laugh. "So… is he gonna be coming our way?" Kato asked as he rose to his feet. "Only if he has no other prior engagements. Everyone else thinks I'm dead. Since that time, everyone thinks he's just been in denial about me since we were tight… on top o' that, I bet it'll take Cap n' over there a while to drag himself back to Atani," Mack laughed as he stood.

Everyone got up and grabbed their stuff. "Ready?" Mack asked before turning around to walk beside Jenko as he led the way. "Asses in gear people and we'll get to Quan before sundown… Mmm I can taste that curried rice and fresh smoked salmon already," Jenko dreamily licked his lips, murmuring as he trotted off.

Sometimes a lie is just an unspoken truth.

Chapter 6: Quan

Quan was like a place taken from a dream, it seemed to be a mirage compared to the wasteland that they'd just drudged past. As they entered the dome, there was a burst of life everywhere. Many amphibious creatures flourished here; frogs, toads, fish and snakes seemed to be everywhere they turned. Trees with long embedded vines wove around each other, bodies of fresh water were everywhere; it was a paradise. Not but at the ocean would anyone expect to see so much blue before them.

Some homes were perched above the ponds, posts of wooden shoots held the houses above the water. They were made of sturdy lightweight beige woods of various types from around the marsh. The homes on land were mostly made of thick cloths draped in the ancient Quan fashion around tall-outstretched harvested tree trunks. The fabrics were colored with natural dyes made by the women of the Quan tribe from the wildflowers the flourished there.

Aromas infiltrated their nasal cavities with enriching scents, Mei thought the town smelled like a spring day just after a heavy rainfall. All Jenko could smell was the fish. A sense of happy lives being lived was ever present in Quan, and they were politely greeted by all as they entered the small village. Women worked heartily preparing food as the men were finishing their hard days labour. The children played, their content and glee sounded throughout the dusk as they ran chasing butterflies and dragonflies.

Kairu held out his hand and a ladybug landed upon his index finger. He'd never seen one before, but felt a kind gentle radiating energy ebb into his system, and a a tame smile stretched across his face. Closing his eyes Jenko breathed deeply, then he quickly urged the other to follow him, "C'mon everyone, grub's this-a-way!" he shook his hand towards a large hut with an opened flap near the top of the stream, and some smoke arose out of it from the cooking below.

As they crossed a small simple bridge from one plateau of land to another, the hideous generator behind the Gargantuan creek brush poked it's ugly head out. It stood out in this haven like a blemish upon fair skinned beauties; it just did not belong. Every head turned to look at it. The harsh metal contrasted to the naturalistic feel of the entire community. Jenko brought them to an abrupt halt, "I forgot. It's Quan tradition to request the elder's permission to stay within the town."

"Uh," Kairu started, "Don't you mean their 'chief'?" and cocked his head to the side. "No. In Quan the elder is the 'All Seeing Eye'. In their traditions he is the seer of souls. He also can tell the future, or so they say. He helps decides what is best for the tribe, as well as the world at large when it comes to decisions," Jenko explained. "So, come on then, show us the way, 'cause I'm-a-get 'n hungry!" Mack insisted, in a laid back rather playful manner. Kato nodded feeling his stomach grumbling. "Alright then," Jenko said, "Ok, this way ladies and gents'."

They approached the most brightly colored hut in the village, it was hues of bright reds and burnt oranges, and it belonged to the chief. As well it was the grandest of them all in size. A smaller hut, mostly blue with a gentle hint of lavender, was situated beside the chief's home. In front of the blue hut was a staff sticking out of the ground, with decorative feathers and bulbous foreign onyx stones tied to it with the local vines. "There's the elder's home," Jenko said.

Walking up, Mack held his hand to the others for them to wait. He saw a tiny chime hanging from the top of the thick curtain door, he hit it and it jingled. A few seconds later a muffled voice from within welcomed Mack in. Looking onward the others waited as they watched Mack disappear within the hut. Vince finally found himself a nice spot of ground to sit down on, but as soon as he' gotten comfortable they were all called inside.

Entering the tent, the strong scent of burnt herbs and incense overcame them. There was a pit dug in the centre of the hut were logs for a fire lay, scorched from prior use, and a large black pot hung above it. Tiny clay pots filled with charcoal based incense lay scattered about; tiny charms and crystals were hanging all around, pinned to the cloth walls and ceiling. A small cot was to the right of the entrance and at the back of the tent the elder sat. His skin was a beautiful tanned color, he had rosy cheeks, a bald head, and a long grey beard with the odd black strand here and there. He wore a woven robe made of the same materials they'd harvested to make their tents and other material type objects in Quan. It was dyed a deep indigo blue, and had a white ring around the bottom. He sat upon a large pillow cushion that matched the robe.

The elder sat there, his small eyes meticulously looking over everyone; he was a man who talked little and listened much. Everyone respectfully bowed, and he kindly acknowledged with the tilt of his head. "Please sit," he finally said. His voice was soft and gentle, yet he still came across with power. There was a silence until Mack finally began to explain the travelling entourage. "We have come from the south. We desire to stay here for a brief period, to recuperate an restock on provisions," he said, not knowing exactly what he should divulge to the old man. The man listened, and only replied, "Why travelling?"

Mack felt stumped and trapped, and took a moment to take stock of the situation. *Is this town for or against the Company? If I lie he'll probably know.* He thought. Having to say something, "We desire to learn from groups of all kinds around the continent," he told the man. The man was no fool and saw that there must be more then Mack was saying.

Nervous chatter bounded back and forth, it was clear to the old man that they weren't prepared to tell him everything. After all his questions he had one final request before giving his decision. "Let me see your eyes," he said to Mack. Mack nodded, neared the man and dropped to his knees. The old man opened his droopy eyelids and peered into Mack's eyes; Mack felt naked completely exposed. After an uncomfortable minute for Mack, the man's old skin yet again sagged down over his eyes. "You may stay," he said, and just like that they were in. After bowing respectfully, they took their leave.

A quick hike took them over to the large food tent near the center of the village. Gentle spices and sauces lavished over the various fish dishes that so abundantly blessed the village. As they walked past those dinning, an overall satisfaction on their faces, they couldn't wait to taste the culinary delights. They were seated on embroidered pillows around a table only ten inches off of the ground with a lacy red clothe over it. They were served camomile tea and fresh water, followed by many platters of food; curried and saffron rice, boiled aquatic vegetables, fried as well as smoked salmon, broiled carp, simmered cod, as well as several other rarities.

Each ate until they felt they'd nearly explode, they hadn't been able to fill their bellies in such a long time, such tasty and abundant food wasn't the norm when travelling. Twilight was upon them as they finished a sweet sugar cane desert. A bonfire was lit in the centre of the village, where the close-knit community would nightly gather and celebrate life with dancing and the telling of tall tales. Jenko pulled out his pouch of gold and paid for their meal, then they walked over to take part in the festivities.

Vince slipped away from the main crowd to go sit by the pond. In his solitude sitting along the water's edge Vince took out his ever-frequented journal. In the light of the bonfire he began to meticulously record the events which had occurred. Quan was the most life filled place he'd ever seen, and he found himself at a loss for words. In the end he couldn't even find the words able describe about the elegance, and was left having to draw the place.

After he finished the sketch he looked up to the stars above lighting the night sky like diamonds. His attention turned to the now waxing moon. The reflection of the moon glistened in the water among the lily pads, and crickets sang loudly. Vince's thought dwelled on Suako. He wondered when she'd be arriving? The next few days perhaps? They were a little early after all.

Mei's laughing suddenly interrupted his thoughts, she was clearly having fun and over indulging in drinks. He began to jot down her transformation after the incident back at the mountains by Ryoko:

After close observation Mei has totally done a complete turn about, not just in her recovery but in her attitude. I believe she is trying to deny her past, which she divulged to us back at Miss Sui Akron's home. Since that time, she has seemingly put on a mask to cover up her feelings. She'd buried those feelings for so long, and after them resurfacing I guess she simply couldn't handle it. I'm worried about her. The looks in Kato's eyes when he looks at Mei makes me think he feels the same way.

Mei is currently getting plastered over by the bonfire with everyone. She's drinking it as if it was water and she was dying of dehydration. I wonder if anyone else notices the tears in her eyes behind that mask she's fabricated? Drowning out the past. I wonder if it'll work for her? It never did for me...

Mack is busy dealing with the C.D.F.P. organisation. I am starting to get the feeling that he has a second objective. I don't quite know what yet. He hasn't given us enough information. Maybe he plans to have it out with Yoshida? Taking down the empire should be enough to get him there. But no... it must be something else.

Suako has...

Before Vince could finish writing his sentence Jenko came over and slapped a bottle of whisky against his chest. "Hey! Get yer butt over 'ere!" Jenko said with a tiny slur. He and Mei had been drinking shots. Vince closed his books and slid it into his pack hastily, while Jenko yanked him over to the bonfire with everyone else. They danced and sang late into the night, enjoying the native's company, as well as their stories before they finally stumbled off to an empty cottage above the lake, which would accommodate them.

The morning sun came all too soon, and as they dragged themselves out of bed, each felt their heads pounding. Kairu, who hadn't touched of lick of alcohol, was the only one who was just simply tired. Rather groggy, Mei stepped outside the front door and saw, by the riverbank side, Kairu practising his martial arts. The thought of that much activity with her overly tired body was more then she could fathom. Kato saw Mei cringe at the sight and gave an effortless wheeze of a laugh. Vince felt well, having built his constitution up to withstand copious quantities of booze over previous years. Mack and Jenko took the longest to get out of bed; once they looked to the centre of the room and saw the tray of food left by the hostess of their temporary residency they soon felt violently ill.

By mid afternoon everyone had finally come around. Mack had gathered them all in a circle within there stay room. "Alright everyone, we need to make a game plan for tomorrow," Mack insisted, He never could stand wasting a day, his days in the military left him restless. If nothing else they would discuss being productive in their investigation to justify not having actually done anything. "Jenko, who are the key players here for us to work on?" Kato asked before taking a sip of an herbal drink.

Jenko, still holding a cold compress on his head, took a moment to think. "Well… the chief… obviously… uhh, lemme see now… well the elder if we can get 'em to say more then two words in a sentence…" Jenko continued in a stunted thought process. In the end they never achieved anything, but it still made Mack feel like they'd at least put in some work that day setting plans.

They lazed the rest of the day away, which almost never happened since they became mercenaries under Mack's command. There was a subtle breeze that played with puffy white clouds overhead. Golden hues blessed the sky as the sun sank down below the horizon that evening. Night befell the village, and the fire was ablaze yet again. While the others slept Kairu attended the festivities. He sat quietly and waited for the stories to begin again.

Morning slowly came, the overcast sky gave the illusion of time being earlier then it really was. A few noisy pelicans announced the unseen sun's presence. As they prepared to embark that day, Kairu suddenly entered the tent. He'd been out all night, but didn't look tired in the least. "I have news," he said in his usual tone.

Despite the lack of enthusiasm everyone took a seat and had a feeling this may be important. "What is it?" Kato asked, thumping against the hard-wooden floor. "I was out all night and met the chief's daughter. I got a lot of information," he explained. Everyone sat starring until Mack finally spoke up, "...And that would be?"
Kairu sat down as well, then he began, "Well, as we noticed from simply being here, there are no modern conveniences..." Mei interrupted, "Oh my god, I didn't notice that," she blurted out in a moment of embarrassment. "Sorry go on," she shook her head. "It seems although they have the C.D.F.P.'s power generator here, but they don't trust technology..." yet again he was interrupted, "Then why do they have that thing here?" Vince vainly gave Kairu a nervy glare. Kairu just rolled his eyes, "Ahem, *as I was saying*, they don't trust or believe in modern technology. They have that here against their will."

Eyes darted back and forth from person to person. "It was just recently installed here, I barely even noticed how new it was when we arrived. That is the Companies very first generator using the new technology, the first to use their new chemical compound. The C.D.F.P. required this land because they had problems configuring the coolant system but didn't want to delay production. The water in Quan makes the air a few degrees cooler here. They can easily pump the water in through the machine as well, rather then expending money and importing water into a location. Hence they chose Quan."

"...And the company has very *persuasive* ways of getting their way," Mack grimly added. Kairu nodded and continued speaking in his formal dialect, "The company offered Quan some gold. At first Okichi's father denied them. Soon offers turned into threats, and the people of Quan, being a small solitary group of people, could easily be forgotten about. The Company forced their way in here using those tactics. Okichi's father couldn't afford a war, he knew it would result in annihilation of the Quan tribe. Rather than risk everything he let them build their 'wicked contraption' as she so eloquently put it. The C.D.F.P. keeps this town poor by inducing heavy taxation to allow them their air filtration dome."

"Damn the company. They always be bustin' in where they don't belong," Kato convulsed. They shared his feeling in a mutual murmur of agreement. "Good work," Mack praised Kairu. "We know where they stand now," Jenko's eyes were deep as he peered back into his memory, "...when I was last here some years back the C.D.F.P. were camped out not far from here. I left before anything happened. Someone mentioned 'C.D.F.P.' and I got my ass outta the line of fire. That must've been when the so-called negotiations took place." He said, eyes lost in searching his mind.

They spent the following week scavenging the town for any scraps of information. Unfortunately, the Quan people were simple and therefore kept their conversations as such, and they didn't care to discuss the generator which they all condemned. The Quan tribesmen were also very superstitious. They believed speaking about bad things perpetuated the bad things to become a stronger role within their lives. This made it complicated as they tried to get more information. Some of the younger generation, who were rebellious to the 'old ways,' were a little easier to dig information out of, though they didn't know as much as those older and politically involved.

It came down to only a few people of whom they had yet to talk to. The tribe elder, being one of the last. Mack didn't know how to approach the old man, he'd felt the initial impression hadn't gone as well as it could have. The old man didn't seem to trust thim, and Mack spent much time dwelling on whom to send in to speak with the elder. He finally arrived at the conclusion that Kairu would be the best choice. Kairu, practically being royalty back in Ryoko, had lived a sheltered life within the mountains. His innocence would certainly be trusted, Mack thought.

Kairu had no problem with this, so he entered the tent, while the others stood outside waiting. The aroma of freshly dispersed essential oils was hovering around the tent; the curtains collected the fragrance as it ebbed out. As Kairu passed through the curtain he felt a sense of calmness wash over him, he bowed, and asked if the elder was taking any company at the moment. The old man looked up over the top of his novel, nodded and Kairu came forth to sit in front of the man. The elder placed his book aside and removed his reading spectacles.

"What do you desire, boy?" The man seemed pleased to have some company. From what Kairu could tell the man lived a rather solemn life, none of the other tribe's people seemed to visit the old man for anything but advice. He was wise, he could read into your mind, and peer into your soul. They must feel uneasy about that, Kairu thought to himself.

"What is your name, wise one?" he asked, unable to stick strictly to his task, the old man made him curious. In Ryoko everyone was close to everyone, no one was excluded; although he somehow felt segregated at times. The old mans eyes glistened, no one had asked about *him* for the longest time. "...Otojiro," he said half stunned. "Blessed Otojiro, would you tell me of your history?" Kairu could not help but ask. This pour soul had been starved of attention. Everyone he'd spoken with for the longest time wanted to know about themselves, now it would be his turn to tell his story.

Otojiro sat there, in a bit of disbelief. Kairu watched the man's expression go from bleak and knowledgeable to the heart of a young man. After a short pause Otojiro began to tell his tales, and Kairu listened intently. Part way through Otojiro fixed them both some tea. He offered Kairu some of his treasured imported dried fruits, which he'd kept hidden in a small safe near a tiny wooden self-supporting bookshelf.

Otojiro told of gripping stories of wars, from back when the continent from the west had claimed this land as their own. The people fought admirably to win back their land to no avail. The old man used to be a grand warrior for the tribe, he led the Quan into battle many times against the new empire before they were forced to surrender. Otojiro was so enthusiast he enacted a few of his battle sequences for Kairu.

Kairu loved hearing his father and grandfather speak of Ryoko in its historic battles years ago. The bandits that used to come and attempt to pirate the old city and escape to the sea was one of his favourite stories: *They came one night while the city was sleeping. They crept around and stole whatever lay in front of them. By sunrise they'd stolen half of the old city's economic property...* and so the story continued, though Otojiro had reclaimed Kairu's attention suddenly as he exclaimed "*Thud!* The enemy hit the ground, and then..."

Hours passed outside and they all wondered what was taking so long inside the tent. "This is ridiculous! What could he be saying that's taking so long?" Vince angrily grunted, fatigue getting the better of him. He was feeling rather envious of Kairu's maturity and entrusted responsibilities, despite his age. Kato was starting to feel a little agitated himself from waiting so long, "Should 'n we be doin' somethin'?" He asked feeling rather useless just wasting time waiting. "Maybe we should go..." just as Mei finished speaking, Kairu slipped out of the tent. Mei, Kato and Vince hustled over to Kairu to see what had been said. Jenko and Mack pulled themselves up from the ground and walked over, stretching their arms as they did.

"So, what did you find out?" Mei eagerly questioned. Kairu stopped moving completely for a second, "Have you all been waiting for me?" he pointed to himself. Mei and Vince vigorously nodded. "So? Common, what'd ya' find out?" Vince asked crossing his arms. "I uh, forgot to ask." Mei and Kato stood looking dumbfounded. Jenko couldn't contain himself, and he erupted with laughter. Mack shook his head, "Oh that figures... Well don't worry about it kid. But, what were you in there so long for then?" Kairu looked up a little embarrassed. "We just talked," he said, then walked off to be alone.

"I don't believe it," Mack laughed. "Waste of time," Vince complained. "Oh, lighten up, he ain't used to interrogatin' people. Besides, he understands formal town structures better then we all do. He'll get us any info we be needin'," Kato said as he started walking off towards their cabin. Mei looked at Vince questionably, her eyes asked *why such animosity?* though her words never reached her lips. She then took off after Kato and went to the cabin. Mack and Jenko strolled off toward the food tent talking about their plans.

Vince just stood there alone for a minute, then walked off into the jungle like area. Using a strong hanging vine, he hauled himself up into one of the trees.

Looking off into the distance he sighed as he watched a few clouds pass overhead. Under his breath he whispered to the wind, "Suako, where are you?"

The floor creaked as Mei entered the cabin. "Mei?" Kato asked turning around. "Hmm?" she looked to him. "What er' ya up to?" He asked, and his eyes asked much more. "Laundry. You have some?" she said as gleeful as any Quan homemaker. Kato shook his head, he looked at her, and he watched her masquerade. He was tired of her always wearing an invisible mask, he saw right through it.

Kato took a moment before he could bring himself to speak his mind. "You've changed," was all he could think to say. Mei laughed, "What are you talking about?" "That's what I'm talking about," her laughter then faded to a grim expression, like a thief being got with stolen goods. She tried to slump it off, "I'm the same old me," she said nervously, turning from Kato to tend to her laundry. Kato walked up to the trembling woman. He gently spun her around to see her tearful eyes weeping. Mei whimpered, "I... I just don't want them... to take anyone else... from me." Her fearful eyes searched his for comfort.

Embracing Mei within his grasp, Kato stroked her head lovingly, "I won't let 'em Mei. Dun you worry." He rocked her gently, and they stood there holding each other for a while. They exchanged no words for the longest time, lost within the sanctum of one another. Mei quivered as she broke drown the barriers of her invisible mask; she was exposed, always, to him.

Desperate hands grabbed Kato's body and refused to release him. "They can't take you too..." Mei sobbed. Kato pulled slightly from her and wiped the tears from her eyes. "They can't have me," He smiled. A tear soaked suffering face looked back at him, her tender heart tried to speak, "But..." in protest. Kato drew near to Mei, and he tilted her head up smoothly and silenced her with his reassuring eyes, then leaned forward and kissed Mei's soft plush quivering lips. Kato was the home which she'd never allow C.D.F.P. to take. Mei was safe within his hold.

Jenko noticed as Mack's eyes scanned the town constantly. After finishing his rice, he placed his bowl down noisily, disturbing Mack's train of thought. Mack turned to look at his companion, and found it off to see him starring back. "You didn't tell them," Jenko replied to Mack's expression of wonderment. Mack sighed, "I couldn't bring myself to say it yet... everything else was fine but, I don't want them to think I'm using them." "They wouldn't. They've all suffered the C.D.F.P., you're no exception," Jenko replied. Mack nodded, "In time." There was a secondary pause. "Well, have you asked about him here?" Jenko inquired. Mack nodded, "Yea, no sign of 'em. I keep lookin' though. Never trust that easy."

Don't let me to ache, I cannot endure to do so again...

Chapter 7: Dark Secrets

Yu-Lee was revitalised to have an apprentice under her wing. Suako was attentive to everything Yu-Lee told her about the planet, magick, and the Universe. She kept a small journal of all she was learning, and Yu-Lee opened up all of her own personal recordings to Suako. Whenever Yu-Lee was busy with someone else Suako had her nose lost in the books. Time slipped away without her even knowing it.

Time seemed to case to exist in this place. Weeks passed and Suako could barely differentiate from one day as it morphed into another, her mind was so focused on the task at hand. After a month of focus on theory, Yu-Lee felt Suako was ready to start utilising the life energies. Suako was excelling as a student, she could hardly sleep; her mind had never been so alive. All she could think about were her studies. This magick was just too interesting, this power, so strong and useful could help save the planet; Suako would make sure of this.

Yu-Lee was fully contented to be teaching Suako, but something wasn't clear about Suako. Suako was a positive soul, always optimistic, and this fit in every aspect of her life, except when she slept. Yu-Lee often found herself awakened by Suako calling out in her sleep, screaming and cursing, overcome by night terrors. She was always fighting something in her sleep. *What could it be that was such a predominant force over her subconscious?* Yu-Lee wondered.

Once day Yu-Lee mustered up some courage to asked Suako about her dreams, but Suako had no reply. She sat there in though for a brief time, then she simply lied. Suako told Yu-Lee, "I don't remember my dreams." Then quickly she tried to change the subject. At first Yu-Lee just gave Suako the benefit of the doubt, but as the night terrors continued Yu-Lee knew something more was at play than Suako was willing to discuss.

As Suako slept on several occasions Yu-Lee would work long hours into the night. She asked the life energy to heal broken straining dreams that affected Suako so horribly. Night after night it was no use, the terrors continued. She attempted preparing a brew of vervain tea for Suako; an ancient sleeping herb, in an attempt to bring her peaceful dream. Suako drank the tea, but it was to no effect that night either.

Yu-Lee knew she was hiding something; hiding, or burying. Whatever she was doing with it, it was festering deep within Suako like a toxin. Yu-Lee knew she needed to help Suako before it destroyed her. One night while Suako was asleep Yu-Lee attempted to call upon Suako's life energy to tell her the story with the nightmares. They painted her a picture within her mind's eye:

It was black, all darkness, but for a single minute light pouring in threw the barred peep hole of a wooden door. The floor was cold, and felt dirty against the bare skin of cold feet; she was imprisoned. Strange inexplicable bitter scents filled the air, and the stale sickly smell of urine and feces mingled with them. Muffled voices could be heard off in the distance, and faint screams echoed off the stone walls. In the corner a prickly pile of hay and matted cotton lay for sleeping. The voices then began to speak in low subtle tones:

"Hurry, they'll be here any minute! I can't die here... not like this... What's taking so long? Common, common!"

"Just let me work it. I've only ever seen this done before."

"We don't have time! They're gonna get us...."

"Just shut up unless you want to die in this cell!" There was a brief silence, and then "Shh... Listen.... Oh shit, he's coming!" the second voice said. Whoever they were they scampered quickly away from the door. They went to the corner, or so Yu-Lee's ears told her. The conspirators panted heavily, frightfully.

Loud footsteps walked up unto the door, and a pair of large devious eyes gawked into the morbid cell. After the eyes spotted a target there was the jingle of clanking keys as the peeping man unlocked the door. Light was almost blinding as the dung swung open. After the blinding light subsided the man was visible, he stood tall and was wide, hair covered a great portion of his gruff body. He wore a soldier's uniform, and carried a gun.

A scream came from within the cell. The contents were revealed, two girls in their late teens, huddled in the corner of the cell. They were wearing loose tattered clothing, and had great scars over their torsos. Both had long matter hair, growing from bloodied and bruised scalpts. Their arms were covered in many clean surgical cuts. "No!" one of them repeatedly screamed and hollered as the other tried to crawl away from the man. He came into the cell, grabbed one of the women and dragged her out, locking the other one in once more.

Through a dimly lit cement passage way they travelled. Many more cell doors lined the corridor.

Petrified prisoners in the calls gasped as the heavy footsteps passed them by. The girl struggled to free herself. She whimpered, and was struck on the back of the skull with his armour-plated hand for doing so. Blue electric light pulsed into the small passageway as the man unlocked the large steel door before them. Big bold letters read on the door: **AUTHORIZED PERSONEL ONLY**. Terror filled the girl's eyes and she clawed at the wall not to be taken in, tearing off finger nails and leaving a bloody trail on the wall. As the young woman turned to do so Yu-Lee caught a glimpse of the girl's face, it was Suako. The door slammed shut.

Yu-Lee suddenly snapped back into reality, and Suako woke up, and sat in her bed, soaked in perspiration. Suako saw Yu-Lee sitting with incense burning about her, and Yu-Lee's eyes focused in on her. They acknowledged that each other knew what just happened. Nothing was said that night. Yu-Lee watched as Suako lay back down in her bed, then followed her lead and went to her own bed; morning would be for talk, this night was for thoughts.

After a sleepless night, they both had an early start to the day. Yu-Lee prepared some mint leaves to wake them both up from their tired state. Suako heard her rustling around and pulled herself from her bed and strolled into the kitchen. The morning was bitter cold. Neither said anything, both were still in the middle of a long train of mixed thoughts and emotions of which they were attempting to sort out within themselves first.

Yu-Lee sat down and passed Suako a warm cup of ginger tea and a small wooden bowl with some mint puree, and the scent alone awoke Suako's senses. They sat staring at their cups. Yu-Lee awaited Suako to speak. Still examining her cup Suako began to speak, "I never meant to hide anything from you... but I'd never told anyone of it. Not a single soul... I know you saw. I know your great powers. You were there, I could feel you there with me..." she trailed of in a bit of a daze.

After giving her sometime to recuperate, as Suako lifted her drinking dish, Yu-Lee finally came out with a nagging question, "Where is... there?" Suako's hand quivered as she lowered the cup back to the table. Three painful breathless words pursed through her mouth, "Torusan... The.... Company..." Yu-Lee had thought that they were the only ones sadistic enough to use people for their experiments but she'd never seen those cells in any of her visions before.

Yu-Lee was about to question Suako on these rooms of confinement when Suako began to speak again. "You saw only what I saw tonight... right?" she didn't await a reply, she already knew, "The other girl... my sister Renee... after that night I never saw her again. They must've killed her... We tried to escape. I couldn't pick the lock in time..." Suako wiped a tear from her blank face, her eyes appeared to be vacant.

Suako paused again. "The rooms you saw... they're on a base level five... the C.D.F.P. building supposedly only has three sub-levels, according to their official documents. They have some of their laboratories down there... we were their lab rats. They stuck IV's in us and gave us drugs to sustain us consciously during many of the procedures... they'd open us up... see what we could live through. They were working on some sort of pain endurance project. Something to help their soldiers.

We were also test dummies for any new chemical products that may be used to enhance the soldiers... I... I had a small capsule inserted within my left arm... it connected right to the vein... it injected me with a drug induced night vision on periodic intervals... I removed it myself when I escaped, I got the sharp rusted shackles that'd been around my feet off and I... I used them to di it out. I nearly bled out..." Suako relived the event within her head. Her once calm tone turned deep and hate filled. After a moment she cooled down and showed Yu-Lee the scar on her arm.

"Some of the more critical operations they put me to sleep for. I don't know all of what may be placed within me. I have a strange impulse to hide the secrets of the miserable time I spent within the tombs of the C.D.F.P. building... I've been mutilated beyond repair," she sighed. Her hand hovered above her stomach, but she couldn't bring herself to touch it. Suako slowly rose up from her seat, then undid her robe slowly and revealed bare skin. Her stomach was covered in precise scarring, the scars you would expect to see from a doctor's scalpel. So many trained across her fair skin she so faithfully hid from the light; hid away from all others sight.

All perfect precision scars, less for one, and Yu-Lee's curious eyes hit Suako. Suako was not shy to share the story of the gorged scar that obliterated its way through several other marks, indenting her skin. It appeared to be a burn of some sort, except for that fact that burn scars to not pattern them selves in such an exacting fashion. Suako explained to Yu-Lee that that scar was the only one she actually didn't mind keeping.

One late night she was taken down to the sterile white laboratory for experimentation. The doctor that ordered her as his specimen had been highly intoxicated. He attempted to use a highly new technology called a laser, a tool he'd never used before. The beam cut along her skin, though she didn't bleed. The doctor was taken aback with its power and accidentally hit the contraption, the laser became intensified, and swung about removing his index finger.

The prison guard came rushing in to assist the doctor. The doctor was so drunk that night he hadn't tied her restraints properly. As the guard dealt with the idiotic scientist she slowly pulled and yanked her way free. She pulled the guard's pistol from its holster, and she killed the guard with a single shot to the head, and pirated a katana from his dead body.

Rage from years of torture didn't leave room for tolerance. Infuriated she held the sword high above her head, over the snivelling scientist, who pleaded for his life like the weasel he was. Suako's patience had been drawn to an end. Briefly closing her eyes and envisioning her sister she whispered just loud enough for the scientist to hear, "This is for you... my sweet Renee..." and he met his bitter end. Suako commented in broken sentences of the happenings before his final breath, her words weren't clear, but one could assume her vengeance to be far from merciful.

Suako's horror stories of her two years within the C.D.F.P.'s entrapment continued through the course of most of the day. Yu-Lee gave Suako her full attention from dawn till dusk. That day the sun never pierced the clouds that rolled overhead. Suako had to remember to stop and breathe the little breath she could take in from the deoxygenated, seemingly toxic air, that the C.D.F.P. had provided the outer world with. The day was as grim as ever, yet in the end Suako felt lighter. Her buried secret was now out, she no longer had to carry the weight on her chest, just the haunting memories.

From the day of Suako's deepest secret being announced she changed; the mask has been shattered, and the fragments thrown to the wind. The fraudulent happiness and fake replies were gone, Suako was a real person again, no longer hidden away. Yu-Lee saw the transformation from cocoon to butterfly, the new woman was strong, and although angry, she seemed oddly relaxed. Suako no longer smiled at everything, nor occupied herself for the full twenty-four hours in her every day. Suako found her self lost in thought as she starred out the beautiful arching windows into the wastelands outstretched beyond her eyes.

The new light shone on Suako's personality left Yu-Lee more at ease. Not as often would Suako toss and turn screaming out into the dead of night. Now Suako was involved in the planet life studies mind, body and spirit.

She could finally link her reality into the life source, she was one with the nurturing earth, and in sync with the ever-flowing universal powers.

Save me from the nightmare before it consumes me, don't let the light fade again.

Chapter 8: Grid One Life

Light footsteps echoed through the hallways on the executive floor of the C.D.F.P. headquarters building in Torusan. There was the sound of the click of a young woman's shoes mixed with the rattling of papers as she flipped through a document. The woman was tiny, and her raven black hair was tightly tied into a neat bun behind her head. Her starched grey suit moulded around her small figure as she walked. She entered the elevator at the end of the hall, impatiently tapping her foot as she awaited her destination. *Ding!* The doors opened onto a single room floor at the very top of the building.

"Ah, Tamiko," a man's voice coyly greeted from behind a large chair. Tamiko stepped out onto the floor and walked up to the desk the man sat behind. Curved windows stretched from the floor to the ceiling within the circular room. The man spun around, and watched as Tamiko swayed in towards him. "How's my favourite Dome and Generator accountant and Maintenance Department Head doing?" he cheekily titled the woman. Scarlet eyes pierced back at him displeased.

The chubby middle-aged man soon saw teasing wasn't a good choice today, he saw the icy glare within her eyes. Swiping his hands threw his greying brown hair he rested his head in his hands. "Mr. Chairman, my department has just completed the construction estimates for the rebuilding the generator in grid eleven," she passed him several papers. "So what's the problem?" he asked taking them from her. "Well sir," she began, but he cut her off. "Please, Tamiko just call me Genjo," he said with a slight sigh. "Ahem, *Genjo,* the issue is that we are falling behind in our tax collection funds. It seems Quan hasn't been paying its monthly taxes for several months now. Of course, the C.D.F.P. has enough funds from other savings to begin immediate construction, that it isn't an issue. My point though, is that we have to dip into our other savings rather than use the tax money we would usually rely on for repairs and building in general."

Taking his spectacles out of his drawer, Genjo put them on and pushed them up. Scanning over the document as he listened, Genjo nodded along in agreement. "Mmm, I see... well I'll be calling a board meeting tomorrow. We'll see what everyone thinks the best course of action is then. I'll be seeing you promptly at 800h in the conference room on the seventy-second floor then," he said firmly. Then turning on his intercom to his secretary, he began to babble orders of who to call unto the meeting the next day.

Tamiko took her leave, and Genjo's voice soon became monotonous behind her. She entered the elevator and pressed the digits 7-0 into the keypad. Tamiko gave a sigh, busy thoughts scrambled about in her overworked head. As floor seventy was coming up she straightened herself out to her usual stiff and formal appearance. *Ding!* The door opened and she stepped out. Busy people scurried back and forth throughout the hallway, in and out of rooms. Work oriented murmurs bounced to and from one person to another.

Tamiko entered her office and gently pushed the door shut behind her. Sitting down at her monitor she immediately began to make up a general report for the audience at the council meeting the following day. Furiously she worked on various projects until hours late into the night; the world outside of her office was oblivious to her. Long nights were her speciality, Tamiko was driven, motivated to be perfect in everything she did. Soon night turned into the early morning hours, and hers was the only light on, on her floor.

Creek! Tamiko nearly jumped out of her skin when her door opened suddenly. "Working late again I see," a deep voice said. A man with ice blue eyes peered in. "Oh, Koto," a sly smirk crept crossed her face. Koto's blond hair intensified his appearance, there was a dark undertone to his nature. Koto fully entered the room and strutted up to Tamiko, sitting down on her desk. Only for Koto would she drop everything in a heart beat. "My dear, may I rescue you from paper?" he asked picking up a few from the desk. "Hey!" she quickly snatched them back from him, "Don't touch! I've been compiling this data for hours. It's taken me forever to put this all together!" Tamiko angrily snapped at him.

The young man's expression went sour, and Tamiko was suddenly fear struck, she turned red from head to toe. *How could I have talked like that to the C.D.F.P. manager? The chairman's son!* she questioned herself. Koto was the only person to whom she'd ever felt the need to submit her power to. Only to him did she feel powerless, yet completely drawn to. "Koto... please forgive me," she bowed her head. Only to her work did she hold such loyalty as to speak up against him. Koto smiled at his prey in submission. Vainly he held his head high, "Shall we then?" He stood offering her a hand to help her up, he nodded, and again all was well.

It was nearly 2:30AM when Tamiko and Koto finally arrived at her house. An hour later, after drinks, Tamiko had her back against the wall, Koto insisted on staying the night. Tamiko enforced her need to sleep before her meeting just over five hours away. "Mmm, Koto... please, common... I need to sleep," she moaned as he caressed her with frequenting hands beneath her robe, and quick moving lips upon her neck. After much swaying, begging, and a final passionate detachment he left.

After waving Koto off from the porch, Tamiko went back inside her grand house. Tamiko listened as Koto's car screeched away down the street, leaving tread marks on the otherwise perfect road. Her house was all pristine white within, furniture was scarce, as was her presence within the large home. No one else was there, she lived alone. Seldom was she home but for to sleep, decor was as bland, as was her black and grey wardrobe.

Tamiko entered her bedroom and looked drearily at her unmade bed. *I wont sleep anyway* the thought and turned to go into her oversized marble bathroom. She drew the water for a bath in a porcelain tub. As the water slowly filled the tub she went into her kitchen. Opening the cabinet, only a few bottles of wine and liquor grazed the nearly barren shelves. As she walked through her atrium she picked up her work bag, which she'd thrown on the couch prior to her bedroom engagement, and walked back to the bathroom with it. She removed her robe and stepped into the soapy bath water, reviewing her work portfolio.

Tamiko sat in the tub reading and sipping wine until dawn arrived all too promptly, the sun shinning threw a stain glass window. The night had been sleepless, as it usually was for her. She washed the soapy water from her flesh, then dried herself off with an overpriced C.D.F.P. embroidered towel. Walking to her room she entered her dressing room, and Tamiko pulled a black dress suit from her closet, along with a pair of leather boots, with a sharp pointed toe.

"...Yes, send a pickup immediately to my residence," she called for a company cab. Tying her hair into her usual tight bun, she dragged dark red lipstick across her plump lips. She viewed herself in the full-length mirror of her hallway, throwing her overcoat over her shoulders she prepared to leave. The cab came and honked its horn to inform of its presence. Grabbing her briefcase, Tamiko left, and the door echoed within the barren home as she pulled it shut.

"Good morning everyone. Please be seated," the weighty Mr. Genjo Anami told everyone as he lowered herself into his head-honcho chair and the front of the oval table. A cluster of important group leaders within the C.D.F.P. had gathered. "It seems the Dome and Generator monitoring department has stumbled upon some facts they need to bring to our attention. Tamiko?" he quickly passed the floor off to her. Tamiko stood up, "Thank you Chairman Anami. I have prepared this for all of you, please take a look," she said as she passed around a fact sheet for everyone.

As the papers were being passed out, Koto finally came into the conference room. "Sorry I'm late everyone, father," he bowed, then took his seat. "What have a missed?" he asked looking to Tamiko as she passed about the papers. She slid him one and said nothing, though strongly desired to reprimand him for tardiness. A few moments later everyone had received and read over their copy of documented facts. "It seems," she started, and attention was immediately given to Tamiko as she stood at the front of the room, "that the small tribe clan Quan has been ignoring its taxes. We usually use tax collection funds for building, or repairing Generators. We need to fully rebuild the grid eleven generator, as well as part of the office building, after the most recent terrorist attacks," She pulled pictures to be passed about of the aftermath annihilated of the generator and damaged office facility.

"We are currently pulling funding from our own saving bonds for the repairs. The construction will begin immediately, there are no issues holding us back time wise. However, the issue of Quan's neglect has now been brought to our attention," she summarized "Great. Thank you Tamiko," the present signalled for her to be seated.

"Now everyone. How are we to collect? We want every departments idea."

"How about we send them an overdue notice?" A young woman sitting next to one of the scientists suggested, which stirred a flurry of responses from around the room, "No." "How could we just do that?" "There'll be more delays!" protested voices round the room. The woman went red and sank back behind her chestnut locks of hair. "How about removing the dome?" another voice came, though no one saw who said it. "Then we are still lacking out money." "No good! No good!" more protesting encircled the table.

A broad-shouldered gentleman leaned forward, his deep booming voice grasped the room. "May I, president?" he asked. "Yes, General Yoshida, please speak," Genji replied. Yoshida stood and leaned his fists on the table, his suit was highly decorated with medals, "As I see it we need to take 'em by force. We go in and straight to deal with their tribe leader. If they don't give the payments we confiscate what valuable items we can and sell 'em to make up for losses." Yoshida sat down. Talk spread amongst the table. "No argument here," one voice agreed.

"If I may," an elder man, with a lab coat on stood up. "Direct action is necessary. Though due to their negligence, should we not enforce overdue fines as well? Charge them interest to warn other domed cities that tax payers are not to slack off in the future?" the pale man looked around. There was a general murmur of agreement. "I say we should also include a collection fee for the deployment of our troops in order to collect the overdue payments," Koto added. "Give our boys a nice bonus as the end of the month, Eh? Ha, ha!" he chuckled.

"Everyone in favour of the proposed, say aye," Genjo asked shuffling his papers into order. A mutual consensus about the room was quickly met. "General Yoshida, when can you spare your troops?" Genjo inquired. "We can leave immediately," Yoshida said confidently. "Good, good. Be sure to file a report upon your return," Genji instructed. The general nodded, "Yes sir." "Meeting adjourned," Genjo dismissed them all and left promptly.

Koto assisted Tamiko up from her seat, "That went well," he smiled. "Thank goodness. This company can't lose face, we'd suffer an intolerable rebellion," Tamiko stated sweeping a few loose hairs back behind her ear. He escorted her down the hall, "So my dear, may I have you for the evening tonight?" he asked. They'd reached the elevator and awaited it. Before Tamiko could answer he went on, "I've reserved a spot at a certain little..." he waved a little card in front of her face. Tamiko looked up and her eyes seemed to sparkle, "Oh, my favourite bistro! Thank you, Koto. Come and get me from my office after work then?" she queried. He nodded.

The elevator door opened, and they were about to step on when the scientist from the meeting ran up to them, "I'm sorry to interrupt. Koto, you're needed." Koto rolled his eyes and turned to look at the man. "Can you not see I'm busy?" he sharply growled. "Yes sir but, we need you *immediately*," he insisted. "I see. Tamiko, I'll see you later then," he kissed her cheek and then followed the scientist down the hallway with haste.

As the elevator doors shut Tamiko felt like she was a few seconds behind lost in thought. *What was so important?* she wondered. The man's eyes were intense with fear, it must've been quite serious. She was curious, Koto often was called away down to the research laboratories, but he'd never told her his reasons. Though he was the manager of the regional areas, why such devotion to the Torusan's research department over the other facilities? Tamiko sighed and just let it go, the elevator had reached her floor.

Slowly the afternoon slipped away, all was well in accounting. Tamiko finished her work and tidying up her things for the night. Koto was on time nearly to the second, as usual. *Knock, knock!* "Hello, my dear," he addressed her in his usual smooth toned manner. He opened the door and leaned against it; he looked smart in his dark suit. His intense nature intrigued Tamiko to no end. Tamiko bounced up from her seat and to his side with a sexy sway, and his hungry eyes watched her intently.

They ripped down the street in Koto's red sports car, the engine roaring. It gleamed in the bright light of the sinking sun, and sparkled under the streetlights. Koto dodged dangerously between cars, speeding down the streets. Tamiko was swept away by his adventurous nature, and dangerous appeal. *How could life be any better? Dating the second to the head of the C.D.F.P.?*

What is it about him that sets my soul on fire? She wondered as she watched him drive. Blonde hair cascading down over his face, around his electric eyes.

They arrived in the heart of grid one's industrial section within minutes. He offered her a hand from the car and took her down the welcoming red carpet into the restaurant. The chandelier in the centre of the establishment twinkled and glowed in the candlelight. The lighting in general was dim, soft, and very romantic, and Koto reserved them the best table within the restaurant them. Koto had money to burn, his father, Genjo, spoiled him rotten. Both his father and he had more wealth then either could spend in their lifetimes.

They settled in at the table, but before conversation commenced he pulled a fair-sized leather box out from his briefcase which he'd brought in. "Here you are my dear," he said pushing it over to her. He reclined in his chair and sipped on some water that was provided by their hostess. Tamiko quickly finished shimmying her coat off of her shoulders and onto the chair. Her smile beamed as she attended to the box, it gave a gentle creek as she pulled it open. "Oh, Koto... it's beautiful!" she exclaimed, pulling a diamond necklace from the box. "Nothing but the best for you, Tamiko," he told her placing his cup down.

The white gold was embedded with at least a hundred tiny diamonds that twinkled and shimmered in the light. Koto stood up and circled around the table. Taking the necklace, he draped it around her neck and latched it on. She got up, threw her arms about him and gave him a kiss. "Shall we dance, my dear?" he pulled his head back slightly as some gentle dinner music began to play. Tamiko was swooning, as she followed him over to the dance floor. It seemed life was nothing but good in the upper class.

After two bottles of the chateau's finest wine, Tamiko finally recalled a question that edged at her mind earlier. Without hesitation she brought the subject up, "Koto, what was the urgency with that Dr. Fumiaki Abe earlier today? Some breakthrough on the psychological floor?" Koto's smile went dim, and he took a minute before he spoke. Tamiko sat there wondering about the delay. Finally, he gathered his thoughts, "Tamiko... if I tell you, there's no going back." Tamiko was taken aback, "What are you talking about?" she asked, confused. He sighed, "I can only tell you if you are going to be going all the way with the C.D.F.P. Are you?" he questioned. Tamiko nodded, this was her life, she had worked hard to get into the C.D.F.P. and live the good life at the top. There was no way was she giving it up now.

"Alright then," he looked her in the eyes, with a slightly sinister appeal, "we can't speak here about it. Better yet, you should see for yourself," he concluded and took his coat, throwing a small bag of gold on the table. Tamiko scurried to get her things together, her intrigue was growing. *What could be so secret?* She couldn't even fathom the possible answer, so she stopped trying to fit the pieces of the puzzle together.

Despite the heavy drinking over dinner Koto drove relatively well, their conversation and where they were headed sobered him up fast. A small smirk lay across his face the entire car ride. Nothing much was said, though Koto stated as they'd entered the vehicle, "Oh my dear, you aren't gonna believe this," he said followed by a devilish little laugh, which soon faded, "too bad you couldn't have seen the entire experiment." The anticipation grew. Tamiko was too drunk to conceive of the possible consequences associated with taking on company secrets.

It seemed to take an eternity, in Tamiko's mind, to reach the C.D.F.P. official building. Tamiko was surprised when they got into the elevation that they were going downwards. "Aren't the labs…" she was about to say, then realised that this wasn't just some wacky science project. They went down several sub-levels to the point of which Tamiko never knew ever existed within the building. They stepped out of the elevator. Tamiko was getting nervous; the light was unpleasantly sterile as they marched down the hall and entered through a large titanium door.

The room was a blinding white. Bewildered scientists eyed down Tamiko as she came in, they were clearly worried by her presence there. The room had several giant test tube type machines built in. Several dead, mutated organisms floated within a liquid inside of the tubes. Tamiko took on her workplace demeanour, "What is all this? How come this floor *doesn't exist*?" she asked firmly. "This is the C.D.F.P. Inc.'s hidden research laboratory. It isn't known because the Western Empire doesn't support it. We also wouldn't want enemies of the Empire, or C.D.F.P., to get hold of any of the technology we have developed down here," Koto explained.

Tamiko nodded slowly trying to make sense of everything in her head. "What are these?" she tapped on the glass window of a test tube. "Part of the emergency earlier today," he signalled for her to walk with him. He went over to a metal table and flipped open a book, pictures, diagrams and scientific jargon filled the pages. He stopped about two thirds of the way through the book. The page was entitled, "Human Experimentation" her eyes darted from the page to Koto.

An empire of such power- let me merge- let me show my worth.

Chapter 9: Into the Freezer

Months had passed, and it was a chilling autumn in Quan, Suako had still not come back to meet up with them as she'd said she would. Vince faithfully awaited her arrival, he refused to leave without her. The others had left him there while they went on minor expeditions to a few petty communities within the Quan region. They returned one cool day under an orange moon.

"Yo, Vince!" Kato called as they walked back into Quan toward the misty swamp. Vince looked up at the tired party as they neared him, and he stood up to greet them, though a grim expression was upon his face. "Still no sign of Suako?" Mei asked, she though knew the answer. "No... How was the trip?" Vince asked solemnly. Jenko dropped his luggage and stretched out his neck, "just glad to have some air in my lungs," he said breathing deeply. "We'll tell you over some fried rice," Mack said patting Vince on the back, "we'll drop off our stuff and head over right away. We haven't eaten anything since early this morning."

After they'd put their gear away they all headed over to the food tent. They all ordered as quickly as possible, they we're tired, cold, and hungry from the trip, and the hot food would warm them up. They sipped some gently brewed teas as they awaited their dinner. The moons broke out from behind the clouds in the sky, and the bright orange of the harvest moon glowed, beaming off of the swamps murky surface.

"So... there's nothing new?" Vince asked slightly shocked, since they had toured for several weeks. "Unfortunately, no. There are just small groups of people that have no real feelings either way towards the company. They didn't have any useful information. I should've guessed nothing would've changed," Jenko sighed. Everyone knew that they'd never planed on going to those places, they sympathised with Vince, but now time was slipping away.

They told Vince briefly of the people they'd encountered, and what the settlements were like, but he could barely keep his concentration. He gazed longingly to the southern horizon line. Their voices were slowly drowned out by his thoughts. He wanted Suako back with him, he wanted to have his companion back. His frustration and worry welled up within him till he was just about ready to burst.

"Vince... Vince?" Mei shook his arm. Vince suddenly snapped back into reality, "Oh, uh, sorry," he said shaking his head. "Vince..." Mack sighed, he couldn't stall their progression further, "Vince, we have to go on. We 'ave to leave tomorrow. The planet, the people... everything's dying. It's getting worse out there," Mack said. Vince shook his head, he'd expected as much but dreaded hearing it, "I can't go," he simply said. "I'm going to go down to Kagawa. If Suako went there, then I will follow. I have to know why she hasn't come back... I was going to leave before but I... if she was dead I... I didn't want to know. But now I need to know, one way or... or the other," he choked out. They all fully understood.

"We wouldn't have it any other way," Mei smiled reassuringly. Mack nodded. "It's alright, we need find out. We're planning to head to the ruins of the old Ryoko," Mack told him. "I'll give you a sketch of my map to take with you. This land is much bigger then it seems," Jenko offered. Vince smiled, "thanks everyone. I know deep down she's all right... but I have to find her."

They spent the evening trying to forget about the worldly woes weighted upon them. They celebrated as best they could with the Quan people this one last time. This refuge had been a blessing, a safe haven for them, in a violent world. Kairu spent the night with Okichi, she loved hearing stories of the world. The two could relate, both being chief children and isolated for it. They sat off to the side, content with just each others company for the evening. The young lady wore her tribal jewellery, and a white gown that her dark brown hair graced over. Kairu spoke quietly to her, hiding his words from eavesdropping ears.

As hard as everyone tried, no one could really forget anything, their mission ahead was tough, and vital. They drank berry wines and enjoyed the evening, disguising what lay below the surface of their exteriors. The night passed slowly, and Vince didn't sleep at all that night, he spent the night writing in his journal, he penned down everything on his mind. He also sketched everybody within the pages to remind him of there ever present beings within his life.

A thick mist covered the cold earth as the sun took its time rising on the eastern horizon, and a brilliant red stretched across the sky. The team awoke, and slowly dressed and prepared to leave, stocking up on as much rice and non-perishable goods as they could carry. Mei stepped out from the cabin they occupied to get some fresh air. As she tied a sweater about her waist she looked up at the blazing red sky. Kato stepped out from behind her, and her low toned words caught his attention, "Red sky in the morning, travellers warning..." He patted her on the shoulder and kissed his on the cheek, "It'll be ok."

They all gathered at the food tent one last time for their final meal in Quan. "I really hope we'll get to come back here to celebrate..." Jenko said grimly. Kairu looked off toward Okichi's tent, as well to look at Elder Otojiro's sitting plainly beside it. "Yo, c'mon ya'll, we be comin' back 'er," Kato firmly looked about the table. "He's right. I don't want all these melodramatics, the planets held on this long, and it's gonna go on a lot longer after we get rid of the C.D.F.P," Mack insisted. "He's right. Once Vince gets Suako they'll be hot on our trail," Kairu optimistically said. Though Kairu was young and fresh to the outer world, Vince hoped he was right.

"Mmm, I think I'll 'ave to live just to eat some more of their soups 'ere again," Kato announced. A weak smile reached Mei's face, and the others gave slight jest of laughter. Then a a revered silence settled upon all of them, of which Jenko finally broke, "Here Vince," Jenko pulled a rolled paper tied with a braid of dried tall grass, "I made you a copy of the map. It's about a four-day journey to the Kagawa region. There isn't any oxygen there, so enjoy your last few breaths for a while here," he said passing him the map. Vince took the map and respectfully bowed his head.

Breakfast was rather dull otherwise, filled with tension. No one knew what lay ahead of them, but they new something was going to happen. They felt it, and they also knew just how badly the earth had degraded in just the past few months. Life was too intense, and they wished for a different reality. To wake from the seeming nightmare of which the world was devastated in, but they never woke up from the nightmare of their lives.

The travellers set off promptly after eating, and they parted ways at the oxygen dome entrance. "G' luck man," Kato gave Vince a bear hug, "Bring 'er back." "You take care Vince." Mei said as she threw her pack over her back. The others said their goodbyes. "I'll come back. We'll find you," Vince said, and with that he turned and left.

After a few minutes of prepping themselves the others prepared to embark on the long week of travel they themselves had ahead of themselves. "Kairu!" a voice called from behind, and Kairu spun about. "Kairu don't go!" Okichi called out in vain, tears streaming down her face. She ran up and flung her arms about Kairu, "you need to finish story telling," she cried. "I must go," he said patting her head. She refused to let him go. "He'll come back, I promise," Mack assured her. She finally let him go, "come back to tell me more stories," she insisted. Kairu nodded and brushed a tear from her plush cheek, and they shared a smile. With that they turned and took their leave.

The humid air encircling Quan worsened the transitioning breathing process. The clouds held on to the sun's heat, magnifying it. Vince covered himself in a cloak shield against the sun, the muggy heat was uncomfortable. The damp air would stick to his lunges, but Vince tried to forget it all by thinking of his dear, sweet Suako.

Vince kept his distance as he crossed back past Atani, walking along the edge of the great canyon by the mountains. Water used to flow there, as stream lines along the rock walls depicted. It looked like a giant crater, the depth was thousands of feet below him. Gigantic rock pillars swarmed within the canyon; it was exhilarating, yet nerve-wracking, to walk close along the edge of such a massive earthly formation.

The second day into the trip he noticed a military regime marching his way, and Vince quickly hid himself within intertwined rock formations. As he waited an hour for them to slowly pass him by, he wondered what the C.D.F.P. were up to. He took it as their response to their attack of Atani soldiers months ago. *Hmm, guess the massacre finally drew the attention of headquarters* he assumed. He silently spoke as if he were with everyone travelling to the ruins, "Be careful everyone."

When he felt the soldiers were safely out of range, he emerged from the rocks, and he started up on his journey again. The sun had risen to its peak in the sky, and the day was virtually cloudless, excluding the smog. He passed by several animals that lay dead on the dry, burnt earth, all appeared to be freshly deceased, without signs of struggle. The heat had finally brought them about to their bitter ends. Vince drank as much of his rationed water as he could to make up for that which he lost threw the paining heat.

The day seemingly had no end. The sun did not cease its onslaught, and Vince now understood why those beasts gave up and died dead in their tracks. Vince set up a tent, unable to endure any longer. Blisters instilled on his feet pulsed painfully with every step he'd taken since he took his leave from his hiding spot near Atani. He'd wait till the sun's retreat below the horizon before commencing his journey again.

The sun was still unkind within his tent. Vince dragged every tiny breath in, and each scorching breath pricked his lunges like needles threw fabric. Drifting in and out of consciousness, Vince realised just how quickly the earth's atmosphere was decaying.

"If life is to only offer this, let it offer nothing."

After regaining consciousness for a third time he knew he needed to stay awake, he had to keep his mind sharp. He took his journal and inkwell from his pack. The heated ink ran quickly from his quill, and the large blots of black stained the page as they dripped. Vince didn't know what to write after he recorded his C.D.F.P. sighting the day. He looked about the smouldering land of which he lay in, and after a moment, his pen seemed to move by itself:

Amanda Rose

"Burning heat from an intolerant sun,
Beating down on the vast plains below,
Red earth as far as the eyes can see,
Grand rocks cover this hellish trail.
The hazing sky above,
Magnify the death of light,
And to the dry earth,
We fall weary,
Breathing fire till the final moment,
Where no more breath do we require.
To the last we fight,
Struggle to survive,
To our ends all we desire is to stay alive.
Nothing for days ahead,
The road is bare,
Seemingly repeating its course,
And it need be asked "This, did I already pass?"
Life is scarcely found about,
Air diminished,
Barely existing within this world.
Impeding life,
For which we thank our brethren,
Come from afar with their curse,
A plague on all."

The sun finally began to dip behind the mountains, and a blanket of a cool refreshing night air soon grazed the earth. But relief soon turned into a new struggle, and the world went from blistering hot to frigid. Only warmth from the smog above gave consolation to the cold. Vince wrapped his cloak tightly about him. The cool air, though tolerable, was no more pleasant.

Seldom beasts would be seen scavenging the lands at night, desperate for food in a barren desert. The chilly night was just as intense as the pounding heat of day, and shelter was essential for survival in the insufferable purgatory. Earthly bounty was nil, it was kill or be killed. They couldn't live to hunt during the day, yet night brought a fatal fatigue on any roaming creature.

The haze of the smog above blurred the stars. The full moon was a light bulb hidden under sheer fabric. The veil of death differentiated the barrier between their world and those above. It was a symbol, it was their invisible cage. They were all trapped within their own chaotic world, and humans left unable to leave until fixing that mess which they'd perpetrated.

As the night neared its end, Vince noticed the ground turned from solid to cracked, it looked like alligator skin. His blisters tormented him throughout the night. The sky began to turn from indigo to hues of yellow and green and the sun's light began its ascent. The sky remained clear. Mist began to rise from the ground as celestial warmth ebbed down upon the earth's surface. The cool dampness of night rose up, and it wasn't long before Vince could not see far ahead of himself. Heat was gathering, so quickly he perched up his tent, and hid within its sanctity. Long hours would pass before he could travel again.

Before the inferno of the day commenced, the last remnants of the cool air of the desert lulled him off to sleep. Vivid dreams of plush lands filled his head, shaped by the stories of his great grandparents, the world before the C.D.F.P. poisoned it. He'd heard these tales which had been passed down to his parents. He heard of green rolling hills as far as the eye could see; of a sky so crystal clear each individual star could be identified; he heard of beautiful animals grazing pastures; of forests so vast, scented of pine and fresh running water of hot springs. These images that he'd collected, collaborated into numerous images within his artistic head. The world had had so much to offer. All that was left now was waste. Vince's motivation had always been a question that he desired to prove the answer to be 'Yes'. The question of 'Can we reverse the cycle of death that is consuming all?' Sweet dreams of the lands of old kept Vince in deep sleep, not even the mid-day baking of earth woke him. Late in the afternoon his hungry stomach finally nagged him to rouse. He fed his starving body and watched as the sun once again made its way down the western horizon. As the flushes of colors slowly became faint he prepared for his nightly excursion across the desert.

Though Vince was well rested and energised, the biting chill numbed him quickly. He remembered and old ballad his uncle had taught before he'd passed away. He began to sing to keep himself warm:

"O 're the hills and mountains high,
Across wide plains where horses tread,
I see the path I must get by,
To get on home and go to bed!"

Vince laughed at the silly little ditty. He thought of his uncle and long days before, and remembered sitting in his tin can of a house, it had been nearly vacant within. He recalled looking through old art diaries of his great grandmother, she had been an incredible talented artist. She'd captured the landscape of her and his uncles time. The colours were grand, the spectrum was exceedingly bright diverse compared to that of the dull world of Vince's time.

Vince remembered spending the rare days his parents and his uncle could get off of working, listening to stories of life as it once existed. Even his parents lived in better days then that world of which he'd been introduced to. He heard fables of times passed, and from these stories he created a view of the world that was devastated by his first site of the new reality.

He remembered watching his parents and his uncle as they slowly withered away, suffering from exhaustion. The C.D.F.P. work force demanded much, and gave little. They were practically slave-labourers, with no other way to get by, but they worked their hardest to keep Vince in good health. They saved every penny towards his future, he was their pride and joy, and they intended to leave everything to him. Upon their deaths the C.D.F.P. seized all their assets and auctioned them off for a company fundraiser, under the guide of borrowed wages that would now not be worked off. Vince was left on the streets to fend for himself at the age of eleven.

Vince tried to only remember the good times that were had, though they were poor, they made due. He remembered all of his birthday gifts handcrafted. On the Birthday before his parents passing, his mother had taken paper from the C.D.F.P. building, collected leaves from tree's malting leaves that blew over onto their grid sector and made him his journal. She used her own hair to create a binding for it; it was Vince most prized treasure. Their hand made items were all he could get from the C.D.F.P., as they couldn't make any profit off of them. After joining Mack's Mercenary group, he left his treasures there. Though he carried his mother's handmade journey and his great grandmother's art journal with him always, never able to part from the images of what he longed to someday see.

Vince continued to rest during the daylight, and travel during the frigid night; the nights were getting longer as winter approached. Despite the lengthy nights Vince had to stop occasionally, making fire to fight off the frostbite. The trip took him an extra day than he had expected. The south he'd assumed would've improved in temperature, though it wasn't the case.

The last night of travel Vince began to notice frequent tremors of the land. He'd heard of the shaking ground from his Uncle who worked farming to the south east as a young boy before the vegetation became completely blasphemous in comparison to it's origins. He'd heard of the earthquakes, but they never were explained to be like these ones.

The rattling ground worsened as he neared Kagawa, they were intense, sending him falling over often. The sun was rising as he was reaching the city limits. As day was about to begin, several engine propelled wagons passed him by. He flagged one down, though they weren't too happy to be held back, a man, women and two young boys stopped, but were impatient to be back on their way.

"Where is everyone going?" Vince asked as he caught his breath. "The earth is acting up like never before. We're all leaving Kagawa now, you should get out too. It ain't safe here," the man said kindly warning him, though he spoke hastily. The woman tapped his shoulder, he eyes urging him to get a move on. "Just one more thing sir," Vince started, "a friend of mine was in town, she…" The man impatiently interrupted him, "yes, yes, the young traveller that showed up a few months ago. She was staying at the temple. She's not there… whoa…" The woman was becoming uneasy as another tremor began. Vince fell forward, catching himself on the wagon. They two young boys cuddled up to their mother, the man began to breathe heavily, desiring to leave for his family. "They left a note," he said quickly. "Thank you sir," Vince said stepping out of their path. "Best of luck to you sir. That land is cursed. Be careful," he said speeding away.

When Vince reached the town it was completely vacant, and the ghost town was eerie. The ground looked as if it had begun to slit across the centre of the town.

Homes all had broken windows, and one house's wall had ripped open. Only the stone temple seemed to stand intact. Vince ran to the building; a note was nailed into the door.

"To whom it may concern,

The temple is closed while we go to Okagwa to initiate one with the magickal knowledge of old. Please be patient for our return.
Sincerely, Yu-Lee"

Vince quickly pulled his map from his nap sack, but unfortunately, his map did not extend further east then Kagawa. Vince hit the door out of frustration until it burst open. He walked inside and quickly he saw Suako's hair comb lying on one of the tables, and went over to it. He knew it was hers for certain; Vince put the delicate comb safely away in his pack. He looked frantically about the temple, and he found a woven map of the entire continent. "Okagwa... where are you?" he muttered to himself as he searched about the map. Finally, he saw it far to the eastern regions of the continent. The journey would take at least two days travel by foot.

Vince scavenged the town for any leftover food and water, and stocked up his pack. Though day was breaking, the tremors were becoming dangerously violent, and he couldn't risk staying. Vince found a bicycle type contraption left on the dirt- street. He covered his skin as best he could, then using all his willpower, he pedalled as fast as he could. The cracked and brittle ground proved a challenge to cross as it shook.

Fatigue swept over Vince's entire body; he'd not rested properly before persevering. The fleeing, panic-stricken townsfolk were reason enough for him to move with haste. His legs burned from the bike combined with the heat of day. His adrenaline was pumping, and all Vince could think of was getting to Suako. He tried to distract himself from the inflicting pain by thinking of the first time he met Suako:

"Ouff!" Suako fell backward after running into Vince. Nervous eyes looked up awkwardly at him. "I'm sorry Miss," he offered her his hand. She hesitated then accepted his offer, and she wiped the dirt from her puffy purple skirt. "No, it was my fault," she said, slightly dazed by his kindness.

"So where are you headed in such a hurry?" he asked smiling at her. She blushed, and her prior mouse like mannerisms seemed to disappear. "I'm looking for a man named Mack. I heard he lived in the grid system here," she said. "Who is he?" Vince asked. "He's the leader of a mercenary group. I'm looking for a job," she explained. "Do you mind some company?" he asked. Her sweet eyes spoke to him in depth. "I'm an artist, looking for some new places to record. Mercenaries travel a lot, don't they?" he inquired. Suako smiled, her eyes lit up. "Yeah, they do," she giggled.

That was they day they met Mack, Mei and Kato, and they both became mercenaries under Mack's leadership together. They were the two youngest and newest members of the group, so they'd stuck together from early on, like peas in a pod. The mere coincidence of their collision on the road always made him happy. How easily they could've missed each other, and he'd have been left on the streets to live, unable to tear down a company that brought his family to an early death. That day he never forgot, Suako's eyes the moment she smiled he constantly tried to capture within his drawings. It was the one thing he drew often, though he never felt he could perfect it.

Vince did not stop to sleep until the following day. He was exhausted, thirty-six hours straight of travel had finally brought him to need sleep. Though he rested the revolting earth would permit no real sleep. After a few hours rest he pushed forward, and within a few short hours he had Okagwa within his sights.

He rushed to the ruins of the long extinct city; crumbled buildings lined the streets, grey stone, once buildings, lay as rubble on cracked cobblestone streets. Dried vines stuck to the few standing walls that remained. Broken pots with long dead herbs and flowers lay cracked in the streets. Though Vince could not tell what it was, there was a strange strengthening vibration he felt empowered by, within the decay of Okagwa.

Vince rushed through the debris-covered streets as fast as he could. He called out Suako's name repeatedly and he frantically searched, but heard nothing in return.

This had once been a vast city, full of hundreds of thousands of thriving lives. As Vince approached the back of the city he noticed a large courtyard encircled by a large limestone wall, that was somehow still fairly intact. He ran within the gates, and Vince was taken aback by what he saw before him.

It was like the pictures from his great grandmother's art journal, life was blossoming everywhere. Vines just like those that hung dead about the rotting city behind him, here they were luscious and green within this courtyard. The sun gleamed down, the sky above seemed clear, and the rays did not burn bare skin. Vince had never seen such a sky, and he'd never truly seen the sun without the distorting glare of pollution.

A colorful bounty of bleeding hearts, tulips, daffodils, and lavender swayed in the gentle breeze. There were rose bushes all about the garden. Butterflies flew about, chirping birds perched in hawthorn trees, and busy bees drew nectar from the apple blossoms, and golden sunflowers seemed to glow. Tiny shrubs grew round and short along the base of the wall. A fresh water spring lay to the back surrounded by carefully placed moonstone crystals. Hues of blue and rainbows within the stones scintillated. Soon Vince recognised the lack of oxygen dome to foster the plants as well, and he wondered how they could possibly be growing. Dancing cherry blossoms seemed to float off of their trees, before they hit the rich earth beneath him. The brutally shaking ground seemed to have stopped as well.

Logic and reason hit him like a pile of bricks suddenly as the euphoria wore off, and he looked ahead of himself. Suako lay on the plush grass, and a woman in pink garb danced spirals about her. Vince was in a state of shock; he was in the wastelands of the world, yet life flourished freely here. "Suako!" he called as he ran forward. Suako sat up immediately at the sound of his voice, and seemed to come out of trance. "Vince!" she exclaimed as he saw him hurtling toward her.

"Vince, I can't believe it's you!" she hopped up and wrapped her arms around him, "this is Yu-Lee..." she began to explain, but Vince cut her off. "There's no time! We have to leave now!" he interrupted, his voice fiercely serious. "W, What? Why?" Suako asked, stunned. "You'll see..." He looked over to Yu-Lee, "I'm Vince, nice to meet you. We have to leave now!" he said to Yu-Lee as he took Suako's arm and began to run forward. He looked one last time back to the garden, then pierced the gate between dimensions back into the real world.

The air seemed toxic after the momentary paradise they'd experienced within the garden's sanctum, and Vince and Suako both started to gasp for air after emerging. Okagwa was as black as charcoal when they came to, the darkness seemed blinding, like walking into a room with no lights on. The complexion of the world was grey, black and muddy brown. Suddenly a strong tremor hit, and Suako screamed and fell to her hands and knees. Yu-Lee came through to the other side just as the tremor hit, and just barely caught herself, nearly plummeting to the ground herself.

Vince assisted Suako back to her feet, "Kagawa villagers were fleeing when I passed through there... it hasn't let up... it's getting more severe... we need to get as far north-west as we can!" He called out to them both over the roar of the raging earth. The women both nodded in understanding. Buildings began to crumble further from the incessant shaking. Huge pieces of the once glorious city crashed down to the streets around them as the three fled, dodging the oncoming attack from above. The ground started to split open; their time was short. Chips of stone flew up and scratched threw their clothing; the wreckage seemed to attack them as they scurried to the city limits. The monstrosity of the city became a maze, streets we're becoming blocked off with debris; Yu-Lee showed the way out as best she could remember.

They struggled but eventually made their way safely out of the deathly entanglement. They continued to run as fast as their legs would carry them until, a few miles away from the city, they fell to the ground panting from exhaustion, with legs that refused to carry them any further. They looked behind them to watch the remnant of the glorious magickal-city enveloped within the opening earth. "Okagwa..." Yu-Lee gasped as she watched in terror, a single tear crept down her cheek.

The earth seemed to be sucking in the structures, the city fell within the now concave earth below. Slowly, bit by bit, it disappeared below the earth's surface, beyond their sights. Last but not least, the garden to the back of the city slowly fell within the hold of the earth.

The swirl of it's colour was pulled away from them; the brilliant moonstones shone one last time before they fell to a new resting-place, far beneath anyone's sight.

There was no time for mourning, the split of the earth that had begun in the center of the city wasn't done yet, and was continuing to collapse the land outside of the city. "We have to go... I'm sorry," he told Yu-Lee helping her to her feet. Her years of wisdom allowed her to put it behind her, to escape the enveloping earth. It was hard to stand with the earth shaking so violently, never the less to try to run on the shifting surface. Vince's bike had perished along with the city, so they were left to travel by foot, with an invincible enemy trailing close behind. "Everyone's headed to the old Ryoko... We should follow, to the north..." Vince called out in competition with the noise. The girls both nodded; anything but the Okagwa region was good for them.

As they started to try and run from the brutally forming pit behind, the earth cracked between them and began to pull apart. Suako found herself trapped behind. The earth pulled her back toward devastation, "Vince!" she screamed. The gap grew in a few short seconds too far to jump across. Vince turned, and looked at her in a panic. He quickly took off his pack and looked through his bag to find a suitable rope.

As Vince searched Yu-Lee got Suako's attention, tith eye contact alone, they spoke. Suako closed her eyes and reached her arms up tall. She began chanting unheard words. Vince couldn't breath, not his Suako; he couldn't have her taken away. He quickly glanced up to take a look at her face, but his heart stopped when he saw her; her eyes closed tight, arms held high above her head, stepping out onto nothing. Vince was about to scream at her to stop, but before he could she stepped off. But she did not fall as she pulled her other foot from the ground behind her. He looked briefly to Yu-Lee, and saw her eyes closed, chanting as well. In disbelief Vince rubbed his eyes, and he saw a brief white gathering of energy pulse beneath her feet like electrical surges as she took each step.

All seemed well, and Suako was a few tiny steps away from their plateau. Suddenly a massive quake brought Yu-Lee tumbling to the ground, and Yu-Lee's sudden loss of concentration disrupted Suako. A heart-wrenching scream gripped their hearts with morbid fear as Suako fell. Vince crawled hysterically to the edge, emptiness bit at his soul. He looked fearfully over the edge, his heart beating through his chest, and saw her hanging from a ledge of rock several feet down. Despite his relief, the darkness below her was still far from inviting.

Life is meaningless if I lose you.

"Suako!" Vince called, his voice was weak and trembling. She looked up to see his eyes burning with his passion to get to her, she fought back her anxiety. The tremor had stopped, for now, and Vince climbed down to her, placing his foot within a divot of the massing rock wall. Chunks of rocks were falling from the rock wall into the abyss below. Suako was within his reaches.

Vince dropped onto the thin rock ledge which she was dangling from, and he took her arm and helped to pull her up. They struggled to get her out of her precarious position, it took all of their strength. Once Suako was safely on the ledge her teary eyes filled with hope and gratitude, and she pulled him close, pressing her body against his. "Thank you," she cried in a whisper. Vince said nothing, simply enjoying his moment in her arms.

Against his will to stay with her, holding each other for eternity, he dragged himself away and helped her climb up the rock face. Yu-Lee helped Suako up on to safer ground once she could reach her. "Vince, common!" Suako called in desperation, holding out her hand towards him. He jumped onto the rock wall just as the ledge beneath his feet crumbled and plummeted downward. He used all his strength to pull his weight up the rock wall until Suako and Yu-Lee could help him fully up and out from the crevasse.

"Vince... Oh Vince!" Suako exclaimed holding him close. The young ones comforted each other, after facing the pain of almost losing one another, but the rumble of the terrain soon drew them apart. Vince swiped his backpack from falling down the cracked earth just before it fell, never to be seen again. Time was of the essence; they hurried away from the forsaken land before any more incidents could take place. The land continued to crumble away behind them as they ran, for a time. Finally, the massing current of exerted energy ceased, and no more earth fall into the new gorge. They paused to catch their breath, turning back to see a gigantic crater.

After a long day of travel under dark cloudy skies, the three longed to sleep when the chill of night slowed the movement of their already tired muscles. There wasn't any wood for fire, and the night was bitter, with fierce winds to torment them. Yu-Lee was rather quiet, feeling the loss of her beloved Okagwa. No longer could she ever visit the sacred garden, no longer could she directly call upon the life energy, the planets sources were weakening. The eastern side of the continent was no longer safe, and Yu-Lee felt utterly lost. She was left without a home to return to, the temple would fall into the chaotic grasp of the revolting planet in brief time. Yu-Lee's heart carried the burden of witnessing all she loved fall to ruin. She was lost in the world.

The night slowly dragged them all to sleep, they were exhausted and it had been too cold to speak anyway. The wind violently whipped the sides of the tent throughout the night, whistling loudly. The three of them huddled together as they slept, to reserve body heat to survive to the next day. The constant swaying from side to side as the wind pulled and pushed on the tent was hard to ignore. The howling of the wind seemed to warn them of the evil plaguing the planet. Vince lulled Suako to sleep with gently sung words in her ear, it was an old song his mother sang to him as a child to help him sleep. It helped them both feel more secure. The day had been one of devastation, all that was left were the people in life to care for.

"Here beneath blanketing stars,
Take us away to the heavens above,
Show me life and love,
Take me up and away..."

Just before morning came, they awoke to numbed fingers and toes that burned painfully with every little movement. The ache of their muscles competed with the stabbing pain of brittle bones. Vince rubbed Suako's arms and his own to help circulate their blood. Yu-Lee followed his lead, and began to rub her arms. "The sun 'l be up soon..." Vince spoke through icy lungs, he breath visible in the air.

Grabbing his bag Vince took out a small container of food which he'd scoured from Kagawa, and he split an apple between them. "We need to find food... I'm running low," he said, looking sadly at the diminishing rations. The sun cracked along the horizon, and the radiant heat soon made them forget the cold, and regret wishing for the heat. After a silent breakfast Yu-Lee was finally ready to speak. "So, who are you, sir?" she asked sipping from a water canister. "I'm sorry... this is Vince. We're part of a group of mercenaries. We've been fighting against the C.D.F.P. together for years," Suako quickly filled in, then turned to Vince, "Yu-Lee has been teaching me about magick and life energy."

"Life energy... wait, does this have something to do with how Suako crossed that gap?" Vince questioned, his voice filled with intrigue. "Yes," Yu-Lee nodded, "yes, that's exactly it. Life energy is a flow of energy that runs threw all living organisms, on this planet, and throughout the Universe. I've been teaching Suako how to manipulate it to her will," her eyes moved away from Vince to the floor, "Okagwa was where the density of life energy was strongest on earth. Unfortunately, Suako will be the very last blessed child from that ancient place. As you saw the garden there flourished without any difficulty, the life energy was able to sustain that small piece of this planet. It resembled what the earth should look like. It seems the C.D.F.P.'s poisoning has finally taken grasp of that last bit of old stable land," Yu-Lee said with a heavy heart.

"That place..." Vince said, his eyes filled with reflective thought, "I've never seen anything like it... but I have a book of pictures from just before the C.D.F.P. rose to power. My grandmother was an artist, until yesterday sketches were the only way I'd ever known the world was different from the rotting corpse it's become," he sighed shaking his head in his disappointment at the world.

Suako was about to take her drink of water, then a question suddenly dawned on her, "Vince, why are you here?" she queried. "We never expected you to be gone for so long... I had to come and find you, we thought you might be in trouble. Everyone else had to keep going. The world's falling apart. We really need your help... I, I needed to get to you," he explained, his cheeks slightly flushed.

Suako took a sip of water to try and disguise her now rosy face. Yu-Lee broke in after allowing them a moment, "Fighting against the C.D.F.P.? How?" she looked to the two of them. "We've mostly been trying to destroy their generators. The only thing is, our group is rather small. We can't knock them all out, and the C.D.F.P. has enough money to build them faster then we can bring them down. We've been trying to gather some intel... Mack, our leader hasn't said it out loud, but... I think he's planning to cross the western ocean to go to the Imperial continent..." Vince told them. Suako's eyes shot open wide, "What?!" she exclaimed. Vince just looked worriedly to her, "...That's why we need to hurry and catch them before they leave. I know they'll wait a while, but the severity of the company's generators isn't only being felt here. As we go north you'll feel just how intense the sun is, most of the animals are dying in their tracks now. We must be careful travelling by day, and by night is best if we can stand the cold..." he sighed, "We can't wait to long though... We won't be able to take much time to sleep or rest."

Yu-Lee sat quietly pondering for a few minutes. She closed her eyes and let out a breath, after making her decision, "If I may, I'd like to go with you. Okagwa is no longer, and it won't take long for Kagawa to be consumed. I may be of some use to you." Suako smiled, "Of Course Yu-Lee, I wouldn't have it any other way. If we can we'll save Kagawa," she tried to comfort her, placing her hand on Yu-Lee's.

Don't suck away all that was once precious on this earth; promise some return.

Chapter 10: Old Ryoko

"Damn Mack, look'it that!" Kato groaned. Not too far off in the distance from where they stood, the earth had an old river canal that reached from the gorge by the Great Mountains all the way to the northern sea. "That's a lot of water to have disappeared so quickly," Jenko added, taking his map out to revise it. "That's awful... those bastards!" Mei kicked the ground. "Guess we should get movin' before we save a place that ain't got nothing left for us to live off then, hmm?" Mack asked and walked on. Kairu looked ahead at the morbid scenery.

A half-hour later they reached the rim of the old waterless river. "Well that's a wee bit of a steep drop, eh?" Jenko chuckled looking downward. "Great. The trench is nearly twenty feet down. Guess we need some rope," Mei said pulling her backpack about her body to retrieve her rope. "Just a little detour," Mack said, lighting a cigar before they would travel on, "at least the sun's behind the clouds today. Makes this easier," he said sucking back on his sweet-smelling cigar.

"Is the world like this everywhere?" Kairu's quite voice spoke out from behind the crowd. His eyes peered wearily at the empty riverbed. "It's getting there," Mei said remembering her old life's sudden halt and retirement. "I see," he wandered up and down along the edge of the swooping scooped out land.

"With any luck we be changin' the lan 'scape 'round 'ere," Kato called to Kairu as he walked away.

"Let's keep hoping. If nothing else the Empire's going to feel the peoples anger," Jenko added. "Kato, help me with this," Mei said as she prepared to attach the rope to the ground. "C'mon Kairu, we're goin!" Mack called as he dropped his cigar and stepped on it with his mighty boot. Kairu slowly meandered back over to the group.

"'Kay, everyone, let's get moving. We'll rappel down the rope, hike across the bottom, then climb up on the other side," Mei said as she secured the rope about her body. She slowly lowered herself down with the rope, hopping off the moist river wall, until she landed in the wet sediment below. The tiny bit of dirty water left in the riverbed splashed up soaking her legs. "Oh great," she rolled her eyes. "Ok everyone, next one down!" she called up removing the rope from around her waist, "Just watch how hard you land!" Mei added.

Jenko was the last to come down, and when he was three quarters of the way down his boot got stuck in the muck of the wall. "Oh, son of a…" he mumbled. He used his other leg to try and propel himself off the wall. After several attempts, with a large suction noise, *POP!* Jenko came loose, but lost his grip on the rope, and he fell several feet landing on his back in a muddy puddle. "Oh my god, are you okay?" Mei rushed to his side. "I'm just peachy," he said rather annoyed. Mack couldn't contain his laugher. "Yea, 'Ha, Ha, Ha!' Real funny Mack," Jenko said as he stood up. The others couldn't help but chuckle too. Jenko's entire backside was covered in grime. "Guess it's not as dry as we thought," Kairu said in his quiet way.

"Oh, not you too!" Jenko shook his head, and their laughter roared.

After a short walk to the other side they all found themselves covered up to their knees in the remnants of the old river bed. They struggled to climb up the other side other the river, their footholds kept sinking down under their bodyweight. It took them an hour to finally reach the top, and by that point all of them head too toe covered in dirt.

As they emerged back onto firm ground the sky cleared, and night was closing in. Purple and magenta hues decorated the entire world in the magnificent sunset. "Wow, would ya lookit that!" Kato exclaimed mesmerised. "That's amazing..." Mei said as she hiked herself up. "This is what we're fightin' for people. Let's move it," Mack insisted.

They trotted across the terrain throughout the night. The air became crisp and cool, and it started to get very thin as they made their way further north. Everybody yawned often, their bodies were starved for oxygen. Kairu kept sipping his water to reenergize himself. Vitality was low, fatigue was high, and the landscape they passed some became repetitive in its scenery.

As the sun was peaking from behind them Jenko couldn't keep going on. "Mack... *huff, puff*... I don't think I can keep going on... without... some sleep," he dropped to his knees and took in several long breaths. "I agree," Mei said resting her arms on her legs. "Yea... I think so too," Kato said with heavy eyelids that were continuously sliding down. Mack turned around just in time to see

Kairu shaking his head in agreement. "Alright, we make camp now. Right after the sun passes its highpoint we move out again," he said, and began pulling his tent from his pack; everyone signed of relief, extremely grateful.

The break seemed to slip away all too quickly; each of them slept like the dead until Mack woke them. Mack had barely slept, he had stayed awake just watching the world around him, deep in thought. His body was exhausted but his mind was sharp, and sleep would not take him. He looked onward, eager to go, and once they were up, Mack marched the party nearly another twenty-four hours before allowing them to rest again. His body was about to give out, and Mack's will was all that was left, driving him to continue. The group noticed his new quiet mannerisms, and once all others were asleep, Jenko stayed awake to speak with Mack.

"Hey buddy," Jenko whispered as he crawled over from the other end of the tent up behind Mack. Mack was shaken by the sudden voice breaking his concentration, "Jenko? What is it?" he said back in a quiet voice, to prevent waking the others up. "What's been eating away at you? Is it *him*?" Jenko planted himself next to Mack. Mack sighed, "Yea... I have a gut feeling that we're close. He knows what I never learned... I tried to get him to come with me, tried to tell him that he couldn't trust the General or anyone else in the Company... I waited for him, but he never came. I never got to find out what it was that he knew. It might be what we're looking for," Mack said, then looked back to the northern sky. "Don't worry," Jenko tapped Mack's shoulder, "we'll find him, don't worry. Get some rest though. You're bushed, so if we find him you'll be too tired to listen to anything," Jenko laughed under his breath, as he lay down on his back. Mack still looked over the horizon for a while longer, "Yea, you're right," he whispered for no one to hear, then finally went to sleep.

The next few days were tiring, despite his conversation with Jenko, Mack had to constantly be reminded to give everyone a break. His mind was so busy time was anonymous to him, so the breaks they did get were short, and commonly restless for Mack. At last, with sore feet, they came up to Old Ryoko.

The city was immense in size; it was wide spread along the coastline. They marched on, down a long hill, and up to the coastal city. The ocean twinkled with golden tones from the sun, water broke gently along some rocks before hitting the shore. City buildings were scattered along everywhere. The outlay of the mining town of New Ryoko, Kairu's home town within the mountains, was obviously modelled after this first location. At the Far Western corner of town a large political office stood. The structures were made up of large limestone and sandstone structures plotted about the city. Small tuffs of grass stuck out of the relatively dry ground here and there.

As they entered the city they noticed a few people here and there, although the city was meant to be vacant, apparently some people decided to come back and occupy the free property. Small clotheslines were strung from one building to another, there was little in this city, unlike in the new Ryoko. They made their way through the city with odd stares from nervous citizens. They heard the citizens whispering about them as they passed by, but no one was friendly enough to welcome them into their city. The group marched quickly through avoiding eye contact with the residents.

All of the Old Ryoko natives seemed particularly interested in Kairu, they starred and pointed at him as he passed by. No one spoke as they travelled through the city any higher then a whisper. "Hey Kairu, what 'r they looking at you for man?" Kato asked quietly so as not to be heard by the people of the city. Kairu shrugged, "I have no idea."

As they made their way further to the back of the city, they saw fewer and fewer people milling about. They noticed the houses become simpler as they neared the waters edge. The homes consisted more of the common man's home, mostly fishermen's land. Since there was no rent to be paid in an empty city, those who remained took the higher classes old homes over the tiny, mostly unfurnished, homes of the poor previous owners.

"What are you doing with that! I told you to gut the fish, not massacre the carcass!" they heard a frustrated young woman tell her husband off as they neared the beach. Slowly they peaked around the corner of a building to see what was going on. The woman stood on the white sandy beach in front of a well-built man, he sat on his knees with a fish and long knife in his hands. Her cheeks were red from exasperated complaints. "Oh Seresuto, I'm sorry," he said giving in to his wife. He hung his head in shame. "Adamu come now! Be a man will you! Hmmp!" she threw her arms up and walked away from him. As she did she noticed Mack and the others watching them, "Hey, who are you?" she called out. Everyone determined her an extreme extravert from the get go.

"We're travellers. Are we interrupting something?" Mack asked, his eyes turning to Adamu. "Ha, ha! Heaven's no!" she abruptly laughed, and flung her sandy brown hair around as she looked to Adamu, "I'm Seresuto. That's my husband Adamu. I swear he's useless," she laughed as she rolled her eyes, and wiped her hands off on her apron.

Seresuto's hair was tied back in a blue bandanna, which highlighted her blue-green eyes. She appeared to have spent a great deal of her life outside, as her skin had darkened from the sun. She and Adamu appeared to be rather poor like the other citizens. Their clothing was cheaply woven cotton, the common people's fabric.

"Please come inside. If you're visiting Ryoko you'll need some shelter. The sea breeze is cold at night," she offered, twisting the doorknob of an old worn down wooden door. Before pushing it in she yelled suddenly at Adamu, "Adamu, we have guests! Gut all of the fish so there's enough for everyone!" she demanded. The door squeaked as she pushed it open, the air saturated their lungs when they entered the small home. They were shocked by what they saw thriving within the tiny domain. There were plenty of vegetables, fruits, and other plants growing all about the inside of the home. "H, how?" Mei was confused. "How d'ya get these?" Kato asked. "What?" Seresuto asked looking around, "the plants?" They all nodded at her.

So Seresuto explained it all out to them, she told them how during the radiation period that destroyed most plant organisms, the people that remained here in Old Ryoko harboured the plants indoors, sealing them off to the outside world. After the radiation levels dropped back down into a safe range they still had vegetation. Due to the high carbon dioxide emissions the plants started to thrive. The oxygen provided by the plants the people considered like a gift from the plants, for saving their lives during the radiation crisis.

The people had kept the plants inside even after that poison left the atmosphere, because of the sun. After they recognised how the sun was damaging their own bodies they felt the plants would die out within days. Living stayed simple when they neglected the need for an air dome; they had plenty of food, and kept their solitude.

"Mm, this is amazing! I haven't had a peach since I was back in my home town," the sweet fruit intoxicated Mei. Juice trickled down her chin, she was in a state of bliss. Everyone enjoyed some of the splendid fresh fruits; Kairu ate plenty of blueberries, which had run out in the New Ryoko when he was still a young boy. Mack contentedly threw grapes into his mouth, the cool sweet and sour juices quenched his thirst. There were cherries, apples, raspberries, plums and much more to feast on. Seresuto dried plums, dates, grapes and apricots in the sun and then stored them in glass containers. Kairu noticed the bottles on the shelves.

"What are those for?" he asked as he sunk his teeth into a shinny green apple. "Hmm? Oh, the dried fruits, we dry them so that they last for a long time. We need them for when we go on trips out to sea... I'll be back in a moment, I'll go see how Adamu is doing with those fish," she explained and took her leave out the door.

Everyone was now at attention. "Hey Mack, maybe they be able to take us 'cross the ocean?" Kato asked, peeling his orange. "I never saw a ship," Jenko said, looking to the others. "Me neither," Kairu agreed. "We'll have to wait and see. Let's not get ahead of ourselves," Mack told them as he tossed a few more grapes into his mouth. *Squeak*! The door opened. "The fish are ready. Come down to the beach. We're starting a fire for the fish. Hope you didn't fill up too much on the fruits," she said then walked back away.

The tender sun kissed the world goodnight, and the stars began to come out and twinkle above. The fire roared under a metal grill plate, which long strips of cod cooked on over the open flame. The group inquired about the city, and any affiliations it might have with the C.D.F.P. Seresuto and Adamu, but mostly Seresuto, told them how the C.D.F.P. didn't even realise that anyone lived in this city since the invasion a hundred years ago. They explained that that was the second reason they maintained to keep their plants indoors, to avoid attention. Seresuto also told them that they kept their relatively large vessel hidden away under a cascading ledge of land that extended over the water a few miles away.

Finally, it was the couples turn to ask questions, "So where are you from?" Seresuto asked in her usual blunt and rather intrusive manner, before biting into a carrot, *crunch*! "We're travelling from Torusan," Mack said. "I'm from Ryoko though," Kairu added, "the new one," he added. "You look familiar, who are your ancestors?" Adamu asked. "I come from the line of chief's sir," Kairu replied. Seresuto's jaw dropped, "Really? You should come to city hall with me tomorrow," she said. Nothing more was said on the subject. Kairu's interest was peaked, and he desired to ask about their excitement, and what they had to show him, but his shy disposition held the words behind the safety of his lips.

The night provided a peaceful sleep, the proper rest was long overdue. The ocean waves gently sounded in the bay, the plants smelt sweet and fresh, and the oxygen was revitalising. Even Mack couldn't stay up that night, and he feel into a deep sleep. They were grateful for Seresuto and Adamu's hospitality. The beds on which they lay were filled with soft fluffy feathers on top of cotton. Silk sheets, left over from the Empires attack vessel within high-ranking officers quarters, were provided for them. The soft sheets glided over their bodies, caressing bruised and tired limbs.

When morning came it took a lot of doing for Mack to get the others to wake up for some breakfast. Kairu was the only one Mack didn't have to struggle with to get out of bed, he was as ready as Mack was to take on the day, and get some answers. Mack practically needed to take a crow bar to the rest them to pry them from their warm beds, and the intoxicating oxygen. By mid-morning the aroma of freshly made applesauce, hinted with cinnamon sugar woke their senses.

As they exited their sleeping quarters they noticed that the sun had begun to take hold of the sky with his golden arms. "Mornin'!" Adamu called as he stirred a large iron cast pot that hung over the fire pit that they had used the night before. Seresuto finished peeling one last apple and threw the pieces into the pot. "Food 'll be ready in a little while everyone. S'down," she welcomed them to sit on logs placed about the fire pit. Adamu passed the spoon the Seresuto to stir, then distributed fresh water around to everyone.

When breakfast was ready Adamu served up for everyone. He kindly gave extra to all of their guests over himself and his wife. The steaming applesauce kissed their taste buds. The luxurious food was like velvet, cinnamon permeated their entire mouths. Not one word was said while they indulged breakfast.

While they ate Seresuto noticed how intently Kairu's eyes had been fixated on her. She read within them the curiosity that had been building up within him over the long night. Seresuto could tell he'd been wracking his brain away, so, when she was nearly finished breakfast she put her bowl down, and stood up. "So Kairu, let's go to city hall," she said, and then immediately started to walk away. Kairu set his bowl down and chased after her, and the others followed right behind the two leading the way.

"What's there?" Kairu asked as they walked through the streets. "You'll see, be patient, will you?" she asked. Kairu interpreted her as being annoyed with him, so he held his tongue for the rest of the way. They walked up to a large building that reflected the recreation in his Ryoko that he lived in with his father.

They passed under the pillar sustained entrance roof, and through tall-carved wooden doors. The interior was much different thank Kairu's home, a thin corridor stretched down the centre of the grand building, and rooms lead off from it. At the end of the long running hallway there was one bigger door, which lead to the grand hall. Seresuto headed straight for that door.

They entered the room, which was just as big as the grand hall in Kairu's home, but this political building was substantially larger overall. He looked ahead to a tapestry that had the history of the city woven on it. He looked over the woven history, as it progressively grew on the long-stretched fabric, and told a long story of the people who had lived here. There was an empty space at the end of the tapestry, left for further recordings, which the Empires invasion never permitted the time for.

Kairu was mesmerised by his peoples' history so plainly available to his desiring eyes. He watched the progression from early construction of the city, to the last battle they'd won against the once small overseas Empire. There was no recording of their final and permanent intrusion that conquered the city, and none of the remaining people would consent to record it, for it would give away that people were here to have sown it onto the material.

"Kairu... hello!" Seresuto demanded his attention, snapping her fingers. He finally drew his eyes away from the wall hanging and plunked them down on Seresuto. She stood at a large towering bookcase, and held a thick leather covered book in her grasp. She flipped through aged-yellowed pages, that crinkled and crackled as they swung about. "Where the hell is it..." she huffed. Back and forth the pages bounced. Suddenly a satisfactory look came over her frustrated face, "I knew it was in here somewhere. Stupid thing," she announced.

Kairu walked around Seresuto, and looked down on the page. There was a picture there of a tall man in heavy metal armour, his Dark locks of hair were decorated in native beads that dangled above his shoulders. The warrior's eyes showed strength, power and confidence, yet were kind and offered mercy. Kairu saw the image, he was staring at it with unvarying eyes, and he could swear that he was staring at himself.

"He was the old town chief long ago, a great warrior as legend tells. You are certainly of his blood. He's the only reason I believed you when you said you were the New Ryoko chief's son. We all wondered when we'd have someone meander into our city, it was only a matter of time. Everyone knows these pages through and through, I talked to some of my friends after you all went to bed last night, they were about to get everyone to flee. We're always on our toes here. If the C.D.F.P. found out about us, well... the bastards aren't kind to non-tax paying citizens, let's leave it at that. Anyway, we knew one day we'd have someone come, we're just glad it's you," She smiled and bowed her head, and Adamu did the same.

Kairu had no words to say. He didn't see himself as a leader, nor did he desire the publicity of it all, "I... I didn't come here to..." he tried to explain but Seresuto silenced him. "We know. We just... just want you to know you're welcome here anytime," And with that she handed him the book and signalled for everyone else to clear the premises.

Kairu stood just gazing at his great grandfather, a true warrior, and though he hadn't been aware of it, he soon saw he shared his great grandfather's name. He stumbled about, eyes glued to the page, until he found a seat. He sat himself down and became consumed by the book, and read of his family ancestry dating back several hundred years. He learned of great men that lead the city through times of prosperity, and of other long deceased relatives that did not have such decent tidings written about their accomplishments, or rather regressions inflicted upon Old Ryoko.

Kairu indulged himself in his family's past, he wanted to know everything there was to know. He desired to have all his unanswered questions be solved. None of these documents could have been saved when the city fell under siege, they hadn't the time while they fled for their lives. Kairu felt that he held the key to the world in his hands. As he read he made himself remembered the courage and triumph of those who succeeded for the people, and the downfall of those who failed, so he would not make a mistake reoccur when he would one day take over for his father.

Seresuto and the others alternated bringing him food and drink; he became enraptured by these old documents and took no breaks. Kairu was too intent on the readings to remember his appetite. He stayed in the chamber for an entire week devouring book after book. When he emerged, he'd read through every relevant book within city hall. He walked through the streets with a new light cast out upon the once bustling city.

Each step he took seemed to echo through his body. As he looked down the road ahead he envisioned the people that once lived there, he stood still, picturing it all. They went about their chores, just as he had read they'd done. He watched the city being built, the great many wars fought, the women wishing their husbands luck out at sea, and the final drive that sent his people running from there homes in fear. He saw Old Ryoko's past up until it's future. *SNAP!* Reality sent him falling onto his back. He looked around. Everything was calm, and quiet, just as it had been the second he'd first set foot into the city.

Kairu made his way to the back down to the beach. Mei saw him through the window of Seresuto's storage room, and she ran out to see him, though he looked to be in a bit of a trance. He sat down on the beach and pulled his legs into his chest. Mei slowly made her way to his side and sat next to him, "Are you okay?" she asked. His eyes spoke of many things, but she couldn't read the foreign language in which they were speaking.

Kairu was silent for a while, but she stayed by his side. The sea breeze swept across them. "I... I saw everything..." he finally said. He told her of the many historical documents, and explained his family history and their devotion to Ryoko. He told her then how he would be devoted to saving the planet for Ryoko, in following tradition with his ancestral history. He had a new determination that he'd never felt before.

"Adamu?" Mack searched the buildings. He found Adamu in the kitchen watering the plants, "Adamu? Oh, there you are," Mack said relieved to find him. Adamu continued working, "Something I can help you with Mack?" he asked turning his head respectfully to show his acknowledgement. "I was wondering what you used the ship for?" Mack asked taking a seat. "We use it to go out to sea for fishing. There's a spot that's not too far away that we find lots of..." Adamu loved to talk, and went on talking about the keen finishing in deep waters. He went on and on until he'd finished water the plants all around the room and had started to chop up some carrots for dinner.

Mack patiently waited until he finally became frustrated from listening to the frivolous details of every possible location available on the great wide ocean. "Uh, Adamu, that's great but I had another question," Mack interjected. "Oh, ok. What is it?" Adamu inquired. "I was wondering if it would be fit to travel... to the Imperial continent," Mack said, eyes dead serious. Adamu's knife slipped from his grip, "D... Did you say the 'Imperial Continent'?" he asked rather overwhelmed, and in disbelief that his ears were being truthful. "Yes I did," Mack calmly said. Adamu left the knife where it had fallen and went over to take a seat at the table with Mack. "What in the world are you planning on?"

Mack told him in great detail the extent of their journey. He told him how the C.D.F.P. had to be taken out to prevent the death of every soul on earth. He reiterated the information that he'd found on the secretive C.D.F.P. documents that had been sent for him to destroy and disregard. Everything was laid out plain as day for Adamu to hear. They needed to get across the waters no matter what, so Mack held nothing back.

Adamu took it all pretty well, and after some thought, he agreed to help them get across the ocean. He went off to get Seresuto to tell her everything. He did not panic, but an obvious grim feeling had been wrenched within his heart.

That evening they gathered around the fire outside, as they ate they discussed their plans, Seresuto and Adamu barely touched their food. Their minds were overly occupied with the situation at hand. "So, I guess all that's left is to decide when to go?" questioned Kairu, his eyes now that of an up and coming leader. "We're lucky, after December twenty-first we'll have the right current to take us over to the west," Adamu said, then remembered he hadn't yet eaten his food. "Not even two weeks... I wonder if Suako and Vince will make it?" Mei unhappily brought up. "Suako and Vince?" Seresuto asked. "They're two travelling partners of ours that have fallen behind. They broke apart from us to get some info... anyway, we were hoping to meet with them here," Mei explained. "Don't worry Mei. I'm sure they're fine," Kato reassured her and kissed her forehead. She put on a faulty smile and sighed, "I hope your right Kato... I hope you're right."

We are a team, how are we to work together when we are so far apart?

Chapter 11: Occupation

"Shh! Do you hear that? It sounds like... screaming?" Suako ran to the top of an incline. She gazed over to Quan, and saw Company soldiers surrounded the entire premises. Yet again the screams sounded. Suako, Vince and Yu-Lee stealthily dashed toward the city, hiding behind large rock formations in between sprints. They discovered a temporarily unguarded entrance to the city that they quickly snuck into.

The city was infested with C.D.F.P. soldiers. From behind one of the tented homes, knee deep in the swamp, they watched as a high-ranking officer attended to tax negotiations with the Quan Chief. Frantic onlookers did not know what they should be doing, mothers took their young ones indoors, and proud tribesmen were infuriated by the treatment of their Chief.

"So, you think you are above the Imperial laws, do you?" the interrogator questioned, his voice booming angrily. It was intimidating to all, and the chief's lack of response, and proud expression, led the interrogator to trip the Chief to his knees. "Father!" Okichi yelled as she tried to run to her father's aid, but several guards hustled over to grab her before she could get to him. "Despicable! You are all in debt to the C.D.F.P. corporation! They have given you the air dome in exchange for a small taxation..." he continued to rabble. The people were fear stricken.

"What the hell's going on Vince?" Suako asked. "I don't have a clue. When I was going to get you, I saw soldiers coming this way, but I thought they were heading to Atani," Vince said. "Why'd ya think that?" Suako asked. "I'll explain later. Look... someone's coming. That must be General Yoshida... something doesn't smell right," Vince vigilantly watched the scene developing before him. Suako sat watching, confused and curious as to what pieces of this puzzle she was missing.

"That's enough Officer Kan," A deep, yet mystifyingly kind, sounding voice dismissed. Officer Kan left as he was directed. As Yoshida walked each step he took crunched loudly beneath his immense frame. "Chief, if I may..." he offered the man a hand up. "Shall we step indoors, the sky is grey, it may rain soon," his voice was coy and mischievous. None the less the chief was no fool, "This way sir," he allowed Yoshida to enter his hut. Several soldiers went to follow, but Yoshida issued them to watch the people, and guard the entrance. Okichi nervously waited for her father.

The crowd slowly dissipated, going about their routines, though with unhappy and worried faces. Most went inside their homes to wait things out. The sky crackled with thunderous rumbling, and rain began to fall from the skies and made the air misty above the water. Otojiro had been standing just outside his doorstep during the commotion, he caught Vince's eye as he turned to go back inside.

"We have to get over to the other side of the chief's hut," Vince told them. He briefly told them how Kairu had known this man, and how he would be someone they could trust. He also gave them a quick synopsis of the unfortunate bloodbath outside of Atani. The veil of mist provided the perfect cover for them to move about Quan discreetly. The water gently swayed and rippled from their movements, so they moved slowly, with caution. Guards were numerous, and after the Atani incident their heads were on the chopping block. The water was bitter cold and nipped at them. The cool late autumn days had chilled the swamp terribly, though the falling rain seemed to warm the water, if only a little.

They slowly made their way around to the side behind Otojiro's home. They waded in the water, waiting for the soldiers to move for quite a while. Each of them felt their bodies numbing as the sun left the sky completely disappeared behind the clouds. "We can't stay here... Move quietly and we can crawl under the back of the hut," Yu-Lee spoke as she moved without a sound onto the rocky ledge of land. Carefully the Suako and Vince followed. The stones gently rattled against one another as they got on to the land, on their hands and knees, and the stones dug into their skin as they went. Yu-Lee heard someone cough and she immediately froze in place, looked around, and raised her hand to signal to the others to be still. She listened and waited but no one came. In a panicked flurry they tried to reach the hut. Yu-Lee got their first and raised up the heavy weave material, waving her hand so that Suako and Vince would rush over and underneath. After they'd gone under she briskly entered the haven herself.

"Welcome," Otojiro said without turning to see who'd come. He sat calmly sipping his tea, and motioned the others to come in, he'd laid out fresh clothes and towels on top of pillows; three seating areas had been laid out prior to their arrival. They did as he willed and found hot tea next to their seats. Each of them bowed to the elderly man. He bobbed his head down in return.

After they had dried off and changed into dry clothing, they came back to take their seats across from the old man. "I apologise Otojiro, but we had no other way to enter," Vince explained. "I know," Otojiro said, and yet again sipped his tea. His eyes kept low so to keep them from guessing at his thoughts. "I'm Vince, Kairu's friend..." Vince continued. "I know who you are. And these two are Suako and Yu-Lee, are they not?" Otojiro cut him off. "Uh, yes sir," Vince replied, bewildered how he could know that. Yu-Lee smirked, she knew he had the power of intuitive insight. Suako did not know exactly what to think about his knowledge, but her training kept her calm, yet attentive.

"We desire to know why the C.D.F.P. is here," Vince asked. "The Company? Yes, it seems we haven't paid our taxes to them," Otojiro's voice seemed carefree on his subject matter. "...But that isn't why they're *really* here, is it Otojiro?" Vince pressed. The old man shook his head, "Yes, and no," he replied. Vince cocked his head to the side and furrowed his brow. "What do you mean?" Suako asked just before the words reached Vince's lips. "They are here for Tax collection. *He* is here for your leader," he replied smoothly. "General Yoshida. Mack knew he'd come after him..." Vince said. "Indeed, but now Quan is in danger, as a whole. We do not have the funds to pay. What our Chief decides to tell him tonight could be very important. Silence or speech it does not matter, both will bring about death," Otojiro said grimly. "What will he say?" Vince worriedly asked. "Who knows? Just to keep in mind, Okichi," Otojiro enlightened them. "Oh no. He's gonna give Mack up!" Vince exclaimed.

Vince stood up to leave. "Wait!" Otojiro stopped him dead in his tracks. Vince, shocked by the intensity in this usually calm man's demeanor, sat back down. "Haste here will just bring about your own end. Stay here for the night, whatever is said, we can learn of in the morning. Hide yourselves well beneath blanketed comforters in case we have unexpected guests," he told them. Vince nodded and drank his tea.

Otojiro cooked up some wild rice for them before they slept. The rice warmed their chilled bodies even more then the tea had; they'd be hungry for days, their food rations being so thin, that the meal came as a welcome respite. They sat around his small fire in the centre of the room, rejuvenating their tired spirits.

They heeded his instruction and carefully covered themselves when they crawled into bed. Vince and Suako quickly fell into a deep sleep. Yu-Lee stayed up to talk with the wise man. He had seen into her past, and they talked about better days the world had seen. Long hours into the evening they went on speaking. They shared secrets of the magickal trade, and the life energy; it was rare to find others connected to the planet during this day and age.

Morning came, and Otojiro was not in the tent. They each waited silently for his return, and wondered what news he would bring. The morning ground felt hard, the night before had brought frost. Bitter wind blew strong and hit hard against the hut, and the bouncing waves of wind against the cloth walls made the sounds of the guards outside minimal. No one said a word, their ears were perked to listen for footsteps and chatter nearby.

They waited as long as they could, but were fated to leave before Otojiro returned. Hard footsteps squished the wet sand like ground beneath heavy boots as they neared the tent. No questions asked, whoever was out there was with the C.D.F.P. No one in Quan wore shoes, except moccasins during the chilly winter months. They'd been prepared to leave at a moments notice, but were disappointed to have to go before they got some more information.

"Common Suako, back threw here. They're coming!" Vince urged her to hurry as he finished helping Yu-Lee under. She quickly finished shoving some water and a container of rice into her bag, she'd found the beg on the way to Quan on the road by a pile of bones. The steps were getting dangerously close. "Sorry," she whispered, and she scampered threw to the other side. Vince rolled under the curtain wall just as he heard the door across from him fall back.

They sat behind the back of the tent for a moment to get a vigil of everyone within the premises. The blustery wind yanked and pulled on the women's hair, blinding their view; Suako and Yu-Lee quickly tied their hair back. Dark overlapping clouds billowed above them, and they heeded warning of storm brewing above.

"No ones there now. Let's go before they come outta the hut," Vince told them. He guided them around the edge of the swamp, and lead them into some thick brush. Twigs and crisp leaves coated the mucky ground; they might as well have been land mines for the trouble they could cause giving away their position. This route was no good, "Let's go back. We'll have to go through the water again," Vince turned around to tell them. They were half way to the water's edge when Otojiro appeared from nowhere, and stopped them with a glance. He entered the bushes as well, "I've managed to talk to the Chief in private," he told them initially, then pointed his finger to a deeper spot that would better hide them, and they made their way to it.

"What's happening?" Suako asked, sitting down on a fallen log. "The chief has exposed the fact that your leader was here. Apparently General Yoshida is planning to leave immediately tomorrow morning, but he's leaving the soldiers here to keep an eye on the people. On top of that, he's taking Okichi with him," Otojiro explained. "Why would he do that?" Yu-Lee asked, she could only think that taking her as a set back for the General, slowing him down. "Leverage, on two accounts. If the information is false that our chief has provided then he has her hostage. On top of that, a young man in your party has fallen in love with Okichi. If the General catches up to them..." Otojiro explained, but Vince cut him off before he could finish, "Then Kairu will offer to be arrested in return for her release, right?" Vince shook his head, angry with the General's tactics. "Indeed, that is correct. You must hurry. He'll be headed toward the old Ryoko City. I will keep eyes away from the water as you leave," Otojiro told them.

"Wait, what about Okichi? We have to get her..." Suako thought aloud. "No, you mustn't! She is heavily guarded. You would not make it far enough before they caught up to you. As long as they know the Chief hasn't lied they won't do anything to the girl, I'm sure. They need her to capture Mack's brigade," Otojiro explained. "May you make it in time," he wished them well. Before he left he pulled from his robe a decent sized package, and passed it to Yu-Lee. She looked at him to see him smile faintly, "Good Luck. I hope we shall meet again." And then he left, straight to the centre of town.

They had no time to open their gift, as Otojiro made a distraction, they entered the chilling water. The cold stung their bodies like millions of pin pricks. "Oh my god... it's so cold," Suako felt all of the air in her lungs disappear, she desperately gasped for air, but the painful breath was seemingly not worth the effort. "We'll make a fire when... when we get far enough away from... town," Vince reassured her as he felt his limbs going numb. Yu-Lee's older body bore the extreme temperate decline fairly well, though her bones bothered her greatly.

After the brief dip in the freezing swamp they were all too eager to get out, and as they crawled out onto solid land they shivered fiercely. The air blanketed them with an immense chill, the wind still gusting strong. As fast as they could, they got far enough from the city to be out of their sites. They found some dried dead wood to make a fire behind some towering rocks that sheltered them from the Quan soldier's view. Vince shook tremendously as he tried to get the friction to smoke, and then light into flame. His muscle spasms weren't helping him start a fire at all. Yu-Lee shut her eyes and tried to focus, she shut the cold from her mind, and started to chant under her breath. Vince found himself able to calm his nerves long enough for him for get the fire going.

Once the fire had started, they removed their wet clothing and tried to lay them flat on the nearby rocks around the fire to dry. Then they huddled, unclad but for their undergarments, by the fire. The heat from the fire dried their bodies and they finally began to warm up. They couldn't speak, nor cold they even think about, anything but the discomfort they felt in their own skins. The intense winds kept the fire from blazing up high and mighty, so they stayed as close to it as they could for heat. When they'd finally dried up Vince grabbed his bag, which he'd lined heavily, and removed some extra dry clothing Otojiro had given him. Each of them quickly pulled the outfits on quickly, and the fabric helped to limit the bitter cool kiss of the breeze.

"We're gonna have to go," Suako forced herself to say moments later. Her words were to her own dissatisfaction. Vince raised his head from which he'd rested on his knee, nearly sleeping, "You're right. We have to warn them about Yoshida A.S.A.P." He uncurled his arms away from the warmth of his core, pushed himself up off of the ground, walked over to Suako and put his arms around her and gently lifted her to her feet. Suako nearly forgot to let him go after she was standing. Her eyes locked with his, and as she stood there, time seemingly paused, if only for a second. He pulled back, with a small and fast dispersing grin for only her to see. He offered Yu-Lee a hand up and then extinguished the fire by dumping some of the earth onto it.

Without rest they scoured across the countryside, stopping only to make their rice and allow their exhausted legs a pause when they refused to continue any further. Suako stirred a pot of rice over a tiny fire they'd constructed. "We have to get to Mack..." she drowsily said as her eyelids rested low. Yu-Lee's body wouldn't let her continue without some sleep, she nearly fell into her dreams the second she lay on the ground. Vince and Suako tried to prepare the rice with their shaking hands as best they could during the dead of night.

"It's so cold... the nights, they're getting longer," Vince said, looking up to the stars glaring down from above. "They'll be getting shorter again soon. Daylight recedes up until December twenty-first, then it reverses, just a few more days away," Suako said. Unable to stand any longer, Vince lay down on his back beside the fire. He pulled Suako gently down to lay beside him, and interlaced his fingers with hers affectionately; the lovers lay cold and tired together on the hard earth.

"Look at that Suako... there's so many of them up there... so many stars and planets. Do you think any of them are going through this?" his voice was weary with the thought of the answer to his wonderment. "I don't know... but I think the life stream has life on other planets... The Universe is so vast, we can't be the only ones... I just hope they're doing better than this. No one should suffer this... no one," she whispered back. "We have to win this battle... we can't hand over the planet to the C.D.F.P. this planet deserves its future," Vince said with conviction. "We'll win. We will, Vince," Suako smiled and turned her head from the stars to look at him, and to see him looking straight back at her.

They lay gazing into each other's eyes for quite some time, like looking into gateways into each other's world. "Suako?" Vince finally broke the silence. "Yes?" She smiled. "What happened to you when you got to Kagawa? What... got you to say?" He asked. She paused to recall the incidents that led to her extended stay. "I was injured... There had been an 'earthquake'; that's what the Kagawa's called it... I remember waking up, I forgot all about getting back to meet you in Quan... anyway, Yu-Lee had taken me into the temple. She told me all about life energy, and how everything is really just one stemming life force and I had to learn more... I'm sorry I never came back. I never meant to scare you Vince, I..."

Vince courageously kissed her forehead, and Suako curled further inward and wrapped her arms around him. They lay quietly holding each other, the small fire crackling next to them. Vince quietly sang to her, "Oceans wide, valley's long, and forests green, come back to me. Canyons deep, deep breaths, sweet sleep, come back to me..." a song his grandfather used to sing to his father, and in turn his father sang for him. The song represented an always hopeful attitude and belief that the earth would return to it's natural state as it was not long ago.

Suako gradually fell asleep in his arms. Vince picked the rice pot up and placed it beside the fire for morning. His body was all too eager to join her in the unconscious realm of sleep, and the stars carried him away. The fire was just warm enough to provide them comfort throughout the long night.

The rest of the journey was quite similar, as they hurried to get to the Old Ryoko. It was a test of endurance, which they admirably passed. Snow began to fall from the grey leaden skies as they persisted northward. They kept moving constantly to prevent the bitter biting frostbite from getting hold of their vulnerable bodies as the days got shorter and shorter. The sun bounced of the white ground blindingly; the glare was nearly intolerable during the daytime.

The final two days they found themselves with Yoshida nipping at their heels. Yu-Lee had spotted them one night when she got up to take a sip of water. His fire was blazing in the distance not far behind them. Without hesitation she woke the others and put out their own fire. It was time for them to hurry ahead while Yoshida and Okichi rested. Luckily, Okichi had been slowing him down somewhat. They figured Yoshida was not a patient man, especially when his long-lost target was so plainly within his reach. His tolerance of her required breaks, they assumed, would to be little to none.

When the three passed over the top of the hill overlooking the seaside city they nearly collapsed from exhaustion. They were about a day ahead of Yoshida, and utterly fatigued from sustaining their lead. They were so overfilled with joy that their journey to their companions was nearly over they ran down the sloping hill. After the exhilarating run they found themselves struggling the last stretch of flat ground before the city walls.

Once they reached the city they felt as if they'd entered a ghost city. A few people then poked their heads from within their homes to look at them. They felt like researchers were eyeing them down. "Stop walking," Yu-Lee commanded suddenly from the rear. "What is it?" Suako asked, her hand at the ready on her gun. "Shh!" Yu-Lee intuitively tried to use a technique Otojiro had taught her. She tried to reconstruct in her mind to the effect of someone inhabiting the town.

Vince and Suako watched, neither had any idea what was taking place. They watched as Yu-Lee's head jutted back occasionally, as if she'd been hit in the face. Suako soon could make out a faint sighting of energy flow coming from the crown of Yu-Lee's head which extended to the limits of Old Ryoko. Upon seeing it she released the hold on her weapon. "It's alright Vince," she told him calmly. He didn't ask what she'd discovered to have made her say that, he simply trusted her instincts, and let down his guard.

"Ok, it's all right," Yu-Lee declared opening her eyes. "What did you do?" Vince questioned, looking between the two girls for an explanation. Suako didn't know exactly what Yu-Lee had done either, only that she'd been in sync with the life energy of Old Ryoko. "I looked into the minds of those living in this place. We are a rarity, people don't visit here very often. There are negative feelings toward the C.D.F.P. I believe they want to make sure the C.D.F.P. don't come here, but it wasn't very clear," she told them. She squinted her eyes and rubbed her temples, images of the town still flooded her vision.

"Are you ok?" Vince asked, as Yu-Lee tended to her head. "I'm fine, I'll just need a moment... anyway, we can talk to these people," she told them. She blocked off the images within a few moments, and they went up to one of the homes where a woman had just exited to commence hanging some laundry. "Excuse me, miss?" Vince asked approaching the woman. Shyly, and with much hesitation, the woman turned, "Y-yes?" her plain face made her vigorously moving eyes all that much more noticeable. "It's alright. We're just passing through," Yu-Lee told the young lady, placing her hand in a caring manner on her shoulder. "Here let us help you," Suako offered and began to help pin up the laundry with Yu-Lee.

"Uh... Th-thank you?" the woman was rather dazed. She felt uncomfortable and pulled the quilted wrap she wore around her shoulders even tighter around her body. "We're looking for our friends. They should've come here a few weeks ago..." Vince began to explain.

The woman's nervousness seemed to melt at that moment. "Oh, you're friends of *the descendent*! Please follow me. They are staying with Seresuto and her husband Adamu," she divulged to them, and swept a tuff of unruly hair back behind her ear.

The woman then sped off towards the waterfront, and they all followed her, trying to keep up with her fast-paced step. "The *descendant*?" Suako questioned Vince. He just shrugged and whispered back, "Hey, don't ask me!" They figured she was referring to someone in their party, but none the less were unable to figure out what the whole title was about.

Through back ally ways, and main streets, they finally emerged at the beach. The woman who led them their walked up to one of the homes and thumped on the door. "Seresuto? Are you there?" she called. The door opened seconds later with a distinct squeak. "Yes? Oh, hey! What are you doing here?" A robust woman answered whom they assumed to be the lady Seresuto, which the townswoman had spoken of. She was in the midst of pulling back her thick head of hair into a ponytail, when she's opened the door. "These people claim to be friends of the visitors you have hidden away in there," she said, showing them off as if they were prizes. "Oh... well don't just stand there, go inside," Seresuto bluntly said to them. As they stepped through the doorways they heard Seresuto thank her friend before re-entering her home.

"Wow..." Vince looked at all of the plant life, and pleasantly inhaled the fresh air within the home. "I knew the city felt easier to breathe in but I..." he paused and took in a deep breath, "...didn't see a dome." "Mmm, the air is sweet," Suako licked her lips. Yu-Lee walked passed the two standing in the centre of the room and over to the thriving plants. Under her breath, so quiet no one could hear, "Okagwa... you live on..." she smiled with her eyes. "Well common now don't just stand there!" the ever bossy Seresuto rolled her eyes and indicated for them to follow her into the next room, and they did just that.

"Vince, Suako!" Mei exclaimed popping out of her seat and rushing over to her friends. "Reunited just in time," Jenko commented to Mack sipping his wine with a huge grin on his face. "Welcome back you two," Mack said getting up to greet them. "Where's Kairu?" Vince asked looking around. "He's over at an old monument. He should be back soon," Jenko told them as he poured some wine for the new arrivals. "Good t'ave ya back," Kato welcomed Suako with a friendly hug, and nodded at Vince with smile.

Yu-Lee stood behind Suako and Vince, quiet as a church mouse. An observer by nature, she was happy to see just how close this group was that she was becoming a part of. "Ah, now who might this be?" Mack examined the new arrival with kind eyes. She intently reached out her hand to shake his, "I am Yu-Lee sir. If I may, I'd like to help you fight the C.D.F.P," he took her hand and in a very gentleman like manner brought it high and placed a kiss upon it. "Well, I'm Mack, and you're welcome to join us Yu-Lee. The more the better," he laughed. They all fell into his spell of guffawing. "Ha! Ha! Well thank you very much!" Yu-Lee said through her laughs. *Squeak!* The door opened. Kairu came into the room and saw the new three standing around the others. "Welcome back," he formally told them. "Good to see you Kairu," Vince smiled.

"Come now everyone, sit have a drink and a bite to eat…" Jenko started to say. Suddenly reality fell like a pile of bricks back onto Vince's conscience. "I wish we could, but we have to leave immediately," he said, his voice no longer pleasant and gleeful. "Whoa! Whoa! What?" Kato looked at him in utter confusion. "We're being followed…" and so he sat and the three of them explained the situation to everyone nearly in full. They neglected to mention Okichi in front of Kairu, to prevent him from acting impulsively. Now it was apparent to everyone that time was of the essence. General Yoshida was not far behind them, the time to act was now. After they were all informed of the circumstances they deliberated in for nearly an hour.

"…The tide is just not ready yet, like I said before…" Adamu shook his head in slight dismay. "It's now or never. Adamu don't be so weak. We'll manage," His wife quickly overthrew the validity of his opinion. "Even if we hover away from the coast where they can't see us until it's the right time, we need to go," Vince urged them. Suako nodded in agreement to back up his plight. Mack sat silently analysing the information presented to him in his head carefully. After a few moments of analytical thought, he came to his conclusion, "Alright everyone, pack up. We move out tonight. It's the only way." And with that everyone fled to their duties.

"Yee haw, here we go," Jenko cheered, and downed the last of the wine from his glass before springing into action.

"Alright I'll go and get the ship. It'll take me a few hours to get it to the shore here. Make sure you're all ready," Adamu resigned to the decision. He pulled a camel colored robe over himself as a shield from the sun, for crossing the land outside the city to the ship's hidden location. He kissed Seresuto goodbye and then left promptly.

Seresuto took on food duty, packing as many preservatives and long-lasting fruits and vegetables away as she could. Yu-Lee helped her. Suako and Vince went to get some fishing equipment that Seresuto had instructed them to get. The others were busy packing up their gear. Kairu made one last trip to the grand political office to pay tribute to his ancestral roots.

The first moment available, Vince stole Mack away from the rest of the group, "Hey Mack, there's more we didn't tell you. Yoshida has a hostage, he kidnapped Okichi." Mack nodded, then shook his head in disgust. "The bastard hasn't changed at all..." Mack signs. "Yeah well, if he thinks that her father lied to him about us being here there's gonna be trouble. We have to leave some evidence we were here... I think we should keep Kairu in the dark on this. What do you think?" Vince said. "For now, we have to worry about getting out of here... Anyway, I'll make sure *he* knows I was here," Mack said as he was walking away, "Thanks Vince." "No prob, Boss," Vince said.

Rushing was something they were all now thoroughly acquainted with. Seresuto left Yu-Lee to finish up with filling barrels with fresh water. Seresuto still had to pack for herself and Adamu for the long voyage. In her usual fashion, she barked at the first person she saw for help, and Kato just happened to be her unlucky victim.

The short hours passed by quickly. Mei was bringing different bags from within the house out onto the beach to await placement on the ship, when she saw the ship not too far off in the distance. "Hey everyone, let's boogie!" she called. Mei jogged back inside and saw everyone looking at her questionably. "Hey common, Adamu's getting close. Double time!" she reiterated to them. The pace was picked up, as they hurried to finishing their preparations.

The ship pulled into the harbour as the sun was nearing the horizon. Leaving by dusk would provide them with a comfortable blanket of cover from any searching eyes. The vessel was a very dark metallic, it's old age was evident from the rust on the anchor. There was a lengthy deck that would make fishing simplistic, the craft itself was thirty feet long. Kairu thought it was quite small for the invading Empire to have sent. He asked and Mack explained it to be an operative ship, used to maintain a base for communication between all the other soldier-infested vessels.

Adamu sounded the horn, and it echoed powerfully through the air. "Everyone, last chance to get anything you've forgotten," Mack reminded them, as he placed down the last of the bags to carry to the beach.

The horn had drawn a crowd of the locals to the beach; the people came to see them off. Kindly some of the stronger men offered to help load the ancient ship, and the group accepted gratefully, and said their goodbyes to the townspeople. Seresuto never got soppy, and found her husbands emotional parting from his only blood family, his cousin, to be utterly ridiculous. "We'll be back in a few everyone. Nothing to see here," she huffed and climbed up a ladder onto the deck.

"Be safe Adamu," His cousin embraced him with a loving hug, "we'll miss you," she smiled. "Thank you, Hitoshi. I'll miss you too… I'll save the world for you and Seresuto," he told her kissing her cheek. He pulled away and boarded the ship, and everyone followed him and climbed on the ship. A big ruckus was made when Kairu disappeared from view of the townspeople.

Mack was the last up the ladder. He turned to wave to everyone, when he noticed not too far off in the distance a couple shady figures at the top of a hill. "Yoshida…" he whispered beneath his breath. He hopped down from the ladder, on to the deck, and ran over to the door leading to the bridge, and knocked on the door. Vince saw Mack leave and looked out along the horizon, couldn't quite make out what Mack did, but noticed the figures as well. "Mack hurry, we have to go!" he called out urgently. "Adamu, we have to leave now, go!" Mack commanded.

They pulled away from the shore and the people returned to their homes. They were informed briefly about the upcoming visitors that they were to receive.

Seresuto and Adamu requested from everyone to act as normally as possible to divert any unwanted attention about their unlawful inhabitation.

They anchored themselves not too far off the coast, just out of sight from the shore of Old Ryoko, to await the turn of the current flow. The water made the temperature drastically cooler aboard the ship; they felt like they were trapped within a tin can that had been placed in a freezer. The metal construction of the boat adapted the temperature of the water that surrounded its body, making the stay within bitterly unpleasant. They huddled under blankets and wished-for heat. Occasionally, Yu-Lee would use all her strength and get the life energy to speed up the particles in the air to warm them up, but such sprints only lasted for about twenty minutes before she'd nearly collapse from exhaustion.

The group spent most of their time in the mess hall sitting around a large table that had been bolted to the floor.

They talked about possible scenarios that could be happening back in Old Ryoko. It would be nearly a week before they could truly depart the continent and begin the journey across the bitter sea. Adamu warned them about how rough and unkind the sea was to those who ventured out onto it. They were well prepared for when the time would come, and until then all that was left to do was wait for the days to pass...

We will cross the ocean to new lands. What will we find? What else exists on this earth?

Chapter 12: Tin Can

"Dear Diary,

We have been riding the current for two horrendously long weeks now. We have been tossed about like a ball in play in a child's game. Yu-Lee has found herself quite ill, much to our disappointment. Her incapacity has prevented her from being able to focus long enough to stir the particles into creating heat. There is a wall of frost that has been slowly developing down in the belly of the ship, we'll be lucky if we don't arrive at the Imperial Continent as ice cubes.

Adamu has informed all of us of what to expect when we are trying to get onto the continent. He says he's fished near there once. He didn't near the shores too much, but he said he noticed that the ports were all saturated with posted guards. Much to our surprise he said the continent itself it minuscule in physical size compared to ours. I have theorised that they must have had too large a population to support on their own lands, and that's why they invaded our continent, they needed the space. Of course, this is just my personal observation. I don't really know why they attacked, and whenever anyone speaks of it is sounds like it was a sudden rather rash decision.

We've all been doing well to make Seresuto's stash of food last, though Suako is looking quite thin. She seems distracted lately. In fact, since Okagwa she's been quite different. I haven't had the courage to ask her what happened yet. She doesn't have her flighty spirit anymore. What could have happened to her?

Mei and Kato have spent most of their time in their barracks. They collected a bunch of dislocated guns from a heap in Old Ryoko which they are putting back together to pass the time. Entertainment has been nil around here. I've been giving Suako her space, I know she needs her time to think. Mack and Jenko are spending their time focusing on coming up with plan after plan for what to do when we arrive. Other then that, Jenko has been preparing to map the continent. Kairu has his nose in the books, which I've often had to borrow to bide the time. I'm glad he brought them from Old Ryoko. Seresuto spends her time bossing Adamu around the hull to "clean the dump up", whenever he isn't trying to steer us about.

To say the least life is rather bleak right now, and I'm looking forward to getting to the continent. I can't even go on the deck much anymore, it's frozen over with ice. Sometimes Adamu will get us to go fishing. It isn't any fun. The only benefit is later cooking it, the tiny stove fire is warm. Since it's the best heat we have everyone will volunteer to fish just to get to be in front of that radiating heat; everyone but Suako that is. I worry about her.

Sincerely,
    Vince"

He placed his book on top of his cot, and hopped down onto the floor. Meandering out slowly, he walked into the mess hall and fixed himself a cup of tea. Jenko sat at the table scaling his map and writing the title "Imperial Continent" as neatly as he could. Adamu came in after setting the ship up to go straight for the next hour; the water was calmer then usual. Jenko and Adamu appreciated the extra cups of tea Vince poured for them, as he passed them their cups. "Thanks Vince," Jenko smiled. "Thanks," Adamu said. The steaming liquid, nearly hot enough to burn the oesophagus as it crawled down into their stomachs, warded off the cold from their cores.

"So Adamu..." Vince began to say as he was sitting down, "how are we supposed to get past these 'watchdogs' on the coastline when we get there?" Vince sipped his tea. "I'm no strategist, we'll have to circle the island and look for a place where we won't be seen I guess," Adamu shrugged. Jenko placed down his charcoal and grabbed his tea, "We'll have to see what it's like when we get there, Vince. A lot can change over the course of a few years. The only thing Mack and I both agreed on is that we have to be discreet, no one can know we're there. Third class citizens from across the ocean wouldn't be appreciated there, we'd find ourselves in the bottom of a cell with a leaky pipe in no time flat," Jenko told him. Vince nodded in agreement.

"If everything is the same as it was?" Vince curiously poked. "We'll do just as Adamu thought; circle the continent until we find a remote area to dock," Jenko replied. "I see... When do you think we'll see the Green Eastern Continent again?" Vince asked with remembrance in his eyes. Jenko paused before he answered, "When we have a way to save it. That's when."

A few weeks later, during the night, the ocean had become treacherous, and no one could sleep through the storm. Adamu spent his night desperately trying to control the ship as the sea tossed them about, like the wind does to an autumn leaf. They held on as best they could to the furniture, in order to keep from being thrown about within the ship, while the wind howled all around them violently. Several times the hatch above the cabin was ripped opened, and snow mixed and sea water poured in, drenching them with an icy touch.

Yu-Lee was morbidly dreadful, spending the entire night in the bathroom vomiting. Jenko stayed with her the entire night through, and everyone else was in between the mess hall and the cabin. "Will it ever end? I'm... argh! Tired of sliding around," Mei complained as the vessel rocked, and she yet again lost her footing. "This has gotta end soon!" Vince said exasperated. "We better not flip over or imma' be pissed," Kato said with a death grip on the pipe above him, "Shi'! Get the door... it's flooding again!" Kato yelled over the howling wind. "Got it!" Mei said, soaked. "Whew..." Kato sighed.

Kairu had held on all night with little more then a peep, simply looking about the room with weary eyes from time to time. Everyone was burnt out from lack of sleep and small rations; another week left on this ship was not a prospect that they were pleased about. The door to the cabin flung open and Seresuto perched herself in the doorway. "Hold on back there! We're coming up to a big one!" she yelled. Vince caught eye of what she meant through the door, past Seresuto, out the front window; they were playing chicken with a massing wave. It was rearing up like a horse that would come back down with a deadly thump. He saw Suako beside him loosing her hold on the bar she'd been holding onto, and he grabbed her and attempted to shield her with his body. The grumble of the sea was echoing off the walls, all that was left was the hit; and it came.

Mercilessly the ocean craft was rendered helpless by the gigantic wave. It plunged down right on top of them with a force so strong that the pressure was crushing the structure. The water crashing above them cause the metal of the ceiling to screech as dented slightly inward. The fury of the briny deep showed them it's power on trespassers, and the ship was swept away. Darkness was all that was left...

The heat, it's burning so strong. Sands stretching on and on, nothing but the sand ahead, nothing but the sand behind. It was vast, all the eye could see in every direction. The light brown ground was glistening under the midday sun, but the calm day didn't stir the malleable grounds of the desert. Only cactuses to break up the baron place; the sand was stretching on into eternity. It hurt the soles of bare treading feet under the fierce sweltering sun; skin felt tight over muscle and bone as it shrivelled in the earthly inferno.

All life roasted under the intense light. Cloudless skies provided no protection for the life that foolishly crept below, and the boiling dry temperatures left a false sense of movement in the distance. Just heat waves in the far off, swaying back and forth, like rippling waves in a pond disturbed by a random skipping stone.

Blazing heat, like fire, prickled on sensitive skin, and it felt as though flesh may as well be melting off of skeletal remains of men and women who dared across the desert. Beading sweat dripped down overheated foreheads, stinging eyes that squinted out the blaring white sun. Exhaustion, so much wretched fatigue, crippled otherwise capable bodies. On and on like machines that wouldn't stop, one painful step after another.

So tired. Sleep… I just want to sleep. Why go on? How long have we been walking? Why keep walking. Maybe if my legs fall off I won't have to go any further… No, then you'd crawl. Still too attached to life… You're such a pussy! You suck! Yeah, I know. But I'm not ready to die, not yet. I will not quit… You won't make it anyway!… Shut up! I'll make it, even if it kills me!… Oh, aren't you the witty one!

"Kato! Kato, hurry! I see it… We're almost there!" A tall woman called down to him from atop a sand dune. Her voice was weary, but it was enough to knock Kato free of the two-sided conversation in his mind. The several other excursionists behind Kato somehow found their second wind at the news, and hastened their speed. Wiping the perspiration off his brow, he looked up to see her, "Tha 's great, Nayu." He panted as he tackled the hill, it seemed almost futile to climb, each step displaced the sand. It took three times as long to hike up these dastardly sand dunes then some regular firm ground. *Press! Sink... Press! Sink...* Aggravation continued to accumulate.

Press! Sink... Press! Sink... again and again. The scalding granules wedged in, and ploughed threw his toes. Each grain inflicting pain upon raw blistering skin. *Press! Sink... Almost to the top. Almost there... just a little bit more.* Kato's trembling legs were on the brink of collapsing. *Can't give in. Not now, not yet...* He made a deal with himself. As soon as he reached the top of the hill he could fall over and just lay there and rest. *Press! Sink... Press! Sink... There! Success!* He claimed victory over the defeating climb, but stayed standing upright. Somehow the motivational promise to collapse had lost its touch when he saw his hometown at the bottom of the dune.

Nayu threw her arms around Kato's wavering body and cheered. Her chocolate brown skin glistened as her sweaty body sparkled in the sunlight. Kato raised his arm and patted hers affectionately with his swelling fingers. Looking down at the small village he longed to get there as soon as possible. He could see the sand building with their cookie cutter square windows and the colourful canopies that stretched out from them. Clothing lines stretched from one house to another, with wet garments hanging from them, left out to sun dry.

The well in the centre of town looked inviting, and Kato would've like nothing better than the cool refreshing water it contained. The stale water in their canteens, hot from the baking sun, had been making him nauseous every time he sloshed it around in around his mouth. Surrounding the well he could just make out the bustling city people as they ran to-and-fro between vendors in the town square. They'd finally arrived back home with their goods.

The rest of the commuting people behind them began to stumble to the top of the mound. They managed to drag up their wooden cart without letting it fall once, as the struggled upward. Celebratory hollers sounded all around. Somehow, they summoned the strength and energy to dash down the steep slope to the gates of the sand built city. It would have been so easy, *too easy,* to have just tripped and rolled down to the entrance to Sheikarah, but they managed to stay upright for the run.

Shade, glorious shade! Free me from the sweltering beating of this hellish heat! Kato's legs nearly tumbled like cogwheels. Nayu ran just ahead of him, and the other merchants found themselves running now just to keep ahead of the cart. Kato and Nayu heard their screams as they dashed, and it had been so funny they could help but to stop running in order to laugh. Their muscles went limp as the diversion impeded them. A mix of the cackling and being burnt out sent them to the ground, their convulsive howling subsided eventually when there was no more energy left to laugh.

Back in town many friendly faces welcomed them home and swarmed their cart for the goods they had brought to town. Money soared high in hands, and bidding wars began before the even reached the market. Nayu and Kato said farewell to the merchant men they'd travelled with, and let them handle the greedy grabbing hands, and tilling the abundant money. They trailed from the crowd to the well, which was now vacant of swarming people.

Gulp! Gulp! The revitalising elixir of life replenished lost strength. The dry patch at the back of Kato's throat started to disappear. Kato offered the pail to Nayu, and she drank the rest. As she lowered the pail, after drinking heartily, water trickled down her chin. Kato smiled her and caught the droplets before they fell. "Common," he tilted his head, "Let's go ge' our cut."

The ventured down a shady ally, and the relief was like stepping out of an oven. His wakizashi blade bounced in its sheath against his desert camouflage pants. Nayu and Kato's matched attire signalled their alliance to the locals. They were well known in Sheikarah as being the best transports through the perilous land of thievery. Praise ran high at their presence.

"...He better not try to cheap out again. I swear if he does..." Nayu angrily shook her fist. Her eye was always on the mark; her pay. She hated being gypped. Kato agreed, they had done an enormous load of work; no *way* were they taking a suckers share. "Dun worry Nayu. I be makin' sure that he's gonna pay up," Kato assured her. "Good," she said as she lifted the falling strap of her neutral tank top.

Emerging out on the other side of the ally it was stepping back into the inferno of the oven. Straight-ahead was a fortress of a place, flower ground paints of red and yellow had been used to decorate the building with triangles encased the building. Two sentries, covered in light linen robes, stood post to the sides of the wooden door wedged between the hardened sand structures rectangular doorframe. Like statues they did not flinch. Their threatening curving swords reflected the sun, blinding anyone looking at it, were at easy access from their hip holsters. The men were prepared to deal with intruders.

Kato and Nayu approached them, and the guards respectfully bowed to them. They were frequent visitors. The man to the right opened the door for them, and into the atrium the entered. The other guard went in and fetched the house-master for them to conduct their business with.

As they waited Kato noticed that the pool in the middle of the room had run dry. Nayu reclined on the red upholstered couch, then, noticing a fruit bowl on the side table, she grabbed a handful of grapes. She began popping them into her mouth. Nayu was not shy by any means, she would make herself at home without needing any invitation to do so.

Nayu had always been that way. Ever since they were little she fended for herself, she learned how to survive. Now in her late teens she was a scavenger. She would make ends meet one way or another, but she always did it in an honest manner. But she had an attitude, refusing to take lip from anyone.

Kato had been orphaned at a young age, when a group of bandits robbed his parents, and left them for dead in the middle of the open desert. "They took their cart and horses... didn't even leave them food or water," Kato remembered the voices of his neighbours, family friends, conversing as he was in their care. They spoke as if he weren't there, "...They died of dehydration." Kato didn't understand what they were saying. He was too young to comprehend what they meant. "...Kato they're not coming back. We're sorry," they told him. So many apologies came to him. *Why? 'Dehydration'? What was that? 'Died'?* "I wan' ma' momma... Where's daddy?" No one answered the child, only sympathetic gazes came his way. It had been his fourth birthday and his parents had been returning with gifts for him.

Kato was put into an orphanage in Sheikarah, where he met Nayu. She'd had the same problem; her parents were killed by bandits. They became close quickly, watching out for each other's back, and as time passed they grew they became closer and closer. Nayu started to learn how to care for herself, not having anyone but Kato to look out for her. Kato was the only person rather than herself that she placed any trust in, and he knew that.

They self taught themselves how to fight, determined to never be at the mercy of others ever again. When Nayu was fourteen, and Kato fifteen, they left the orphanage. The overcrowding made it easy for them to decide that they were better to set out on their own. So, they left, taking what little money, their parents had left to their credit. They decided to try and open a fruit stand in the market to make ends meet, and they had arranged for transports bring them exotic fruits from across the dessert. Unfortunately, it did not work out as they had originally planned, and the two found that they were losing money, because their cargo often didn't make it to them. The pillaging outlaws struck any travellers they found and took their goods. In the end the had to close their stand, and were getting so short on cash that they could barely pay for shelter and food.

The annoyance of the bandit attacks sparked an idea between the two of them. It was a cognitive thought: *If the bandits hassle everyone so much, why don't we do something about them?* And just like that they started they own escort service. They accompanied travelling caravans, families, private officials, and anyone else in need, as their acting bodyguards.

After several close calls they managed to ward off the raiding gangsters. With each successful crossing their popularity grew, and word spread fast. In no time at all they found more people than they could possibly accommodate trying to hire them. At that point, for Nayu, it came down to whoever the highest bidder was.

And that's how it was. The last three years they had spent constantly going from one place to another. Their journies were always harsh, but the rewards had become phenomenal, not to mention the treatment from their renown. People revered them everywhere they went, especially in Sheikarah they were highly regarded, and well respected. They were treated so well, Kato supposed, because they ensured the livelihood and safety of the people; a security that for so long did not exist.

"...Care for a grape?" Nayu swayed the stem of juicy warm fruit in front of Kato. The purple skin was transparent in the daylight. He shook his head, then crossed his arms and leaned against the wall. The cool surface conducted through his epidermis, and the relief was heavenly. He crossed his right foot over the left and just enjoyed the drastic change to the feel of his skin. His body tingled from the cold. Nayu was always moving, either tapping her foot, or looking around. In a hyperactive way she was always on the look out, as if always waiting for the ball to drop, and something horrendous to occur, though she'd never admit to it.

Kato yawned and rested his eyes; he'd personally had rather headed straight home to bathe and sleep before attending to business. Unfortunately, Nayu lost her edge when she wasn't with Kato, and she couldn't rest until she had her cut. Her uneasiness extended to a whole new level, she wanted to get her payment as soon as possible. Against his own desires he usually folded to her will; they watched out for each other, and that wasn't about to stop now.

Kato rubbed his eyes to refresh himself, and moments later, they were finally beckoned forth. They went through the left corridor, past two rooms, and entered the third. It was an office, sand shelves, of the same concoction that formed the walls, extended from the walls of the study and held many books and a few miniature trinkets. On the desk ahead, made of the rare island red-wood, some more trinkets lay, and a special one caught Kato's eye, it was a carving of the extinct animal Kato remembered to have been told was an elephant, made from some sort of animal bone. A man sat behind the desk scribing in a bound book of parchment.

As they approached, and their feet stepped off the carpet and clicked against the hard floor, they got the man's attention. He book-marked his page and then placed his work aside, removed his spectacles, and a grand smile stretched across his face. "I see you've made it back, a day early too, my thanks," he turned his head and nodded to his guard. A chest was presented before them, "Here is your fee." Nayu wasn't shy to open it and count it.

"I trust you had good passage?" he made small talk. "Yeah. Wasn' too bad Gakushi," Kato replied. Gakushi was a prosperous salesman; wealthy, but a weasel with a tight wallet. The man's smile was sly. Kato glimpsed at the chest and soon realised why, there was at *least* an extra ten-percent in there. *Something* was off, Gakushi was *never* overly generous; In fact, it occurred to Kato, that it was rare if they even got their just deserved amount.

So, what's the catch? Kato's eyes glared at Gakushi as he leaned forward on the desk. The man laughed and stood up. "I see you noticed your bonus! I have a special job for you. My daughter is to go inland to Torusan to further her education at a higher-level school, funded by the C.D.F.P. Company. I want you to escort her across on the boat, and every step of the way to her destination. If you do that, I'll triple your usual bounty. What do you say?" He put forth the job. That was the first Kato had ever heard about Torusan, or the C.D.F.P.

Without hesitation Nayu accepted, "Great, when do we leave?" she asked, her eyes always on the loot. Kato turned to look at her in shock for not even asking him his opinion. "Excellent, in three days come back here, and be prepared, it's a long journey," Gakushi said. No questions at all, it was done; the deal had been made. At the time Kato's only qualms had been that he wanted some time off, and to have been consulted first.

They finalised the arrangements with Gakushi, and then left with the chest. They got home, back out of the sun, and Kato's full sense of fatigue set in. Nayu had been ecstatic with the job they were about to take, but even she was beginning to feel the extent of how run down her body was. It was time to rest, but first they hide their gold away.

Down to naked skin, they stripped off all their layers of sand and sweat stained clothes. They then entered the carved pool in the floor, under where the ceiling opened to the sky above. The rain naturally kept the pool filled with fresh clean water for bathing. Light blue sky with wispy clouds passed on by overhead. The water was cool, and washed off the sweat. Nayu squeezed a sponge free of its retained water, and the droplets trickled down from the top of Kato's head. *Drip, drip, drip...*

Drip, drip, drip... Little drops of freezing cold water fell onto Kato, and they slowly woke him from his memory of a dream. He looked around, but Nayu was not before him. He was in a tin can, as he had been before. *Before when? Before the wave!* He was no longer hot, he was freezing. He realised he couldn't feel his hands of feet at all; His extremities had been completely numbed.

It was the morning after the storm. They awoke to find themselves bumped, bruised and scrapped, but miraculously alive. The whole ship was resting on a downward slant. "Ugh... Where are we?" Mei groaned, placing her hand on an enormous bump on her head, "sss, ouch... oh man..." she said, pained. "I need some help 'ere!" Kato called from behind Mei, in a bit of a struggled pant. He'd just noticed his injury, and Mei turned to see him with the large metal hatch resting over of his left leg. "Oh, shit! We gotta get this off of you!" she rushed to his side, and struggled to try and lift it without success.

Vince opened his eyes and felt blinded by the light coming in from the cabin above. After his eyes adjusted he looked down to see Suako still safe within his arms. To his left Kairu lay with a large gash on his chest; he hadn't yet awoken. Seresuto lay over one of the bolted legs of the mess hall table, and Adamu still was seated in the captain's chair as he had been before; both of them were still unconscious from being tossed about like rag dolls.

Creek! Down the corridor a bathroom door swung open, from which Jenko and Yu-Lee stumbled out. They were extremely disoriented. Vince gently placed Suako against the wall and climbed the steep slope over to help Mei with Kato. "Here, lift together..." Vince said, "one, two, three! Argh!" *Clunk!* The meal hatch hit the ground hard. "Oh, thank god it's off," Kato signed in relief. "Oh, Kato, look at your poor leg!" Mei looked down with teary eyes. His knee looked out of place, the skin had split open in several places under the weight of the door, and his calf was most definitely sprained. "I'll be ok. Need a brace though..." he looked around.

Jenko entered the distorted room slowly, trying to find his footing, and Yu-Lee followed close behind. He soon analysed the situation and noticed a stray piece of metal sticking out from behind Suako. "H..." he tried to speak but coughed. "Wah! Ahem, here, I found something we can use for Kato's leg," Jenko said pointing. Vince got up and helped him to get it. "I'll go and get something to tie it around with," Yu-Lee said turning to go back into the vessel's barracks. Mei kneeled beside Kato and squeezed his hand. "We'll fix you up," She smiled at him. "Imma countin' on it," he smiled back.

Jenko let Vince handle the rod, and made his way up and over to Adamu. He checked his pulse, "He's alive! He's pretty banged up here though. The glass from the window cut him up pretty badly... but he'll live," Jenko sighed. Then he tried to look out the front of the window, but the rock that had broken the window had wedged itself inside, and he couldn't see anything past it except for a small piece of the sky. "Hey..." *Sniff,* "Hey, I can breathe well... like being in a dome?" *Sniff, sniff!* Jenko said breathing deply. "You're right... Wonder why?" Vince said, confused.

Vince woke up Suako and she moved aside, stiff and groggy. After several minutes she started to get a grasp on reality. She inched her way up to Seresuto and slowly removed her off the table. Seresuto's abdomen had a long deep purple bruise stretching across it, and when Suako moved her the muscles twitched.

"Uh... What happened?" Kairu asked as he came to, looking at the ruins around him. "Don't move Kairu. I'll be there in a second," Suako instructed as she placed Seresuto down. He looked at himself and noticed his chest wound. "What happened last night?" Kairu asked, trying to remember. "I saw a tidal wave. It came right down on us," Vince replied. Yu-Lee came back holding strips of a blanket she'd pulled apart for Kato's brace. "Yu-Lee can I have a piece of that? I need to wrap up this cut," Suako said, kneeling beside Kairu. Yu-Lee nodded and threw her a piece, "There you go... here Vince let me help you," she said slowly making her way up the floor to him and Kato.

"Hey where's Mack?" Suako suddenly asked, flinging her head up and looking around. No one answered, and they all looked about too. "Kairu finish tying that, I've gotta go find him," Suako said and she got up and left him with the innovated bandage. She made her way as quickly as she could down the slanted floor and to the hallway. Suako checked every room along the way, until she arrived at the engine room. She looked all around, and noticed two legs sticking out from behind the power generator. "Mack! Shit!" she scuttled over to him and tried to pull him out.

As she tugged him around he slowly came to. "Huh? Wha'…" he looked around. He'd been lying in a cold puddle of water that was gradually leaking into the ship. "Mack, you awake?" Suako asked. "Uh, yea… I uh, I can't feel my legs," he said, not entirely coherent. "It's ok, we'll warm you up. I'll see if I can get a fire started in the other room," she said, and rubbed his legs to start the circulatory flow in the mean time. "Is everyone ok?" He asked. "Seems so. There's a few injuries, but otherwise everyone seems to be alright," she told him. "Where are we?" he inquired. "We don't know yet. After we get everyone conscious we should get outta here if we can. Right boss?" she said, "we have to find out what's going on. This ship is gonna sink sooner or later. I don't think we can fix it."

"Why were you down her anyway Mack?" Suako asked. His body shivered menacingly in her arms, "Before the black out I heard some clash, I came here to check it out. I think we hit some sort of rock or thick coral… anyway that's what started this leak," he explained. "Is he ok Suako?" Jenko called down the passageway. "He's alive! Can you start the fire in the stove? He's freezing back here!" she hollered back. "Sure thing! Then I'll come help you carry 'im out!" Jenko replied. "Thanks, Jenko!" Suako said.

Several hours later everyone was awake and huddled around the stove. Seresuto was nearly immobile, her stomach kept her from being able to move too much.

Adamu was practically a hundred percent all right, his mutilated skin aside. Kato could walk with help and Mack was warmed up just before the point of hypothermia. Luck was seemingly on their side for surviving such an event with such minor injuries.

The ship echoed with creeks and cranking metal as it slowly filled with water. It was time to get everything and everyone out of the ship. Vince, Suako, Mei, Adamu, Yu-Lee, and Jenko went around and collected all the tangible goods that they could and got them all placed by the hatch. They made certain that they had all the food, artillery and tent equipment. Jenko climbed up to the hatch, twisted the porthole open, and extended the hatch up and over.

Jenko poked his head up and looked around; to the rear of the ship was the wide-open sea, which had turbulently pushed them about. As he turned around he saw a city built above water rocks on the coastline, that stretched on quite far before he saw land. They had crashed near to shore, and he noticed a port not fifty yards away. No one stood post there, though there was a city situated behind it; it seemed eerie that no one was there, and that no boats were in the harbour either.

There were more trees, though not many more, then there were on the Eastern Green Continent. A thick foot of snow coated the ground. It seemed like on gigantic air dome covered the continent, it was so easy to breathe. Tiny snowflakes fell on him from the white-grey sky above, and their falling made the far distance hazy. He looked back to the city and wondered if maybe there had been guards posted at the harbour that were coming to retrieve them from their crash. Whatever the explanation may be, he had a foreboding feeling about it.

"Hey what do you see up there? We're not stranded, are we?" Suako called up. "No, we've hit land. I think we're at the Imperial Continent already," Jenko called down. "What?" Adamu was shocked, "We were still a week away!" Yu;Lee walked up beside Adamu, "The sea helped us get here faster. Maybe it sees just how hard we're trying to save it and the planet," she smiled contentedly. "We'll let's get the hell outta 'ere then," Kato called from the back.

First the more able bodied of the group lowered the goods off of the ship and onto the ground. Next was the challenge of getting Kato and Mack from the ship when their legs were temporarily useless. They slowly helped get them up the ladder, onto the deck, and finally onto the snowy shore. Mack's legs slowly were become more sensitised, tingling with a burn from within.

They rested exhaustedly on the bank after escaping from the ship. They listened as the hull of the ship filled faster and faster with water; it screeched as it scratched its way down the rocky slope. Finally, it slipped beneath the rippling waves until only three feet stayed above the water. The bottom of the ship rested on the shallow rocks below it. The sun beat down on them, but it wasn't brutal on them like in the plains of land in the East Green Continent neglecting air domes as cover. When the rays touched their skin, it did not burn them.

"I guess we're finding a different way back," Adamu tried to make light of the situation with little success. "Sorry you lost your ship Adamu," Mack tried to be a comfort to him. Adamu sighed and just starred out to his sunken ship, silently paying tribute to his sunken livelihood. After a moment of silence, he walked over to his wife who looked onward to the ship that she'd called her home so may times. The others looked at it two, each with the same two thoughts in their heads: *It's a shame they lost their home away from home. How are we going to get back?*

The wind started to become bitter and they knew they needed to make their way to the town quickly. They decided that they would pretend to be travellers from a city on the other side of the Imperial continent, seeking shelter within the city. Kato rested on Mei as he hobbled on his weak leg, and Vince and Suako helped Mack while his legs were slowly replenishing.

When they got closer to the city they noticed it was much too quiet for its size; In fact, it was noiseless. They read a sign hanging just in from of the entrance onto main street, *"Welcome to Kukotan"*. The homes were tall and wide, made of some sort of dense clay. Dark wood sectioned off the homes, and was also used to make the roofs and window shutters. The town was vacant; recently abandoned they assumed. Knocked over fruit carts and other random items were scattered across the paved streets.

After they'd searched the entire city, to find no one was there, they pirated it for food and supplies. They found a grand home, situated around the town square, with an outlay of flowerbeds in front, beneath a layer of soft fallen snow. When they entered the home, they were taken aback. The walls were in good condition, and the home was furnished with intact furniture. Lavish curtains hung over the windows, which stretched up the twelve-foot walls. This was something few of them had ever seen this close before. They knew that the C.D.F.P. on grid one had the good life, but they never knew exactly what the rich lived in, but now they could well imagine.

Within the house, it took some time before they got over the shock of the lavish appeal. They were mystified when they found the remnants of a flame burning in the fireplace of the entrance hall. "How long ago could they have been here?" Mei asked as she sat down Kato on a sofa near the fireplace. "Couldn't have been too long ago," Vince said suspiciously, looking about. Vince went to search the upstairs of the house, and came back down shortly after to report that he'd only found a cat, which he carried downstairs to feed.

They found a hardwood chair that would be suitable for feeding the fire. Jenko and Vince pulled it apart and threw it in, and within minutes the heat emitted by the newly rekindled fire became noticeable. Vince had also found a pipeline that run into the ground. He told them it was able to extract water from its source, and bring it directly into the house. They drew it into a cast iron pot they found and placed it over the fire to boil, in order to ensure it was sterile. Kairu cleaned and removed his bandage, and poured some of the water over his cut.

They bantered about ideas trying to conclude the strange vacancy of the city, but they reached no such conclusion. Whatever had caused the evacuation they would have to discover later on. Meanwhile Seresuto, Kato and Mack rested by the fire, and Yu-Lee prepared warm soup in the pot for them with some potatoes, leeks, rutabaga and carrots that had been lying in the street. Having had scavenged the kitchen there were some unusual and rare spices available for them to try. The meal was much appreciated and warmed them from the inside out.

Suako and Vince volunteered to stay up the first half of the night watch. With the oddity of the seemingly sudden leave of Kukotan's residence, they could not be too careful. For the first time in weeks everyone slept soundly, while the two group guardians found it hard to keep their eyes open. They didn't say much but sat and stared at each other for over an hour.

"Suako?" Vince finally broke the silence. "Yes Vince?" Suako responded. "...What is it that you won't tell me?" his voice was timid. He sounded nearly betrayed, yet not spiteful by it. Suako turned her head to look away. How could she possibly answer to such a needy plea? It took her a while to group her thoughts; she felt he deserved an explanation. She'd wanted to tell him for quite some time now about her shady past that haunted her in whole now. Before, she'd repressed her painful memories, until they had nearly fled from her mind.

Though her soul would not allow her mind to forget for good, and when Yu-Lee had resurfaced her past, revisited it with her constantly. She knew it was time to open up to Vince about it.

She let him hear it, all of it. He was horrified by what he heard, but it explained a lot of things that never added up to too much before. She felt rather numb afterward, tears streaming down her face. He rocked her in his arms and told her she was safe there. She was tired and gradually fell asleep shaking like a quivering arrow shot from a bow. He laid her down on the couch they'd been sitting on, and covered her with his coat. Then Vince got up, and quietly tip toed over to the window. He gazed out at the hazy clouds over the dark blue-black night sky. The moon, nearly at its peak, shone intermittently through the fleeting grey clouds of night. He couldn't remove the images of Suako's whimpering eyes from his mind.

"So, she finally told you," a voice from behind startled Vince. He gasped, spun around and just about fell over. Yu-Lee was standing a few feet away, and once he had a moment to realize, he took in a long breath and sighed, "Yea. She finally told me... I always knew something was there but I..." He looked to his feet. Yu-Lee walked up to him. "But you never expected this," she nodded. Vince trembled as he took in his breath, "Yea. I thought I knew so much about the C.D.F.P. but this... they have no morals... and Suako..." Vince's eyes welled up with tears. "She has been through hell, and back again. But now she's released the chain around her tongue that contained the secret. Now she can begin to heal," Yu-Lee said, comfortingly.

"I shouldn't have pushed her to tell me though..." Vince said, feeling guilty. Yu-Lee placed her hand firmly on his shoulder and looked him square in the eye, "Don't you say that. She needed a reason to tell you, I think she's waited to tell you for a long time. Don't feel that you forced her to say it. She isn't one to fold under pressure, and if she didn't want to she wouldn't have. Now get some rest, you have a lot for your mind to digest," Yu-Lee instructed. "But the rest of the watch..." Vince began to object. "I'll take over, just ease your mind for the night," Yu-Lee smiled. "Thank you," Vince said with gratitude. "Remember it is the will of the life energy, this is how we learn to better the whole of our existence. She suffered for all of us. You should be proud," Her words were that of the wise. Vince nodded his head and found a spot on the couch next to Suako. He wrapped his arms around her waist. His mind had been working full tilt, but the night slowly carried him away.

The past does not dictate your future- you are not your past- you are what you took with you from your past.

Chapter 13: Civil War

They were provoked to rise when morning came and a sweet scent encircled the room. The smell was warm and delicious. The air tasted like confectionery goods; the scent was rare and hypnotising. Yu-Lee pranced into the main living room from the kitchen happily, "Mm, what's the delightful smell?" Jenko asked as he was taken away by his stomach. "I found a book in their kitchen about 'Baked Goods'. It seems to be a common thing on this continent. They had supplies of flour and other such things in a large; uh... oh what did my mother call it... Oh yes! It was the *pantry*. I haven't seen one of those for years," Yu-Lee said delighted.

Seresuto blinked dumb, "What is a pantry?" she asked eyeing Yu-Lee questionably. Jenko and Mack laughed. "Seems only us old folks remember," Mack chuckled. Seresuto only looked further confused. "Ha! Ha! Oh, it's a room used to store long lasting foods. It's just beside the kitchen," Yu-Lee explained. It took a while to convince the others that is had no other purpose then to store food. They weren't used to space being designated for the soul purpose of virtually only one use, especially when food was so scarce.

They feasted that morning on delicious apple cinnamon bread and honey scones. They found that Seresuto's preservatives that they'd salvaged from their ship were a divine addition upon the luxurious flavours that tortured them with pleasure. They stopped talking about strategy for the time being and simply enjoyed the moment. Jenko, Mack and Yu-Lee shared stories over breakfast about their childhood and of their parents; stories were heart-warming and helped them forget everything else.

They sat, talked and laughed for the first time in over a month. These times were all there was to cherish, and it was these moments that gave them the drive to continue, that they fought so hard for. This was the life experience that wanted everyone to have. No more needless violence, ravaged earth, and imposed taxes, nor grieving over pointless deaths.

After the leisurely meal it was straight back to reality, and there was much to do. Kato's knee needed to be placed back in its joint; there was no other way for him to go on. Jenko gave him his leather belt to bite down on, and he gritted it tightly within his jaw. Mack counted to three and then jolted the dislocated limb back into its proper place. There was a loud *pop*, followed by a deep growl from Kato. The pain was excruciating, but he endured it well. After the initial sting the throbbing pain that had been swarming the area fled. He gave it a moment and then tried standing on his leg again.

Mack had most of his sense back in his legs, though his nerves were still recuperating. He was all right to walk, which was good enough for him. He was readying everyone for departure already, no time was to be wasted. They'd been out a month travelling the waterways, and Mack was determined to make up for the time.

Unfortunately, Seresuto could not be healed so easily. She had suffered a massive blow to her midsection, and they feared she had internal damage. She was beginning to show signs of an oncoming fever. The situation did not bode well with any of them. They discussed their next deployment and what they could do concerning her injuries. Adamu asked for him and his wife to be left for a moment alone.

Following their discussion, he called the others back into the room. "We can't hold you up, you need to go ahead. She won't be able to travel like this, and I can help her better here. We'll stay here and wait for you," Adamu explained. Seresuto lay sprawled out on the couch. He looked back to his battered wife and went to her side, and kindly he pulled a blanket over her icy legs and swollen abdomen. Mack look Adamu in the eye and saw his resolve, "You do what you feel's best. We'll have to come back to leave from this port when we leave. Here..." Mack pulled a few automatic weapons from a case he'd brought along, "Stay safe." "Thank you," Adamu graciously accepted the guns. "Common everyone. Let's gather rations and get a move on," Mack ordered, pointing toward the kitchen.

Quickly they finished preparations, said their goodbye's to Seresuto and Adamu, and left. As they walked the empty streets, the abandoned city stilled felt quite out of place. The sky had cleared, and was blue for the first time they'd seen in weeks, letting the sun glare off of the snow like light off of a mirror. When the reached the city boarder the saw snow stretching out seemingly forever in front of them. Evergreens, spruces and naked summer trees coated in white powder snow only broke view of the endless snowy plains.

Trudging threw the deep snow they cautiously began to cut across the land. The blustering winds of the prior day regretted to show up again, but the chill was still in the air, with a nipping cold bite. They weren't an hour's march away from Kukotan when they heard screams and gunshots. It came from the distance, somewhere beyond the forest of trees ahead.

They scattered for cover behind the wide based trees of the pine forest. Suako immediately began chanting beneath her breath, "Defendre operire..." over and over. Suako could see a vague shield of light cover them. "What's happening? Can anyone see?" She asked, prepping her gun with bullets. "It's comin' from the west just 'head of us," Kato used his ears to place the sounds. "Stay here until I give my word. I'm going in for a closer look," Mack ordered them. "Here Mack." Suako tossed him a cartridge for his pistol, "Be safe." "Right," he nodded, "Stay here till I come back everyone."

They listened as the snow crunched beneath Mack's feet as he trotted off. The gunfire in the distance echoed. Mack's movements were soon out of earshot. They stayed covertly hidden behind the trees and remained quiet. The frequency of the shooting increased drastically, and they were anxious to get a move on.

Though it only took minutes it seemed much longer. Mack returned, "Everyone huddle round me... ok, good. Listen, about a kilometre that way there is a drop into a valley. There's a small town there. All hell seems to be breaking loose there. I think we should go and see what's going on. Might be something interesting for us there. No one can see us back here, but that doesn't mean we should let our guards down. All right? Good. Move out!"

He led them down the snowy trail, past the trees to the forest's edge. They stayed behind the borderline for camouflage from eyes gone amiss in the action below. It was hard to see anything specifically, but the picture was clear enough. It looked like an all-out slaughter down below. Though the townspeople fought back against an onslaught of armed soldiers, they were no match. The women and children were being killed just the same. Some homes were being set ablaze, and the black smoke climbed up into the sky.

"Mack, we can't just sit here and watch this..." Mei's eyes vividly watched the violence. "You're right Mei. Ok everyone, we're going in. Be discrete, we can't afford to be found out. Let's just stop that shit from going on," Mack commanded. A simultaneous "Right," returned from everyone in favour. "Ok now, Mei and Suako take the left flank, Kato and Vince the right, and Jenko with me straight into the centre. Now..." Mack scavenged through his pack, *Happy birthday everyone*, scare the troops away with these," He sarcastically said, then tossed each party two grenades. "Now for you Yu-Lee, Suako told me that you were able to protect your town from the C.D.F.P. with some kind of magick?" Mack asked. "Yes, that's correct," she confirmed. "Well when the soldiers flee I need you to do the same thing for this place. Can you do that?" He asked. "Yes," Yu-Lee nodded. "Good. Stay here in the hills so you can see when it's time, then come down to the village afterward, Mack Instructed." "I will," she agreed. "Great. Boys and girls let's get a move on," Mack said.

The pincer attack commenced. They crept down the hill, staying low to the ground; they would quickly infiltrate the city from the front and on both sides. The sped up as they came into the clearing to avoid getting spotted; they were dark targets along the snowy white hill. Suako and Mei were the first to reach the town, followed by Mack and Jenko. Kato and Vince weren't so lucky as to go unnoticed.

A lone soldier had obviously seen something, and was coming towards them full tilt. He looked rough and rather barbaric as he plodded towards them. As he passed behind a building they were temporarily out of sight, and Vince noticed a miniature slope of snow around the foot of an evergreen. They ducked back behind the slur of snow quickly for cover. Vince pulled a knife from his belt halter and cut a branch from the tree and threw it out to where they'd been spotted.

The soldier tore around the bend, and came sprinting up the hill. *Crunch! Crunch!* The footsteps neared. They began to slow until they came to a full out stop. Vince sat with his back pressed against the cold snowy mound behind him, Kato right next to him holding his breath. Vince's heart rate escalated, and he held his knife, ready to attack. They heard the branch rustle about. Vince was nearly ready to pounce out and charge the intruder, but Kato touched his arm and shook his head 'no' with warning eyes. Vince nodded and took a deep breath. *Crunch! Crunch!* The man moved about inspecting the curious area.

Then again, the footsteps went to leave, but something was wrong, they stopped, and then they returned. The soldier had spotted some of Kato and Vince's incriminating footsteps in the snow. The guys knew something was wrong when the receding walk abruptly stopped. Vince prepared to go once more, but yet again Kato held him back, and whispered to him in a firm tone, "Hey man, if he calls out, then everyone's finished. Hold yourself back, Vince!" They heard the man talk to himself, "Hmp, guess I'm crazy." Then he turned to head to back the town.

Suddenly an explosion permeated the area with a flash of fiery fury. Kato released his grip on Vince, "Go, now!" Kato told him. Vince ran at the man from behind, who was in shock watching the explosions in the town streets below. The man was about to turn and go back after the target he'd suspected, when Vince caught him from behind and forever silenced him with his knife. They hid the body behind the rift that they'd been using for cover, and then rushed down to the town.

They were halfway down the hill when Kato stopped straightaway, "Vince, start firing!" he told him, struck with swift inspiration. They fired off several rounds high into the air, and the noise boomed, and gave the illusion of a coming onslaught. The soldiers were hastily fleeing the town. Vince and Kato remained on the hill and waited for the soldiers to leave. Then they cautiously made their way down the hill, until they finally reached their destination.

"Hey what happened?" Mack asked as he met up with Suako and Mei. "No clue. Where're the boys?" Mei asked looking around herself, knifes at the ready. "I have no idea..." Mack replied, when they suddenly heard bouncing footsteps coming towards them. "Hey we're here! Sorry we're late," Vince puffed as he and Kato ran up to the others. "What were those shots from?" Suako asked, constantly checking around herself. "Calm down, it was us," Vince explained. "We wanted to get them outta 'ere before the fires ate up everythin'," Kato replied, "So, where they keep their water?"

They scouted about for some water barrels, but when they found them they were partially frozen, so they found themselves throwing snow onto the bursting flames. The fires burned furiously, and was not willing to go out without a fight. It roared on, and seemed to be even stronger after their attempts to extinguish the flames. It took some doing, but when the townsfolk realised the attack had ceased they helped as well. Until nightfall they all worked hard to save all they could. They managed to save all but one home, which had been the first one set ablaze. The flare reached high up into the celestial sphere above, lighting it up and blocking the view of the stars.

They met back up in the center of town, exhausted. "Phew, finally they're out," Mack wheezed and coughed. "Yea... Mack you really need to stop smoking," Jenko laughed, just as tired as Mack. Mack starred him down, "Shut up." Jenko laughed and shook his head. "Ok, they're ok over there," Mei announced as she, Vince and Suako jogged back over to the main group, Kato following close behind. "There's one on da other side of town... It's no use. It's gone anyway," Kato said wiping the charcoal soot from his arms as he walked up.

They began to discuss what the best course of action from there would be. "Excuse me..." A voice converged into their conversation. They turned to see a short young woman standing behind them. "You helped us so much. I saw what you did. Thank you," she held her hands up to her chest, fingers interlocked and bowed to them. "Please come inside where it warm for something hot to eat," she offered with watery eyes that spoke genuinely. They followed the young woman to her home. Suako paused a few steps from the girl's door. "Oh, Yu-Lee!" she remembered, "I'll go to the outskirts and bring her here. Ok Mack?" "Oh, yea, go ahead," Mack nodded. "See ya in a flash," Suako ran off.

The rest of them entered a cozy log cabin. It hadn't suffered any damage from the fire, unlike many of the other local homes. The interior was just as glorious as those houses back in Kukotan; the splendour inside was of silk fabrics, frivolous frills, and desirable shiny decorative gems that hung about the interior. A crackling fireplace welcomed them with the scent of stew that was heating above it. "Please take a seat," the girl offered. They did just that, weary of dirtying the fineries though.

She was a pretty girl with almond shaped eyes and cupids bow lips. Her attire was alien to them, though it was to be expected. Her clothing was rich, and modern, unusually designed; velveteen, leather and suede coated her body. Her skin was fair, and fine, never having had endured strenuous physical labour. This was a life, an existence, that stirred emotions them within. *These fineries should be offered to everyone* became the collective thought.

"Dinner should be ready soon," she said while stirring the pot with a long silver spoon. Turning around to face her guests, she took a seat in the master chair in front of the fireplace, facing the two couches to either side where they sat. "My name is Masumi," she bowed her head. "My name's Mack... what is this place?" he asked. "This is Uwajima... And what are your names?" her bright eyes asked looking to the others. "I'm Mei, this is Kato, that's Vince, and Jenko over there. The girl who left is Suako. She should be back soon; she just went to meet up with one of our comrades by the woods," Mei explained. "Hello everyone, nice to meet you all," she smiled sweetly. "Nice to meet you too," Jenko said. "Thanks, fer lettin' us s'all in outta the cold," Kato said. "We appreciate the hospitality," said Kairu.

Mack opened his mouth to speak when, *Thud! Thud!* there came a knock on the door. Masumi jumped up from her seat and excused herself to go open the door. Suako and Yu-Lee came in rather chilled. "Thank you," they told the girl. "My pleasure, my name is Masumi. Please come in and take a seat. Dinner should be ready," Masumi said as she walked back over to check the stew. Suako and Yu-Lee did just that, and the fire's incandescence soon heated their exteriors. Masumi pulled out some white china dishes from a wooden cabinet with fine glass inlaid windows. She filled the grapevine painted bowls with the savoury scented stew and passed the plates out to her guests. The stew was admirably delicious, it seemed to melt in their mouths, and filled their hungry stomachs. They found themselves heated from the inside out.

"We are grateful for your hospitality young one," Yu-Lee bowed her head. "No, not at all. I'm grateful for all you have done for Uwajima. They've been attacking for months now. I guess they finally got organised to take us down once and for all. If you hadn't come, I'm sure no one would be left here. Thank you so, so much!" she cried. "Oh, don't cry now, it's all right. We couldn't just watch them massacre this town," Suako put her stew down and went over to comfort Masumi, "Really, we couldn't let that happen to anyone. You looked completely defenceless. It wasn't just a warrior's battle; it was a blood bath from where we were looking from."

After Masumi had calmed down, Suako passed her a handkerchief that was lying on the end table beside her. She whipped away her tears, "I'm sorry, it's just... *sniff*... my parents, they killed... my parents," She grimly said trembling, "Who Masumi? Who killed them? And why?" Mack questioned kneeling down by her. Suako held Masumi's hand and rubbed her back to release the tension. "The Imperial army, because of their ties to the East Green Continent... That's what father told mother and I. He said that the company the, uh..." she shut her eyes to think. "The C.D.F.P.?" Mei tried to help. "Yes, that's what he called it. He said that 'the *traitors* here finally are able to show their true colours and betray the heart of the Imperial system'," she told them, wiping tears from her red blotchy cheeks. Mack stared at the wall behind the girl with wide eyes.

"This doesn't sound good. Hey Mack, I'm worried," Mei uneasily looked to Mack hoping for some sort of response. "Yeah Mack. If the C.D.F.P. is gaining power over here..." Suako started. "Don't make assumptions," Jenko stopped Suako, "Masumi... I know this is a hard time for you. We need you to be strong. We can't bring your parents back but maybe we can help their deaths to have not been in vain. How did your dad know what was going on?" Jenko asked. "He worked under the Imperial officials... *Sniff*, he used to escort them to different places," she said. "Did he tell you anything else about the attacks sweetie?" Yu-Lee kindly asked. "No," she replied. There seemed to be a collective sigh of frustration around the room. "But... He kept records," Masumi told them.

Masumi showed them down the hall, into the den, where there was a second fireplace happily burning down there. She walked over to a sculpted masterpiece of a pine desk, and reached into a cubby-hole. When she pulled her hand out she revealed several thick black books. She scanned inside the covers of the books until she found one that seemed to satisfy her. When she did, she placed it on top of the stack and carried them over to a central coffee table in the centre of several large cushioned chairs. "Here are his documents. I put the most recent one on top. You're welcome to go through them all. I'll bring you some blankets and coffee," she told them, and then tore left.

"That poor girl... she's trying to keep busy... trying to forget. I know the feeling," Mei sympathised. Kato wrapped his arms around Mei from behind, "It's all right Mei. Everything s'ok." "I know. I'm fine, really... Well let's get a head start on these," Mei said. They all found a seat. "Mack read it out loud to us," Vince requested as he cuddled next to Suako. "Yea Mack," Kato chimed in. "Good idea Vince," the others agreed, seconding his idea. They'd all been too tired to want to read themselves anyway. "Alright. Let's start from the beginning I guess," Mack agreed, and picked up the books and looked through them until he found the first one. He flipped the book open and began to read aloud:

Book 1 Entry No. 1

I, Nakazo, have just been hired to work as a guard for the political head of the local Imperial army, General Kai. I have sold my farming plot. Now with this new job I'll be able to keep my wife and daughter better fed. I am in charge of guarding the office and escorting him to and from meetings around the continent...

Mack stopped. "This isn't any good. Too far back..." He put the book down and picked up the next one. Masumi came down the stairs with a pile of blankets in her arms, and she passed them out. "Thank you Masumi," Yu-Lee smiled as she accepted the blanket. "You're welcome," she replied, then went to disappear back out of the room, and upstairs to the second floor. "Here let me help you," Yu-Lee offered, and they went up together. Mack flipped the second book open to a random page and began reading again:

Book 2 Entry No. 238

The winter has been brutal. General Kai has been summoned to many meetings. His other transport has been ill so I've had to take double shifts. We have to leave again this Wednesday. I doubt I'll be back in time for Masumi's fifteenth birthday...

Mack sighed. He flipped the pages and read to himself short sections. He continued to flip the pages, unable to find a satisfactory entry to read to everyone. "Here Mack go with the final one," Jenko picked up the book and passed it to him. Mack grasped the book and opened it halfway, and after clearing his throat, he commenced once more:

Book 3 Entry No. 672

After our last trip General Kai appeared to have a great burden on his mind. He refused to divulge it to me at this time. He seems to be troubled by it. I am worried for my family...

Everyone sat up with expressions of interest. "Bulls eye Mack!" Mei exclaimed. Mack flipped onward several pages. *Thump, thump, thump!* Masumi and Yu-Lee came down the stairs with trays in hand. They passed out coffee around the room. "Did I miss anything?" Yu-Lee asked pouring Mack his coffee from a copper kettle. "You're just in time," he replied picking up the cup and blowing on the hot liquid to cool it slightly. They fixed their drinks with sugar and cream as they desired before they continued onward into Nakazo's documented excursions. Masumi sat with the group, next to Yu-Lee. "I'd like to hear too," she said mildly. Mack reopened the book and embarked upon the pages once again:

Book 3 Entry No. 680

Today General Kai finally told me the concerns of his meetings. It seems there have been some politicians who have joined with the C.D.F.P. Company on the East Green Continent to make some profits. This has never been brought in question until now. Apparently, the company spreads death with its productivity.

Kai is deeply disturbed by the movement of the political views. He is strongly against the movement.

We have been trying to put a stop to our distant neighbours in general after discovering the negative infliction they've been causing. Talk of their possible growth is not a good tiding. General Kai is to go back in a few days to discuss with the council about the proceedings...

Mack looked at the following page in silence. He took a sip of his coffee and rubbed his tired eyes. He flipped a few pages further:

Book 3 Entry No. 686

We just got back from a town meeting that Kai held. He explained the situation to citizens. We anonymously agreed as a community to rebel against the growing view of joining the C.D.F.P. Corporation. The continent is divided. General Kai announced that civil war was declared early yesterday morning when a city against the seemingly popular view attacked a politician on the road in an attempt to stop the C.D.F.P. from building one of their 'reactors' on the boarder of his city. The C.D.F.P.'s strong force took up arms and is now deploying against all rebelling groups.

Book 3 Entry No. 687

General Kai just received word that the East Green Continent has sent over troops to help "deal with malcontent nonconformists" as he put it. We have quite the war to fight. The odds are not in our favour...

Mack closed the book. "I think we get the picture. This wasn't swift, the dispute was growing till it got violent," He placed the book on the table. "At least we're not the only ones who want to see the C.D.F.P. stopped," Jenko said with a slight bob of his head. Mack yawned. Masumi stood up. "I think you all need a good night's sleep. You can talk in the morning. Rest now, I'll be in my room upstairs on the second floor if you need anything. Good night," she bid them farewell, bowed to them, and then took her leave.

"She's right. We're all bushed," Vince yawned. "Let's call it a night Mack," Jenko pulled the blanket over himself and lay back on the sofa. "Ok, everyone, rest up, we'll discuss everything in the mornin'," Mack followed their lead. He momentarily massaged his temples, trying to rest his busy mind, then got up and turned off the oil lamp. Only the gentle light coming from the fire kept the room alit and comfortably heated. The mild crackling of it lulled them off to sleep.

The morning sun was rising, awakening them to see Masumi standing by the fireplace stirring a pot of cinnamon hinted oatmeal. Apparently, Mack and Jenko had gone outside temporarily, so Mack could have a cigar to ease his nerves. A red teapot with a gold rim steeped with rose leaf tea, and a matching set of teacups encircled the pot stationed by their bedsides. Mei sat up and placed her feet on the plush ivory carpet. She yawned and stretched her arms as she allowed herself to try and recall all of last nights discoveries.

"What's on your mind Mack? Don't say it's nothing, I can see it in your eyes," Jenko said pulling his jacket around himself. "*He* was at one of the council meetings Nakazo wrote about.," Mack took a long inhalation on his cigar. "I see... Mack it's time you let everyone know. You've held out long enough. They *need* to know. You know it's important," Jenko pushed him. "I know, I know..." Mack sighed. "I'll tell them when we go back in," he consented to comply. "Good, it's better that way," Jenko reassured.

Mack and Jenko slowly came back into the den, and found the group sitting around eating their brown sugar sprinkled porridge and talking amongst themselves. Mack took his seat with a loud *thud*! that drew everyone's attention to him. His face showed his mind's preoccupation. Jenko sat between Yu-Lee and Suako. "What's going on?" Suako whispered. "Just give him a minute. You'll find out," Jenko assured her, his eyes glued on Mack.

"Listen up guys. There's somethin' you gotta hear. It's the piece of the puzzle missing from the story I told you about when I used to work for the C.D.F.P...." Mack started. "Wait, what?! You worked for the C.D.F.P.?" Yu-Lee exclaimed. "I used to work for their military brigade.

To make a long story short, it went sour near the end when they asked me to destroy some documents on the pollutant effects of generators. It had an estimate of the earthly demise... anyway, like I said there's more to the story then I told before," Mack sighed. "What is it Mack?" Mei had a shroud of worry present in her voice. "I wasn't the only one to see those disturbing documents..."

"When I joined the Company military, I joined with a friend. His name was Kazuo, we'd been close since we were kids. He and I worked our way up the chain of command, and our services and skills were equally recognised. We worked well as a team and always got the job done; I watched his back, and he watched mine. When we went to work with Yoshida, it seemed perfect. For a while we worked as a unit, and if there was an important job to do, they'd get Me, Kazuo and Yoshida to do it."

"When we were assigned to destroy the incriminating documents, we feel apart. Yoshida didn't want to question anything on the documents, he just wanted his promotion. That was all he cared about. Kazuo and I weren't so easy going about it. Kazuo decided was going to talk to the leader of the C.D.F.P. about the records. The next day I heard, from a buddy I'd helped out in battle, that Kazuo was imprisoned and that they were searching for me. That's when I faked my death and got the hell out of the Company. Like I said before, Yoshida never bought the cover. He knew I wouldn't have been done in like that... He knew me too well..."

"Well, this journey has been twofold. I've been searching for Kazuo ever since I heard he was taken away. I have no idea where he is, but he found more papers. He was taken before he got to show them to me. They must be important. None the less, I owe it to him to find him. He's been imprisoned for years. The Company's going to pay for what they did to him. So, now you know. That's it. That's all there is…" He shrugged, let out a huge sigh and searched for a distraction. He picked up his breakfast and started to eat.

"Wow… 'ey Mack, why didn't ya tell us before?" Kato leaned forward. "No reason… Too hard to tell I guess," Mack replied. "Don't you worry Mack, we'll find him," Suako smiled. Masumi sat blank faced by the fire. "I guess this *company* has been causing a lot of pain for a lot of people… I never knew," she said meekly. "They've killed lots of people. We're trying to get back at them for what they've done to the people of East Green Continent… no, to the world. They've been killing the planet just as much as people, animals, and plants… We're going to stop them," Mei assured the girl. "Good," was all Masumi did say; vengeance was in her soft-spoken voice.

"So, what's next boss?" Kato asked after a simultaneous group pause. Mack looked up at him but gave no response. Yu-Lee scooted forward on the couch, "Before I came down to the town I saw the soldiers fleeing north-west up the other side of the crevice. It looked like they had quite a few wounded. They wouldn't have gone too far before setting up camp. We could probably catch up to them," she suggested, then leaned back. "Well if we follow them we could make it to their headquarters probably," Vince put the idea forward. Murmurs and nodding heads sanctified the mutual agreement.

"Good theory Vince, if the C.D.F.P. started its dirty roots from here there's no doubt in my mind that the same kind of people are in power here. If we can follow them..." Mack began. "Wait, wait, wait!" Masumi protested, cutting Mack off mid-sentence, "If you want to go to Tomakomai I will take you there. I may only be sixteen but I am no child. I wish to avenge my parents. Take me with you," her voice was firm, not allowing 'no' as an answer. Mack looked into her eyes. They burned with an unwavering determination. "Tomakomai is the capitol then?" he said, his eyes agreeing to take her on their travels. "Yes, my father took me with him once to go and visit the massive city. Let me prepare my things so we can go," she said, and hurried out of the room. "Right, everyone, we leave at dawn tomorrow," Mack said.

The day went quickly, and Masumi did her best to pack her valuables up. She took a picture from it's frame off the mantel downstairs and put it within a cubby in her bag. "Masumi?" Vince inspected her pack. "What is it?" She asked. "Is that... oh what did grandfather call it... um... l, leather?" Vince inquired. She looked confused, between the bag and Vince, "Uh, yes. What, you've never seen leather?" she laughed. Vince blushed and her laughter abruptly ceased, "You've *never* seen leather?" Masumi was astonished, "What kind of place is this 'East Green

Continent' of yours?" "It's a barren wasteland of what used to be a glorious land. The C.D.F.P. spreads disease and destruction like a plague," He explained. "I never knew it..." her voice trailed off, then changed entirely, "Come with me. I need you're help carrying some things"

Masumi handed Vince a coat, once belonging to her father, he put it on, and they went out into the street. The day was sunny, as well as crisp and cold, with no wind. It was like the calm after the storm syndrome upon the town; people were in the streets cleaning the wreckage the armed force had inflicted yesterday. They saw Kairu helping a family to fix the hole in their burnt roof. The town was in shambles.

Ring! The door chimed a bell as they entered a store. All the buildings were the same residential looking throughout the town, so the only distinction to indicate it was anything other than another home was the sign that hung outside that read: **Convenience Store**. They entered and caught a whiff of delectable chocolate. A lovely wooden counter stretched horizontally across the room toward the back. Pine shelves were lined with goods; bags of flour, sugar, jars of jams, apple and cherry preserves, bottles of fine aged wine, and much more. A shelf to the left was graced with fresh breads, scones, croissants, cinnamon buns and other freshly baked goods. To the right, there were some odd looking devices Vince had never before seen.

Crinkle! A young man stood up from behind the counter, and Masumi waltzed over to him. "Oh Masumi, hello!" he welcomed, with a cheery grin. "Hi Kyoto, good to see you're safe," she said. "Same with you. My store miraculously survived without anything but a few stolen goods. I figured it'd be most helpful to be open today for everyone in town. Bread is free today, and everything else is on sale," he informed them, then looked at Vince, "Who's your friend?" Masumi smiled, "Oh, that's Vince. He was just passing by yesterday when everything was happening, he helped save my house." "Ha! He could've picked a better time," Kyoto shook his head and laughed as her wiped the counter, "Thanks for helping Masumi," he said to Vince. "So, where's your mum an' pop today? Fixin' up the home?" he asked. Masumi's expression faded and she began to jitter and shake. "Mom and dad... they didn't make it," she fought back her tears. "Oh no... Oh Masumi, I'm so sorry," He circled the counter and gave her a hug.

Masumi shook off the emotional purge before tears could come, "Thanks Kyoto but I'm fine." "You're a tough nut to crack Masumi... Would you two care for a cup of hot chocolate? It will help ease your mind," he offered walking back behind the counter to a large brick oven. "That'd be great Kyoto," Masumi smiled. "What about you Vince?" Kyoto asked. "Yes, thank you," Vince said, scanning his eyes over the immense supply of unusual items before him.

Making his way slowly up to the counter, Vince couldn't help his eyes moving frivolously around. Kyoto retrieved three porcelain cups and set them on the counter. Then he pulled a steaming pot from then stove and poured each cup full of the rich brown brew. Vince reached the counter and smelled the sweet drink. "I haven't had hot chocolate since I was just a boy…" he fondly recalled his uncle coming over to his home with a small bar of chocolate, at which point they melted it in water and poured the drinks. Chocolate was rare on the east Green Continent after the C.D.F.P.'s radiation incident. This drink looked different, the liquid was not as dark, and looked to be a softer brown. He sipped it and the creamy drink pleasantly tingled as it burned down his throat. "Not since you were a kid? You must be from down south. Must be nice to be warm down there huh?" Kyoto took a drink from his cup. Vince just nodded along with the assumption.

After a nice time of petty talk, and simply enjoying their drinks, Masumi got right down to business, "We need climbing equipment. Your best stuff, show it to me Kyoto." "A-alright. This way," he led her over to the wall of awkward looking instruments. She picked up several funny looking metal instruments, as well as some sturdy looking rope, a few gun like machine's, among other unfamiliar things.

Masumi told Vince, who adamantly was looking over foods he'd never seen before, that he could pick up whatever he wanted. He was modest, and only chose a few items. He brought a jar of cherries, a bar of chocolate and a tiny bag of maple sugar candies up to the counter. Masumi smiled. "Ok now help me with the regular rations. We'll need canned goods, a loaf of bread…. Maybe two, uh… what else?…" They gathered everything they needed and made two trips back to her house in order to carry everything back.

Everyone else from the group looked onward at the mountain climbing gear with sceptical eyes as it was placed in the center of the room. Masumi explained it to them, "… So, you see, this helps people to be able to climb rock walls. We need these so we can climb the Snowy Peaks in order to get to Tomakomai. Now let me show you how to use everything… this is a type of gun that will bolt these metal hinges," she held it up so everyone could see, "… directly into the rock face. Then you can tie some rope from your harness to it and that way if you fall you wont die… next we have…" she went through everything. Bit by bit they got the layout of these foreign devices and the concepts behind them. Her father had been a professional mountain climber in his profession with the local politician, General Kai, so he'd needed to learn very well how to manoeuvre through the mountains. In turn he taught Masumi everything he knew, and she was a sufficient climber. Now they were set to go, and Masumi was their lifeline of information.

Masumi pulled, from a cedar chest, many furs. They were left over from the animals that had their lives taken in order to feed her family, friends and neighbours. The soft plush hair felt heavenly on their callous fingertips. "You need to line your boots and clothing with it. I have parkas you can have instead of those jackets you're wearing, you'd freeze to death in them," and so, she dealt out needle and thread around the room. Long hours passed which they worked away in preparation.

Amanda Rose

As day turned to night snow began to fall from the sky. They watched and anticipated the worst; the hike would be hard and long enough without a storm to slow them down. None the less time was against them and they'd have to leave the next morning regardless. All they could do was watch, hope, and wait to see what would become of it.

One does not require many years to their credit to be wise.

Chapter 14: The Long Trip

Orange tinted the top of the eastern hill as the sun began to rise the next day. The snow had been brief and barely dusted a new coat of snow on top of that already there. They were grateful that the snowfall hadn't come to cause them any grief. They bundled up in the furs Masumi offered them. The temperature had dropped dramatically and hurt to walk out into. As they walked through the streets, up the town, they saw ladders tilted against homes for repairs, blood stained snow, and other remnants of the not so long ago battle. They crept through the sleeping town with only the soft sound of the compressing snow beneath their feet to signal their presence. Masumi turned and said goodbye to her home, and her innocence.

They trudged up the steep hill. It was tiring, but the party from the East Green Continent found it to be somewhat of a lesser challenge with the fresh air to bless them. The cold air nipped at their exposed skin. Each of them felt the burn of their legs as they pushed upward, tired muscles from the cold ached agonisingly with each little movement.

When they had reached the top of the top of the hill they were in for quite a treat. "Oh my god... Vince, look at that!" Suako exclaimed. "Suako that's incredible! Everyone you have to see this! Hurry up!" Vince called down to the others. "What is it? What's all the fuss… about… wow…" Mei looked on in awe. They all peered outward, standing still, as if to hope time would do the same. "I have to come back here and draw this…" Vince said wishing he'd had the time to do so then. Kairu inhaled the mint air and was reminded fondly of the mountain paths of Ryoko.

The cascading valley below was swarmed with snow covered spruce trees. Rolling hills stretched on for miles, and sunlight danced between the branches, through the puffy white clouds that stood timeless in the sky. The grandiose furs, spruces, and pines reached their arms tall to touch the forever-unattainable blue above. In the distance snowy peaks stretched as far as the eye could see in either direction. A draft blew the fresh powder snow along the tops of the mountains. Far to the base of the mountain ridge ahead the faintest view of some sort of house like structure stood out against the white outstretched snowy ground. The condensation from the mountains picked up the hues of the sun's rays, and rainbows played merrily about within the vapour as it dowsed the earth.

"Remember this everyone… this is what we fight for," Mack said after gazing longingly. "We have a long day ahead of us if we want to make it to the traveller's cabin by nightfall," Masumi insisted. "The *traveller's cabin*?" questioned Jenko, slowly pulling his eyes off the peaks and to Masumi for a second. "Yes, everyone in

Uwajima loves to climb the mountains. We built a cabin there because the journey is so long. We can stay there the night if we make it in time," she explained. "Oh," Jenko replied, looking to the heavenly scene in front of him, a medley of colours. "Also, try to keep it down, the wolves aren't out as much during the winter, but they still hunt sometimes," she warned. "*Wolves*?" Kato raised his brow. "Uh, Masumi, are your animals mutated? Was there ever a time the Imperial Continent didn't have an air dome while the C.D.F.P. was in operation?" Mack asked with inquisitive eyes. "Uh... no, I don't think so... mutated animals?" she asked. They explained to her the radiation that the East Green Continent endured and how their unsheltered plants and animals were affected, and mostly killed off by poisonous fumes.

Masumi ingested the information well, though it left her feeling ill, and rather naive. Her entire Empire had been deceived by the C.D.F.P. Deception ran thick within the Imperial's political system, and her father had fallen a victim to this treachery; Masumi was deeply angered. Unable to decipher her emotions she just shook her thoughts away and decided to ignore her muffled mind until she had time to straighten everything out.

"Ok everyone, I guess you three," she pointed to Yu-Lee, Jenko and Mack, "Know a bit more about wolves. Everyone else," she turned her attention to the others, "They're like dogs, but not friendly by any means. They're vicious. Their teeth are really sharp, and they're quick too. Keep your voices down while we pass. If you hear them coming, they pant when they run, they bark to intimidate their prey, and howl to call each other; a gun is your best bet. Knives might scare them off, but are hard to fight with," she explained in the words that she recalled her father using when he first told her about the beasts long ago.

They began the escapade with the sun to their backs, as they headed westward toward the Snowy Peaks. They passed through an ocean of trees. The darks blue between the clouds showed its face continuously throughout the day, a never-ending game of hide-and-go seek. Heavenly images used the clouds as their pallet. They heard the flow of a small stream trickling beneath a sheet of ice as it moved around the stones in it's bed most for of the day. They moved in relative silence, avoiding anything much louder then a whisper to avoid becoming lunch. The forest was equally silent, it seemed nothing but them stirred between the trees.

They went as quickly as they could, though Kato's leg was still far from healed, which slowed them down. Vince and Mei switched off helping him to keep the pressure off of his leg. Kairu had been awarded a slick bow and arrows crafted out of birch, a woman in Uwajima had given it to him for assisting her with mending her burnt roof. Kairu had been taught as a child to use a bow, so when he saw a gallant bird soar high into the sky, he quickly drew back and shot. The arrows whistled and the stone-carved tip spun upward and punctured the bird's heart. It fell like rock to the ground, dead. After a brief scouting they found the bird, a large crow, which they bundled up and carried along with them for a later meal at the cabin.

They took a short lunch break. Masumi had prepared them some sandwiches with the fresh bread she'd got the previous day, with some cheese. Everyone was curious about the odd substance, they starred at the cheese with ogling eyes. Mei sniffed the cheese. After some in depth thought Yu-Lee provoked a memory of having her father explain about how much he missed having cheese when he was a boy. Masumi explained to them it was made from the milk a cow produces, and subsequently explained what cows were. Hesitantly they tried the sandwiches. Everyone less Mack enjoyed them. Dairy of any sort apparently wasn't Mack's cup of tea. He held himself over with an apple and one of his beloved cigars.

Although they'd been making exceptionally good time, the days were still relatively short from the recession the sun had gone through leading up to the first day of winter. Days were now getting longer as February was at their doorstep, yet the hours still seemed to fly by. Recognising the fact that regardless of how fast they paced they wouldn't make the cabin by nightfall they took a well-deserved rest at their lunch break. Kairu showed Mei and Suako, who had been yearning and asking constantly to learn for quite some time, how to do some Jujitsu. Kato watched happily as he sat with a blanket over him and a cup of tea Masumi had boiled using a portable burner. Jenko and Vince scattered around collecting pinecones and other natural wonders as memorabilia.

Vince would put it into his journal and Jenko's into a box, which he'd painted the words '**World Travels Collection**' back in his house in Torusan.

"So, Masumi..." Mack began, sucking back on his cigar. The embers at the tip of it glowed an orange red. "Hmm? What?" she looked away from Kairu's swift moves and to Mack's rough face. "Where do we need to get by tonight? I don't want to have to deal with running into anything while we're trying to get some shut eye. Where's safe?" he inquired. "There's a place just a few miles away from here. We'll make it there in no time. It's a spot just above a slope, the hill is small and heavily embedded with trees. My dad used it a lot when he travelled. Plenty of cover within the pines, and the scent will cover up ours," she told him as best she could.

As she found others relying on her for her opinions and information, she found a new sense of strength, growth, and overall maturing within herself. She was without parents to guide her now and had to become independent. She thought about a lot in that short bit of time. It was but a brief few seconds, but it was an eternity within her mind. "Good, good. We'll move out in an hour or so. Great memory, Masumi." He said and patted her on the back. *Snap!* She popped back into the moment. "Oh, uh... No problem Mack."

They set off just as planned. Mei and Suako play fought with their new moves as they walked along. Kairu's regular emotional shield was let down, he was enjoying himself, and the people he was with. They reached the campsite in quickly, just as Masumi had said they would.

There was still a while before sundown, so Mack gave everyone his or her chores to prepare the campsite. Mei and Suako went to scour for dry wood for a fire, Vince and Kairu were to set up the tent, he asked Yu-Lee to make a magick shield to protect them from listening ears if she could. Masumi ran after the girls to help gather firewood. Kato went through his things searching for the flint he'd packed before they left, and Mack and Jenko searched for the stream they'd been hearing to get some water.

"Mack..." Jenko began. Mack couldn't help but let out a mild-mannered laugh. "What's funny?" Jenko asked. "Ha, nothing really. Just... tired. Nothing left but to laugh... phew, hehe," Mack said unable to hold back his laughter. Jenko couldn't help but crack a smile, so they walked along chuckling. They searched until they sighted the brook down in between two sloping ridges. They carefully made their way down to the water's edge. Mack took out his gun and beat the protective ice sheet with it's butt, and a snowflake like pattern sprawled across the icy coat. The sheet slowly cracked apart, and Mack continued to hit it again and again until he got threw to the water beneath.

They dipped their canteens into the frigid water. "So Jenko..." Mack began. "Hmm?" Jenko looked at him. "What were you going to say earlier?" Mack asked. "Huh? Oh Yea... Sorry hehe, you'd lost me for a second there. I was going to ask if you thought Yoshida crossed the sea to follow us?" Jenko replied. "Oh..." Mack sighed, "I never told you about the Naval Unit's advancements they'd been working on when I left..." Jenko's interest was suddenly stroked, "Naval Advancements?" "Yea. They realised how inefficient waiting for the current change is to travel, so they developed a new kind of ship. It was nearly complete when I left... I have no doubt they finished it. Anyway, it's got a strong engine so it can go against the current. They could've made it here in about a week. I have no doubt he's not following us; he's waiting for us," Mack said grimly. Jenko was slightly taken aback by the news.

Mack plunged the cooking pot into the stream, and as he submerged it a great big air bubble ruffled the surface. "You think that's why the support is here for the civil war?" Jenko asked. "Not really, Jenko. It sounds like the plans have been going on longer n' that... Help me yank this up, get the handle... ok, on three. One... Two... Three! Argh!" They hauled the heavy-pot onto the snow bank. They hobbled back to camp where they found everything set and ready to go.

The tent had been pitched between the trees, a pit had been dug where the firewood was being stacked, and Kato had his flint prepared to go. Yu-Lee looked pleased, which indicated to Mack that her magickal spell crafting had worked. As Mack got into the small circular orbit of camp he realised just how noisy everyone was. He was bewildered that he hadn't heard them sooner; apparently Yu-Lee's grin was one well earned.

"We have some water. We'll boil it and make some coffee," Mack said as he plunked the pot down in the snow before attending to help set up the fire. "I'll get the cups and coffee," Masumi said bouncing up and over to her satchel. "After that how bout roastin' that bird Kairu caught, eh?" Kato said licking his lips. "Sounds good. Someone wanna pluck the feathers?" Mack asked preparing a rotisserie above were the fire would be burning. Yu-Lee, who'd been doing nothing but stand posted against a tree, quickly took up the task of de-feathering. She took the bird aside and first off thanked the soul of the bird for giving its life for them. She opened her mind's eye and watched it slowly morph its life with the universal life energy. Mack hung the pot to boil while the poultry was being prepared.

The wood was set, so Kato banged the pieces of flint together, and sparks began to rain from them. Repeatedly he continued to clash them together. Bronze specks exploded like fireworks, then sank slowly to the ground. A tiny branch started a little flame, which hey kindled, and nurtured as it grew. Massing with haste it soon consumed the entirety of the wood. The light glowed within the trees' sanctity. They stayed close to it's mothering warmth.

As the sun said goodnight, it made the mountains glow, and the snow turned to gold. The mountains looked like they were on fire. The indigo blue of night, that showed the beginnings of silvery stars behind them, slowly creep forward. The sun was being chased away by the moon and the night, and ran away too, but left in its wake a lasting impression.

Masumi took a sip of her coffee and then pulled from her bag a small canister of brown sugar, which she coated of the bird with. Masumi then filled the birds centre with some bread which she'd picked apart into small pieces, seasoned with parsley, salt, pepper, mixed with chopped onions and doused with butter. No one had any idea Masumi had brought along such extravagant food. She was an inexperienced traveller, and was carrying an excessive amount of waste. They'd have her leave unnecessary baggage at the cabin the following night. Until then they'd enjoy the fact that they had such extravagant pleasures to enjoy.

They skewered the stuffed carcass, and hung the pot of left over water, in which they boiled the birds innards to create a broth, over the fire. As the bird cooked over the open flame the sugar melted and created a glaze over the skin which darkened and became crispy thin. They sat in the silver moonlit night and watched the roast. The fire diluted the cool climate, and as the evening morphed into night the fire projected their shadows against the trees. As time passed, the aroma of the bird spread through the camp, it was a strong scented bird, but the stuffing within dulled down the pungent smell, and the glaze masked it with it's caramel like appeal to their noses.

Late into the evening they enjoyed themselves. Masumi gave them another surprise when she pulled a bottle of fine aged red wine out for them to enjoy with their feast. They pulled the bird off of the spit and emptied the stuffing onto their plates. Then they tore it apart; the meat flaked easily, seemingly falling off the bones. "Masumi this looks excellent," Suako salivated over the dish before her eyes. Masumi blushed, "My pleasure," she giggled. Jenko bit into the caramelised skin and entered a blissful state, "Mm, this reminds me of being in Quan..." he happily reminisced. "Thanks, Kairu, this looks great," Vince said as he placed his meat on his plate. "No problem," Kairu remembered the long nights in Quan and was distracted by his memories of Okichi.

The tender meat melted on their tongues. The crisp delicate skin crunched gently between their teeth and infiltrated their entire mouths with intense flavor. The rich soft stuffing swarmed with the taste of the bird cooked right into it. "This is 'licious man... Mm... You be a great hunter Kairu," Kato said in between lustful mouthfuls. "Oh, this is orgasmic," Mei laughed in supreme taste-pleasure. They filled their bellies, eating slowly, feasting for hours in the enjoyment of each other's company. Merrily they laughed the night away, washing down their sinfully heavenly meal with the precious full-bodied crimson wine.

"...So, Kairu ran off and then comes back holding this enormous buzzard... ha, ha! With this totally innocent *I didn't do anything* look on his face!" "... As you can imagine, I looked like an absolute fool! I was running through the city, totally lost, looking for my pants, and then..." the stories went on long into the night.

With full tummies they were drowsy and hit their pillows and to sleep quickly. Vince asked Suako if she'd join him on a starlit walk through the forest on the cloudless night. She accepted and he offered her his hand to help her stand up. She dusted the powder snow off of her coat and then walk off with him. As they left the safety of the encampment they were startled a by the sudden orange flare and crinkle from behind. They turned to see Mack leaning up against one of the trees puffing his cigar. "Don't wander to far you too," was all he said. Vince nodded and took Suako's hand in his, guiding her onward.

They walked alone through the trees, the night was quiet and soothing. Their breath fogged before them as they spoke, "Thanks Vince... I wasn't sure how you were feeling about me since Kukotan... You've barely spoken to me..." she timidly told him. "Oh Suako, I, I'm sorry I didn't mean to be distant. It was a lot to take in. I needed time to think. I was just so angry that they... did that...." he stopped before he would well up with tears. "That's good to hear. I was starting to worry," She said relieved. "Whatever the C.D.F.P. did to any of us would never make me think less of any of us for it. It's their entire fault, no one but theirs," Vince assured her. "I know that Vince I just... Don't want you to see me as the slab of meat that they saw me as, because of my deformities-" he stopped her and stepped in front of her. Dead locked with her eyes, he said nothing. They had an understanding beyond words. She smiled faintly and nodded her head. "I could never see you in the way you think I could," Vince said. "I think... I think I knew that already," Suako smiled.

He took her hand once again and walked along with her. The long outstretching branches of the ferns brushed against their shoulders as they passed threw a narrow path. The snow fell off the trees and onto the ground like pixie dust falling. Suako picked up a tiny handful of the powder like snow and stopped Vince. "Watch!" her eyes excitedly flared. She took a moment, and chanted under her breath. Then she blew the snow from her hand and it formed into a heart as it fell. She looked to Vince who stood there blushing.

They walked on, sighted a hill free of trees, and began heading to it. "So what other little tricks did Yu-Lee teach you?" Vince asked. "Not much really. When I focus I can see Life Energies, I can sometimes focus to make things happen but I'm really still just a novice," Suako said. "You're incredible. Don't think so little of yourself," he tapped her chin up. Suako struggled and lost the fight against the smile it conjured. "See, you know your amazing... I still, when you crossed that chasm..." he said in awe. "Yu-Lee really helped me a lot with that though, and we were right by Okagwa too, but thanks you," she said. "You're welcome," he smiled.

They climbed the hill. As they reached the top the crescent moon beamed down on them. Vince playfully spun Suako around to face him; perched on top of the hill in the dark, moonlight glowing in her eyes, Suako looked like an angel. Vince ran his fingers through her auburn hair. Affectionately she reached up to brush his cheek with her long soft fingers. In turn he did the same, their eyes locked squarely with one another's.

Vince slipped his other hand around the back of her waist and pulled her closer to him. Heart fluttering, Suako couldn't even blink. "Suako I've loved you since you ran into me on the street when we first met," Vince confessed. Overwhelmed with emotion her breath was taken away. Lovingly he reached his hand from her cheek to behind her head. Suako was swept away in the moment, she was a rag doll in his control, and she loved it. He pulled her close and kissed her soft sultry lips. Like satin they kissed his moist lips back. Infatuated with one another they would not separate. Suako bushed her chest firmly against his as he stole her heart away. Pulling back, she looked into his deep dark eyes, "I loved you since you said you'd come with me to find Mack," she said as her heart beat against her rib cage as if it were playing a drum.

They refused to let each other go, like doves they were inseparable. Vince pulled his lips away, "Suako, I got this for you when you weren't looking in Ryoko at the market. Here..." he pulled from his journal a small thin package which he handed to Suako. She looked from him to the package and back again. "Open it," he whispered, a hint of excitement in his words. "Ok..." she slowly unwrapped the brown paper, and it crinkled as she did. From it she pulled an amethyst pendant. It was carved into a rose, which spoke of Vince's artistic nature. "I'm sorry I couldn't afford a chain for it, I..." Vince began to explain, but Suako rose her index finger to his apologetic lips to silence him. "It's beautiful Vince. Thank you. Help me put it on my I.D. chain, ok?" she smiled. He did as she bid.

Vince undid the back of her chain and slid the amethyst pendant on. Latching it back together he shimmied the stone down, and it hung between her breasts and twinkled as it caught the light. Leaning forward she kissed him. Both of them back into a mesmerised state of being, their unified hearts beat as one. Love ebbed and demonstrated itself with every caress, gentle brush of hot lips, and bodily compression. Every single little executed touch, every single movement significant in its own special way. Delicate breathing became calls demanding for gratifying air to enhance the pattering of passionate hearts. It was an intoxication of overwhelming desire.

Too attached too notice they were anonymous to the sight high above them, the aurora of light started to wave like a flag in the wind. Hues of vibrant greens, pale blues, bright white and dusty purples graced the earth. A slight of the eyes grabbed Suako's attention. Turning and looking on in awe, they absorbed the colours through the portals of their eyes. "Look at that... It's so beautiful..." she said, carried away by the immense sight. It was breathtaking, and it only enhanced the night from its prior perfection-like state to an even higher level.

Mack, still awake at camp, caught glimpse of the tremendous display in the night sky. Looking over to the slump of tired bodies snoring soundly away, so innocently sleeping, he couldn't bring himself to wake the crew. Turning his attention back to the northern lights, shinning like phosphorescent electric lights, he'd never seen such a thing before. Looking once again at the mound of sleeping bodies he found himself able the wake them from their peaceful slumber to witness such magnificence. With one loud whistle they all jolted awake, and Jenko's snoring ceased. Stumbling out from under the tent they wobbled over to Mack. "What's up boss?" Kato yawned. Mei rubbed her arms to heat herself after leaving the comfort of her warm spot under the blankets. "Yea, what's so important?" Masumi pouted. "Look…" Mack said pointing upward.

Heads turned and jaws dropped. "Oh… uh… wow…" Mei was at a loss for words. Kairu inhaled the colours through his observant eyes, and Masumi's youthful being was just as respectful of that of the elders. Yu-Lee saw through it the power of the Life Energy and felt an intense magickal vibe pulsate through her entire body. Kato stood behind Mei and wrapped his arms around her muscular torso, and held her close, staring up. She placed her hand on his forearm, eyes unwavering from the lights. "Hey, thanks Mack," Jenko said tapping Mack on the shoulder. "Ha, of course!"

The next day was an easy hike, just as the day before had been, as they made their way towards the travelers' cabin at the foot of the mountains. The wind had picked up a little, and scattered clouds decided to come out, but the day was other wise delightful. They meandered along the countryside, in no hurry. They took another leisure lunch break, and once again Kairu taught the girls some new moves. They picked at left over meat from the bird and sipped the broth they'd made the night before.

Love me tender and nothing shall get in my way.

Chapter 15: Mountain Climbing

"Psst! 'ey Mack," Kato whispered as he ran up from the flank. "We ain't alone, sum 'un 's following us," he told him, as he looked around his perimeter. "I know," Mack whispered back. "I heard them this morning after we started out. A few of the soldiers from the fight in Uwajima apparently didn't flee," he calmly told him. The rest of the group took notice of the whispering voice and decided it best to follow that lead. "So, what's teh' plan?" Kato asked, looking in a paranoid manner, attempting to situate their followers. "I want you to discreetly inform everyone, and tell them to prep for battle, *but* not to be obvious about it. Alright?" Mack directed. "Gotch 'ya boss," Kato nodded.

Kato drew back to share the news. It spread like wildfire over dry bushes under a high summer blaze of the sun. Shifty eyes scouted the immediate area, and Kato returned to Mack for further instruction, "Right boss, everyone knows. Now what?" He lowly asked. "Everyone's ready?" Mack asked. "Yea," Kato replied. "You're sure?" Mack confirmed, his voice serious. "Yes," Kato told him, equally serious. "Alright then," Mack stopped dead in his tracks and drew his shotgun from his hip holster. He spun around and aimed it between a gap through where Masumi and Yu-Lee stood. The others stopped walking, instantly assuming battle stances, and readying their hands on their weapons.

"Whoever you are come out! We don't want any trouble!" Mack bellowed. The pursuers' footsteps ceased to sound. They we very close, hidden within the shadows, the trees shielded them from sight. Only the bleak whistle of the wind made any sound. Nervously he waited for some sort of reply. Soon that answer came, like a crackle of thunder, a shot was fired, and it buzzed by Mack's ear, just missing the skin. *It was game on!*

As if orchestrated they fled for cover behind the trees, and everyone armed prepped his or her piece. The minute sound of the clicking of metal objects simultaneous started and ended. Jesters for their game plan were going around as fast as children playing a game of hot potato. For now, they would hold position and wait. When the anonymous enemies advanced, the attack would begin.

Yu-Lee dragged Masumi too the side. "We're not going to fight, alright?" she strictly told the young girl. Masumi went to talk back, *Why can't I fight? I'm not too young!* She initially wanted to protest, but after some reconsideration she thought the better of it. She knew she may not be too young, but she *was* too inexperienced. Masumi sighed and then shook her head in agreement. "Good girl. We have to stay out of sight, stay with me, we'll look out for each other, ok?" Yu-Lee attempted to give the girl some feeling of responsibility to help combat the feeling of being unworthy for battle.

"Right," Masumi agreed, taking the bait as Yu-Lee had hoped.

No sounds came; the enemy wasn't advancing. They held their ground, staying on their toes. An hour must had passed, and it was becoming tiresome for mind and body to wait. More time passed. Still nothing sounded but the wind in the trees, but they continued to wait. Another agonisingly slow hour passed by; their followers were patient whoever they were.

"Yu-Lee," Mack whispered from several feet away. "They're just not coming. Can you do something to force them forward?" He'd come up with the idea after the long stretch of nothingness that left only room for thinking. Yu-Lee thought about it, and an idea suddenly inspired her. "I'll try!" she replied. Turning to Masumi, who'd been sitting in the snow next to her, Yu-Lee said, "Now I need you to be very still, and stay quiet, ok?" Yu-Lee's majestic face and lively eyes held something that peaked Masumi's interest. "Ok," she replied.

The older woman took a stance with her feet spread apart, and her arms stretched up tall. Her creamy white eyelids enclosed around her marvellous eyes, and her cherry red lips muttered chants to quiet for Masumi to hear. Out of the corner of her eye she noticed Suako in a similar stance, only her palms were in direct alignment with the top of Yu-Lee's hands.

Yu-Lee summoned all of her strength, her repeating words more powerful with each repetition. "Element of fire, I call ye forth! Bring our enemies out from where they hide!" again and again. She began to hear the spirits of old around her whisper the words. Like a choir of voices more and more joined in to help. Yu-Lee could feel the energy building up between her curved hands; the life energy was responding to her will to call it forth, becoming stronger and stronger, and more physically composed with each passing second. Yu-Lee soon sensed Suako's influence and thanked her within her mind. Echoing spirits regretted to simply whisper for her to try and hear them. They began to chant louder and louder. Tiny sensations of prickles on her fingertips vibrated vigorously, then throughout her evoking body. As the spirits grew louder, so did she, without even realising it.

It became evident to the others soon just how powerful Yu-Lee could truly be. Before they knew it, they could hear the spirits too! Utter disbelief, then acceptance swept over them like a thin veil revealing its treasures that seemed too good to be real. They looked up to Yu-Lee with the innocent eyes of children exploring something new for the first time.

The followers in the woods behind could be heard murmuring through the thick sounds of chanting spells. Their words were not clear, but the tone was; they were in a panic. The chanting was intimidating them, it was evident that they felt quite uncomfortable. Some obtrusive voices rose above the rest, which they assumed must have been that of some of the higher-ranking officers trying to keep their men in line.

Masumi hadn't blinked the entire time. She was intent on seeing everything; but when she saw what she did she had to rub her eyes to make sure she wasn't seeing things. At the centre of Yu-Lee's forehead she could see and transparent vertical eye open, but not only that, from the pupil emerged a blossoming lotus flower, which sprouted open instantly. Masumi's eyes fluttered away and then shot open to gaze at the miraculous spectacle.

An unexpected thing happened then, one that would never be forgotten until the end of their days. It was if billions of minute specks of red tinted flecks appeared in the air. They were more concentrated and bright near to Yu-Lee's cupped palms. A long stretch of condensed energy specks created a visible line between Suako and Yu-Lee, like a river's flow, the energies glided down to Yu-Lee where they pooled together. The swell grew larger and larger, and the voices became more, and louder. The red light was shinning consistently brighter, till it nearly blinded onlookers, and their elevated heart rates took a jump into overtime. Then the chant, one last time, enunciated firmly, and clear from Yu-Lee's lips, the voices ceased, and Yu-Lee's eyes shot open after the few seconds of silence. The last resonant sound was her words, "So mote it be!" The gathering power from Suako jolted from her, sending her stumbling backward. It then joined with Yu-Lee's every gathering force. The red energies shone suddenly white light, and then... it happened!

Like a lightening bolt it left Yu-Lee, sending her flying backward several feet, and as if a cannon, it blasted forward into the trees. *Boom!* Like a bomb the exploded into flames. The energy moved, as if alive, only to where it was needed, then dispersing as if it had never been there. People fled from their positions, and most of the pursuers ran away, screaming, devastated with fright. The fire left almost as quickly as it had come, without having harmed anyone, nor leaving any trace behind of it's existence. It had barely lasted a minute, but it had done the job.

Simply three men were all that were left after the others had fled. Those three came fleeing forward from their hidden locations to charge them, carrying powerful Gatling guns, and wearing navy blue uniforms which did up with a single gold button at the collar. "We don't want a fight!" Mack yelled. But the men did not slow down, and they started screaming battle cries as they continued their frantic charge toward them. "Kato, Suako, Jenko, we're on!" He issued them out, passing Jenko a handgun. Mack tumbled out and took aim; he fired three shots, which took out the first man's right knee. The blood squirted out and rained down in tiny droplets, staining the snow below. The man screamed, cringing, as he fell frontward onto the cushion of snow beneath him. The second man came at Mack, attempting to revenge his fallen companion. Mack took aim again. *POW!* The man fell as dead as a stone onto the ground, but not by Mack's hand. Jenko had taken aim, like a sniper, from the tree he'd hidden himself behind.

"Ready?" Kato asked. "Yea, I got it! I got it! Go!" Suako exclaimed as the third man came at them. Kato stepped out from cover and raised his gun. The soldier pointed his gun to Kato, but then Suako hopped out and shot a bullet straight between his eyes. Kato took aim at the soldier with the shot knee cap, and swung his weapon up t point at the man's head, who was in the midst of lifting his gun to take Mack out. *POW! POW!* Two shots ended that.

The crackle of the ammunition fired boomed and echoed in the valley, resounding again and again, more faintly with each reverberation. It was an utter mess lying before them. Blood and brain scattered the once clean white snow. Masumi ran and threw up in the bushes, remembering her parents' recent brutal slaughter. Kairu went to her side to console her, and she shook vigorously. "Fuck..." Mei sighed as she peered around the corner at the stomach churning sight. It was a royal disaster all right. "Why the hell couldn't they have turned around?" Mack asked shaking his head, quite pissed off. "This sucks," Kato tried to blur the images from his mind. Vince sighed, "Good job you guys," he thanked them despite the unfortunate events having to happen.

Tears streaking across her young face, but Masumi managed to pull herself into a straight train of thought. "We... have to... we have to leave. The noise will attract the wolves," she muttered as she wiped her cheeks clear. Yu-Lee went to question the girl's wellness, but upon seeing her face she held her tongue. Masumi's eyes had gone vacant; she put up a temporary brick wall to shield out the nasty world from her sights. Masumi walked off, and they followed. After they left it behind them, they never mentioned the upsetting scene again.

By twilight they had made it to the cabin. They entered the cabin, it guarded them from the wind, and once they started the fireplace it gathered a great deal of warmth within its walls. In the centre of the one room cabin there were two inward facing couches with a carpet laid between, by the walls several beds were set up. An armoire against the back wall beside the fireplace held linens. To the right of the entrance there was a mini kitchen with a small brick oven, an icebox, and cabinets filled with canned goods, flour, sugar and jarred fruit jellies.

Setting their items down it was time to relax into a comfy warm night. Masumi took to searching through the cabinets and baked them some new bread to replace that which they'd already devoured. They rested fully and restocked their packs; their stay would be short, but well enjoyed. Masumi went over the basics of rock climbing once again before they slept, and bedtime was early, for the next day bode the need of much energy and strength.

Vince lay holding his precious Suako. Her hair smelled of fresh mint. He stroked her hand with his fingers, and as she was falling to sleep he sang just loud enough for her to hear:

> *Ocean of crystal blue,*
> *Drag me across to you.*
> *Silvery moonlit sky,*

Across it I would fly.
Anything to get to you,
Please love me when I finally do...

The melody dithered on in a blur as dreams swept Suako away.

In the morning they rose with the sun as usual, once it cracked its rays through the frosted windows and stirred Mack to rise. In turn he followed up by inducing his troop to wake up by making hot coffee, the strong smell couldn't help but wake the others. They drank and munched on goods from the cabinets, which they hadn't any room to carry further on. Then they dressed and left the cabin just as it had been when they'd arrived, despite a few missing items from the kitchen.

It couldn't have been a better day had they constructed it themselves, it felt almost warm with the sun beating down on them, and the louds were scarce, and if seen only were as wisps. It was a simple mile hike to the base of the mountain ridge. There, Masumi explain they'd have to climb a quarter of the way up the mountain. At that point they'd reach a ridge a few feet wide which they'd use as a road to circle around to the other side. From there they would need to decent about a hundred feet to reach a wooden bridge the connected to a mountain on the other side. After crossing the bridge, they would make their way around to the other side of that mountain and then finally climb down.

"...That's all and we'll be on the other side and back on the road to Tomakomai," Masumi finished explaining, while securing her rope holster around her waist. "Ha! *That's all* she says," Kato laughed rolling his eyes. Suako joined and Vince helped each other suit up with their safety harnesses. Mei stood there staring upward, and Yu-Lee joined Mei, raising her hand to block the sun from her eyes. "Well it looks like we've got quite them climb ahead of us, hmm?" Jenko raised his brow as Masumi handed him his harness. "Yea, it'll be a pretty long time. It's a few days to the other side," she informed, tying back her rich brown hair into a ponytail. "I see. Well Mack, hopefully this weather will hold fast for us," Jenko said as he turned to look at Mack. "We can only hope my friend," Mack agreed.

Kairu found himself right at home with manoeuvring his way up the rock wall. Mack, Jenko and Masumi helped Yu-Lee, who was struggling to find the upper body strength to pull herself up when she lacked footholds. Vince climbed beside Suako and both watched each other, to insure for their own consciousness that the other would be all right. Kato and Mei seemed to dart up the mountain like they'd done this all of their lives; they practically were racing Kairu to the top.

Every so often the disorienting pops of the bolting gun boomed through the otherwise still air. The noise swarmed through the sky, extending it's reach far in all directions. Masumi kept her eyes on everyone, having been the only one to have ever done mountain climbing in the extreme before. Kairu was used to climbing a few feet up the rock walls in Ryoko from his childhood play, but was otherwise as new to it as everyone else.

Krrry! A screech from behind etched its way into their ears. Mei gasped and looked around herself, and everyone flung their heads around to site the maker of such a gut-wrenching noise. Suako lost her hold in the shock of the situation. "Ahhh!" she screamed as she fell. Vince turned only to see Suako's pleading eyes fearfully focused on him. He reached his hand out as far as he could just in time to grab her hand. Fretfully Suako started hyperventilating. "Suako!" The others called, trying to get over to help her. "It was just an eagle, don't worry, we're not in danger!" Masumi yelled as she helped Mack to have a good hold on Yu-Lee. Masumi locked her eyes on her target, and then went up to offer her skills to help Suako out of her awkward predicament.

"I love you Suako..." Vince said as his finger tips finally lost their grip, and slid off from the icy stone rim from which he'd been holding onto. The two fell like stones. Mei nearly jumped off of the wall to get to them herself, but Kato held her back. "Suako! Vince! No!" she shrieked. "No Mei, it won't help!" Kato desperately tried to hold her back. Yu-Lee turned her eyes away. Masumi froze in place and watched with eyes wide open.

"Oof!" Suako had the wind knocked out of her as her harness stopped the fall from being fatal. Vince gasped, feeling as if he'd been hit with a boulder to his chest and stomach. The fall caused them to drop their bolting gun, and Suako's backpack. The discarded items bounced off the mountainside below noisily clashing off of the rock until the final loud thud that they endured upon hitting the hard ground far below. They hung like puppets suspended in the air hanging from the metal bolt they'd last inserted into the rock face. Jolted horribly from the experience, pain surged throughout their bodies; but they were alive. Suako hung a about a meter above Vince, and therefore took most of the impact. Yu-Lee looked back down to them and breathed a sigh of relief, but they were far from danger yet. "Are you ok?" Mack called from below. "Uhn... yes, but hurry..." Suako moaned in agony. "Hold on!" Masumi called to them, about twenty-five feet left of the metal saviour Suako and Vince shared.

Masumi began to move but then hugged the wall placing her ear against it. Something was wrong. "Everyone, be quiet," Masumi ordered. She heard something that seemed muffled at first, her gut told her what was wrong, but her head refused to believe it. Slowly the noise grew, and as is became louder it was clearer. Soon the noise apparent to her and her heart jumped. With slow exhalent breaths she dictated her uncomfortably twisting inner feelings, "I... I forgot to tell you before, to keep your voices down..." she listened further in hope that she was wrong. Everyone watched her, now able to hear what she did.

The mountain began to rumble terribly. Masumi looked up to see fluffy snow, followed by boulders of ice and snow chucks was falling from the heights above. With a racing heart she called to the others, "Avalanche! Stay as close to the wall as you can!" "Oh shit!" Kato used himself as a human shield to Mei. Mack, Jenko and Yu-Lee huddled together. Kairu pressed himself up the chilling rock face. Suako rested on her ropes above Vince, and watched as the tumbling snow came crashing down, pulling her arms and legs in to protect her self just before it hit.

For the most part the snow flowed like a waterfall a few feet out from them. Still small dustings fell upon them, and the occasional large chuck managed to get near them. The cold snow got into every crevasse, down their coats and shirts onto the bare skin of their backs, up their sleeves and into their shoes it forced its way in. Warm skin shuttered as the now packed itself in. The unpleasant wait seemed to take an eternity to pass.

Eventually the massive wave of snow slowed down. Below them, the path they walked up to the base had disappeared below the newly formed snow bank. Uncomfortable bodies attempted to rid themselves of the unpleasant snow that commenced to sting their skin. "Everyone alright?" Mack raised his head after hearing the last of the snow crumble below. Voices checked in, in response. Suako had been bombarded by lose snow and minor clumps of hard snowballs. She'd bared the brunt of it above Vince, shielding him from it. Suako swept the heavy build up of snow that rested on her chest and abdomen off of herself. As it floated down it picked up the sunlight like miniature crystals.

Masumi breathed a sigh of relief, "Thank god that was a minor one..." she said stealing all eyes to her in amazement by the words that slipped out. "...Suako, Vince are you alright?" Mack asked when they hadn't yet replied. "Uh, yea Mack... Sst ah damn that hurt..." Suako breathed steadily out. Her ribs were sore from one particularly hard blow. "I'm fine Mack. We need help is all," Vince called. "... You sure you're ok?" Vince asked just loud enough for Suako to hear. "I'll be fine. Thanks," she smiled at him.

Masumi edged her way over, and Jenko climbed up and over to help as well. "We're coming! Try not to move to much!" Masumi called in a low voice. They hung there doing just as she asked and stayed as still as they could, though from their fall they found themselves still swaying from the momentum. The stress was having it's wear on the bolt. Suako was fixated on it, and Vince saw her intent eyes glued above and caught site of it himself. *Crank*! The metal began to disfigure from their weight. Suako tightened up. "Masumi, it's not going to hold!" Vince calmly reiterated his panic into words.

"Here!" Masumi said unbuckling a few odd-looking metal pieces with gear like ends, and tossed them down. Suako caught them, "What are these?" "Listen, see that deep sliver? No, not that. Look over there, the split in the rock wall... Yes, that's it, I need you to gently sway and shove at least one of those cams into it. Attach your rope to the end of it. If your safety goes, then that will hold you. Ok?" She explained as she shimmied over. "Right... ready Vince?" Suako gulped. "Go for it," he told her. She agreed with the look in her eyes, took in a deep breath, and began to sway the rope to allow her to reach the wall. The bolt above squeaked as it slowly pulled loose.

"Almost… argh! Just a little… further…" Suako squirmed. She brushed the wall with the spin-wheel ends. *Ping!* The top of the safety came loose. Immediately her attention went up; Masumi was just out of reach, and Jenko not far behind. Suako tried once again, legs flailing behind her, attempting to propel forward. The rope began to crawl toward the edge of the metal bit, and the metal started to bend, and then, let them fall.

Suako managed to stick the cam into the wall just as the metal bolt gave out, and as she did her hand was caught in the loophole it provided. When they fell her wrist caught all their weight, the jolt dislocated her wrist, and she cringed and let out a weak cry. Jenko was now just next to them, so he took his gun out and bolted a metal hold into the rock. "Suako, toss me the end of your rope," he told her. "Ok," she threw it to him. He began to tie it when the gear that Suako's limp wrist held them up with started to slide downward. "Jenko, hurry!" she cried nervous and fear struck.

Jenko kept his focus, and tied the rope as quickly as his fingers would permit. Again, the bracing cam slid down, Vince's eyes narrowed in on the shifting support, "Suako… don't move…" he forcefully told her. Very slowly she tilted her head to look at it and came to see the strain that their weight was having. Perspiration trickled down Vince's forehead, and burned his eyes. Staying cool, calm and collective was the name of the game. Ice crystals and small stuck stones pulled free of the rock crevasse as their brace edged its way down.

In a split second they came loose, but Jenko wasn't yet done the knot. Masumi had made her way to them in the mean time and had grabbed a hold of Suako's arm just before the fall. Suako bit her tongue in order not to scream from the surging pain she endured as Masumi squeezed her injured wrist. "Jenko... hurry, I can't... can't hold them for long," Masumi flexed. Vince and Suako's combined weight, along with the force of gravity, was doing quite a number on Masumi.

"There!" Jenko exclaimed after the knot had been completed. Masumi released the two and they dropped slightly, and swung against the rock wall. Masumi rubbed her arm, which had uncomfortably cramped in place, strained to it's limit. Finally, they were able to help Vince and Suako back onto the wall. Jenko and Kairu, who had climbed down, helped to get them out of their swinging pendulum-like situation. They pulled them over to the wall and allowed them time to get a good foot and hand hold. Jenko then secured a second safety guard, just in case.

"Holy shit!" Suako exclaimed in shock. Vince could barely catch his breath; the entire situation had completely blown their minds. Their grasp on reality had temporarily been shaken, and it was taking some time to stop the fear. "Ha! Hardy two you are!" Mack laughed from below. Anxiety turned into good hearty laughter among the two as the world slowed its delirious effects until it came to a stop. "You two are the luckiest little... I don't believe it!" Mei shook her head, her heart still pounding away. Vince and Suako starred at each other, the adrenaline was pumping full tilt. "That was…" she started slowly speaking, "…in-freaking-credible," he finished her words in the same slow and mesmerised manner. "Are you ok Vince?" she asked suddenly. "Um, uh, yea… yea I'm fine," words were hard to conjure. "I'm sorry," she said, still dazed.

After Masumi helped wrap up Suako's wrist, they moved up the rest of the way to the top as a tighter group. In case of any other odd happenings they would be able to deal with it swiftly in the new formation. Kairu shared his bolting gun with Suako and Vince until they reached the cliff ledge they'd aimed to reach. After the avalanche they kept their voices low as they ascended. Suako grit her teeth as she forced herself up the rest of the climb with her throbbing injuries.

Nearing the end of their ascent they got to see a real sculpture, naturally beautiful an awe inspiring. Where they would camp the night appeared as if someone had taken an enormous ice cream scoop to the side of the mountain. The inner wall had formed rough, exactly like the remnants left by an ice cream scoop. It was odd, yet extremely intriguing and pleasing to the eyes and to touch. The slight overhang would provide them with a wonderful roof to shelter them from any weather that might come, or any more snow that might fall.

Upon arrival Yu-Lee rebound Suako's wrist and cast a healing spell to help her recuperate quickly. Setting up camp for the evening they began a fire. The whole experience that day had been rather overwhelming for everyone, but Suako and Vince were making light of it all, exhilarated by their intense near-death experience. That night they all talked about it. Suako told them how she knew she was in serious trouble when the gun and backpack fell as they clinked and clanked down the hill, and how easily that it could have been them tumbling in spirals to an undesirable fate. Making light of it all was the only way to recount the story.

They set up their sturdy tent once more, and had a strong fire going, over which they'd placed the broth they carried along, which was soon boiling. Masumi threw vegetables into the pot to make a soup, as well as lessen the weight of her load to carry since the root vegetables were heavy. She unloaded a few potatoes, some carrots and onions. She looked for her spices but then remembered how she had to leave it behind at the cabin.

The entire day had been quite exhausting for everyone, and after dinner they slept like rocks. Suako stole Vince away; she'd been more affected by the fall then she'd wanted to admit to anyone. They sat by the fire, shuffling to find comfortable spots on the hard surface, they sat together with a blanket about them. "Vince, I know I said it before, but I'm really sorry. I could have killed us both..." she gazed into the fire. Vince cut her off short, "It's okay Suako, really..." he tried to no avail. "No Vince, it's not. We came this close to being some animal's dinner. So, I'm sorry. I should've been more careful..." she lowered her head into her hands and began to weep.

Vince held her and just let her to cry; he knew nothing he could say would do much right now. Nor could he think of what would be the right thing to say anyway, so he just held her, gently rocking back and forth. She eventually pulled herself together a lifted her head, he wiped her cheeks free of the salty tears. No words left their lips, and in their silence, came about an understanding. He kissed her forehead and held her close to his body, the lovers sat nurturing each other with unspoken love.

Clouds rolled in and light snow began to fall. The entire sky became the top of an orb; the clouds looked like they had a blood red colour behind them that they were masking with grey. It was a gentle snowfall at first, but the night brought bad tidings. A storm had blown in, and the temperature drastically dropped.

"V, Vince I'm freezing... what is this... I'm so cold..." Suako shivered. "This isn't right," he said looking around. The sky was no longer just there above them, it was like an attacker closing in on them. Vince had an awful warning in his gut telling him this was a bad tiding. It was as if howls of the wind were war cries to scare the enemy; and it did what it set out to do. "Help me cover the fire!" Vince called to Suako who could barely make out his words as they were being swept away just as fast as they were coming out of his mouth. They stood and did they best with a few spare tent rods to tie the blanket over it. The wind thrashed the blanket about, nearly dragging it from them.

Snow beat down in pellets at them, the wind was, at least for the moment, steadily pushing in from the north, along with the storm it decided to bring along. "Get the others!" Vince yelled. Suako couldn't make heads or tails of what he said. "What?" she screamed back. "Mack, get him!" he pointed toward the tent, where miraculously no one had yet emerged from. "You want Mack? Ok!" she confirmed and jogged over to the tent. The snow scratched at her face as she went; the only thing on their side was that the mountain blocked the north wind.

Suako went to shove the cloth tent door open, but it fought back knocking her onto her backside. Frustrated and slightly dazed she pulled herself up, and finally got it out of her way. Entering the tent, the walls blustered about, ripples twisted their way down the side of the tent. "Mack!" Suako yelled, surprised to actually hear her own voice once more. Everyone woke up as if hit by lightening by her yell, and as if the rude awakening hadn't been bad enough, soon the fact that the tent being treated like a battering ram became all too evident. "What the hell is going on?" Mack asked catching a brief glimpse of the red lit blizzard bitterly taking its toll outside.

Grogginess left him like a drunken man suddenly snapping back to a sober state. "Oh, what the fuck is it now?" Mei grunted rubbing her eyes free of sleep. Suako ignored her, "Mack we're in trouble. A storm rolled in, and fast. You can't even hear yourself think out there. Vince is trying to salvage the fire, we gotta help him A.S.A.P!" she told him. "Right, Kato, I need you now. Everyone else stay in here, but be prepared for anything," he told the others, strapping his leather boots around his feet. "Here," Suako helped him with his coat. They swam through the blustery curtain to get outside.

Just as directed the others wasted no time dressing themselves. "This sounds bad..." Kato did up his coat and left the tent pulling his hood over his head. Mei watched him follow the others, and felt a sharp pain in her heart as she did. Ignoring Mack's instruction, she followed Kato out into the tormenting night. The storm cackled at them helplessly stranded there. Mother nature had provided such beautiful clear days for them, which now seemed as if they must have had been a trap to lure them in.

Mei stepped outside, and she felt as if she'd strayed into a bad dream. She looked all around herself, staring at Suako, Vince, Kato and Mack as they struggled around their only heat source to keep it alive. Her attention then changed to the clouds. Billowing above her, the clouds were not as dark as a clear indigo night, but still intimidating, not showing a shroud of what would be the otherwise visible starry sky. The night growled angrily, and it seemed time was almost going in slow motion in Mei's eyes. In a very prolonged way she gradually rotated her head, finally pulling her eyes along. The tent next to her was barely standing. *Wham!* Time nearly went in overtime, catching up for it's prior impediment. Mei dove into the tent, "Jenko, I need you! Now! We have to pin this tent down, or we ain't gonna have a tent left any more!"

They both darted outside, their eyes searching for something to pin the tent to the ground. Stronger and stronger the wind grew, it came to the point when Mei thought they'd nearly lift off of the ground and would be carried away by this gale force. Words were useless, neither one could hear the other. Jenko pointed over to a huge chunk of ice that must've been left from the avalanche. Mei followed him over to it, one leg being forced to step, then the next. The struggle to reach it was overcome only with great effort. They broke up the enormous ice chunk and then, faced the wind once more as they made their way to the tent to pin down the corners; it was a night straight from hell.

Are we so right to continue? Does this planet desire our help? Why can't we escape disaster?

Chapter 16: The Ice Cavern

The rest of the night was best described as a blur. After attempting to save the fire, they all ducked into the tent. They rode the night out under blankets trying to preserve body heat. No one slept as the viscous winds howled all around them. The hours passed painfully slow, and it was not until many hours later did the storm cease to beat away at the tend walls. Day never seemed to come.

Once the wind had died off they left the tent one by one. They were entrapped within a newly formed ice cavern. Their fire had not been so lucky as to withstand the torrent night, the blanket shield they'd set up had been carried away, never to be seen again. A few cracks in the snowy cavern roof emitted just enough light in order to let them make out objects a few feet in front of them. Mack went straight to the fire after inspecting the new surroundings.

Jenko soon noticed Mack and tapped Mei to go with him to help. After about a half-hour of trying with the flint the sparks just refused to catch flame. Masumi had an idea, she took a piece of extra fur from her bag and placed it on top of the leftover pile of sticks and twigs that Kairu had collected from hibernating trees along the mountain path ahead the night before, which now were out of reach. Once again sparks flew, and finally a fire was the resulting factor.

"Well aren't we in a mess," Vince said starring up at the ice barrier. "Yea, talk about a sticky situation. This really blows… how the hell are we going to get out of here?" Mei sighed. Kairu walked up to the wall of snow and ice, examining it closely. "What do you see?" Yu-Lee noticed him, and took up an interest. "Come here…" he said as he touched his hand up against it. "What is it?" she said upon approach. "It's thick and the inside is completely ice. Before the fire went out it probably heated the snow closest to it, and then when it blew out the melting snow froze," his wise words theorised. "I think you're right... this isn't good," Yu-Lee said feeling the wall just as he had.

Mack rose from the fire and looked around, "We're going to have to dig our way out, lots of force to get threw the ice sheet..." before he could make the start of another word Masumi jumped in, "Whoa, you have to be careful with this! If you pound it too much it's going to collapse in on us," she offered her expertise. "We're in trouble," Mei huffed. Little did they know just how right Mei would be; they *were* in trouble, a heap load of it.

Their fire dissipated slowly away until it was not much more than a flicker. They continued to add items they could spare to keep it burning, but the fire consumed them as quickly as they hit the flame. Then finally it ceased, on the third day, and that was when the cold began to take its wrath out on them. Becoming brutally tired they noticed their bodies being drawn to sleep. They could only chip at the ice during the day now, by mid-afternoon when the light shone appropriately on their dig site. The rest of the time the danger was too high for a cave in, so, for those few hours they summoned their bodies to work for them, against the fatigue through sheer will.

They rationed their food, and snow they had melted into water until there was no more fire, before resorting to their canteens. They sat chilled in nature's freezer, knowing they needed to escape fast, or they would die in this place. Within the first fire-free day Yu-

Lee became quite ill; she'd been asleep near the fire before it had gone out, and the heat had melted the snow near her. When the fire dyed the water began to freeze on her body. The shock had rendered her morbidly ill, and her weak constitution was working against her. She coughed harshly until they noticed her start to bring up phlegm. They gave her extra water, and she used her magick connection to try and help herself to be aided, as well as to guide them to be freed from this death trap.

Suako got Masumi to take care of Yu-Lee during the hours they all worked to carefully chip away the ice. Masumi cared for Yu-Lee as a nurse would her patient, tending to her with water and the left-over broth. In between keeping an eye on Yu-Lee, she went out to watch them dig and make sure the ice wasn't cracking up above their heads. Slashing away at the ice with knives, and random crude objects, they were making some headway. Ice flung this way and that, attacking the chipper with sharp shards; small cuts were etched into the skin of whoever had been working on the tunnel.

Just living out the hours of the rest of the day was agonising, their skin became red-raw in their entrapped climate. It wasn't long before the others began to show symptoms like Yu-Lee had first shown. Their lunges became saturated with their own bodily fluids, and the liquid seemed to double the intensity of the frigid air they brought into their bodies. The rest of the day and the night stretched on into an abyss of time.

The feeling of claustrophobia was slowly starting to agitate Jenko, who longed to wander the great wide world. He distracted himself by working on his map of the Imperial continent, for as long as the dim light stayed around. The others tried to encourage him with the idea of escape into mind. With great struggle he contained his anxiety, but after his ink became to thick to utilise, his desperation for escape started to nag at him. Mack tantalised his brain with distracting conversation whenever he could muster up the thought capacity to do so.

Kairu stuck by Masumi. He felt the need to protect her, and he offered to help keep her warm and share his blankets. "Thanks..." Masumi, quite jittery, crawled under the partially warm weave. "You're welcome," he told her. In silence the group sat most of the time. It was a difficult decision on whether to use one's voice or not, for either choice was twofold: talk and be distracted from your mind's lonely contempt, but struggle and aggravate an already weary body, or, stay silent and rest the body, but overwork the mind. "S... so, tell me a, about your home..." Masumi stuttered.

Suako slept on her side next to Vince, as she lay their, her breaths were rashly taken in and exhaled in a raspy fashion. Vince watched every little movements her body made, listening to the heavy struggled breaths. Her once soft porcelain skin cheeks now red and dry. Her chain hung about her neck, the amethyst pendant rested on the ground near her slightly outstretched arm. Her hair lay down her neck and face gracefully, framing her face like a portrait. Ruby red lips looked like candy, deliciously tempting candy begging to be had. It was so amazing to him that so much beauty could appear in such a brutally treated being.

Despite the dissipating light Vince held his journal open to a blank page in his hand, and with a piece of charcoal in his hand, he began to grace the sheet. Dark strokes morphed into a gradually shaping form on the paper; Suako began to emerge in his book. The sleeping beauty of the snow cavern, each hair he placed with much thought and caution. He looked at his subject, his grim heart aching with every cough her gentle frame endured. Suako, recreated from all time within those moments, would ever remain in his sacred book. Her symmetrical features pleased the critical eye. Ruffled sheets below shoulder covered the rest of her body. Besides her face, the only other skin showing was her hand next to her pendant. Long graceful fingers stretched out, slender but not bone-like, they pressed against the floor. Her curvy nails complimented the already outstanding glory of her angelic hands.

Vince looked about their prison. He saw Mei and Kato sleeping, pressed up against one another. Their mutual heat kept them within a comfort zone, if such a thing was possible to achieve within this morbid cavern. Masumi and Kairu sat side by side talking, chilled down to the bone. Yu-Lee slept to his right, Mack paced around, and Jenko working, intensely focused in on his map.

We're were birds trapped in a cage... Birds need to be free to explore. They were given wing so that they could fly. Birds that are caged always die unhappily, and much before their time. Caged birds lived with heavy hearts, always dreaming of the wild. I want our freedom back. No way in hell are we falling victims to this cage! Vince thought, his blood heated from the anger for the first time in a while.

The sun had reached the peak, and Vince was on a mission. Freedom was his goal. He would not watch his friends die in this place. He would not submit himself, he would fight to survive until his last breath; nothing could get in his way.

Throbbing fingers took grasp of a long metal pole. Marching over to the icy door they were opening, he was ready to finally get through the damn thing once and for all. Vengeance glittered in his determined eyes. Raising the pole up high he brought it down hard, striking their work site. *Wham, Whack!* The pole struck repeatedly. Adrenaline drove him on. "I," *Whack!* "...Will," *Crack!* "...Not," *Crunch!* "...Die," *Whoop!* "...In," *Wham!* "...Here!" with one last beat down on the ice it finally shattered into a million tiny pieces.

Vince stood there, heaving from exhaustion, looking at what he'd done in a state of disbelief. He wondered for a moment if he'd just been dreaming, his heart pounded his chest from his angry breathing. Then suddenly he began coughing, as his weary body had been through a lot. "You did it Vince!" Mei exclaimed coming out from the tent. They all flocked around him. Together they dug through the few feet of snow on the other side, praising Vince as they did. And then it came: Light! Glorious light peered in and lit up the dark cave; the door to the birdcage had swung open, and now they could fly away.

They took down the tent and packed their things quickly, then crawled out to freedom. Carefully they pulled Yu-Lee threw, who lacked the energy to make it by herself. Blinding light pierced their unadjusted eyes, but after several disorienting moments, once their eyes stopped stinging, they could see the outside world once again. The sky above was as blue as it had ever been, the ground all around was covered in deep snow, and slippery ice sheets lay below that. The warmth felt tangible as the sun heated their near-death bodies; instant relief overcame them all.

Hoarsely breathing, Masumi made out what she wished to say, "On... On the other side, side of the bridge... there... there's a cabin... blankets... fireplace..." coughs followed. "Good. Let's go," Mack insisted. Hiking Yu-Lee onto his back, Mack carried her for the entire duration of the trip. Trudging along, the snow tired already tiresome bodies. They circled to the back of the mountain in hastily. Just as Masumi had told them before a rope bridge connect the two mountains.

They looked toward the rickety bridge with questioning eyes. "This... will, 'll actually hold? Masumi?" Kato asked, examining it. "Yes... my father crossed it... many times. L-look... see? The cabin..." She replied, pointing across. Her legs were barely able to support her. They all turned. And saw the cabin, which appeared minuscule in the distance, but they could see it regardless. Mack passed of Yu-Lee to Vince. "I'll test it first... everyone follows after me," Mack commanded. "We're right behind you boss," Mei quickly pushed her words free of her lips in a single gasp.

Cautiously Mack tested the bridge. He applied his foot and gave it a strong pus, which made it creak like an overly used floorboard in an old house. The snow hadn't piled much on the surface of the bridge, the wind had blown it off while it gusted the stormy night. Ignoring the noise, he recognised that it took the pressure well, and stepping on with his full weight he felt supported. Looking down between the wooden boards beneath his feet he could see the sharp icicles shimmering like threatening daggers hundreds of feet below. He raised his head and regretted to look down again. Taking in a deep breath he shuttered and continued onward; the rope guard-rails clenched in his fists. A quarter of the way across he could tell the bridge was sturdily constructed, so he called back to the others and they began to follow.

The bridge swayed as they crossed. The sheer elevation, and that they were above the ice below was eyrie, sending shivers down each one of their spines. Kairu and Masumi supported each other as they crossed. Speedily they went, travelling with light steps. They each felt that the faster they were on solid ground again, the better. Uncomfortably they heard each sound being amplified as it echoed throughout the gorge far below. Mack was closing in on the snow covered rocky edge ahead. Thoughts of food, shelter and warmth permeated his thoughts. He was contented to be so close to luxury, but also thought of the need to get the others the cabin because of their desperate need for a healthy environment. Yu-Lee was ghastly white and barely conscious the past day.

So many thoughts swirling around in his busy mind Mack wasn't watching his step. *Whoosh!* He found his feet sliding and dropping off the side threw a gap in the criss-crossing ropes. Luckily, he had a death grip on the rope with his hand, though the wind seemed to tease him with its sick sense of humour as it whisked by his tangling feet, whistling as it went.

Mack felt the nothingness surrounding his dangling limbs. The icicles below looked ever so much more sharp and pointy in this position, like starved dogs that are held back just by a cage, they seemed to antagonise him. The precarious way in which he hung strained his arms. Looking down he watched his feet swish to and from his line of sight.

"Mack!" Mei screamed frantically. Kato was about to make his move toward him, but Kairu had been a step ahead of him. Like a cheetah he ran, pushing past the mental and physical barriers of lethargy. The others hobbled as quickly as numb limbs, and unresponsive muscles, could endure to take them. Kairu soared across the bridge, his legs felt like glass bending just before it cracks. The ache was horrible, but presence of mind prevailed.

Suspended in the air, everything seemed to slow down for about the first thirty seconds for Mack, each movement lasted an eternity. Not until Kairu hovered above him, hand extended toward him, did life revamp itself into its natural flow. "Mack, here..." Kairu said clasping down on Mack's forearm. Kato caught up and helped Kairu to yank Mack back up. Mack felt the pressure of their fingers press into his skin, and the gradual elevation; upward his limp body went. His body tingled where they had grabbed onto him as he was laid on the bridge.

Bam! The sudden realisation struck light a bolt of lightning. "Are you ok Mack?" worried voices asked, and dwelled on him. He sat there with his thoughts for a second, then he looked up at them all to see them staring down at him. He trying to stand, and Kairu and Kato helped him to his feet. He then addressed them, "I'm fine. Let's just keep going." And from there he walked on, not desiring to discuss the intense reality check. Looking around dumbfounded at each other, all they could do was follow and pry with continuous questions of his well being. Repetitiously he dismissed their questions, insisting he was fine, and then returned to the path they were on.

Eventually they accepted their defeat in getting him to talk, and they followed their leader as steadfast as ever. Her took them to the end of the bridge, where each of them was thrilled to be leaving the slippery, wobbling suspension they'd had to cross. Masumi then guided them the rest of the way to the cabin. Forcing leaden eyes open wide enough to watch her step, their only motivation was the destination that lay ahead. *One foot in front of the other Masumi... almost there...* she told herself as she stumbled forth leaning on Kairu.

Not to long after departing the bridge, it was there; just feet ahead the cabin rested. It was a simple cabin, more like a hut, it's construction was simple, and wood walls quite thin. The lead weights on her eyes seemingly migrated down into her legs just before the reached it the cabin. Mack headed it on, and opened the cabin. Masumi ceased walking allowing the others to pass, and Jenko carried semi-concious Yu-Lee inside. He happily displaced the extra weight from his back as he placed her down on a soft, at the far side of the cabin near an empty fireplace.

Once everyone else had escaped the cold outdoors Mack scuttled indoors as well closing the thin door behind him. The outer world was now shut out. The dark of the wood had absorbed the sun alone, making it warmer immediately. Somehow Mack found some energy, and dragged himself over to the pilled wood and picked u a few logs, then with every last ounce of strength he could muster took them over the fireplace. Jenko felt a bit of a second wind after releasing Yu-Lee. *Clash! Clank!* He hit the flint together. Finally, luck was on their side and the caught quickly, roaring upward with strong curling flames, it looked as if it had just been a prisoner freed after years of captivation.

They helped each other heat some water and distribute it amongst the deathly ill mercenaries. Humbly they took it. It may as well have been the nectar of the gods, instantly the sloshing fluid radiated heat from their centres outward. Taking their own share, then one last time checking on Yu-Lee, they found themselves at the mercy of their bodies. Falling on plush pillows, they were soon carried away into their dreams.

Death will NOT consume me here.

Chapter 17: Recuperation

How long has it been? "Mmm… Unn… Uh?" *It hurts to breathe…* "She's awake…" "Good. It's been days…" "I was so worried!" *Where am I? Ah, the sun… too bright…* "Ooh…" "Shh, take it easy." *But what's going on?*

Someone just tell me what's going on! "But… where…" *My throat's so dry… What happened?* "In a safe place… Here we have some water and soup for you if you want?" *Yes! Water, sweet juice of life how I want you! And I'm so hungry! It hurts… Feed me!* "Y… yes please…" "Then let's sit you up." *Oh, but my sides ache… Well my stomach hurts more. Fine sit me up, just let me eat!*

Light was all there was. Sheer light, so bright it was blinding. Stressing the eyes, straining to keep eyes open, reflex fought her. *Blink, blink!* Fluttering lids shielded delicate pupils. The haze finally faded gradually away, and Yu-Lee opened her eyes wide and looked around to everyone hovering by her side, everyone except for Suako. Jenko slide a pillow behind her back to sit her up. She had a better view of the room between the bodies that encircled her. She was in a poorly built cabin lying on a faded forest green sofa, which despite appearance couldn't have possibly been any more comfortable. The curtains were spread wide-open over thin windowpanes. It was late afternoon, and there were four beds scattered around the room and a plaid recliner chair which had definitely seen better years. She looked to her feet when the crackle of the fire pulled her attention briefly.

"We were so worried!" Masumi said, smiling at the sight of Yu-Lee regaining consciousness. "Give her room everyone!" Suako insisted sliding through the crowd holding a bowl in one hand and a cup in the other. "C'mon I said! Shoo! She needs some space to breathe!" she insisted. "Good to have you back with us," Suako said, as she took a seat beside Yu-Lee. "You gave us quite the scare for a while there!" and other such comments came from concerned, yet relieved, companions as they left to give her room.

"There, they finally went. Here, you must be thirsty..." Suako smiled with kind eyes as she put the cup to Yu-Lee's dry lips. Diving into her the water, cool and delicious, wet the desert of her throat. *Gulp, gulp, gulp!* She drank as if she'd never done so before. After consuming a quarter of the glass, the water tickled her throat and she began to cough. "Whoa... take it easy. Don't worry, you can have as much as you like. Take it slowly," Suako assured with honest eyes.

Gathering her thoughts together, she just had to know what was going on, even though the food tempted an empty belly that begged for nourishment. "What happened?" she made out through heavy breaths. "Well... what do you remember last?" Suako asked before jumping into tale. "I remember..." *What do I remember? Think! Think goddamn you! We climbed the mountain... Suako slipped... we reached top... The storm!* "The blizzard... we were snowed in... everything else is a blur." Suako nodded, "I could see how that would be. You got really sick, and you weren't awake very much. We were stuck there for days. No one knows how long. It was getting pretty dicey, but Vince got us out of there. We carried you across the bridge to the second mountain Masumi told us about, remember her saying that? Well we've been here about two weeks now, and you've been in a coma since we got here. We fed you the rest of the broth we had till we ran out, and then made some more from some frozen vegetables we found left here and have been giving that to you..." Her maternal expression faded. She stayed quiet, just looking to the floor, "I wasn't sure... I didn't know if you'd make it. I'm glad your all right," Suako said getting all choked up. Yu-Lee looked upon the girl as if at her own daughter. Yu-Lee offered wide-open arms to comfort her. Suako placed the dish down and wrapped her arms around Yu-Lee with tears of utter joy streaming down her cheeks. "I'm so happy you're safe," her weak voice muttered.

They held each other shortly, and then Suako returned to her seat. Wiping tears from her face, she couldn't help but let out a timid giggle, laughing at herself for crying. Looking for distraction she remembered the soup and lifted the gently steaming bowl from the floor. "Thank you, Suako," Yu-Lee squeaked out of her crackling throat. Deep eyes ensured sincerity in Yu-Lee's thanks. The message was well received, but there was no more time for exchanging words, it was time for Yu-Lee to fill her begging tummy.

The silver spoon reached her lips, and the scent of food was intoxicating. Taste, incredibly overwhelming to a lonely tongue. It soared down to her stomach, and Like a trigger it began to increase her already bothersome appetite. Grumbling it sounded, calling for more. *Slurp!* Flavour blasted in on its way down.

The soup disappeared before the hunger. Disappointedly, Yu-Lee eyed the empty bowl. "Good, you finished everything. I'll get you some more in a little while. You still need to rest. You only started to get better after you stopped coughing up phlegm the day before yesterday," Suako informed her. Kindly she tugged the blanket up and tucked Yu-Lee in. "Sleep now," her voice said. Yu-Lee hadn't thought she could, but after closing her eyes the conversation behind her became muffled, and then darkness drew her in.

"...Man she's a tough one," Mei commented as she lay down a playing card on the table. They had found the playing deck left behind by previous tenants of the cabin, and it had been a welcomed distraction for them. Mei, Kato, Masumi, Kairu, Vince and Suako sat at one end of the table playing. *Plunk!* Kato dropped down his card. "No kiddin' Mei. Must 'ave a damn strong will t' live." *Plunk, swish, and plunk!* The cards slapped against the table.

Jenko sat with Mack down at the other end. Jenko was working fastidiously on his precious new map, and slowly he perfected it to his own specifications. With his thawed ink, which now ran too freely from the additional ice crystals that had built up and then melted to mix with his precious scripting ink, he carefully he detailed his map, making sure not to let the ink run or smudge while drying. Mack's cigar supply was running low. He'd been lucky enough to find one left by the fireplace in its wooden box, and though it was stale, he still enjoyed the taste. He lit it intermittently, enjoying it here and there as the days trailed on. He longed to buff up his diminishing supply, which now only numbered three. He inhaled one long drag of the cigar and released the smoke after he could no longer contain it, and skillfully produced tiny smoke rings. He then extinguished the remains. Standing up from the table he walked it over to the mantel. Setting it down, he'd leave the last bit for the next day. He marched back over to the table and fell into the chair.

Yu-Lee stirred in her sleep, and Suako's eyes jumped from the game to Yu-Lee, "She really is getting better," she said. Suako, who had not abandoned Yu-Lee's side, even while she was herself recovering, was finally starting to feel at ease. She warded off the others, feeling the need to care for her solely. While the others were sleeping the previous night, she'd cast incantations to help Yu-Lee; and her pleas were heard! Yu-Lee woke the next day, though exhausted, with a definite zest for life still within her.

"Suako… Suako?" Masumi tapped her arm. "Hmm? Ah, oh! Yes? Sorry. What is it?" Suako said, coming back from her thoughts. "How well do you think she's doing?" the innocent youthful girl had returned in Masumi. "Oh," Suako giggled, having thought she'd been needed for something more urgent. "Quite well," Suako told her. Mack took up an interest in the conversation from across the way, "When will she be able to go?" he asked. "I'm not sure, but she's been doing really well. A few more days and I think she may be able to handle it. A week at most," Suako estimated. "Good," Mack nodded.

Yu-Lee woke up some hours later, and again Suako tended her with soup, and now with a tiny bit of rice, which they'd found among a few other non-perishable goods within the shelter, to settle her rumbling tummy. Energy returned to her as her body absorbed the rice. Dedicatedly, Suako fed Yu-Lee and kept her company. In and out of consciousness she drifted, always to happily find Suako by her side when she woke.

Once Yu-Lee fell victim to her bodies will to sleep, Mack insisted Suako turn her maternal care toward herself. He fixed her a bowl of rice and had her come from Yu-Lee and join the others at the table. "Girl you need to rest. Yu-Lee's fine. We'll keep a close watch on her. You finish that up and grab yourself forty winks, eh?" Mei leaned her elbows on the table as she spoke. "She's right. Now eat up an' get t' sleep!" Kato seconded the motion. Like a big brother and sister, they watched her back, looking out for her.

Suako caved in and did as they suggested, though she strongly desired defiance. As she ate, Kairu brought a blanket and placed it over her shoulders. They were right, despite her will to never admit any form of weakness, she was about to work herself sick. It had always been in her nature to do, Suako never knew when to quit. She always worked until the job was done, taking her body to extremes, it suffered often for her die-hard iron will. She was not easily detoured from a path she'd choose to take. They were her family, and always watching out for her, and they knew if they didn't slow her down, she would not do so on her own. They cared, and she knew it, and because of that she would occasionally bend and heed their advice.

Her body longed for a nice comfy bed more then it willed to finish eating. She set the bowl down, stood up, and stumbled over to a bed. Flopping down on it, the bed welcomed her like she imagined falling onto a fluffy cloud would feel. It was welcoming, and already warmed from Masumi who had been laying there not ten minutes ago. She wished herself to flip onto her back, but her body just ignored her intentions.

Just leave me here forever... I don't want to leave. Let me stay, let me be...

The week passed, and Yu-Lee mended tremendously as it did. By the end of the week she was ready to go just as Suako had predicted. They prepared to leave the very next morning. In that last night Kairu had been fortunate enough to come upon a straight razor, so they could groom before they left. Kato trimmed his beard, Vince redefined his goatee, Mack shaved his face entirely, as did Kairu revealing his baby face once more. Jenko passed it up, quite enjoying the lengthy beard he'd grown. Mei had Suako cut her hair short once more; she detested it much longer than an inch or two after her family was taken from her. Her husband always stroked her long hair; it was too painful for her to keep it long.

Now, all spruced up, it was time to focus on vital survival supplies. They had little grace on time, all food, except a half bag of rice, some carrots, two potatoes, a few bottles of preserved fruits and the sweets Vince had brought from Uwajima, had been eaten. They still had a couple days ahead of them just to the base of the mountain, not to mention how long it would take them to reach another town once they were down. Rations were low, and stomachs grouchy. They'd asked Masumi about where they would next find civility, but she only knew of Tomakomai's location, besides that she was just as new to the countryside as they were. She informed them it was about a nine-day journey to Tomakomai, and that there may have been a town in between, but the young age she had crossed at before left little ability recall for the small things along the way.

"...So, this is all that's left." Mack plopped down the left-over rations on the table. Everyone's eyes looked depressed upon seeing the remnants. "Well... let's just hope Kairu finds something else to kill," Kato laughed, breaking the mood, if only temporarily. "We need to tighten our belts, and..." Yu-Lee interrupted Mack before he could finish. "Wait a minute!" She got up and went over to her back. Rummaging through it, she grunted as she pulled things free, then tossed them aside. She then pulled an oblong package, which she stared at for a while. Yu-Lee developed a wrinkle in her brow as she did, until a sudden overall remembrance overtook her expression.

At long last she pulled free a good size bag of flour which she'd stored. It was enough to provide two meals, small meals, but meals all the same, for the group. *Thump!* She put it on the table along with the other few things they'd had left. "We can mix it mix some water and cook it to make some flat bread. It isn't great, but it'll keep us going," she said. Analysis provided an understanding of roughly three to four days worth of food. It was nine days from where they stood all the way to their destination.

"We're going to be in trouble if we don't find something on the way," Kairu lifted his eyes from the table to meet Mack's. "You're right," Jenko nodded, "we'll stick to a strict diet. If we plan it out right we can make it last," the food adoring man sighed. "Half you're regular portions everyone. It may get nasty, but we'll just have to deal with it," Mack added authoritatively. They all agreed, without having a choice to do otherwise, regardless of desire. "Right everyone… Common let's back up. The sooner we leave the sooner we reach a place to stay, and some food. Maybe we can cut a day or two off if we go long days. Get ready, and then get some sleep. We'll leave at first light," Mack told them. Chairs discontentedly squeaked across the floor as they got up from the table. Prospects didn't look as pleasant as they'd hoped.

Yu-Lee went back to her bed. "Suako? Vince? Would you please join me for a moment?" she asked with her backs to them. They looked to each other and then meandered over. "What is it?" Suako queried. "We never opened this…" she presented the package before them. It was what Otojiro had given them before they'd left Quan. "Shall we?" the maternal yet quirky Yu-Lee asked with a grin from ear to ear.

Like children Vince and Suako's eyes glistened; gifts were rarely given to them. Yu-Lee pulled the twine string from the rough silk wrapped package, and as it came loose the material flopped open. Within her lap lay an oak wand with quartz décor, a double-edged dagger chipped from granite and a rare pistol, a collectors' item from its age, gleaming as it mirrored the flame from the fireplace. Each lifted their new weapon for closer examination.

Vince lifted his blade, testing its sharpness on a few strands of hair, and it cut threw them without any pressure. It was as sharp as the best crafted Samurai sword would. Vince practised with it, indulging into a fantasy fight with his shadow. The dagger soared here and there as he whisked it threw the air. At the end he bowed respectfully as he would to an actual partner, and then carefully hitched it onto his belt.

Suako raised the pistol in her hands. Below it lay a white box, she picked it up and snuck a look inside to see it contained silver bullets. This truly was a rare piece of mechanical glory. It was weighty, and it would make a good kill shot she figured. The metal had embroidered rose vines across the barrel; immediately she felt connection to it.

Yu-Lee had watched them discovering their precious wonders. She lastly picked up the wand, and it zapped her with a dose of intense magickal potency the second she lay her hand upon it. Her eyes rolled back in her head, as the blissful power ebbed into her. When she came back around to opening her eyes she looked down at the wand in her hand, and as she did she noticed another package wrapped in the lavender silk the others had been. A small wooden piece of bark had '**Kairu**' scribed into it. Placing her wand aside she took the package in her hands and walked over to Kairu who had been conversing with Masumi with much laughter.

Yu-Lee tapped taped Kairu's shoulder, and he turned sharply to see the older woman. "Otojiro had given this to me to give to you. Take it," she held the package forth to him. He first looked at it, then his arm slowly crept upward and wrapped around the package. Kairu picked it up and looked wide eyed at it, then he looked to Yu-Lee, to whom he bowed. "Thank you," he said in his maturing voice. More and more he shed his quiet, reserved voice and began to sound like a leader. "You are welcome," she smiled, then left him to enjoy his present.

Kairu took a seat on his mattress. Masumi looked over his shoulder, "What is it?" her youthful curiosity begged to know. "Who's... Who's, uh?" she couldn't recall the name. "Otojiro," Kairu helped her along. "Yes! Who's he?" she pondered. Kairu thought long and hard about how to label him. He eventually came up with his answer, "...a friend." He unravelled the package to find folded papers. He pulled them apart and found within it a letter. "A letter? ... well I'll leave you to it then," Masumi blurted out and returned to her packing.

Kairu began to read the ill hand-written ledger of a man whom seldom put pen to paper:

"☐☐☐☐ ☐☐☐☐☐,

☐☐☐ ☐☐☐☐ ☐☐☐☐ ☐☐ ☐☐
☐☐☐☐☐☐☐☐ ☐☐☐☐☐☐☐
☐☐☐☐☐☐☐☐☐☐☐ ☐☐☐ ☐☐☐☐
☐☐☐☐☐, ☐☐☐ ☐☐ ☐☐☐☐☐ ☐☐, ☐☐☐
☐☐☐☐☐☐☐☐ ☐☐ ☐☐☐ ☐☐☐'☐
☐☐☐☐☐☐☐· ☐☐ ☐☐☐☐☐☐, ☐
☐☐☐☐☐☐ ☐☐ ☐☐☐☐☐ ☐☐☐ ☐☐☐
☐☐☐☐ ☐☐☐ ☐☐☐☐ ☐☐☐☐· ☐☐☐
☐☐☐☐ ☐☐☐☐ ☐☐☐ ☐☐☐☐☐
☐☐☐☐☐☐ ☐☐ ☐☐☐☐☐☐☐☐☐☐ ☐☐☐
☐☐ ☐☐☐☐☐☐☐☐☐ ☐☐ ☐☐☐☐ ☐
☐☐☐☐ ☐☐☐ ☐☐☐ ☐☐☐ ☐☐☐☐
☐☐☐☐☐· ☐☐☐ ☐☐☐☐☐☐☐☐ ☐☐☐
☐☐☐☐☐☐☐☐ ☐☐☐☐☐☐ ☐☐☐☐☐☐ ☐☐
☐☐☐☐· ☐☐☐☐☐ ☐☐☐·

☐☐☐, ☐☐ ☐☐ ☐☐☐☐
☐☐☐☐☐☐☐☐☐ ☐☐☐☐☐☐ ☐☐☐ ☐☐☐☐
☐☐☐☐· ☐ ☐☐☐☐ ☐☐☐☐☐☐☐☐ ☐☐☐☐
☐☐☐☐☐☐☐☐☐☐ ☐☐ ☐☐☐ ☐☐☐☐
☐☐☐☐☐ ☐☐ ☐☐☐· ☐☐☐ ☐☐☐☐ ☐☐☐
☐☐☐☐☐ ☐☐☐☐· ☐☐☐ ☐☐☐☐ ☐☐☐
☐☐☐☐☐☐☐ ☐☐☐, ☐☐☐☐ ☐☐☐☐☐☐☐

□□□   □□□,   □□□   □□□□
□□□□□□□□□□ □□□ □□□□□, □□□
□□□□□□□ □□□□□· □□ □□□ □□□□
□□ □□□□'□ □□□□· □□□ □□□□ □□
□□□□□□ □ □□□□□□, □□□ □□□□□□
□□□□   □□□□   □□□□□   □
□□□□□□□□□□ □□□□□□□□□□□·
□□□□□□ □□□ □□□□ □□□□□
□□□□ □□□□ □□□□ □□□□· □□□
□□□□□□ □□ □□□□ □□□□□□
□□□□ □□□ □□ □□□□□□□ □□
□□□□□· □□ □□□□□□□□□□· □□□□
□□ □□□ □ □□□ □□□ □□ □□□□
□□□□□□□· □ □□ □□□□□…"

That letter went on, but Kairu had to reread the second paragraph several times over. It baffled and worried him all at the same time. *What was it that he saw?* he could not remove the question from his mind. It nagged at him, and dwelled there until he finally couldn't think about it anymore and finished reading his letter. The question was always infringing on his thoughts from there on.

Two shadowy figures stood by the window. The curtain was halfway closed, the night was still, and constellations shinning brightly. Soft murmurs of slumber mingled in the background. Peering out, not a branch stirred, and there were no clouds to block the sky. No beasts prowled the mountainside. The only lively business was that of the two shadows by the window.

"...Are they all asleep?" Mack asked. "Yes," said, looking over the sleeping bodies. "Good. They should get as much rest as they can... Their energy's gonna be gone quick," Mack said, worry in his voice. "Hmm, yea. We need to boot our asses down that mountain, Mack," Jenko nodded, sharing his concern. "I just hope Masumi's right. We're in some serious shit if it takes longer. Hell! We're in trouble as it is... anyway... the sooner we get to Tomakomai the better," Mack sighed. "We'll need to be careful my friend. If the civil war has spread all over we need to watch our step," Jenko warned. Mack paused before he spoke, "...I know. I'm not expecting a warm welcome. If my prediction's right then we'll have someone waiting for us." "...Mack?" Jenko eyed his friend. "What is it?" Mack asked. "You've been keeping to yourself, more then usual. What's on your mind?" Jenko asked.

"I can't hide anything from you, can I? Heh. Never could. Hmm... Well, a lot. I've been thinking about what's going to happen if... if we fail... I remember my parents talking about their childhoods. They told me stories that I'll never forget, I know you know what I'm talking about. Hell! Even when *we* were young the East Green Continent was at least green! Well some of it was... it's just that... even seeing the world over here, it isn't enough, and it won't last. We both know that. The world is falling apart. The people deserve trees, air... they deserve life, but they've been denied by the god damned C.D.F.P. and it's fucking disgusting!"

"I want to be able to breathe without some stupid dome. I want to not have to worry about my skin melting off when I step into the sun. I don't want to see any more morphed freaks of animals trying to kill whatever it can to survive. I'm damn well tired of seeing people working themselves to death for the Company! I want to watch that piece of SHIT Empire fall to the ground and see what its like!" Mack held himself back from yelling with much restraint. Pulsating blood pounded threw veins, perspiration over red skin, heavy breaths and bitter eyes replaced the calm and collective leader. He trembled as he stood there. Slowly he allowed himself to cool down. *Inhale... Exhale... Inhale... Exhale...* Jenko said nothing, just standing there with him.

"...If we fail, all that was ever good about this planet is gone, not to mention the planet itself. It won't be long. It's like a time bomb that'll implode... if we fail, what chance is there? There isn't one. We're it, all there is... it's just... just getting a little overwhelming. Sorry... I shouldn't have..." Mack fought back his feelings. "Mack, don't, you're right. Yes, you're our leader, but you're human too. Those bastards have been toying around too long. We *are* the last hope. We can't fail, and we won't fail. I have faith and you should too. Look around you!

Everyone here has lost something or someone dear. They would follow you to their deaths to bring the Company down. We *will* succeed. We *will*," Jenko's sincere words were like a comforter providing relief.

"You're right. It will be fine. Thank you, my friend. Let's call it a night," Mack smiled. The shady figures moved across the room, and their bodies, as noiselessly as possible, crawled onto couches. The hushed timid tugging of their blankets shuffled meekly across their clothing. Heads pressed down against borrowed bed pillows. Tomorrow would come all too soon...

Hope is what we cannot afford to lose. Hope is all that is left sometimes. Life is what we shape it to be. If we can't even hope to change it, it will never happen. Hope is what we cannot afford to lose.

Chapter 18: Descent

...And it did. It seemed a blink and the sun was up, peeking over the mountains from behind. Waking the others, Mack began the day, trying to forget the negativity that had overcome his thoughts for so long now. It was time to think positively, for if he couldn't believe in this renegade group of freedom fighters, who could?

They readied themselves, and skipped breakfast altogether. Saying goodbye to the cabin they travelled with the light. It was tiresome, and bodies were still weakened from their time stuck in the ice cavern. Yu-Lee had a stable cough that never seemed to leave her be. Ideally another week or two would have provided sufficient rest, but it was simply not and option.

Trudging forth they ploughed through the knee-deep snow. The high rock wall to their left, and the other random snowy peaks to there right, they were surrounded by rock in all directions. The path curved around the mountainside, and several trees poked their upper halves above the snow along the path. As they went along they collected dry branches for their fire that night. They followed the trail for hours around to the other side. Snow enjoyed crawling down into boots, nipping at their skin as it melted and became like glacial water dripping through their socks. Exhaustion tuckered them out, still less than fully recovery, long slow wheezing aerated their bodies. Lively conversation died by late-morning; their high spirits faded along with the sunlight, for as they twisted around the side of the mountain pass the high peak cast its shadow over them. The temperature from the light unto the shade bore great significance, at least fifteen degrees.

Intermittent breaks spruced up out of necessity, as their stubborn limbs protested the anguish. Much to Mack's approval Masumi urged them to keep moving. "We, we can't stop everyone. You need to keep moving or... or you'll, your blood will get thick... Common!" she expelled as much in a breath as she could. Grunts and moaning resounded all around as they followed the girl onward.

Hunger pains started to compete with sore muscles and the feeling of oncoming frostbite. *Crunch! Crunch!* Was the only sound that was present along the curbing pass, aside from the random cough, sneeze, and distressed huff. All they wanted to do was get to the next stop, set up tent and cuddle up in warm furs with something to fill their empty tummies. It was the race to get to the end of the day, a race being played in slow motion.

By early that afternoon the sun had risen high enough to fill the separation between the peaks, shining onto the trail. The heat was a blessing and was like receiving a second wind during a marathon run. The heat radiated onto their skin pleasurably, teasing them with its sensuality. Caressing, feeling, alive, it was a grand occasion, like the festival of lights. It was the first pleasant break of the day; little did they suspect that luck was on their side.

A little further down the path the snow wasn't so deep, as most of it had been swept over the edge by the wind. It was only ankle deep, so as the merged from the deep snow it was as if stepping into a new pair of legs. Movement was so much simpler, numb legs began to warm up and started feeling motion again, as the blood began to better circulate through them.

On and on, the path was cleared for them. They walked in the warm ebbing light from the sun for hours. As they cornered the bend, around sunset, it was clear a storm was brewing from the south. Threatening cumulus clouds lined the distant southern horizon. Slowly the mound of clouds were migrating closer and closer, edging their way toward them. The oncoming clouds had stolen Mack's attention away. He started to calculate the time that had passed since they departed Ryoko in late December. It had to be the first week of February. *February...* he thought, *...the month of storms...*

"It's coming too quickly. We'll never make it! It's coming too fast! Mack, oh god! Don't leave me here! ..."

The blue and green pastels of the sinking sun flared across the sky. They had achieved their destined goal for the day, and would climb down from this spot the following day. Stretching out ahead of them were plains and plains of winter white fields, all the way to the ocean they could see over the flat land to the south-western corner. To the north-west, toward Tomakomai, the land was rougher, hills rolled creating a distorted distance. Faintly they thought they could see the monstrosity of the great city far off from them. Whatever their eyes perceived, it stood as a speck in the distance.

A second dark speck among the rolling hills caught Masumi's eye. She squinted, and thought herself delusional at first, "Hey, everyone!" she waved them over. Mei, Vince and Kairu attended the call. "Do you see that too? Look... just below that sixth mound... You see it? You see it, don't you?" she exclaimed. The others looked vividly until it also came into visual recognition. "I see it!" Mei asserted excitedly. "I see it too, but... what is it?" Vince squinted harder. Kairu looked on with his hawk like vision. "Is that what I think it is?" he asked Masumi. "Yea!

Hey Mack, come over here! Quickly, common!" Masumi impatiently persisted.

Mack shook off his daze, went over to his crew, and the sight automatically caught his eye, but he couldn't quite make it out. "Good job," he praised, "what is it... is that?!" he finally felt a giant weight lifted from his shoulders, which he thought, must be fraudulent at first. *A mirage?* he questioned the validity of his eyes. But no, it *wasn't* a mirage! It was real! Down between the hills a new underground train station posted itself. A tunnel had been burrowed beneath the land, which was otherwise invisible if not for the station post. Not a moment later a train pulled into the station; it was operational! Maybe, just maybe there could hustle and get to it before the storms spitefully began their bitter onslaught, just maybe...

"Everyone, come here!" Mack hollered. They set the tent they'd been erecting aside. "What is 'e boss?" Kato asked as he abandoned the woodpile he'd been stacking. "We're in luck! Ha-ha! Theres a transport for us, and where there's people theirs gotta be some food! So, tonight let's cook up a storm! Leave just enough for tomorrow, cause tomorrow's gonna to be a long day. Ha-Ha!" He was so exhilarated he went and worked intently on the fire just so he could light his cigar. Their leader was back, and they all knew it.

It was a night to remember indeed. Even though their meal was poor, it was a banquet to them compared to what they'd been living on. They had boiled the potatoes in water they'd melted from snow, then tanned them to a crisp golden brown in their frying pan. They made a tortilla like flat-bread from the flour, and although bland, the crunchy warm bread gave them an enormous energy boost. For desert they cracked open the third bottle of fruit preservatives; the cherries, that Vince had brought from the cabin. They left themselves the carrots, rice and last two bottles of fruit preservatives for the next day.

Though the feast was quaint, the company was excellent. A ray of hope, a new energy, permeated through each of them. Vince and Suako entertained them with song about their adventures, switching back and forth with the verses. Suako began the little jig:

"Down into the depths below,
The troops, they wandered to an' fro'!
Came out atop the upper land,
To find thee Earth was only sand!

Between the mountains of the south,
Met a jujitsu master,
His heart was sound and stout,
But he had a quiet mouth!

Onward yet they ventured on,
Onto the other side,
Looked around for a new place,
Rejected at Atani, accepted at Quan!

Across the angry shaky land,
Came across a magickal ma-am,
She took me in and healed me up,
When the earth played just too rough!

Met up with them at the end of the world,
Pulled them from an imploding place,
With little time,
And lack of grace!

Ran back just as fast as we could,
Stumbled to the ship at port,
Set the sail and aimed the cannon,
'Cause Yoshida's a mighty bad man!

Came across onto new lands,
Wasn't our initial plan,
Crashed our way onto the shore,
Split our party up once more!

Heaving through the snowy fields,
Until the trees would reveal,
Our rivals we assumed behind us,
Got here first in time to blind us!

Met a cute mountain climber girl,
Brought her along to take a twirl,
Turns out she was a mighty climber,
Can barely keep up behind 'er!

Up the peaks we climbed so high,
But to the eagle we almost died,
Good thing for our loyal friends,
Or we'd have met a bitter end!

Locked up in an icy prison,
Days went by,
The sun did glisten,
Until from it we had risen!

Over the bridge to the other side,
Ran to the cabin before we died,
Turned up the heat; and crawled under blankets,
Hid there till the food couldn't bide us!

Out once more we travelled on,
Tired; starving,
It was no fun,
But we just kept pressing on!

Then we reached the other side,
Where good tidings for did lie,
So now we sit around the fire,
Giddy and full of laughter!"

Vince and Suako came together at the finale to finish it all off, and laughter roared among the entire group. The pair had acted out the scenes comically, which everyone responded to by holding their sides as they laughed out hysterically. It was a time to remember, and even better yet when Jenko found a bottle of rum from Quan he'd forgotten about at the bottom of his satchel. "Hear, Hear! Bravo you two! We even have terms a reward for you!" he called out, then held the bottle high to curious eyes. "Wohoo!" Mei cheered clapping her palms together. He brought it over and twisted the tin lid from the top of the glass bottle. The warm rich colour of the rum chug-a-lugged and sloshed around as it entered glasses held high to be filled. Even Masumi was given a small glass of it, to join in the merriment; they had all been deserving. Maturing seemed to be rapid in those that took on challenging roles in these rough days.

"A toast!" Jenko held his glass high after serving everyone up, "To our magnificent performers!" "Aye!" everyone cheered, and then took a swig. Vince put his arm over Suako's shoulder and kissed her cheek. No one noticed, but she blushed under her already hot red cheeks. More cheering prevailed on, praising one person to the next for all that had been done. The excitement over the railroad had been so uplifting, that they felt as good as if they'd already decimated the C.D.F.P.; well, *almost* that good.

"Everyone, I have another surprise! I was saving it in case we got desperate, but that doesn't matter now!" Vince gleefully announced. He pranced over to his pack and sifted threw to the bottom. He pulled out a bag, which Masumi recognised automatically, and from it he pulled a rectangular package. "Chocolate!" he smirked. Eyes lit up around the circle. "Enjoy," he threw it into the jumble of bodies. Mei snagged the bar and cackled giddily. "Ha-Ha!" Vince laughed. As they all sat preoccupied with it, Vince grabbed Suako from them, and pulled his finger to his lips signalling her to keep quiet. Although flustered at first, she did just that.

He led her away from the others to a moonlit spot; the yellow glow of the fire could be faintly seen between a lively spruce tree's branches to their right. Her heart fluttered with anticipation as he practically swept her off her feet. He pressed her against the rock wall, holding her hands to her side, and then without warning, intimately kissed her before even saying a word. Everything was happening so quickly that it took her mind a moment to catch up. Once it had, she just relaxed into it, and let him take her away. Her heart was his, there was no doubt in her mind.

He pulled gently away from lips desiring even more. He kissed his way across her jaw and to her neck where he commenced to merrily whisper an unsung piece from their song:

Came up with a sharp new arrow,
Shot it deep into bone marrow,
At first I'd thought that I'd gone stupid,
Then I realised it was cupid!

Suako giggled at his silly verse, then bit down gently on her bottom lip. Her eyes were wild for him. He nibbled gently on her ear lobe erotically and it incited her even more. They necked like doves; two birds in love, their two hearts beating in unison. *I love you* were words that didn't need to leave the lips; like the unspoken knowledge, it was out there, and they both knew it.

Infatuated with each other, they refused to pull apart in the least. Desperate hands longed to touch, and tender skin quivered at the touch of wandering fingertips. Internal infernos erupted as their bodies begged to be held, felt, touched and ultimately loved. Their emotions ran deep, they had so much to say to each other, but no words in which to describe their feelings existed.

It was an invitation into Shangri-La, to be offered such an unspeakably endless swell of devoted mutual appreciation, only a fool could refuse. Lust was an undeniable motive, but there was more to it. Their attraction came from a deep understanding between two people; it was a once in a lifetime connection that not everyone is blessed to discover.

Love me forever. Join with my soul. Never leave me lonely. Never take away this feeling you've injected into my very being. Stay by my side, till death do us part, and beyond into the abyss of the afterlife. Hold me close... just hold me in your big wide arms. Explore me, learn all there is to know. I'm open to you, I shan't hold back for you. Pull me into the euphoria of your love. Feel my heart beat against your chest, while I feel yours echo into me... Love me... Just love me... If this is not Utopia, it does not exist...

Was this night to good to be real? The thought wandered into Suako's mind. Could she have dreamt all of this? Was she dreaming back at the cabin, wishing that this were what was to become of the day to follow? A hallucination possibly? No! It *was* real. It was mystical and romantic, and for once in a long time she was not consumed with worries, or uncertainty eating away at their innards. It was simply... bliss.

"Mmm... Oh my *God!* That was *so* good!" Mei exclaimed. The chocolate had practically been orgasmic. Everyone had taken two squares and slowly enjoyed them as the sweet rich textures had gradually melted on their tongues. The warm sensual feeling it summoned in their bodies was soon heightened by the caffeine boost that followed. "That was great... H, Hey where's Vince...? Uh, Suako's gone too?" Masumi asked looking about. They all looked around themselves. Mack looked around the corner with Jenko, and then turned back to the other with a big grin on his face, "Guess we'll have to save our thanks for later," he chuckled while the others looked up puzzled at him. "Hah!" Jenko let out, taking a friendly jab at Mack's arm for the comment.

An innocent smile crept across Kairu's face as he imagined Vince and Suako caught up in each other's gaze. Looking next to him, Masumi sat comfortably leaning against him with his arm about her shoulder. He suddenly had a flashback from Quan, and he remembered Okichi vividly, as if she stood before him with the warm air buzzing about, and the rippling waves that manipulated the moon's image behind her. He recollected the sway of her brown-black hair across her tanned skin, and the way her dark eyes lit up when he spoke. Then the smell, as if he could be with her then, that provocative, zestful scent she allured to him with, eradicated anything else from his mind. Spices of curry and saffron... and then nutmeg and cinnamon with a hint of ginger. He could almost sense her there, with her sweet voice pleading to hear one of his stories. An untamed look of delight beamed from his face.

The lively hyper mood of the group faded as the hour grew late. Jenko noticed the conversations dying down, and since he was earlier captivated by the landscape, he neglected to retain his ambition any longer. He heated his inkpot up with the kindling flames of the fire, and a few moments later it was ready. Pulling out his map, he started his artistic and precise art of mapping. He began by detailing the train station down below, using his special quill pen, he dipped it into the black ink and stained the page. It was absorbed instantly into the sponge-like parchment paper.

"It's amazing," Yu-Lee said as she snuck up on Jenko. He jutted backward, almost sure his heart had stopped, but was fortunate enough to pull his pen up, rather then destroy his map. "What is?" he jolted, and snapped the automatic response out at her. "Oh!" she gasped shocked, and then laughed. "I'm sorry," she giggled, "I didn't mean to scare you, hehe," she raised her finger to her lips to try and halt the laughing fit. He turned his head away and blushed as he felt his heart start again after the temporary arrhythmia.

After gathering himself together Jenko looked back up at the woman. He laughed at himself, and the thought of how silly he must have looked. "Heh, what can I do ya' for Yu-Lee?" he put on his charming smiling. "I just caught sight of your map there, and it reminded me of just how far we've gone. Amazing, don't you think?" She asked, taking a seat next to him as she peered at his masterpiece. "Yea, yea it is," his head bobbed up and down.

Jenko offered her the map of the Imperial green continent to take a look at. Her eyes flew around from place to place, and she noticed that the far south-eastern corner of the map was incomplete. "Jenko," she placed a hand upon his shoulder to grab his attention. "Hmm? Yes, what is it Yu-Lee? Something wrong?" He asked. "No, no, it's just..." she took her hand off his shoulder, and pointed her pale long finger to the map where her eyes had landed. Her lengthy fingernail dragged his eyes to it. "Nothing wrong, just not yet finished. You've never ventured past here I assume from the lack of this corner, right?" she tore her eyes off the page to look at him. "That's correct. In fact, I'd not even been into Kagawa, I've only camped near by," he explained. "That's understandable. No one ever travelled to the Sacred Lands without one of the Kagawa Priestess'. There was a city, close to the ocean, beyond the dry desert lands past Kagawa, but... the earth gobbled it up before my eyes..." she felt her heart sinking. "It still deserves to have been remembered. Would you..." she hesitated to ask him to modify his life's work for a now non-existent place.

"What is it? Yu-Lee, please go on." Jenko lifted Yu-Lee's head with his index finger beneath her chin; his eyes were reassuring. "I know it's not there anymore but... if I... if I described it to you would you put it on your map? It was the dearest place to me... I, I'm sorry I shouldn't have asked. It's not fair," she began to talk at a faster pace. "Yu-Lee, Yu-Lee, just relax. I'd love to. Nothing has ever made me as unhappy as having this corner empty. It would be an honor," his cheeks wrinkled just slightly as he smiled. Her scarlet eyes lit up and she swooped back her long black hair, which shone with purple hues in the moonlight, before she poured her hearts happiest memories out to him in all the detail that her brain could muster.

Masumi crawled into the tent, quite exhausted, and Kairu followed suit not long after. Inside the tent Masumi and Kairu lay facing each other. They had had a wonderful night talking and enjoying the celebratory dinner. Kairu's smile didn't last when the illusion was discovered to be just that; an illusion. The chipper mood faded into the old heady thought-filled boy from Yokutan. Masumi noticed immediately. "Kairu...? What is it?" she asked looking up to him with insightful eyes. "Nothing... it's nothing," he lied, as he shook Okichi free from his mind. Masumi looked at him longingly before accepting the claim, but even then, not fully. Silence filled the air, and the two slowly drifted off to sleep.

Mack lit up his second cigar that evening and puffed it to relax. He plunked himself down across the fire from Mei and Kato, who had huddled together beneath a blanket to stay warm. "S' how's the leg mending?" Mack asked between puffs. "Pretty good. She's take 'n' care 'o me," Kato smiled nudging Mei who playfully nudged back.

"Good," Mack said, and took another suck back on his cigar. The sweet burning taste filled his mouth. "How 're you two holdin' up?" he questioned, having had not addressed his troops as friends as much as he'd have normally liked to in the past few weeks. "We're keep 'n' it t'gether Mack. It's been hard, but ch'ya never led us wrong before. We trust ya with our lives boss. Ain't no mistake 'n' that," Kato began. Mei kept her eyes on him, then shifted them onto Mack. "He's right. We've always trusted you," she included then let out a great big yawn, "oh, I think I'm ready to hit the hay," she giggled as a sleepy haze overcame her body. "Yea, I agree. Night Mack," Kato said trekking behind Mei. Mack flung his head back, teeth gritting down on his cigar, "Night you two," he managed to say around the oblong object.

A flurry of smoke, mixed with his-own condensing breath, rose up into the cold air, mingling into puffy cloud like formations. He'd felt at ease, and relaxed up until this point. They *believed* in him. They *trusted* him. Those words interchangeably took their turn resting on his shoulders. *Was it to be taken more seriously to lead? Did it mean the job was already well done?* He wondered. No resolution presented itself. He felt the buzz of the alcohol wearing off as he tried to search for an answer he desperately desired, but it did not come. He shook it off after getting held up on it. *Another puff,* relaxing him like a drug-like induced mellow overshadowed his aggravating unanswerable question. He looked overhead at the blue-black starry night sky. He bunched up a random blanket that was left next to him, and used it as a pillow. Mack laid back to rest while he pondered, and before he knew it he'd fallen asleep.

Leadership is a difficult path…

Chapter 19: The Train Station

"Mack…? Hey Mack, wake up!" he could vaguely hear the ruffling of his shirt as the gentle tug of Masumi badgered him awake. He felt slightly out of sorts, barely remembering falling asleep beside the fire. None the less, he was wide-awake when she waved a bowl of sweet smelling rice beneath his nose. His stomach replied immediately with a rather insistent grumble. "Here you go," she merrily placed it beside him.

At first, he wondered if his sense of scent had simply deceived him, but upon the first bite of the rice, the mouthful proved to taste just as good as it smelled. He looked around in wonderment. Masumi noticed his thought-invoked eyes quite quickly. "It's not your imagination," she said like a mind reader to his surprise. "Vince picked up some maple sugar in Uwajima, so he gave it to us to use with breakfast," and then she added, "I remembered how my mother showed me to prepare maple rice. All we're missing is the cream," a contented expression spoke of her pride in her cooking abilities, which Mack would not deny, was well deserved. He praised her accordingly, and the beaming turned into a magma hot expression. He winked at Vince for the contribution, then reverted back to eating his bowl of rice.

"How goes the map, Jenko?" Mack asked, peering over to his food-loving friend as he gobbled up the last of his morning meal. Between muffled mouthfuls Mack thought he could hear him make out something that sounded like it might be the word 'good'. Jenko was quick to share the fruits of his labour in progress. Elegantly illustrated and well proportioned, the path of their route was outlined on the paper. The black ink, ruined as it was, did not stray across the page. To the untrained eye it displayed perfection. "It's incredible Jenko," Kato tapped him on the back respectively. "It's all right... the mountains are too close together, and Uwajima is too big..." he modestly tried to deflect the praise of his talent. Mack couldn't help a smirk from emerging.

For the first time that day, Mack noticed the sky. Enclosing in on them was that distant storm that had threatened from the far south the previous night. His smirk faded, and the magnetic feeling of the air was beginning to emerge. He quickly downed the last of his breakfast as fast as he could bring it to his mouth.

"Alright, we're leaving. Common everyone, up. Now!" he stood dusting off the powder snow stuck to his behind.

Jenko curled up his map and stuck it away in it's protective tube casing. The group had the packing already completed before Mack had been woken up that day. Even Mei had taken the liberty to get his things together for him. They were all set to start out down the rock face. Securely they attached their ropes around stone holds, and Masumi checked the knotting. She ended up fixing one, but the rest were fine. It now was time to shimmy down to the ground. They got dressed in their harnesses, and Masumi clipped them onto their ropes. Nervously Suako and Vince looked over their shoulders to the land so far below. "Phew!" Suako shuttered. "Hey," Vince got her attention, "It'll be alright," his smile was assuring.

"Ok everyone!" Masumi addressed them, "Y'all got your gloves on? ... Good! Get a good hold on your rope, make sure the leather palm is touching the rope, it'll help you hold on. Have one hand up, and one below where I attached your harness. Shift the rope threw your hands to move down, like this," she demonstrated for them. "Use your legs to push off of the side to help you move down. Now, if you slip..." she went on explaining procedures for any possible situation. Mack was growing impatient, constantly keeping the storm within his sight. Her words seem to linger on, and he was just about to speak out when she wrapped it up. "...that's it! So, follow my lead. Just push off with your feet like this and loosen your hands a little from the rope," she showed them as she began to lower.

It was like a leap of faith as one by one they went. Suako shut her eyes closed tight and then, *swoosh!* The air caressed her ears as she went over the edge. Safely her legs plunked back against the firm stone. Opening her eyes, she saw everything as Masumi described it to be, and Suako felt like a bit of a fool for being so fearful. She couldn't help but let out a tiny giggle. She pushed out again, *swoosh!* She went down again. It was actually quite a bit of fun, and she found out that going down was *much* simpler then climbing up, *Thank god for that* she thought. *Huh? What the...? Snow?* Suako found her self baffled when they reached the bottom so suddenly. It had seemed like they'd only just first taken that first little bound a second ago. She sighed miserably as she unhooked her harness from the rope. Then looking around she realised she was the only one there. *What?!* Shock grabbed her. She spun around, and then finally looked up to see everyone else was still a good twenty feet up.

A minute later they came down to join her. "Hey!" Mei called down to Suako, "Hah, our late starter turned out to be as fast as a flying bullet!" she laughed. Mei planted her feet into the snow, "I guess nothing puts you out for long," Mei smiled. "Yeah," Suako forced a fraudulent smile. A flash back of falling nipped at her as she blinked. The others came down before Mei could pick up on the subtle signals Suako had briefly given off.

"Let's just leave the ropes here for when we come back," Yu-Lee said, exhausted at the thought of climbing back up that darn thing once more. "Good idea," Jenko agreed detaching himself. "Right. Now we should…" Mack's eyes silenced his mouth. He turned, looking out over the endless mounds of snow that stretched out to the ocean. It had come; just starting, sparse snowflakes came down from the dark sprawling clouds overhead. The other noticed his displeased attitude, and took notice of his interest in the weather. Though to the inexperienced traveller the light snowfall heeded within itself no danger. He turned to look for the train station; it was at *least* a few hours trek away. Darkness was settling in for the night.

Mack felt an overwhelming anxiety. *What should I do?* His brain refused to answer. Again, he scanned around, but ideas were not promoting their existence. *Damn! Damn it! What the hell are we going to do? If we camp we'll be buried alive. I don't trust those goddamned clouds… but if we go, we'll be stuck out in the storm. We'll never make it!* No peace was available within his brain. Again, eyes longed for a solution, and again, nothing presented itself willingly. Or *did* it?

It was *so* obvious, so *plainly* there before him. *Why didn't I think of this before? How could I have been so blind? What's wrong with me?* But no time to answer such monotonous questions. It was time to solve the 'x' and 'y' of this equation. It was…

"Is everything alright Mack? What are we going to do?" Kairu asked as he bundled his gear. *Damn it all to hell! So brilliant, so perfect! It was… it was… it was lost. Now what? What the fuck were they going to do now?* Frustration edged him on until his right eye began to twitch. "We're going for the station now," he answered bitterly, and then commenced to walk toward it. It was the only option available. *If* they were lucky, they wouldn't be trapped in the month of storms furious temper. *If* they were lucky, history wouldn't repeat itself.

The wish he had been praying for almost seemed as if were going to come true. The day stayed in a maroon-like darkness as the sun sank behind dark clouds far beyond the mounds of snow, and the ocean waves past them. Spread out like the diamonds of stars that peeked out between the clouds in the sky, the snow fell. It was magical. Even when it came down faster, like falling pixie dust, it hadn't been awful by any means; but the serenity did not last.

Gusting winds soon decided to join the fray, and like bee stings, the snow flew up at bare skin. Exposure was so awful they even tried to cover their eyes with their scarves. Unfortunately, the storm had a mind of its own, and it seemed to derive a sick sort of sadistic delight in torturing them. Morbidly, they trudged on against the northern gale force winds.

They could begin to feel the icy deep freeze within their bodies. Lunges, if only in their imaginations, salvaged the recollection of being fluid filled, so they began coughing and wheezing as they went. The maroon sky got even darker, and the snow so thick that the station was out of sight. Something had to be done, they would not last the night in such conditions.

Mack could not help but recall the brutal past that haunted him every February. Trying to block it from his mind, he found himself unable to combat the intense images from showing their ugly faces. They were burned into his skull. The sky just the same as that above him now...

It had been Mack's second year working as a soldier for the C.D.F.P. He'd been on a training exercise, far to the north of Torusan. His Commander had issued the party into five groups of three men each, and each team had been assigned to collect three red flags, which were buried in chests beneath the snow along with extra rations as incentive. The objective of the mission was to be able to use their issued maps in order to locate the chests, as well as to practice survival skills.

Initially it was only meant to be a three to five-night practice drill. They had been given appropriate rations to last them the five days, a tent per group, flint and the such, to last them through. It was a routine drill, and when they set out it had been an enjoyable day; cold but still beautiful blue-sky sunny day. The first day had been excellent. Mack's party's group leader had been an excellent map-reader, and they had reached the first chest in good time. After stopping for a late leisurely afternoon lunch, they decided to keep going toward their next mark in order to have less to do the following day.

Each flag was made to be harder to find. The first bit of terrain they covered had been relatively flat, and the snow not much higher then the top of their shoes, rarely to their ankles. Up ahead of them lay the rocky uneven grounds of the granite rich lands. The north-western corner of the East Green Continent had rocky sections surfacing through the dark abounding soil. The hike was taking its toll on their legs, and by nightfall their hamstrings were burning and ached deeply. Steep hills were unkind to unfamiliar travellers using them as their road. They sat by their campfire and enjoyed their prized rations obtained from earlier that day.

The next morning a beastly overshadowing cloud shut out the light from the sun. Nothing could penetrate threw the thick sky, though they thought nothing of it. It was dismissed as just another nasty looking snow cloud; It was winter, and it was just as expected for that time of year, even if it wasn't something anyone coveted. They set out again across the snowy plains, stretching out sore limbs.

"Heh! Hey Mack, at this pace we'll be the first ones back. I can see that nice fat juicy bonus already, eh? Man, this is sweet!" A younger first year soldier rubbed his hands together greedily. He was energetic and, by speculation, only cared about women and how he looked at every second of everyday. He was a bit of a hot shot, but otherwise the life of the party. Mack and Kentaro, their precious map guru and temporary commander, both liked him a lot.

"Yea Jiro, I can see it now." Mack had no trouble feeling the same. Some extra cash, to cruise the town and go bar hopping with? Sure! It sounded great to him in his young years. He was barely Jiro's senior, though had maturity to his credit. A break from work would be just *fine* with him. Kentaro wasn't about to disagree with that idea either.

"I know some *real* hotties downtown grid sector five. There's a bar they always hang out at. It's called... it was..." Jiro snapped his fingers as if to order his brain to spew out the name. "Ah! That was it, *'The flying Dragon'*. Heh I can't wait till we get back to Torusan. I'm not leaving till they kick me out- unless one of those sweet gals wanna have some fun," Jiro said, spoken like a true playboy. The one talent Mack wasn't as great at. Kentaro and Mack kept giving each other sideways glances; Jiro's enthusiasm drew curly-cue smirks.

Jiro continued "...The beers cheap, and the music's great. I know the guy there so he can get us a discount at the inn upstairs. So how about it, are you in?" he swept back his long sandy blond bangs back from his blue eyes. Not just a playboy at heart, he had the image to pull it off. "Sure," Mack replied. "I'm in too," Kentaro concurred. Why not? If they were with mister handsome maybe they could, just maybe, have some luck with the ladies too. "Great. We're gonna have a blast. When you meet..." he was full of energy and continued rambling on about everything. Kentaro and Mack just listened, continuously giving each other those lip biting, near laughter, sideways glances.

As they travelled onwards and the clouds began to drop their snowy flakes down on them while morning was still early. The wind picked up, but they continued to pay little attention to it. Jiro's mouth went on flapping about so many frivolous things. With the wind blowing as it was, Mack was relieved to have Jiro's stories to distract him. Anything was better than being left to simply dwell on how awful that wind was.

Still, they continued to ignore them storm front. They reached their second chest at noon on the second day. It was shielded under a piece of the granite, jutting free of the snowy earth. The large granite piece blocked the bitter wind, so they made a small fire and heated the soup they found inside the second chest. Mack had shoved the second red flag into his backpack. The hot soup warmed them from the inside out, and it was enough to motivate them to finish the job, once their bodies had shed the nasty chill.

The warm mouth of Jiro now had strength again to continue with silly miscellaneous stories, when they started for the third chest. That afternoon the land migrated its state once more; steep rolling hills, deeply covered in snow proved to be the next challenge. It was all down to willpower at that stage for them to persevere. *Just get it over with, then go to 'The Flying Dragon,'* was the thought that kept them all going. They were all healthy and young, and figured that they could endure a little bad weather.

Mack and Kentaro occasionally shared some of their stories too. It was almost like a challenge to see who had done what, and therefore who was more of a man's man. It was a silly testosterone game between them. The crown was ultimately handed over to Jiro; the most foolish of them all, ultimately became the 'hero', and consequently the winner.

The snow began to fall thickly, it was a white out in every direction. The sky above was a maroon haze through the muffling flakes. Not long after the heavy snow started, their compass went wacky, and with no way to see landmarks, or anyway to know which direction kept them on course, it was no use to keep going. They couldn't see two feet in front of themselves, how could they ever certain they were travelling in a straight line?

Against the forces of nature, they attempted to set up camp, but Mother Nature had other plans. The tent wouldn't hold up, and they had no way to secure it down with the snow being so deep, no anchors presented themselves. Once again, stranded with nothing. Now what? They'd freeze to death if they stayed there. Pink skin began to be hindered to a bluish-purple colour. On top of that, the degraded air was already becoming a challenge to breathe in those days, but the ghastly damp northern storm air proved to be attained in a brutally painful fashion by weary bodies.

Then the cave; a random flash back to the cave. How they got there Mack could not recall. It was small, and didn't keep the wind from gusting inside. Jiro was suffering, the most, he was in critical condition. Somehow, he'd broken a rib. Another part that white out erased from his mind.

They were trapped; outside they couldn't see two feet in front of themselves, and inside they were slowly freezing to death. The wind was too strong for them to build a fire. Their options were nil, they had to wait it out. *Would they be able to wait it out?* Mack couldn't help but wonder as he saw Jiro's lips turn blue as he quivered, like a bow after releasing an arrow.

Huddled together beneath sleeping bags their mutual body heat was all they had to rely on. It was nearly unbearable. As light cracked in occasionally he could see ice begin to form on their eyelashes, eyebrows, and any other hair exposed to the condensation from their breathing. It was freezing, yet somehow, they were surviving. Somehow, they hadn't fallen into an endless sleep. Somehow...

The next day wasn't any better. The numbing of body parts was giving off extreme warning signals of immanent death. They couldn't stay there any longer, but when they tried to move Jiro he gasped. The pain caused him to shriek, in a weak airless manner. Things did not look so good; they had to leave, or they'd all face the deathly fate of becoming human ice cubes.

Kentaro and Mack had no choice but to take turns carrying Jiro on their backs. They left the cave and went back out into the whiteout of a storm. The snow, now mixed with ice pellets, nicked and scratched at their skin. As they headed against the storm they found their skin being torn open by the sharp winter blades. Blood dripped until it froze to their faces. They continued, headstrong toward a cabin on their map; it was their only chance of making it through this.

As feet plunged down again and again into knee deep snow, the bottoms of their legs began to feel awkward. They could only feel the slightest sensations below their knees. Jiro was wheezing as he bounced up and down on his transport's back. Every step down insured a sharp scrutinising pain, like a stab wound pulsing through his chest, as he bounced against his carrier. Jiro cringed at every single change to his bodily position.

After a while Jiro's breathing slowed, but Mack, who had been carrying him at the time, didn't notice. It was too noisy outside to hear much else but the wind, never the less the subtle sound of someone inhaling and exhaling. Kentaro was slowly fading in health as well; dark circles under his eyes looked terrifyingly unhealthy. Nothing but the will to live kept his legs moving forward, as Kentaro looked to the map every now and then, Mack wondered if hi friend's eyes could even make anything out in the state they were in.

Abruptly Jiro's hold around Mack's shoulders went limp, and Jiro fell back into the snow, behind Mack. His body indented the thick snow when he hit the ground. Mack called out to Kentaro, using all of his strength to produce any sort of sound, "K... Kent... Kentaro!" was all he could manage from a frozen throat. He turned and his legs wobbled as he fell to his knees. Kentaro struggled backward to them. It was too late, Jiro was dead, his face was already frozen. He was mummified by the storm, his skin was an eerie pale blue, which made Jiro look like some sort of porcelain doll.

With no other choice, they left him there, with grieving hearts that sunk low. Guilt followed them for not having even buried their comrade, but there simply wasn't time, they were on death's door too. If they'd had

had any feeling left in their numb torsos they would've felt a great emptiness within. They barely knew Jiro, yet it was just as if leaving a very old friend behind. Tears froze to their faces.

On and on they went, *will we _ever_ find that cabin?* Mack wondered, amongst his image of Jiro etched into his skull. That face, it didn't look real. The life had been sucked right out of it. It seemed as if they'd never find it, that they'd die out in this horrendous storm just like Jiro. The weather just seemed to worsen. Ahead he watched as Kentaro fell face forward into the snow. Mack quickened his pace to get to him.

Mack turned him over and rested his head on his lap. Kentaro was in horrible shape, and his eyes were the only indication that he was still in his right mind. Lips chapped so badly they'd cracked and bled. Kentaro complained of his legs. Mack checked them, and saw his feet had severe frostbite that was spreading up his calves. It was a miracle he'd gone as far as he had. Scared eyes looked up at Mack, and his weary voice came forth to admit his mental defeat, and his fear, "It's coming down too quickly. We'll never make it! We'll never make it! Mack, oh god! Don't leave me here! ..."

Mack opened his eyes. Everyone was following him, and he knew they were going to have issues reaching that train station in time. Already it was getting hard to pinpoint where it was through the snowfall. He remembered carrying Kentaro to the cabin, and the bitter operation that left him without his legs from the knee down. All to well he remembered the life like doll of what used to be a man. He wasn't prepared to relive that.

Mack looked around himself, and he waited for some sort of solution to present itself. "Common... Common, give me something... anything please..." he pleaded with some invisible force. Nothing came to him. "Please!" He yelled out. Still nothing came. The feeling of defeat was tugging at his ankles, but he refused to give in.

Rage infused into his voice as he began to curse the storm, the C.D.F.P., and the entire state of life. Everyone had stopped behind him, and huddled together. They all heard ranting, but nothing was clear through the harsh winds, it was as if listening to a radio when the fuzz was just to strong to make out more then one or two words. "...Damn.... I hate... Bastards... Mother f..." it went on and on.

Mack took in a deep breath and cursed one last time. Yu-Lee had been spending that time heaving her way through the snow to him, and finally, she had reached him. Her eyes met his. He looked at her rather confused for a moment, and then suddenly knew, that she *knew* about his last experience. He didn't know how she knew, but he knew she did.

Yu-Lee took his hand. As their palms met Mack felt a surge of energy pulse through his body. He understood, to some degree, what he should do. It was a *knowing* that he could not describe, it was just there, and that's was all that mattered.

With a small indicating gesture of the head, Mack began. He stood facing against the storm winds, pushing in from the south. Harshly he jolted their connected hands up, and took a moment to focus his thoughts. He wasn't exactly sure what he was going to say. Everyone saw the pyramid formation of their arms, and they watched with wonder.

Mack looked on. into the storm, and he thought about the many things that made him upset about it, and that helped him gather emotional strength. In the end all he could think of to say was, "I will not let you take anyone else from me!" Although it had appeared as if he was talking to the storm, deep down the statement was guided toward the C.D.F.P.

Like a successful oil dig, a light blue, almost white, energy spouted out from them; up and out at the grey overhead. Mack felt like a conductor rod for some sort of electrical current. A prickle sensation titillated throughout his body; the feeling was remarkable, and left him invigorated.

Higher and higher the energy ray climbed, until it was reaching beyond the clouds. It had appeared as if it had gone up, and up and done nothing. Mack kept watching, and with one final emotional boost, he finished off the chain. The energy wave pushed out of them, and sent Yu-Lee and Mack to the ground. Up and up it went. At the top, it disappeared. There was nothing, and then, a lavender glimmer pulsed across the sky. *Boom!* Like a nuclear blast, the energy began to work it's magick. *Whoosh!* It spread outward in all directions. In a perfect circle the clouds were pushed back, further and further, until they vanished beyond the horizon; past the mountains and over the ocean it receded. There was nothing left of the storm but minute wisps of cloud against a blue sky. Instantly the sun warmed them, and the temperature skyrocketed up. The storm was gone, and the crest of the waxing moon looked like a cloud amidst the day sky.

Mack just sat in the snow looking upward, as his brain refused to compute the happenings as real. The snow, as if a light powder, rested on their clothing and red flushed skin. There was a long silence. The others lowered their hoods and looked around in awe. Oddities had become more of a normal thing on this trip, but this by far had topped everything they'd seen off as of yet. "Whoa…" Mack finally said, then burst out laughing hysterically.

While everyone was still distracted Mack turned to see Yu-Lee, and she returned the stare. 'How?' he mouthed the question without a sound, not desiring to have anyone else pry into his painful recollection. She turned away and then looked back, holding up a wand. Then she mouthed a single word back, 'Otojiro.' That was all there was to say, until he stood up and offered her a hand to help her up. As he did she whispered to him, "Don't worry, your secret is safe with me. I won't tell a soul," she assured him, and she kept her word.

The past will not haunt me anymore…

Chapter 20: Death Trap

After the storm had been sent away, the group had found their way easily to the station. At the top of the hill, above the train station, they spied down. It was apparent that the train was being used to transport troops and supplies for the Tomakomai distributed regiments, and, of course, the C.D.F.P. that were helping; this was no civilian train.

The sun was setting behind the station, making everything glow with a frame of bright orange light. The station itself indicated it was in use, before its military inhabitancy, for leisure travel for people across the Imperial continent. It was a very dark stacked stone building, which had dark forest green sign with gold letters, illegible from the distance Mack was at, resting above a glass window leading into the station. A beautifully crafted, recently shovelled, wooden platform sat next to the train. Tall lamp poles, and benches sat on top of the platform, and some soldiers sat on top of them. The faint scent of burnt coal lingered in the air.

Dark green uniforms, best for fighting in the forests to the east, like at Uwajima, suited the soldiers. They were armed, but not heavily. Everyone, even though the event had happened hours ago, looked as if to still be questioning the bizarre clearing of the storm. Every so often someone would point up and say something to the person next to them, who would, in turn simply shrug their shoulders, just as clueless about freak occurrence.

They had a few lookouts, but they weren't looking their way. In fact, they looked like they might just be pretending to be on the watch. Posted to watch out for a civilian attack? *Likely*, but what were the chances of that? There weren't any towns to close to here, and Mack's small outfit had enough difficulty manoeuvring over those damned mountains.

Many cargo carts of the train were being loaded with numerous crates. It looked like they were empty ones, perhaps to be sent back to be refilled at their base. Only a few of the soldiers appeared to be taking the train besides the conductor. *Perfect,* Mack thought, *all we have to do is hide in one of the carts and wait until we get to Tomakomai… Now, which cart?* Carefully he searched the train with his eyes, and he saw that the soldiers were working towards finishing loading the carts closest to the front.

"Everyone listen up we're hitching a ride, now take a look... see near the back they've already finished up loading. We're going to go for the third one from the rear, it looks like the door is still open a bit. We have to keep low," he paused to smirk, "Looks like they're all looking up," Mack said pointing to the sky. Many little snickers, sarcastic waves of the hand, and rolling of the eyes ensued towards the remark, as if to comment, "Yeah, yeah... show off!" all in good humour.

Mack lifted his eyes up to see what was going on down below. He held up his hand, index and middle finger extended with the others curled in. He made quick movements, in two tiny warning jolts. Then he signalled it was time to go.

They sprinted down the side of the hill to the lower ground. They seemed to have been moving faster than their legs were able to go, the downward momentum propelling them ahead. Now, up against the snowy banks near the tracks, they pressed their bodies. As slim as possible, they tried to hide themselves. Mack then eyed the way again, and he waited. Ill-fated, the lookouts did actually peer out every now and then. Now was one of those times, so they'd have to be patient and wait.

Whooo-Whooo! The train whistle sounded, and it was about to pull out of the station. Of all the luck, the damn stacking didn't require all of the carts as earlier hypothesised. Well, they'd have to do what they could. *No use complaining now,* Mack just wanted the obstacles to stop. He was ready for a break; his body wasn't as energetic as it used to be.

The surveillance recessed. "Go!" Mack ordered the first three people he saw. He held the others back, it was too visible, and too risky this close up to go all at once. Masumi, Kairu and Kato hurtled over to the train. As fast as they could, they got to the train car and managed to drag open the door, and jump in.

Just in time. Mack saw the watchmen looking in that direction just as Kato sank behind the shadows. Sweat began to bead on Mack's forehead. *Whooo-whooo!* The whistle blew again, but this time another sound followed. The train shook, and seemed to make some sort of rattle. A black puff of smoke came out of a funnel near the front of the train; it was about to start out. *Common, Common! Look the other way damn you!* Mack ordered in his mind, as if thinking it would make it happen. Leisurely the lookout eventually turned. The wheels had already started to move, they had to hurry.

Mack pointed to Mei, Suako, and Jenko. "Go!" He frantically demanded. They scampered off. They were three quarters of the way there. *No problem... Good...* Mack saw one of the lookouts was about to look their way. "Get down!" Mack called in a yell-whisper as best he could. They plummeted back behind a big crate that had been left behind. Their furs seem to match well with the crate, and they went unnoticed.

Jenko kept his eyes on Mack, waiting for the signal for him to go. Mack was about to have a heart attack. "Phew, I can't breathe," Mack tugged at his collar, but it was reluctant to loosen up. Mack's eyes gazed back and forth. The coast was clear, he waved his hand, and Jenko nodded, and the three of them dashed the rest of the way towards the train.

The wheels were creeping slowly against the metal tracks, gradually picking up momentum. It was now or never. Eyes averted... "Now!" Mack commanded, and the last commission bounded forward. Mack kept looking all around, ever vigilant. Vince thought Mack's head might fall off if he kept it up. *Almost there! Almost there! ...* Mack's eyes were plastered on the goal. *Boof!* A mild sound came from behind. *What the hell was that?* Mack halted and turned around. Yu-Lee had tripped and fallen in the snow.

Mack spurted back hastily to her, and Vince turned to help too but Mack pointed to the train, "Go, I'll take care of this! Just run!" Vince accepted the command, this was no time to argue. The wheels hummed along grasping the rails. It began to pattern its cycle of movement, and the cycle gradually went faster and faster with every rotation. Vince could hear it doing so; he didn't have to look to know. He reached the cart, and Kato and Masumi helped to hoist him up. They looked back, with worrisome eyes to see how far back Mack and Yu-Lee were.

Yu-Lee was pushing herself up, and Mack took her by the arms and hurried her up, lifting her to her feet. She tried to thank him, but now wasn't the time. Not allowing her any time to dust off, he took her hand and persevered onward, nearly dragging her behind. He continued to watch for eyes prying. Those evilly condemning eyes that would do them in. The train chugged along, and it was picking up speed.

Yu-Lee struggled to keep up from behind. She felt like Mack just might tear off her arm if he pulled just a little bit harder. He realised he was tugging furiously, but he wouldn't stop; their destination was getting farther away. A feeling of abandonment put its icy unwelcome hand on Mack's shoulder...

The train's gone. We're were <u>*too*</u> *late. Yu-Lee's fall cost us our ride... Shit, we're out in the open! All eyes, all of those condemning eyes, focused in on them. They were like two black sheep among a heard of white. "Throw down your weapons!" the lookout aimed his sniper riffle at them. "You have to the count of five!" He warned. "One! ..." They'd been had. There was no way out of this pickle. "Two! ..." Everyone else was looking at them, one by one guns were raised. "Three! ..." His voice rang in the air. Hills repeated his words as they echoed, like children passing a ball back and forth. His voice was deep. "Four! ... This is your last chance!" Yu-Lee shivered fretfully. Mack still had his gun at hand. He still searched for a way out. He did not wish to surrender... "Five!"* **POW!**

Mack shuddered. His imagination could be brutal at times. If they didn't get on that train, and it pulled away, they'd be exposed. If they weren't shot dead on the spot, they'd be taken hostage, and be interrogated and tortured. He knew the scenario in his head wouldn't be that far off from the truth. The fear of abandonment, and what it meant in the long run, gave Mack the extra *oomph!* He needed.

"Heave… huff… pant…" they were exhausted by the time they finally caught up. Yu-Lee was just about to try and get in when she found herself rather disoriented. She gasped, and the train whistled again. It took her a moment to settle down and recognise why her feet were no longer touching the ground. Mack had whisked her up into his arms, and just as she comprehended this, she found herself in mid-air being thrown into the caboose. *Thump!* She hit the baseboard hard. She winced, and Mei helped get her out of the way.

Mack was falling behind slightly as the train continued picking up speed, but he was determined to make it regardless of the odds. Then he fazed out; he didn't remember it very well afterwards. Somehow his legs went even faster, a fall would have sent him brutally skidding through the snow. Suako could barely believe just how fast he was going. It seemed surreal as they watched; he caught up and grabbed the metal bar of the door with one arm and reached for Kato to help him in with the other. They managed to get him in just before they entered then tunnel. *Wham!* They slammed the door shut, and the darkness encompassed them all.

Mack's eyes were blazing with intensity as the adrenaline coursed through his veins. He felt like he'd just woken up from a dream. He stood there shaking, and he couldn't stabilise himself, his legs quivered. When Kato released his hold on Mack he nearly tumbled over. Kato grabbed him again to keep him from falling. Mack's breaths were deep, and heavy. "Are you ok?" Jenko asked. Mack blinked speechlessly. A moment later he gathered his thoughts, and his breath, enough for him to speak, "I'm fine." The much-delayed answer came in a vague tone. They sat him down. Mack then couldn't help but laugh. The adrenaline had wiped his mind for a moment, and he found it extremely humorous at the time. He was an inch away from captivity, and he found that funny too. Everyone knew he was fine.

Masumi had found a lamp, which she'd lit just before they went into the pitch-black tunnel. The light was dim, but at least they could see. Small vents to either side of the train let in the now potent scent of the burning coal. Minor amounts of the smoke came in threw the vent; the smell was sickening and made them all feel light-headed and dizzy.

The cab was nearly full of crates, so the amount of room left was uncomfortable to suit nine people. Needless to say, it wasn't as if they'd had an option upgrading to first class seats, or even coach for that matter. It was chilly at first, but they were so close together that their body heat soon made the entire cabin quite warm. Mei, Suako and Jenko ravaged through the crates. They had been empty so far, but they kept looking.

"Well, we be home free," Kato grinned, "S'all thanks t' you boss," he patted Mack on the back, "smooth sailin' from 'ere till Tomakomai." Mack nodded at Kato, "Thanks Kato," he said between his uncontrollable chuckles that were just then dissolving. Leaning against crates or walls, most of them sank down to the hard floor to rest.

There was a constant rattle, as the treasure hunters went through the crates. One by one empty boxes were thrown aside. Yu-Lee had to lean slightly to one side or the other as she sat, trying to get comfortable, for she'd bruised her tailbone when she'd landed. The thrashing Yu-Lee had withstood had left her sore all over, and all she wanted was to rest. Jenko was frustrated with not finding anything in the crates yet, so he tossed one last crate aside and then went to sit with Yu-Lee. He took off his vest and gave it to her to sit on; her sore rump was more then grateful.

Slowly Yu-Lee was drifting off with her head comfortably situated on Jenko's shoulder, when suddenly, "Jackpot!" Mei bellowed out of the blue. An indiscreet noisy rumble of several crates crashing to the floor followed her impulsive disruption. Yu-Lee just about jumped out of her skin. She was finally agitated enough that she had to restrain herself from yelling apprehensively at Mei. *Fump!* A heavy carton hit the only clear space on the crowded floor. Goosebumps lifted on Yu-Lee's skin, and her eye began to twitch.

"Look everyone. They're a few bags of stuff... Let's see, what do we have?" Mei squinted her eyes to try and read the already poorly written labels of stitched bags in the dimly lit cart. "Figs, dried apricots... pecans, cashews and... raisins," she placed the five bags down. "Guess the Imperial army fighters think they're too good for dried fruit n' nuts," Mack coherently laughed. Yu-Lee, now to antsy to sleep, snatched the figs and greedily ate them.

The natural sugars gave them a boost; compact nutrients gave them much needed energy and strength. They munched away happily as they settled in for the night. The dull drone of the wheels on the rails became strangely soothing. Though it was still rather early, the day had been long, and huddled together, they slept soundly.

Vince found himself the first to wake the following day. He pondered over the time, and he wondered if it was still night. There was no way to tell, though he still felt tired. He rubbed his bloodshot eyes and groaned. Vince looked around to see that everyone else was still sleeping like babies. Suako had been using his leg as a pillow, so he tried his best not to disturb her as he loosened his coat and scoured through his pockets. He wiggled his journal free, and pulled it out.

"Dear Journal,

We're on our way to the Imperial Capitol City of Tomakomai. We've snuck aboard a train. It's travelling beneath the earth in some man-made tunnel. Since we're underground I can't even tell what time it is. It's probably the middle of the night, everyone else is still sleeping. The exhaust fumes from the coal they're are eking in here are giving me a nasty headache.

Food has been hard to come by. We found a few half-eaten bags of some nuts and dried fruit, they should last us until we get to Tomakomai. I don't know what to expect when we get there. I've built it up I my mind to be some extraordinarily grandiose place. I suppose time will tell.

This trip has proven to be much more then I have ever thought it would be. I have seen things that no one could ever fathom... I have to stop and ask myself sometimes if they actually ever happened. Then I look at Suako, or one of the others, and see the same questions in their eyes and I know it was true because they saw it too. I wonder if anyone will ever believe that the stories we'll have to share aren't just fabricated delusions?

The power that this planet, no, that life in general, wields, makes me wonder what else can be done by the hand of man? It also makes me worry, what if the C.D.F.P. learned how to use it? The life force of the Universe is open to everyone Yu-Lee has told me, because everyone is part of it. If they learned how to gather the energy I can only imagine the terrible things they would try and do with it. Their greed exceeds that of anyone, or any other group, that I've ever known. It brings extreme disgust to me.

I'm sorry for my vagueness leading up to this. I am still in a bit of shock over it. I'm not sure if it's over the act itself, or the one who did it. Mack saved us from a storm. Yes, I know that 'wow whoop-de-do, what's so incredible about that' is the reaction to that right? Well than listen to how he did it and you'll know why. ...

...And so now we're here. My hands are cold, but other than that everything is fine. Suako's sleeping with her head on my leg. She looks like an angle. I have to wonder about her poor mind sometimes though. She's been through so much sorrow. I suppose we all have endured some kind of torture from The Company, but... none so literally 'tortured' as Suako." Vince put his pen down and brushed some hair free from her warm pink cheek. His expression was grim- eyes lost in disillusion. He pulled back his hand and picked up his pen again.

"I have to wonder what some of the injections they had forcefully given her did. Her emotional stability is as rickety as a picket fence. One moment she's fine, the next her eyes are empty and she distances herself from everyone... She also sometimes seems like she forgets everything that the C.D.F.P. did to her, but she may have blocked out those images as a sort of self-defence mechanism, an overly happy naive artificial personality takes over her. In fact, it wasn't until after I saw her in Okagwa that she first dropped down that shield. It was like meeting her for the very first time then. I can't explain it...

Another thing... I've been reluctant to mention it. I guess once it written it becomes more of a reality for me. Suako has always seemed to have a low immune system in some regards. Ever since I first knew her she's had a deep growl of a cough. It's become worse lately. Also, random fainting spells, not severe, but still, they... they scare me. ...

...Kairu is looking more and more like a leader everyday. He has grown inside. And I suppose that's all there is to report up until this point.

Sincerely,

Vince."

Vince stuck his pen in a nook by the spine of the journal. He then closed the book and tucked it back away in his jacket pocket. The callus on his middle finger was beginning to ache from the pen having had pressed against it. It throbbed deeply as if the pain was coming from the bone, he attempted to settle it by rubbing it with his thumb, but it only made it worse.

Vince's lower back had a gap between it and the wall, and his spine felt as if tiny needles had been placed in it. An annoying twinge became agonisingly present at the slightest movement. He was tired, but his pains refused him rest, so he sat there miserably caught in transit.

Suako flinched and startled him. Her sleep was violent, and Vince could only imagine what taunted her in her sleep, though he didn't even want to try to picture it; he felt helpless when it came to aiding her. Indecipherable babble conjured between her slurring lips, then more flinching, and what Vince made out to be, punches and kicks of struggle. Whatever she fought against in her troubled mind, her efforts seemed to be futile against them. A dark unsettling feeling swept over Vince, he couldn't pin point why, but it was there.

Closing his eyes Vince prayed for sleep, but the harder he tried the more he failed. Coaxing himself to sleep was as beneficial towards falling asleep as trying to recite a sonnet, it simply didn't work. His body was jiggling from side to side as the bounding transport wobbled about. Like a zombie, he just sat there in a vexatious mind frame. It got to the point where tired urges led to making him quite pissed off at circumstance.

I'm so tired. God damned train, stop shaking! ... *My back is fucking killing me. When will this be over?* Not soon enough. *You can say that again...Why can't I just sleep?* Maybe if you stop talking to yourself it would help. *Then shut up.* Shut up! *Shut up! Urgh! This isn't working...* *And what the hell is that freaking hissing!*

His cranium-concealed banter was starting to drive him slightly wonky. He rubbed his temples, but the pressure of his fingers increased as his headache persisted. The hissing sound wasn't helping, in fact, it was getting louder. He didn't know what it was, and he didn't care, he only wanted it to go away. He was tensing up as a bitter irritation, pent up within, grew. Vince just wanted some peace for his overactive psychological state.

Hiss! It just kept coming. Vince was about to erupt but found that his mind was suddenly whisked free of all prior concern as a new situation presented itself. Sudden circumstances called for his immediate attention. He was at full alert.

There was a noise-drowning suction sound that was followed by an ear wrenching squeal. Vince held his hands over his ears, and everyone else came to life at that point. The tunnel was being torn up from above them. Vince could hardly believe his eyes, snow dumped in threw the newly forming holes. A red light began to flash inside the cabin.

Everyone was in a bit of a panic. It was unreal; they could see up through the vent past the sheer veil of falling snow to a star shinning between the newly forming clouds above. Something was *very* wrong. The hissing and squealing took over all thought. Vince jumped when Suako reached up to squeeze his hand. He looked at her for a second then back up through the vent. It was hard to make out much between the metal bars. The train was speeding up. Mack tried to stand up, and he could feel the intense pull on him to fall backward at the speed they were going. The others followed step to get up onto their feet.

"What's going on?" Masumi yelled over the overpowering strength of the hiss. "I don't know!" Kairu yelled back. They stabilised on each other to keep from falling over, it was petrifying. Gusting wind-flow surged inward and began to ravage the cabin mercilessly. Crates toppled over, and hair blocked eyes; the glow of red stained everything in its tinge.

Mack climbed over the crates and pulled himself up to the vent shaft. His eyes dried out from the wind blowing into them, his eyelids batted up and down to try and keep the moisture in. He peered out through the slant of an open left eye. They drove threw an enormous forced opening, and then, he saw them.

Pillars of wind circling round and round reached up from the ground all the way to the hazy grey sky above. He could actually *see* the wind, that once invisible force held sustenance now. Snow flew in at his face temporarily stunning him. He quickly whipped it away. Between the breaks in the tunnel he watched the tornadoes as they wrecked the land. they brought destruction to everything in their path, eating up objects and then spitting them back out with tremendous force.

The devastation they were causing was immense. The odd tree, that stood amongst the nearly uninterrupted stretch of snowy fields, was uprooted ruthlessly. Mack watched as it plucked one up and took it for a spin. He wondered what could cause these twisters, and then he thought of the C.D.F.P. and the global warming process a scientist once told him about...

"You see Mack, the pollution emitted from burning coal produces a gas called 'carbon dioxide'. This gas rises up, and then gets trapped in the atmosphere. It works the same way as that greenhouse I showed you earlier, it traps heat. So, when it's sunny, it captures the heat and takes longer to part with it then clean air... Hmm? The effects you ask? Well, from my observation it manipulates weather patterns. It may induce some severe uncommon weather, but only time will tell. It also has been the cause of our deteriorating oxygen..."

Mack remembered his words well. The man had been in a lab accident, a chemical fire, just two weeks later, with all his research destroyed by the flames. Mack now wondered if there had really been an accident. Mack cursed the Company. He returned his attention back to the *'severe uncommon weather'* in front of him. It was sweet justice that these twisters would come at the toxic gas producing train; it just happened to be bad luck that they were on it at that specific time.

Mack's attention was on that single tree that had been taken up into the funnel. He watched as three of the twisters tossed it between them. Then snow flew into his eyes again, and Mack wiped it away with his forearm. Looking back out with a wet face he tried to find the tree with his eyes again, but he didn't see it, until it was *too* late...

There was no time to move. Mack's eyes bulged, and then it came! Slamming against the train with it's side, it rumbled the entire cart. Sharp thin branches with their still intact twigs shoved their way in threw the vent slates, and one of them pierced Mack's left eye. Mack let out a ghastly sound that they could hear even over the howling storm winds. He fell backward lifting his hands up to cover his bloody eye. Jenko crawled over to Mack.

Then train was speeding up even more, trying to outrun the whirlwinds hailing from the heavens. The twisters screamed, and the high-pitched shrieking deafened listeners. "Stay away from the vents!" Vince yelled after catching his first glimpse of Mack. His voice was a blur, if it was heard at all by anyone. Blood poured out from under his cupped hand, *red tears* Vince thought, then shuttered and held Suako tighter.

The bolts holding the roof down started to creak; they sound of the screeching metal tearing away above now had competition. The thin roof began to wriggle itself free. *Ping!* A bolt flew loosely away. "What's happening?!" Masumi screamed in utter terror. Kairu threw her to the floor and flung himself on top of her as a human shield. "It'll be ok!" he called out. Tears streamlined down her pale cheeks.

Ping! Ping! More bolts came loose and left with the velocity of a bullet. One from the bolts, from the front of the cart, came free and pierced through the metal wall into the back corner of their cabin, sparkled in the red light and then, *Ping! Ping!* Exited out the other side. Yu-Lee ducked down with her hands over her head for protection.

The wobbling of the metal sheet above their heads did so with distinctive sound. It looked like it fought to stay attached to the cabin, but the twister fought back, and it didn't play fair. It savagely pulled at the metal roofing, and as the metal sheeting lifted up and down it let in waves of blustery snow. The battle raged on for several minutes, the roof was not going to give in so easily. One of the train carts behind them was lifted up off the tracks, and carried off, long before their roof would even consider defeat; triumphantly it seemed to hold on.

One frustrated blow finally uprooted it and it flew off. The lamp flew off the crate it had been perched on, and crashed, throwing glass shards down like rain over Kato and Mei. The glass tore at their coats, which they'd thrown over themselves just before the shit had hit the fan. Crates flew up and out, twirling as they did. A few of their packs nearly flew away but Yu-Lee pounced on them before they got away.

Windburn dulled the senses of the perceptive skin. Only the crackling of dried skin brought forth any source of sensation, and that even went easily unnoticed. Pounding dreadful nippy flashes of wind gusts made the epidermis tingle, until eventually turning it numb.

The stoplight red was no longer contained inside the cramped space. Each of them tried to find something to hold on to. Looking up they could see straight up to blue skies; they were directly in the eye of the storm! To the sides wind circled around the calm centre, it seemed very odd. Suako and Vince looked up eagerly with enriched hearts. Most of the others hadn't caught the view, determined to cover themselves from any free-falling dangers that may find their way into the open caboose.

It didn't last long; blue sky was disappearing from their line of sight. Green, brown and white hues imbedded within the grey funnel, obstructing the sky. The velocity of the wind was speeding up, and the sheer power was scary. It was starting to pull at them, into the fury of its wrathful gusts. Their bodies began to lift, only anchored down with the minor hold of grasping hands. Suspended in mid air they felt temporary weightlessness, and it was as exhilarating as it was devastatingly frightful. "I love you!" Vince yelled to Suako, conceiving of his more than probable death. She couldn't have possibly heard him in all the commotion, but she could swear she had.

Thud! Against the metal they fell, and the light faded. Only the agitating red light, now flickering horribly, provided any light for them. The warmth of the concealed tunnel thawed skin quickly. Aches and sharp dry awareness returned to their bodies. As much to their discomfort, as it was to their pleasure it came back, for the one good thing about pain was that it was the one assurance that they were *still* alive.

As much as the twisters spun around, their mental conditions twirled about, the disorientation was strong. Every move felt odd and slightly out of their control. Limbs were still shaky under their guidance. They shivered and twitched as their nerves were revalidating their bodies. Odd prickly vibrations under the skin made them feel like blobs of cytoplasm, feeling all the functions of a cell at work take place.

An unforgettable moan from Mack ended everyone's self-directed attention; Mack was injured *badly.* Kato and Mei stood up, and glass tingled as it fell off them and hit the floor. They made their way over to Mack quickly. Jenko had been by Mack's side the entire time, he had saved his *life.* "Jenko! Is he ok?" Mei asked looking down with a wrinkled brow in slight horror. "He's is rough shape…" Jenko replied morbidly. "Shi'… Mack…" Kato looked down sympathetically.

"Yu-Lee?" Jenko called over to the mangled mess of bags and protruding legs in the corner. They moved, and an undefined noise came from below them as she began to stir. Kairu pulled himself free of the grasping-shaking wreck Masumi, who clung to the floor still yet for dear life. Kairu went to help Yu-Lee, lifting the bags free, off her covered body, and offered her a hand up. On her feet, Yu-Lee felt light-headed, but it soon settled. She grabbed at Kairu's hand and balanced on him as she lifted a hand to her head.

"Wha..." Yu-Lee began to say, then shook her head and regrouped. "What is it Jenko?" she asked a few seconds later. "I need a cloth for making a bandage," Jenko replied. "S... sure," she nodded, and then turned to look for one in the baggage. In spinning around, she engaged the instability she had before and toppled over, luckily landing mostly on the soft cushy baga, but she also bumped against something blunt which she grunted about. Kairu helped her back up. "Thank you," she said notching her neck. With a little body shake she straightened herself out and went back to look, *carefully*.

Emerging, successfully and without another fall, she went over to Jenko and handed him the cloth. Uneasily, Jenko moved Mack's hand away from his face, the muscles on the left side of Mack's face clenched tightly. Jenko hesitantly pressed the fabric gently down on the gory mess, the cloth's pure-white color absorbed the blood, migrating it to velvet red. Mack's hand tightened to a fist, soaked in crimson blood, and protruding veins stood out on his fisting arm. *Drip! Drip!* As he squeezed the blood dripped onto the floor. Suako and Vince just sat there watching with sympathetic hearts.

Mack eventually passed out; there was a final grunt and he lost consciousness, and his tensed muscles went limp. They were grateful for that at least. Jenko used some water to clean the wound, the gushing had finally subsided. Then he got Yu-Lee to get him find a fresh cloth. She handed him a small cotton washcloth. Jenko used some twine and tied it down over Mack's eye.

None of them could get back to sleep after the terrifying events. Masumi had released her death grip on the floor, but she was still in shock. They all sat around silently, nothing seemed to be the right thing to say. The red light continued to flicker, and the open cart was getting cold. They put on their coats and leaned against the walls. The space was now wide open, cleared of the once cramping wooden crates.

Mei leaned her head against Kato. Then pulled it back away, "Ouch!" the silence breaker drew everyone's attention. She had a minor nick on her cheek which she touched with her hand then pulled it away to see a petite speckle of red. Kato tried turned his head to look at Mei, and then knew why she'd jumped away from him... *he couldn't turn his head*. "Kato, you're neck! Oh shit!" Mei looked at him fretfully.

A piece of the shattered glass had wedged its way into the crook of Kato's neck. He hadn't even felt it until now, and it wasn't bleeding much by any means. The muscle appeared as if it were a base to a trophy. The base incision was large, and forming up from the base the glass came to a point, making a pyramid. Mei ogled at it.

"Ya' need to ge' it out," Kato said, head facing straight forward. "Ok..." Mei got on her knees and prepared to pull it free. She reached up, nervously biting down on her bottom lip. Mei placed her fingers on it. "D... Does it hurt?" she couldn't help but ask first. "Nope," he replied, swallowing his fear, eyes forward. Mei pulled, and

Kato didn't even flinch. It came free with a gushy sound, which disgusted Masumi. It left a shallow two-inch gash, though Kato couldn't feel any pain. It had missed the nerve they figured. Not knowing what else to do she handed Kato the glass piece.

Yu-lee waddled over to him on her knees. She had a metal coil, which she'd straightened, and had some thread, which she untangled from one of her sweaters. Kato eyed the glass. "Here, I'll sow you up," she said attaching the thread to the improvised needle. Mei scooted aside to give them room. Kato looked down to try to see the gash before she began. *Stitch, stitch, stitch...*

Uncomfortable hunger leered inside Masumi, but she refused to say anything. It felt selfish at the time. Oddly, she almost felt a bloating sensation in her stomach. The hunger was playing tricks on her mind. Her stomach grumbled, and she crossed her arms and leaned her head back against the wall with eyes drifting shut, trying to ignore it.

Kairu wondered when Mack would wake up. There was a puddle of blood that his head lay in, and although Jenko was cleaning that up, it smeared across the metal ridges in the floor. The grotesque images revolved around in Kairu's mind vividly. *Flick! Flick!* The red light finally went out and they were enclosed in a darkness that reflected on circumstance perfectly...

Whooo-Whooo! The whistle sounded. They had reached Tomakomai at last.

Commitment calls for self sacrifice...
The natural world is collapsing... Are we too late?

Chapter 21: Tomakomi

They surfaced from the underground tunnel, and the bright light of early morning stung their eyes. After what may as well have been an eternity after the red light dimmed out, there was finally light. It took a while for eyes to adjust accordingly, and Mack was even beging to stir. After their eyes adjusted they could see a light smog covered the sky like a fog. The black of the burning coal trailed upward.

Vince looked up, and he felt like he might be looking unto heaven. It was so large and grand, more so than he had expected. It made him feel very small. In this foreign land, sitting there, Vince looked up and felt his breath leave him.... *Tomakomai was unreal.*

Mountainous building stretched on and on, further than the eye could see. Sitting in the train cabin, Vince couldn't see the bases of the buildings, nor even begin at this point to imagine them. The tops seemed to touch the sky they were so tell. The buildings were all reflective with glass windows, between their concrete structures, which sparkled like crystals under the bright sun. Structures of various heights towered upward, and many neon signs labelled the buildings. Tomakomai was quite the spectacle to new eyes.

One place stood out in particular, it lay ahead, and was in the centre of all of the other buildings. It was taller, much taller, than the others, and at *least* five times as wide. Something about the way the light reflected on it shone a spectrum of orange, pink, yellow and green that captivated Vince. The colors danced as the train moved him closer towards the building. Gold tints twinkled here and there radiantly, and he was lost in the bliss of colour.

Suako looked on at the city; the immensity of the central building was unsettling. She wondered how anyone could ever construct such a thing. It had lacked feeling, it stood cold, and intimidating. The building commanded power, and obedience.

Had they spoken about it, she'd have known Yu-Lee and Mei looked at it with the same regard. Masumi had never thought about it. It was always just a big city to her, some happy memory of a childhood excursion, but seeing it now, after all they'd been through, it struck her for what it really was. Kairu didn't know what to think as he looked on idly without prejudgement. He simply absorbed the sights.

Jenko peered up to look, and at the same time, he took in a nice clean breath of air; it was revitalizing to be under a dome again. He wondered how this 'City of Light' could be so different from the dark depths of Torusan. Mack strained his right eye to see, though from the floor not much presented itself in his line of vision, but he had seen the glorious light. Mei stared at the city with one thing in her mind... *revenge*.

Vince darted toward the vent, and he pulled himself up and looked out the slits. Sparkling buildings glittered the way leading up to the climatic city. He could see marvellous homes around the outskirts of the city. The houses had frosted windows, and were mostly three stories high. Beautiful yellows, rich maroons, cactus greens and soft blue hues colored the houses splendidly. Parks that were filled with glorious hedges, benches with black metal that curved into slender vine-like patters, and trees of all sorts pruned to look perfect. These parks were interspersed here and there as they based through the residential area, and even in the winter, covered in snow, they contained a few people walking through them. Vince could see the people in their extravagant clothing; fur coats, cashmere, suede, leather boots, wool hats and gloves. Sparing no expense, these people got the life that everyone deserved to get.

Then, further inward into the metropolis, minor factories from which bellows of white steam and smoke rose, scattered around freely. They were quaint in their setting, and from these factories, many roads began to open to the rest of the city. Vince was flabbergasted by all the automobiles, back in Torusan, only in Grid One back in Torusan had he ever seen an accumulation of them, but this was *much* different. There were hundreds of cars that he could see from the distance he was at. Yet further inward towards the city center began the tall building of mirror glass, and finally, the central mega-building from which the entire city spiralled outward.

Vince inhaled the images through his eyes; it was like a breath of fresh air for his soul. The images kindled his heart. He had previously imagined that he'd be coming up to a dark place from which hatred spawned from. But this was no such kingdom of evil, at least not visually.

Vince felt his sleeve puff in as a gentle hand placed itself down on his upper arm. Suako decided to share the view. "It's so beautiful…" she said in a breathless exhale. Her eyes glossed over; this was a moment she would *never* forget.

Mesh fencing obstructed their view suddenly. *Whooo-Whooo!* The whistle went. Then it repeated itself again, and they could feel that they were slowing down. The train station approached not far in the distance, the same deep dark green covered this one too. "Time to leave," Jenko said getting to his feet.

Jenko and Kato helped stand Mack up. Their leader was light-headed and slightly woozy. The others collected their things and prepared to disembark. Mei yanked at the large metal door, her muscles flexed and popped the veins to the surface and she exuded the strength needed to pull. *Twang!* It finally came loose and opened. The sudden momentum of it practically dragged Mei along with it. She regained her footing quickly, then swiped her fingers through her short hair, the intense red of it highlighted by the magnifying sun.

A gust of snow blew inside causing squints all around. The scenery passed by still with much speed, and they knew had to wait a little longer before they could jump. The cushion to their fall would have to be the snow, which all and all, didn't seem *that* bad. They would have to judge wisely, not jumping while the train was going too quickly, but also not waiting until the train was too close to the station. Either fault could be fatal.

The smearing of objects in the eyes slowly stopped as the train slowed, things stopped flashing by, and finally took shape. There were plenty of trees nearby to take cover in. The whistle blew again. Mei stuck her head out to look forward and could see the station was approaching. There was no time left to wait for the train to slow down; they had to jump now.

"Everyone's let's go!" Mei yelled over the clanking metal of the wheels as they chugged along. Mei helped everyone out. The falls weren't as soft as they had anticipated; bruises were sure to show up the next day. Jenko and Kato got Mack out as best they could, cushioning his fall. Lastly Mei fled the cabin, tumbling into the hard snow below.

Their bodies felt stiff, and each of them would have loved to have just lain there and recuperated, but it was not an available option. They gathered their scattered luggage and headed for the sanctity of the trees. Mack, under the natural light, looked quite pale, and rather yellow. The two men helped him carefully away, disappearing like shadows, they vanished into the trees.

A safe distance away, laying Mack down, they were finally able examine him properly. Jenko removed the bandage; it was messy. "Mack... Mack we need you to open your eye," Jenko told Mack. With slight apprehension he complied. The lid opened up, and Jenko covered Mack's right eye with his hand. "What can you see?" the grim question came from Jenko. His mutilated eye searched around. "Nothing," Mack replied, then closed his eye. There was a solemn feel in the air. "Mack..." Mei lips parted as she drearily looked to him. Suako took his hand in hers. "We're so sorry..."

Jenko re-bandaged Mack's eyes to prevent infection. Yu-Lee had pillaged the train for the nuts before she'd left, and she fed Mack once Jenko was done. He needed to regain his strength; as unpleasant as it was, they *had* to keep going. Mack would have to heal up quickly, bite the bullet, and continue onward. For now, though, they'd let him grieve his blind left eye.

Pain gripped at Mack occasionally. It was dull mostly but the odd sharp needle like throb would occur, and those spasms were the most discomforting of all.

Their first bit of business would be to find some medication to prevent infection. Being winter, there weren't any herbs freely about to pick. They'd have to search within the city limits. That afternoon Mack declared he was ready to go, and though they were weary with his discoloration, he insisted they leave.

Mack denied any help, he would walk on his *own*. and he was persistent. They finally caved and let him do it. Besides the frequency of his walking into objects his peripheral vision could no longer pick up, he did quite well on his own. Yu-Lee continued to have him fed, as stubborn as he was to have his way, she was just as forceful to feed him. His color improved by it, and she was not one he found easy to trifle with; her willful nature was too strong.

Along the outskirts of the city limits they saw no one. Still they hid in the nearby brush as they walked, they had come too far had they come to risk it all now. Suako kept her gun handy. She took the rear and kept an eagle eye watch in constant motion of all directions. Kato watched the front with a silenced pistol; there was no room for discovery in their plans.

They followed along the train tracks, and after twenty minutes of forest bound hiking, they reached the end of the fencing. With dedicated observation they checked out the area. No one was close, a few people in a park ahead, but they were specks in the distance. They prepared themselves to cross into the city. Masumi halted them.

"Wait!" she held out her arm in front of Kairu who was just about to go. "What is it?" Kairu asked startled. Masumi huddled the group together. "What is it Masumi?" Mei seconded the question. "It just dawned on me, you can't enter the city. Not wearing those clothes. We'll be noticed," Masumi explained. They looked at themselves and supposed she was right; their clothes were torn and dirty from their travels. "She's right," Yu-Lee said gazing at her robes, "Good eyes little one," she smiled commendably.

"Ok –S' what d' we do?" Kato looked up, rather peeved at the complication. "Well..." Jenko started and then fell silent, "I, uh, I dunno," he turned away and scratched his head. "What if," Masumi began, eyes envisioning her plan, "What if I go in and I can get you the garments? You could just wait here until I come back. I should be back by nightfall..." she suggested. "It's risky," Kairu cut her short. "But it's a good idea," Vince commented, seeing no other way, "besides, she's dressed like everyone else here and she didn't get her clothes messed up in the fighting. It isn't all that risky, really." "I agree, It's the best option," Mack spoke up. Kairu uneasily said no more. "Good, it's settled then." Masumi pulled her loot bag free of her backpack.

Before she ran off Kairu pulled her aside, his guardian instinct for her was in full gear. "Listen Masumi, make sure you go to different shops, that much for that many different people, you know sizes and that, well it'd look suspicious, with the war on. Be safe," he hugged her. A warm tingling sensation overcame Masumi. "I will Kairu.

I'll be back soon," her eyes speaking deeper meaning than he saw. As she left, Vince stopped her a few feet away from the others, and they discussed something no one else could hear.

Off she went. Dark against the snow, she quickly got across the open area. Up the hill she climbed, crossed the train tracks, and circled around the fence. Running at full tilt she reached the start of suburbia. Between houses she entered, and from there she left Kairu's sight.

Yu-Lee, without openly admitting it, couldn't have been happier about the delay; it kept Mack from overexertion. They waited in the trees, feeling useless. There was nothing to do but prepare their gear, which took no time at all, and once that was done, there was nothing to do but wait. And wait they did...

Not until the wee hours of the morning did Masumi return. At sunset, before she came back, they watched as light streamlined across Tomakomai. The city turned to gold, glorious, brilliant and shinning. It reflected gold onto the surrounding area, the warm hue turned everything it touched to beauty. Yu-Lee got to her knees and began chanting, tears running down her round cheeks. It was a blessing, which each of them recognised it as so in their own way.

Later, Kairu started up his mini Jujitsu class again to pass the time. Suako and Mei had fun play fighting one another, testing out the new movements. It was quite entertaining to watch as well, for the others. As it got dark, and stars painted their constellations in the sky, they sat in a circle talking amongst themselves. They were hungry, there hadn't been much left to eat, and most of what they had was given to Mack to give his body the energy to recuperate. Yu-Lee wouldn't have had it any other way, and in the end nor would have anyone else.

Sounds kept gun fingers alert. There were animals, *actual* animals, here; they weren't disfigured or starving at all. They were alive and vibrant, and they played together, not trying to kill each other for food. Mother birds nurtured their freshly hatched eggs. Squirrels giggled and toppled about, chasing each other in circles. They even saw a few floppy eared rabbits hop by them, that were just as white as the snow they hopped on. Life was serene here. It spoke of the natural, or rather the more natural, way of the world. What it was. What it *should* be.

It was cold, but bearable. They had seen colder days. They had moved slightly further back into the treeline and started a fire after the sun had gone down. It crackled in a soothing way, and glowed magnificently. They sat around, starring into it, each reflected on themselves at times when conversation faded. Vince had pulled out his journal and fastidiously recorded his first image of Tomakomai into it, he only wished he'd had color to elaborate it. Jenko worked on his map while his memory was still fresh.

"Do we have a plan, Mack?" Suako asked sitting next to him. "I think so," he said. Everyone's ears perked up. "I was thinking we'd make our way into the city. I want to check out the influence of the C.D.F.P. here. I have a feeling they've wormed their way in. After we scout, I want to go to that big place in the centre of the city. We'll see some action there," he stopped to cough, then cleared his throat, "... I'm sure of it. It's not much I know, but I don't want to make this complicated. Simple is best," he hoarsely coughed again. "... And Kazuo?" Suako sheepishly asked. His right eye zeroed in on her. "I can only hope..." a pause, and the eye idly drifted away.

Crunch! Crunch! Crunch! Someone was coming. Suako drew her gun and did a 180 as she stood. It was Masumi, and the young girl's eyes bulged nearly free of her skull at the sight of the gun pointed directly at her. She dropped the parcels at the sudden ambush. Suako lowered her weapon, "Oh Masumi, I'm sorry... Here let me get those," Suako collected the brown paper parcels, wrapped and twine-tied, from where they had landed. Masumi breathed a sigh of relief, her heart pithier pattering inside her uncontrollably "N, no It's alright. I should've said something... Let me help..."

Gathered up between the two of them, they presented the articles to everyone else. Before opening all of them Masumi took one out of the lot to be first. She let Mack open it, for whenever she had been sick her father would give her a gift to make her feel better. She instinctively wanted to help him feel better, and it had always lifted her own spirits. The paper was torn away to reveal a conglomeration of decadent foods.

Eyes ogled, and mouths salivated, at the assortment before them. They had smoked salmon, smoked ham, a real expense, pork was so rare, and some canned sardines, which could last for a long time preserved in their tins. Then there were two loaves of freshly baked sunflower seed bread, and vegetables galore, potatoes, celery, carrots, string beans, broccoli, to name a few. Some fruits, tomatoes, a few lemons, oranges, apples which were dipped in a caramel glaze, cherries, and a few bags of nuts; after having some on the train Masumi found she'd been craving more. Then some *real* treats, Masumi had gone all out. She'd got butter, salt, pepper, sugar, white, brown *and* maple, a few of her favourite herbs, including rosemary, and a gourmet box of truffles. To top it all off she'd managed to fudge her age and brought two bottles of red wine for Jenko and, her pride and joy of it all, a small wooden box...

Speechlessly starring at it, all the felt to be in a dream. Masumi picked up the box and offered it to Mack. "Here. It's for you, A get well present," she smiled cheerily, with a sense of pride. Placing it in his hands Masumi then lowered to her knees to watch him open it. Mack pulled the small metal latch forward and then pulled open the lid. A sweet aroma slid out and tickled his nose. He closed his eye and enjoyed it as it tantalised him. "Cigars... mmm, thank you," He looked to her happily. She could see the weariness in his face. "Enjoy," she smiled.

Then feast commenced. Pork flaked from the bone with ease, butter smeared across the bread, toasted above the fire, and melted into every nook and cranny. Jenko was reminded of Quan as he ate away at the salmon, sprinkled with dill and drenched in lemon juice. Apples crunched and the caramel slowly saturated their mouths with flavourful sweetness. Seasoning highlighted everything. Wine was passed about like the elixir of life. Lastly came the memorable truffles, eaten and slowly savoured. The feast went on just short of two hours. Happy people with full tummies now sat around the encampment; it was the calm before the storm.

Once the food had been put away out came the other packages. Ripping off the paper and twine revealed briefcases, queer looks glared at them. "Well, open them up will you!" Masumi excitedly urged them on. Without question they did. *Snap!* The latches popped open. A scent, not common to the newer generation of the East Green Continent, poured out from inside. It was a factory 'brand new' kind of smell. It was unique, and they thought they liked it.

From there they pulled their new clothes out, the new fabrics slide across their skin; they were fine, very *fine*. The group examined them. "They're suits, business suits," Masumi explained to them, "We're going into the business sector, so I thought these would be best," she looked at them with anticipation. *"Weeelll? Try them on!"* For her amusement they went and did so right away. She joined them to get on her own formal attire.

Re-appearing in the circle they looked open each other with speculating eyes. They saw each other in a different light. The men, snazzy in dark suits and loosely buttoned shirts, pulled off the get-up with surprising ability. Pants draped, the heavy material held relatively uniform shape. Their blazers added a dash of charm. The deep plum Masumi had chosen for Kato was a royal match.

The ladies came out feeling the snug spandex, rayon and polyester blended skirts and dress pants hugging tight against their hips. From there, pencil skirts came to the knee and pants hung long and swayed seductively as they walked. Blouses with jackets went with pants suits, and formfitting sweaters with cardigans topped off the skirt ensembles. All together they were a fleet of 'mock employees'.

"Hey not bad," Mei said checking herself out, adoring the feeling of the pants as they glided across her skin. Suako straightened the collar of her blouse. Other than slightly gruff around the face, the guys looked great. Masumi had even found a black eye patch for Mack to compliment everything. "Hey, Masumi, great find!" Suako smiled as she saw Mack's eye patch. "Oh yea," Masumi was distracted. She found the pencil skirts a slight challenge to walk in at first. She was used she her casual clothing which allowed freedom in her stride.

Lastly Yu-Lee came from behind the trees, and she really stood out. Her raven black hair let down was long, and took years off her face. The sexy, yet subtle exposure of skin, her defined calves were elegant. Her deep violet sweater accented her amethyst eyes; she was a poised woman and she walked as one too. "Yu-Lee you look amazing!" Masumi gasped, feeling slightly envious, she desired to be as distinguished and pulled together. "Thank you," came the reply, her voice even differed to a slightly lower tone. Chills went up and down Jenko's spine.

"So, uh, we be ready?" Kato asked, struggling to adjust himself to the odd textures on his body. "No, not yet," Masumi let him know. He looked around and everyone looked all right to him. "...Why?" Masumi couldn't contain her giggles. "Hehe, your ... haha... your hair! We need to fix everyone up. Hehe, need to look professional," she explained. "Oh," he felt himself turning red having had not thought of that.

Masumi fixed everyone up, starting with subtle make up on all of the ladies. After that, she worked on their hair, she pulled Suako's hair back into a bun, and did the same for her own. Yu-Lee looked so fabulous she hesitated and then decided she would just leave it long on her. With a jelly type concoction, she slicked back and styled Mei, Kato and Mack's hair, and despite the length, simply slicked back Kairu's hair as well. Once she completed tight ponytails on Vince, and Jenko they we're finally looking the part.

Moving everything from their tattered and worn bags into the shinny leather briefcases was the last step. "Oh, so that's why you got these," Kairu said as she started shifting items from one place to another. "Hey, Masumi?" Jenko looked at her. "Huh, what?" she asked continuing to work. "How did you carry *all* of this stuff here by yourself?" It had finally dawned on him. The feast of food and nine briefcases stuffed full of clothing. There was no *way* she could have done it. In fact, he doubted anyone could, it would be too damned awkward.

"A man from one of the shops I went too lent me a trolley. He said I could bring it back today. I told him I lived on the other side of town but would be back in a week. He was quite pleasant, he had a beard like yours, only his was more salt and pepper. Anyway, he said I could return it then. So that way he won't get suspicious when I don't show up today. I figured a week was plenty..." she prattled on as she continued the migration of objects. Her actions were just as if it was any regular day in her life, quite was innocent.

Once everything was cleared from their bags, they were thrown onto the fire. *Leave no trace.* After it finished burning, they snuffed it out, and covered it with snow. With any luck it would not be found. It was time to leave.

No matter how dark the night, morning will always come.

Chapter 22: Recon

Briefcases in hand, they crossed the danger zone, exposed to the world. With haste they crossed, no one was around, and they station was far enough away. It wasn't even daybreak yet, so being seen was at minimum risk. But *being* seen meant a discommodious situation. How on earth could they explain themselves, nine businessmen and women scampering about the countryside? Indeed, they were certainly out of place. As well, complications would be harder to address, for concealing weapons within these clothes proved to be a perilous task. For now, most weapons had to be kept in the briefcases. It was not good for a sudden assault; all-the-more reason to take every precaution.

Once across, they slipped between the houses, and entered the city. It was the dawn of a new day as Masumi guided them between the endless rows of houses. Through many streets, and past many artful homes, they discovered dreams could be real. Things only imaginations could manifest on the East Green Continent came to life in this place. It felt like entering a fictional world; a chamber within their minds.

The sky was yellow when the sun began its daily rotation. The tall executive buildings, which melded with the night sky, began to reappear like water absorbing a reflection. The chameleon-like city welcomed the day. Faint sounds of motors from the city streets started up, and factories began their production lines once more; early risers were the money-makers.

For being in the midst of a civil war, the city seemed to lack the boarder control. Infiltrating couldn't have possibly been easier. They were either unconcerned about damages, and certain that their forces could demolish any enemy attack, or *very* certain that no one would dare to attack their core. Regardless of the answer, Mack thought it foolish to allow pride to blind sight them.

They passed through a shovelled walkway of one of the parks. Lovely climbing equipment for children scatted around, slides and monkey bars. The families were offered wonderful things to live here and work here, after all, a small sweet flower attracts the bees away from their nest. Envisioning the Empire growing did not take much. A second look at the swing sets found an engraving: **Compliments of C.D.F.P. Incorporation**

"So, you've bought your way in have you? Hmmp!" Kato grunted as he kept on with the rest of the crew. He told it to Mei and she spat disgustedly at the jungle gym. The C.D.F.P. was always scheming, but that much they had already known. The fact that their roots sprang from this place lessened the shock that this Utopia of a world would actually allow such a plague to wriggle its way in, and start to spread its poison thickly from here.

Mack wouldn't allow it; if this place was the only place fit on earth to save, they'd save it for those not involved. If the earth was still to crumble despite their efforts, at least they could ease the intensity of its demise. Life was too valuable to say fighting for one more day, one more hour, one more minute, or *even* one more second wasn't worth it. It *was* worth it. It may have been vengeance too, but in the end, it was for *humanity*.

From the park, down some concrete stairs, they entered a parking lot. Automobiles parked there were few, for the day was still young. There was a clank sound from inside the building the parking lot led up too, followed by a time of whizzing noise. The noise grew and grew, and then a puffy grey cloud started rising out the top of two tower smokestacks on top of the brick building. They walked past it. Back in Torusan, besides small businesses in the higher numbered grids, there wasn't much to see, but here there were real factories; machinery was for the rich.

The city air was surprisingly clear for the amount of waste emitted. A later finding had them discover ventilation that had to have led out a distance from the actual city. Large fans induced suction near all of the main factories that pulled the pollution to an exhaust at the edge of the dome. The air seemed naturally pure, unless an exhaust was close by. A smart development, yet still not eliminating the underlying source. But there was something-different even about the release of the factory output here, it wasn't anywhere near as potent, and it didn't feel as sickly to the body when inhaled. They didn't understand it.

Mack pulled them aside once they were well into the heart of the downtown region, "We split up now. Everyone goes solo. Our cover, we're surveying the area to find out whether or not the general public wishes to endorse the C.D.F.P. to build power generators here. Build off of that however you will. Low profiles, you know the drill, I won't bother with the spiel."

"At five tonight we're meeting up at a hotel Masumi scouted out for us last night. It's large so we won't have to worry about being found out. She's already reserved us the rooms. Meet in the lobby. Be punctual, we're *supposed* to be anal executives after all," He smirked, and they all chuckled. "OK, Yu-Lee, Masumi, Kairu Jenko and I are under Kairu's last name, *Hiroshu*. I'd use mine but I bet that that Yoshida has made word to watch for my name... Anyway, Mei, Kato, Vince and Suako you're under Mei's married name, *Yoshini*. Got it?" Flurried nods and several *yes* and *yep* reply answers flew at him. There was a solemn look on Mei's face, with eyes to the ground; her eyes lifted to meet his, and a slight of the head thanked him for the respect of her dead husband. "Then be there at five. Go," Mack commanded.

Before Masumi got away, Mack grabbed her arm gently. She turned and saw him looking down at her with a truly thankful expression. "I know you've spent most of the leftovers of your parents' money on us. I don't know how we can make it up to you..." he started to say. "Just try to bring down the C.D.F.P. Just do your best at that. *That* is worth more than any amount of gold to me," she interrupted. "Thank you," he bowed to her.

Ding! The door opened in to the sales counter of a metal works factory. The metal could be tasted in the air. From practical, too sculptural, they had all sorts of pieces on display for sale. The electrical whizzing of some processing machine was a droning white noise in the background. In waltzed a model, even *without* a magickal spell of glamour deception. Tight skirt around her sensual hips, Yu-Lee approached the counter where a twenty-some odd year-old man stood behind the counter, trying desperately to keep his jaw from plunging to the floor. He was her pawn from the second she shook her thick hair around her face of rose leaf complexity...

Thump! Thump! Thump! Kato waited behind a door that no one seemed to answer no matter how long he pounded on it. *Thump! Thump! Th-* "Yes sir? What is it?" Some hot shot, red in the face, employee poked his head out the door. "Hello Sir. I'm surveying the local municipal companies 'bout the building of C.D.F.P. Incorporation Reac-" He didn't get to finish his speech before the guy was calling for the manager. He told Kato to wait a minute and closed the door. Kato rolled his eyes. "This ain't f' me..." he shook his head. Changing his vocabulary, turning away slang, was becoming more of a challenge then he'd expected. It would be a *long* day...

Two down, a good start. Jenko Thought to himself as a kindly gentleman opened the door guiding Jenko out. "Come back anytime sir. And thank you for considering the people!" He was actually *thanked* for coming by. Kind people, or at least in their treatment toward him. Rub anyone the right way and they'll open-up. Jenko began to travel down the sidewalk, where salt had been sprinkled and melted wintry deposits off of pearl white snow on the sidewalk squares. Light bounced up off the melted snow puddles brightly, and only dirty patches mellowed it down. Hard working labourers passed him as he went. The click of his shinny 'Corporate Man' shoes stood out amongst the heavy thuds of work-boots. These small back streets were pleasant, the air was crisp, and the day was beautiful. He took it all in preciously. For who knew what tomorrow held in store. For today, all that mattered was the day itself...

Kairu found himself still not vocally projective, or assertive enough. He'd felt he'd come a long way from his secluded depth of self when he had left Yokutan, but apparently, he'd not changed as much as he'd felt inside. He had to call for the storeowner, those brutes working their noisy tools just didn't seem to hear him. After the initial feeling of displacement upon entering a place, once he was settled, all went well. Sitting down in the intact plastic covered seat, it crinkled beneath him, within the office he'd been scooted into. "How can I help you Mr. … ?" the man started off. He had a bushy beard and wavy grey hair pulled back. A pencil rested in the crook of his ear, though he wore a shirt and tie he looked as rough as his workers. Just as Kairu had won over the heart of Otojiro, he placed all attention on the owner, and got to him too…

Down the roads of back streets Suako walked on. There was a certain charm here, unlike when she fled the C.D.F.P. building, and entered into Torusan's garbage heap of grids through the water-main system. Back there, Suako had found herself intimidated by the trash scattered around, the towering buildings in the distance that she had left behind, and the darkness of *everything*. She had been in a city she'd never seen before, abducted from her home with her sister in a far-off land that she couldn't even remember, due to some of the experiments messing up her long-term memory. Torusan was scary, and unfamiliar. Tomakomai was unfamiliar, but inviting. She felt like a little girl again and wanted to play; she wanted the childhood she'd been robbed of. With eyes as wide as saucers, exploration was on Suako's mind, she'd excavate for questions later…

"So, ma'am, with that statement shall I presume you are for the construction?" Mei drilled. She stood, with her short-slicked hair and suit giving off a masculine appeal, even without the merciless questioning. "Uh, well... Ahem, yes I am," the lady replied almost bewildered by the intensity and strength in Mei. She was certainly efficient in her data collection. The first three people she'd interviewed so far were most uneasy, rather terrified, by her dynamic eyes. Green and sharp, they threatened like a blade.

Mei's blood was boiling. She wanted the next day to come, she wanted to finally avenge her family. Her patience was running thin for these silly side line jobs, and she had to stop and remember just to breathe. She looked up and noticed the woman almost squirming in her seat, on the verge of perspiring. *Clam yourself down!* Mei demanded of herself. "I apologise," Mei improvised, "the Intel board is breathing down our necks. It seems this 'C.D.F.P. Incorporation' is impatient to get their building permit. That's why I was so harsh," in her words she accomplished two things: An excuse for her own overwhelming emotional attack, second she managed to turn this woman's view on the C.D.F.P. The lady leaned forward, tables on her desk. "I see..."

Squeak! The old wooden door rocked on its hinges as it was pushed inward. Jewellery presented itself in unique and interesting ways, draped over ceramic models and crystals, hanging from pins in the walls, and under glass cases. Shinning stones, glowing gems, and polished pearls intertwined in fabulous silvers and gold, or strung on chains. Masumi closed the door behind her to avoid letting in the draft. The lighting was dim feeling Romanesque. Behind the counter stood the merchant.

Walking as carefully as possible in heals, *oh so awkward*, and her conforming skirt, Masumi slithered up to the counter. She knew the major factories we're being bombarded, and that the majority of people in the regular city shops used power too, in some form. Putting on an adult front, or so she hoped, she was ready to try to get some information from the common people...

Tired of hearing such high regard for the C.D.F.P. Vince took a break. He found a vendor on the street selling hot drinks, so he rummaged up some cold, for his foreign coin would give him away, and exchanged it for the brew. Frothy coffee, topped with whipped crème and cinnamon, tipped toward his lips. The hot and refreshing flavour came in and energised him. The burn of the coffee allowed him to feel his oesophagus as he drank. Vince waltzed into a nearby park and took a seat. He sipped at his coffee as he watched the coming and going of people through the park trail.

A red cardinal flew up and rested itself next to Vince, landing on the bench. Vince looked down at the bird, and it looked back. He'd never seen one before. It's bright red body and distinctive black throat melded gloriously. It seemed it to not be afraid in any manner, so Vince pulled a piece of bread from the suitcase and tore free a morsel and tossed it to the bird. Pecking away the cardinal pulled free the seeds and finally consumed the rest of the tasty tidbit. They sat peacefully together for a long while. He'd never experienced such non-hostile wildlife...

"... This way." A cold hard slam cast out the bright light. Shadows enveloped the body belonging to the voice. The dark figure, free of detail, led the way, while the echo of footsteps bounced off stone walls. Dim electric light above slowly had eyes adjust to them. There were no windows. Past the titanium door there wasn't much but stone and steel, both anonymous in the blackness. The hum of electricity, and the sloshing of flowing exposed pipes, permeated throughout. The stench of urine dominated the foul and stale air.

Around the corner came a rattle of keys, followed by a screech as a barred door pushed forward. Entering the next section of the hall the man behind Mack re-locked the caging door. "Go ahead an take your time sir," the man said. "Thank you," Mack proceeded in. Through well kept steel doors, the inmates looked to Mack. His eye was straining to see in the dim light, and he was developing a headache from it. Searching face after face, prisoner after prisoner, Mack marched down the corridor. Mack had visited another prison already. His mission varied from that of his warriors; his *true* reason for the group division...

Five o'clock rolled around faster than anyone had expected. For some it was a blessing, for others an all-too soon end to a free day. They gathered in the lobby as they'd planned. At 5:22PM the last, Mack, finally arrived. "Sorry. I got held up," Mack apologized as he walked up. "So much for punctuality," Mei rolled her eyes, the stress taking its toll on her. Kato couldn't help but laugh, there was nothing else he could do to release the tension he felt. It sprung a chain reaction, and soon everyone was laughing, as discreetly as possible due to location and status. Not everyone even knew why he or she was laughing, all they knew in the end was that it felt good.

It was time to check in. Mei and Kairu handled getting the rooms while the others sat at the end of a of the room, in a semicircle couch, which trailed just slightly away from the main lobby. They were served complimentary tea for there business there. They examined their surroundings as they waited. The marble floor was so well kept it gave off reflection. Rose trees were potted indoors, and bronze trim coiled around the room, accenting it. Scarlet paint, that tricked the eye to look like velvet, covered the walls. Paintings and tapestries hung here and there decorated the interior.

A sheen seemed to appear on everything under the soft lighting. A low fire crackled, barely heard under the mingling voices of guests and hotel workers. The fire was framed by hand carved cherry wood that hand been covered in some sort of reflective wood protector. On top of its protruding mantle rested three vases, the outer two filled with lavender and the inner one with lilies. There was a green house not a block away from the hotel that had kept them in good supply of bountiful plants and flowers.

In the centre of the circular lobby a chandelier of crystals and candles sat above the heads of passing clientele. Cascading rainbows, and water-like reflections, projected from the chandelier onto the floor and walls, just like magic. On the ceiling, from which the chandelier emerged, was an enormous and all-consuming mural. It was midnight blue, and the constellations of the stars had been carefully detailed on it in a silver that shinned. On top of it being critiqued to perfection with artistry, the dimensions of the ceiling alone drew the eye upward. In the circular lobby it domed in, and throughout the halls it fell concave.

Everything was polished in this place, not a hair was out of place. From the couch they sat upon, to the flowers, and the wardrobe of the staff, it all flowed and seemed paradisiacal. Kairu and Mei returned with keys in their hands. The click of their shoes against the floor drew back everyone's attention, which had been lost to flawless mastery.

"This place is amazing," Mei said twisting her head this way and that as she came back. "It reminds me of my old house... only *much* better," Kairu said, remembering those doors to his home which he'd examined so thoroughly as a boy.

"So, we're all good?" Mack asked standing up once they were in good ear's reach. "Yep, no problems. Our rooms are neighbours. We're in 216-" Mei started.

"And we're in 217," Kairu finished. They passed out the extra keys. "So, anything else today Mack? I'm tired," Mei said, her eyes speaking the droll truth of her words. "No. We'll talk tomorrow morning briefly before we go," he replied placing his key in an inner pocket of his blazer. "Ok, I'm leaving then. Kato, you coming?" Mei asked rubbing her dreary eyes. "Yeah, I could use a drink," he replied with just as long a face. He tossed his suit jacket over his shoulder and carried it as such. "Later," she said as they left.

Everyone dispersed from there. Mack ended up entering the room first, and alone. Everyone else sharing his room had headed out to explore the city some more. He'd taken the bags and placed them in the room, then turning on a lamp by the bedside, it lit up the room dully. With the illumination a full-length mirror, standing across the room in a corner by the window, could now be seen. Mixed feelings guided him to the mirror standing at the other end of the room. Avoiding a coward's denial, he brought himself to see his reflection.

He was it was not as dreadful as he had suspected. His rough face accepted the black patch in almost a mysterious and intriguing way. Tiny corners of white gauze peered out from the sides while it healed. Still, it wasn't enough, it wasn't him; the patch was a cover-up. Mack had to see what *he* looked like beneath it all.

Slowly but surely Mack brought fourth the courage to pull the black patch free of his face. The gauze stayed stuck to his face, red in the centre where he had last bled. A hesitant hand reached up and pulled the gauze away. He closed his good eye as he felt the gauze come free of his flesh. Reopening his eye slowly it focused and gazed at the image, which was his face.

It was wet, with translucent fluid. His eyelid had been cut threw entirely in numerous spots. Pulling gently on the recovering glossy skin he looked to his eye. It was a ball of mush. It was as blind as it was when the eye was shut. It was an odd yellowish color, and swimming in bodily fluids trying to mend it. He let the mangled lid close. Searching desperately, he found some new gauze, placed it on the eyes and then covered it with the patch. Looking back into the mirror, he stared reproachfully at the left side of his face.

Retreating to the sanctity of the bed Mack shunned the mirror. He cursed the truth. Accepting his disfigurement proved more of a struggle than he had imagined. Never having had considered himself to have been one aesthetically oriented, he hadn't realised how much he cared. He verged on self-pity. Recoiling a moment later, he tried to focus on his mission. Mack needed his full attention for tomorrow, but still, his mind wandered back to the horrid image...

The burn tingled and popped as it trickled down the throat. Intense artificial grape flavour intoxicated taste buds. Bubbles played hopscotch on tongues. The sweet scent of the drink was not strong, but it lingered on. Suako let go of the pinch on her dainty straw and placed down her glass on the table.

Vince sat across from her with a white dress shirt and a tie, with his suit he'd worn that day. They were in a fancy restaurant, which was part of the hotels facilities. Their small table was covered with a warm sunflower yellow tablecloth and decorated with a small amber lampshade over a tea-light candle. The table itself rested against a crème colored pillar. Subtle music played from a violinist, which created a delicate yet desirable mood. The electric lights from the ceiling hung on brass chains, matching the other brass incorporated within the hotel, and the minute light let out came through tiny cut outs of stars on the metal ball containing the bulb. Other light sources, used more for their mood defining characteristics, came from candles in mounted holders on the walls.

Lighting up the room, Suako was the bell of the ball. Vince had managed to get Masumi to get him a special dress for Suako. It was strapless, allowing attention to fall on her amethyst heart pendant, with a deep plunging back. The scarlet satin curved around her body. It fit close to her, with a tulip flare, as it drew near to the hard-dark wood flooring of the dinning area. A wide canary yellow band of satin circled her waist and tied into a bow in the back, the ribbon of which stretched the full length of the skirt portion. Suako was radiant.

"So, will you tell me *now* why you're doing this. You've been keeping me in suspense all night. I don't think I can be patient any longer," Suako said, reaching for her carbonated flavour pumped drink once more. The clear liquid tingled down once again. "Well, you're just going to have to wait some more my dear," Vince grinned reclining in her oak chair. She rolled her eyes and put down the glass again, "Oh, *fine* have it your way."

Click, click and click. "Hello. I'm Yuri, I'll be your waitress tonight. I have your menus for you here. ... Would you like to hear our specials tonight? ... All right then. Tonight, our chefs are preparing a special lentil soup appetiser. It is made with some fresh onions, carrots, and celery leafs chopped finely and some imported garlic with cayenne, bay leafs and thyme to taste. Our other special appetiser tonight is garlic bread with the imported garlic we just got in. It comes with melted Parmesan cheese, soaked through with our butter mixture."

"Our first entrée for tonight is a honey-roasted ham, which has been slow cooked over the spit for the day. It comes with a small side of baby bok choy, and golden roasted potatoes. Next, we have a yakitori dish of skewered chicken, green peppers and gingko nuts which are glazed in a tare sauce and then grilled over charcoal. Once they are finished cooking one of our chefs pours cool beer over them and sprinkle them with schichimi and serve's them with steamed leeks. I've had it *several* times; it's absolutely scrumptious! And the last of our special entrées tonight is a large shiitaki mushroom stuffed with mozzarella cheese and shrimp, then baked in our brick oven, and that comes with steamed asparagus, eggplant and squash."

"Shall I give you a moment to decide?" The not-even-winded waitress, Yuri, asked, with a smile plastered on her face, yet it was genuine. Her hair was pulled back into a tight bun and she wore a black uniform with simple red trim around the edges. It had a sheen like everything else within the hotel, and appeared to be silk. "Yes, thank you," Vince replied. Yuri bowed and then left them to look over their menus.

"Ok, Vince, don't tell me *why* we're here, but at least tell me how you're affording everything!" Suako insisted with a giggle. Fizzing bubbles danced on top of the drink. "You remember when Mack used to pay us? Well, I found out why the pay stopped. He had been using his own savings from the years he'd worked in the C.D.F.P., anyway, I had mine stashed away. I traded paper money for gold currency, and then traded with Masumi. This is the last bit of my savings that I had hidden away," he simplistically explained. "Oh..." Suako hadn't realised what he was doing for tonight. It was understandable, quite possibly their last night in leisure, but still, the last of hard-earned savings gave the evening a certain depth. Not knowing what else to do Suako reached for her menu and opening it up. This dinning experience was something neither of them had ever experienced before; it was like stepping into a fairy tale. All of the eateries they'd ever been to before had been in informal setting. In Torusan there were only old run-down places, which used to be *Rich Men* C.D.F.P. turf, before they had abandoned them for the even better constructed Grid One sector. They had rusted metal walls, and de-fluffing barstools around a food stained counter. And then places like Quan, sitting in the sun on a cloth while one of the Quan natives simmered up some cod on a grill, or some other magnificent dish that produced a therapeutic scent.

As it was here, the aromas were of many different kinds, and they called forth all sorts of reactions. The amount of diversity offered here was astounding. All sorts of cuisine ranged here, and it was all authentic Imperial Continental in origin, but that's where the similarities ended. Everything imaginable seemed to be listed on this menu. It had *three* pages *just* on their regular appetisers! Suako couldn't believe her eyes.

Explanations went into great detail, and everything sounded so delicious. Suako looked up, almost feeling dizzy, and *very* hungry. Vince lifted his head in time to meet her gaze. A grin swept across his face. "I've never seen so much to choose from in my *life*!" Suako snickered. "I know," Vince looked back down at the page, "I can't even choose what to start with. Any ideas?" "Nope," a swift reply flew from Suako's painted lips. She was on the verge of another giggle.

Click, click and click. A woven basket with a graceful assortment within it was placed in the centre on the table. Egg rolls and a few pieces of complimentary garlic bread with gooey cheese dripping over it spiralled around the innards of the basket. Salivation commenced instantaneously.

"So, have you decided?" Yuri pleasantly asked, a small notepad and pencil in hand. "Uh... We'll need a few more minutes," Suako nearly looked embarrassed, her hot cheeks slightly red. "Certainly. Can I bring you anything from our wine racks in the cellar?" she asked before leaving. Suako looked to Vince, who, in turn, looked up to Yuri, "Yes please. Do you have a good fruity plum wine?" "Indeed. We have well-aged Ume-shu that is quite nice. I'll bring you some right away sir," she bowed and excused herself.

"She came back so quickly. I guess people here are used to these kinds of fancy places... Must be nice..." Suako dreaded the thought of leaving. She was enjoying herself in this kingdom of dreams. So much beauty was entangled there. "Well, let's keep going through it while she's gone," Vince lifted his menu back up.

Pop! The cork flew off the bottle to release the sweet and tangy beverage. "May I?" Yuri raised her brow. Vince nodded. She filled one of the mauve glasses partially with the champagne-coloured wine. Vince took the glass, swirled the drink around, releasing the vapour which he inhaled, and he could almost taste it then. He sipped it and the sour flavour was washed away with a sweet and fruity aftertaste. "Delicious," he put on his imaginary mask and become a different person in front of Yuri; he was enjoying being an actor for the day. His confidence was appealing. Their glasses were filled and the green bottle placed in a stationary holder next to their table.

"So, may I take your orders now?" she asked once more. "Yes. I'll have the gyoza to start —the dumplings sound wonderful. And as my main course I'd like the sweet pork and rice balls," Vince told her with a sense of conviction. Yuri scribbled down notes on her paper, "Alright. And you miss?" "I'd like the cucumber and shrimp salad and then the salmon sushi dish," Suako took her turn using conviction in her speech and thoroughly enjoyed it. "Good choice, we just got in a fresh batch of seaweed in today. Great choices! I'll be back later with your dishes."

It was relieving and yet somewhat delightful to have so boldly spoken. They shed their slightly more grotesque habits and refined themselves in order to conform to this *high-class society*. It felt good to be treated like royalty. It was a refreshing experience that left a great and everlasting impression. The chime of glass radiated threw the air, as a toast was made several tables away.

I wonder what he's thinking. I really wonder why we're here... Hehe my heart is going to beat right out of my chest of fall onto the table if it goes any faster. Suako lifted her hand to cover her mouth and the monstrous giggle welling within. *I feel like a princess... I guess I can see why the C.D.F.P. don't want to change. Who would want to? This is just so, so... I can't even think of a word for it. Oh, Vince looks so handsome. This can't be real. It must be a dream. I'm going to wake up back in Torusan any minute now... now... now? No, maybe it **is** real. I hardly believe it though.*

Mmm oh how delicious... It's like heaven on my tongue. Yes, heaven is having a party on my tongue. I've been blessed. If only I were hungry. I don't know why I'm not. I barely ate today. I was hungry before we got here, no wait... it was before the dress I suppose. Oh, I feel warm and tingly. Was I drugged? Someone put something in my drink? No! What the hell is wrong with you? You weren't drugged!

Wow... so soft... I've never felt this before. I feel so pretty. I wonder if anyone can see my scars? Oh, who care's...Look at the colors... They even shine... Suako smiled. She continued on, in her mind, conversing with herself. It seemed an eternity within the depths of her flowing thoughts, yet it was next to none at all.

"You're beautiful, Suako," the soft brush of Vince's fingers, as they slide over her long-fingered hands, brought the cloud-hoping Suako back down to earth. Her toes could reach the floor again, and a dreamy sigh pushed from her. "Thank you... for everything. This is just... thank you," no other words would do. They sat holding hands with romantic gazes that spoke more than any words could. They memorised every last detail of each other, as they were that night, to be forever kept locked away inside.

The first course came and was lain in front of them It wasn't food, it was art! The arrangement was dazzling. Sprinkled herbs and coloured sauces dribbled along the rim of the dishes. Color hues integrated perfectly, and even structural placement deserved the highest praise. It felt shameful to ruin this decadent piece of art.

Enveloped in taste it was hard to admit that a few bites in and neither were hungry. Though beyond scrumptious, the sheer happiness of the night filled them up inside. Vince stood and placed his napkin down neatly beside his plate. He circled the table and held his hand out to Suako, who looked up to him questionably.

Since they'd arrived someone came and played the piano with the violinist. "Dance with me," he said, looking at the vision of perfection before him. She slid her hand into his and took to her feet. Vince led her through the tables to a floor space. It was wide and circular like the lobby, it's shape was depicted by a tincture change of the floor, and the pillars that encircled the skylight. It was magic. The tables didn't penetrate the dance floor. The only different between the restaurant and the lobby was that the lobby had a painted night sky on it, but here, it was the real thing. A spectacular class ceiling looked up to the celestial bodies above.

Standing there in the centre of the room Suako felt embarrassed. Vince took her hand in his and placed his other hand at the small of her back. Never having had danced before Suako didn't know what she was supposed to do. Vince's grandfather taught him as a boy, so he leaned toward Suako and whispered softly in her ear, "Put your hand on my shoulder. Then I'll lead you. Alright?" She nodded and refrained from the urge she had to bite her lip.

They began to dance, and like angels, they swept across the floor. Everyone watched them. Exhilaration pulsed through Suako's veins. Vince leaned forward once more putting his mouth to Suako's ear. "The reason we're here," He started, "Is because I saw a calendar today..."

Suako felt puzzled. After a short pause he went on, "It's March seventh... Happy birthday."

"Couldn't you just drink that sunset in. It's fabulous," Mei munched on some grapes as she and Kato stood on the balcony of their hotel room, overlooking the city. "Hmmm. Yeah. S' pose I could," Kato replied. Mei finally let down her tense nerves. The day had been a little much, and it was time to let it all go she figured. A cluttered mind wouldn't think clearly the next day. They leaned against the balcony wall, in revered silence. They watched the city turn into that streamline gold again, and like sponges, they soaked it all in.

Water... warm... mmm... Yu-Lee stood in the shower. The artificial rain ran down her firm skin beading up along the way down. Cleansing and revitalising water washed away the accumulated grime and grit. She closed her eyes and put her face directly in the line of the nozzle's spray. Pounding water streams bounced off her skin. Showers and baths had been limited on this journey, and this was a pleasure. Yu-Lee just stood unmoving, like a statue, letting the droplets plummet down on her, they seemed to nurture the soul.

Yu-Lee lathered sweet smelling soap over her torso. As shampoos and gels came into the line of water they emitted their scents of vanilla, lavender and ginseng. The shower washed the soap free of her breasts. Then that vertical wave carried down the rest of her body, accumulating the rest of the bubbles at her feet. Suds spiralled round and round as they went toward the drain. Twisting her hair into a funnel, the water squeezed out and flowed in a stream. The water was milky at first but eventually became clear. This was heavenly bliss, encapsulated as earthly bounty.

Tomorrow will come... but for now let's just enjoy the now...

Chapter 23: The Attack

Day did not announce itself. The sun hid like a child shielding its eyes, as it rested behind the clouds. Mack was up early as usual regardless of the run, he was habitual. He watched Kairu, Masumi, Yu-Lee, and Jenko in sweet slumber, and he did not wake them. Slipping open the glass door, he stepped out onto a balcony. A chair sat there, which he rested in. He starred at the central building. It was a mass that matched the sky, which looked grim and uninviting. It was darker than the clouds it so eagerly portrayed.

The day was lightening up, but the clouds did not part. It was nearing eight o'clock, and Mack knew it was time to get going. Stirring from beneath warm sheets the others became re-animated with life. "It's time to go," were the only words Mack desired to say before exiting the room to get Kato and the others.

Mei had awoken early too. Her blood sizzled in her veins, yet she retained at a certain level of calm, collected control. Everyone there had been ready to go since an hour before being beckoned by Mack. Weapons had been sheathed, and bags were packed. Their business guises of the previous day hid their combat garb underneath. They followed Mack back, entered his room.

The late sleepers made haste in preparing themselves, and were ready in minutes. "Alright everyone. We're going for the main building. We need to keep a low profile. We're going through the main doors, as I'm sure you've guessed by the way you dressed. We're going to proceed to the top and go and see the man in charge. Our best plan is to take immediate action. After we've taken control of their official, then we're in control. I want this to be simplistic," Mack explained.

"Mei and Suako I need you to be a separate faction. I want you to sneak into their sub-levels. I want you to look for Kazuo," he continued. "Mack, I think if we're taking dominion, and seizing this place, then we can look for Kazuo afterward. We need to stick together Mack." Mei conjured the excuse to keep herself involved in the immediate action. Mack sighed, "Fine," he reluctantly replied. "After we have control, then we'll go from there. Just focus on the task at hand. Let's go," Mack said.

The morning chill was damp, like that of spring, yet still cold in winter. Wet snow sloshed beneath shoes, and splashed upward. The busy people frequented the streets as they started their days, busy ignorant people, that went on with their daily activities around them. For those people it was a day as any other, for Mack and his small infiltrating rogue group, it was history.

Climbing higher and higher the skyscraper building went, as they surrounded their capitol's government. As they proceeded up the steps of the political-military base, they could hear their footsteps echoing off the front face of the building. It rung in their heads. So close to a long desired enemy base, it became a battle against impulse to draw forth weapons and charge in.

Composure in check, the doorman opened the glass door for the 'executives'. Four secretary posts created a broken semicircle around the entranceway. Behind pine desks the four women worked fastidiously, like machines; efficient. Walking past the secretaries, through the carpeted pathway, they went on in. Elevator doors in dull copper lined up in threes on either side of them. Straight ahead an architecturally renowned staircase scaled, made of glass, and rails of the same copper that made the elevator doors. Randomly placed potted plants, like those in the hotel, could be seen around on the main floor. The over all impression of the initial viewing was that of prestige. Deep green wallpaper, like the color of the paint they had seen coating the railway stations, rose above a cream-colored panelling that extended the room at the bottom of the wall.

There was no time for sight seeing now. It was time to... "Hello, may I help you?" Mack was startled by the strange voice. He turned around to see one of the secretaries standing behind him. He stared blankly at her for a moment, as her intense blue eyes impatiently waited an answer. Mild voices could be heard speaking to her through an ear-piece. Staring at her still, she looked anal with her tightly bound blonde bun of hair and her grey suit. "Ahem. Yes, we are here to see the chairman," he improvised. "You have an appointment?" she asked bitterly. "We're with the C.D.F.P. and need to speak with him *immediately,*" Mack insisted.

"Oh, he's been waiting for you sir. I'm so sorry. Please, up to the top floor, then make a right out from the elevator, then go through the doors directly ahead of you. You will have to use the executive elevator. Please follow me. I'll take you there," she heightened her pace as she led them around the corner, and to the right, behind the stairs. Mack had been sweating bullets; he felt it a miracle the *drill sergeant* of a receptionist didn't catch on to his act.

The secretary swiped her employee card down a scanner, and an electronic device lit up a green sign that said "Confirmed". *Ding!* The doors opened. One by one they stepped into the elevator. Apologetically too, the receptionist got in to escort them up. Kairu whispered to

Jenko in the back of the portable room, "Didn't she say '... he's been waiting for you sir'?" Jenko nodded. The words did not bode well with either of them, but it was too late now.

Ding! Fump! The doors peeled open. With her usual sharpness, the secretary exited and guided them the way she'd previously dictated would be the path. Ahead tall thick wooden doors, with copper handles, stood like the barriers between them and a plague. Every step was heavily weighted. *Closer, closer... there*!

The secretary pushed both doors wide open, and in they entered. Mack's heart nearly jumped from his chest. Mei was just about ready to toss the cases she held onto, in order to grab her dagger. Tension eroded at their very souls, but then all at once, the stress was cut and left.

A long oval table stretched out across the length of the massive room. Red cushioned chairs were placed every couple feet around it, encompassing the table. Curtains were drawn back from the floor to ceiling windows that looked out over the city. "Please have a seat. I will get Mr. Kane for you now. It will be just a moment," pulling the doors closed behind her, she left.

A mutual sigh blew heavily out. Masumi's hands were shaking. Kairu plopped down on one of the chairs, next to Yu-Lee. "This is it," Mei said, conviction was in her eyes and breath. "Just don't get trigger happy," Jenko warned. Mack sat at the far end of the table across from where Mr. Kane would be. The cushion swallowed him into the chair. "No un would 'appin' t' have a tension ball, would they?" Kato asked as he sat into his chair. Much needed unilateral laugh spread, but as it faded, there was nothing but silence as they waited.

Minutes later footsteps approached, and in entered a middle-aged man. He was handsome in his own way, with a thick head of hair, just long of a military cut. He was not a heavy man, nor a thin one, and his perfectly tailored suit screamed money. It was soft in the subdued light of day, navy blue complimented with a lighter blue dress shirt. He looked stern, and had the air of importance following him through the doors.

Solely, he came in and excused his receptionist. She closed the doors behind herself and left, the click of her heels marking every step as she walked away. "Good morning gentlemen, ladies. I'm Mr. Kane. You can call me Keiji," he introduced himself as he took a seat in his master chair. His voice spoke supremacy. Mack introduced himself and the others, keeping his true identity a secret. "I was expecting you a half hour ago. I am glad you finally made it. Shall we get right down to it then?" Keiji asked. His patients had obviously been worn down from the wait for his true appointment.

"Indeed," Mack nodded. The others kept quiet for the time being. "Right then. As per your building permit proposal, tell your superiors that I accept. They know how to do good business. As for locations..." on and on he went talking about prior proposals, discussed offers, and prices with them. They got an overall view of the C.D.F.P. infiltration, and they learned about the war. It seemed to have been sparked by the C.D.F.P. All and all it became more and more present just how little the Imperials actually knew about what the C.D.F.P. was actually doing.

It was time was Mack to make his move, he looked to Suako, who took definite notice. Then gave one other glance to Kairu. The message was received. Kairu stood, up breaking Keiji's concentration, and swiftly he darted to the doors and guarded them. Keiji reached for his intercom to call for security, but Suako had already shoved a knife threw it. It was slightly crushed, and short-circuiting from the impact.

"Don't be alarmed Mr. Kane. We are not here to hurt you. We need you to listen to us, that's all," Mack explained. "We're not actually with the C.D.F.P. My real name is Mack Yamamoto..." before he could continue Keiji interrupted him, and looked fierce. "I see. You're the ones the C.D.F.P. is after. What do you want?" Keiji seemed to be calm. Keiji was a businessman through and through, and he must've realised he had no other options available at the time. For a man in his position, he was quite respectful in listening with his full attention.

So, they gave it to him straight, the whole story. They told him about the rise of the C.D.F.P. and how the world outside of the Imperial continent was falling to destruction and darkness. Each person shared their horror story about the atrocities the C.D.F.P. had committed. Mack told him about the documents he'd found during his time employed by the C.D.F.P. military division. If Mr. Kane had been a sponge, he was dry when he walked in there earlier, and now was sopping wet with information. Finally, Mack explained why they were there,

"Originally, we thought you were involved when we heard about the civil war and proposed building of the generators. It seemed to me that you didn't know the effects. You see, you live with your entire continent protected by an air dome. This has been slowing down the effects of the carbon dioxide poisoning. I say 'slowing' because on our way here there some... bizarre weather..." Mack remembered his eye when he'd mentioned the twisters, but he fought it back to keep his composure, "On the East Green Continent it's nothing but a wasteland. Outside of the domes it feels like death has his hand on your shoulder. It's a struggle just to breathe and-" *Bamm!* The doors flew in, sending Kairu flying to the floor. Several C.D.F.P. soldiers swarmed in, guns readied. Mack and the others were quick to draw their guns forth. The game was *on*!

Thud! Thud! Thud! Yoshida walked into the room. His arms were crossed and he had a wide grin on his rough masculine face. The site of him enraged Mack, and he snared at the general. "Long time no see," Yoshida said. "No shit," Mack angrily replied. He aimed his gun right at Yoshida, but did not fire; the tense predicament did not allow for one bullet to fly alone. It would be a chain reaction. "Now, now Mack, there is no need for profanity," Yoshida cockily said, with a grin still on his face, "Oh, and by the way, thanks for the consideration old friend..." Yoshida reached in his pocket. Mack looked confused. Yoshida tossed him his I.D. tags that he'd left behind in Old Ryoko. Mack just looked down at them as they slid to a stop on the table.

"Sorry we're late Mr. Kane, there was an incident we had to tend to. Mack, Genjo Anami wants you imprisoned for treachery my old friend. He wants your entire terrorist group for that fact. I've been in charge of getting you back to Torusan," the general explained. "I see," Mack said without any sound of surprise. "My dear old friend, you should really be more careful," Yoshida said coyly pointing to one of his eyes. *Fuck you* Mack mouthed without sound.

"You know Mack, I always knew you'd faked your death. No one believed me, thought I was paranoid. You did a good job; no forensic evidence could have proven otherwise. Only my hunch ever caught you. It seems my instincts have served me well," the grin still glowed, now with pride. "Congratulations," Mack's tone was just slightly darker than monotone.

"I never understood your decision to leave, Mack. You had earned yourself a glorious living and status within The Company, then you gave it all up. What on earth for?" Yoshida's inquiry faded his grin. "All of the money in the world can't save this planet from its decomposing fate. I wasn't about to sit idly by and let the world crumble around me," Mack replied with conviction. Keiji turned his attention to Yoshida. "Mack, I don't know what you're saying. Nothing's happening, you're delusional," he flat out lied. Mack gave no sign of response, it was useless.

Tired of a futile game Yoshida was ready to take his prize, "Well enough of this prattling on. It's time to leave. Lower your weapons," he ordered. Mack Laughed. "You don't have the upper hand here my friend. We're on an equal playing ground. We are not going to simply surrender to you. We didn't travel across two continents and the ocean for nothing," Mack couldn't shed the humour from Yoshida's direct command. "I thought you might feel that way," Yoshida said in all confidence, his words would be followed. He walked out of the room and just around the corner where he couldn't be seen. Mack cocked his head to try and see what he was up to. "So, I brought along a little insurance..." his dulled voice came from around the corner. He re-entered the room with a firm grip on Okichi's arm and a knife to her throat.

Kairu's eyes grew wide, and his heart nearly exploded inside the cavity of his chest. "Okichi!" he screamed and tried to get to her. The sound of guns releasing their safeties stopped him dead in his tracks. "Now you wouldn't want me to have to harm our dear friend here, now would you Mack? I'm sure the Quan chief wouldn't be too pleased to have you compromise his daughter's life," Yoshida laughed.

Okichi stood there trembling, her white dress was stained with mud along the bottom rim. Her elbows bled threw cracked dry skin and her hair was matted badly. A wide split in her plump bottom lip contained a scab of dried blood. Mouse-like she coward away from Yoshida, knee's buckling terribly. Desperately Kairu wished to go to her.

"Throw down your weapons," Yoshida ordered with a firm voice. Mack tried to think, paining as he scraped at his brain to find a solution. One person was a small price to pay to save the planet, yet there was no justification that could leave him feeling good. He just sat there in thought, but he couldn't lower his weapon.

The clanking of Kairu's gun on the floor was as distracting as shattering glass amid the silence. Teary-eyed Kairu slowly rose from the floor, "Everyone drop them! Please!" he screamed in vain. A soldier seized him and another gave him a pat down. Mack's forces were weakening. Yoshida pulled the knife tighter against Okichi's throat, drawing blood. She yelped, and tried to pull away, which caused Yoshida to pull the cold metal up even tighter against, and into her. Kairu screamed for the group to conform once more looked to Mack for resolve. There was too much pressure. Mack spun his gun on his finger, releasing it as surrender. The rest, neglecting the desire, followed his example.

Like lotus the soldiers swarmed them, patting each of them down for weaponry, just as Kairu had been. Yoshida let down his knife. "Let's go," he told Okichi, his hold on her arm still as tight as ever. "Sorry for the disturbance Mr. Kane," he told Keiji who sat there the whole time speechless. "Take care of the rest," he addressed his men and left, dragging Okichi with him. "No!" Kairu yelled. Then the darkness came...

Expect the unexpected.

Chapter 24: Imprisoned

Dim... I can't see... What happened? ... Where am I? ... It's so dark... My head hurts...

"Everyone drop them! Please!"

The words echoed. Memory blurred as it came back to Kairu in scattered pieces. *Cold... It hurts to breathe again... I'm not in an air dome... Where...?* Moving fingertips, they pressed against a frigid metal surface on which he lay. It was hard and rough. His ribs dug into the floor as they expanded with impure oxygen, and the poison filled his body. Lazy eyelids fought to open. *Blink. Blink.* It was dark. There was nothing but shady figures that couldn't be made out.

Drip! ... Drip! ... Drip! The repetitious fall of something sounded like a leaky faucet dripping. It sounded hollow in there. *Where?* His eyes began to adjust. Something was blocking his vision. With a sore arm Kairu reached forward to decipher what it was. "Bars..." he whispered to himself. He was in a cage.

Using all the strength he could muster he pushed himself up onto his hands and knees. He flinched once he was up, noticing an IV dug deep into his arm. He regretted to pull in free, he strength waning. Everything was foggy within his head. Reaching back with one hand Kairu felt the back of his head. Gummy-like drying blood stuck to his fingers, which he rubbed around in a circular motion. He felt a deep headache sprawling from the location; it was deep and agitating.

More things were becoming apparent, as his eyes adjusted to the dark, Kairu's was picking up more detail now. Past the bars he could see wooden crates with the writing **FRAGILE** on them. There were stairs beyond the crates leading up. From the top of the staircase came in the only light, which was faint at best. A sloshing sound started to make sense. He was in the cargo hold of a ship. They were on the sea, heading back to Torusan. His head started pounding.

A few moments later he was back to exploring with his eyes. Kairu saw other cages surrounding him, everyone was there, except Okichi, and each was being held in their own separate cage. He was the only lucid one. He saw Masumi in the cage next to his. He lay down on his back. Masumi was on her side and he thought her awake.

"Hey Masumi… I'm sorry," Kairu began to speak. "I didn't mean for this to happen. I… I'm in love with Okichi. I know the planet and all but… I couldn't let them kill her." He turned his head to look at Masumi. Masumi didn't respond, she was quite still. He called her name, but she lay unmoving. It was now clear she was laying face down, not on her side. Her head was turned in his direction with locks of hair gracing over it. Kairu reached through the bars of his cage and hers, and he took her hand. She felt as cold as ice. "Masumi," he called to her gently again.

Kairu rubbed her hand vigorously to warm it up. The heat would not keep. "Masumi… Masumi!" he yelled, but she didn't stir. His voice echoed in the tin can. Reaching as far as he could into her cage, he swept the hair away from her face. Her eyes were wide open and looked lifeless, she was staring his way with black inkwells of eyes. In the dark he could just vaguely make out a bruise on her temple. It didn't look fatal. Then he heard it, the dull raspy breath exhumed from her slightly divided lips. "Masumi!" He screamed.

Masumi's body let free a deep cough. She had no energy. Masumi looked as if she'd lain there in agony for hours. Dripping out from her lips a puddle of saliva mixed with blood had formed. Her eyes blinked. Helplessly she lay there in vain. "Masumi... Oh no..." he looked on with horror. Slow breathing. *Inhale... ... ... Exhale...* It terrified Kairu.

Death had placed its unwanted hand on Masumi's shoulder. Slower and slower her breathing dyed off. "Masumi, stay with me! Masumi, look at me!" he told her, fighting the lump at the back of his throat. Her eyes looked to him and she tried to speak. Nearly unheard, she spoke, "K... Kay... Kairu..." she coughed bitterly, "F... finish... wha... what we... started... It's... so pretty..." Her eyes still transfixed his way, she could see something beyond him. A moment later her eyes dropped shut. Kairu called for her.

The words of Otojiro's letter came rushing back to Kairu:

"...You will be given a choice. Either road will cause a devastating consequence. Either way will bring loss into your life. The result of your choice will not be visible at first. Be forewarned. That is all I can say on this subject. I am sorry..."

No... No! Oh god, please no! "Masumi wake up... Please wake up..." *She's just sleeping, just sleeping that's all!* "Masumi, I'm here now. Wake up!" *Just unconscious, she's NOT dead... she can't be...* "Masumi... Masumi?" Kairu's voice fell weak and he began to weep. Looking upon her in denial he prayed to see her stir, but no such movement came. He rubbed her hand between his vigorously. Masumi lay on the cold floor limp, her body was as still as a statue. Not even her chest expanded; she was no longer breathing that Kairu could tell. Kairu gave a tug on her arm and she joggled like a rag doll. He lay staring blankly. She *was* dead.

The persistent throb of his headache flourished. Migrating partially to his temples and forehead, each thumping pound swarmed him. Tenser he became. The intensity continued to rise. He couldn't sort out his thoughts. *The throb... The emptiness... The dripping... Make it go away. Just make it all go away...*

An ill sickly feeling built up within Kairu; he felt nauseated yet empty inside. Kairu squeezed her hand firmly in his. Tears welled up and began to stream down his face, down onto the floor. He curled into a ball and sobbed, refusing to release her hand. "Masumi..." he moaned remorsefully. Guilt overshadowed his conscience.

Kairu felt the anguish building within. *Why...?* he kept asking himself. His heart felt a piercing go through it. Eventually some soldiers came jogging down the stairs. He started screaming for them to help her. Kairu was hysterical in nature, and they looked down on him like a vile rodent infected with disease. "Please! Help! D, Dying! She's sick, dying! Oh god, help! Help, sick, god... Oh dying!" He rambled. One man inserted his key into Kairu's lock. "No!" Kairu screamed, extremely pissed off. "Not me, her!" he tried to explain. Still inward they came, towering over Kairu like giants, they looked down at him and then rose the butt end of their weapon high.

Darkness…

Every decision has a consequence…

Chapter 25: The Escape

"Kairu?" *What happened?* "Kairu, wake up!" *I don't remember anything…* "Come on, time to get up!" *Why can't I think of it…? What was it?* "Kairu!" *The light hurts. I can't see… Oh, it's dark in here. The drip is gone. The sloshing stopped. Drip!? Sloshing!? Masumi!* "Masumi!" Kairu screamed and bolted up to sitting upright, cutting his arm as he did on a jutting piece of wood, sticking out from the bottom of a thick door. He didn't notice the cut, his mind frantic; everything came back in a flash.

Kairu's heart started to race, and he began to pant as he hyperventilated. He could only see his resurfacing memories. The chilling sound of Masumi's last words rung inside his ears, *"F... finish... wha... what we... started... It's... so pretty..."*

Kairu began to cry uncontrollably. "Kairu? Kairu what's wrong?!" Suako's voice came from the cell across from him. "What's wrong with Masumi?" she inquired after his comment. He let out a dreadful noise on anguish, as he felt that paining emptiness resurfacing. He could barely hear Suako, her words would not pass the chatter of his mind.

She... she looked so calm... so ready, ready to die. S, she was so innocent. Her last breath... she just compressed... like, like a balloon... Masumi... Denial left him, but acceptance was harsh. Every detail played in a sort of slow motion picture show in his mind. The horrible graphics did not cease. "Kairu!" Suako's voice freed him. Silent tears streaked down his cheeks.

"She's dead," Kairu's morbid voice said regretfully. Rustling from the cells all around him alerted him to the presence of everyone else. Individually caged like animals, they were trapped in the poorly lit cells. Through the tiny square-foot whole, on the bar on the door, torchlight brought a glow to the room. Kairu was alone in his cell, and he figured that they had all been kept solo. It didn't matter now, Masumi was dead, and all other concerns seemed petty, and wrong to even think about.

"What happened?" Yu-Lee's compassionate voice reached to him from some distance. Kairu lay back down on the hard floor. "You were all unconscious... we were on a ship. I... I woke up..." Kairu's voice began to tremble fiercely. "Masumi had been beaten... she was sick... she must've been lying there for hours. No, not hours, *days...* in the cold, on the hard metal floor... In pain... The sound of her breathing, oh god... Masumi died right in front of me... I held her hand. With her last breath, s... she pleaded for us to... finish what we started..." he choked up and could go on. The dreary sound of sobbing infiltrated every cell, and sunk already lessened hearts. "I'm so sorry," Kairu whimpered, wracked with guilt. Lower their spirits sank. The only other voice that came was the solemn one of Kato, "Kairu, I'm so sorry," The exhaustion of Kairu's emotionally distraught body finally gave in, and then a third darkness came; that of sleep.

"Kairu? Kairu? ... I think he's sleeping now. He said he woke up on a ship? Where the hell are we?" Jenko said with a weighted heart. Suako shuttered, "We're in Torusan... the bottom of the C.D.F.P. headquarters..." Suako said meekly from within her captivity. "How do you know?" Mei asked. Suako closed her eyes. *"Let go of me! No! No! You are not taking me back there! No! ... Argh! No!" shrieks emanated.* "Because this is my old cell..." she whispered, terrified. She pulled in her knees and held them as she rocked back and forth. Again, conversation halted.

"Mack?" Vince's voice travelled quietly from the cell next door. "What is it Vince?" Mack, depressed, returned the call. "What are we going to do now?" Vince asked sadly. "I don't know... I never expected this. We'll have to get out I suppose. Though, I don't know how..." Mack's voice was vague, that of a ruined man. His vision of their supremacy over the C.D.F.P. had been dissolved. Mack was still coming to terms with it all, and he felt lost. A real sense of devastation swept over him, and now compounded with Masumi's death, guilt was now riding on his conscience.

Vince said no more. Looking around his tomb of an enclosure he felt drab. The floor was dirt and stone, and a tattered blanket lay in the grit of the floor. The walls were stone, cool and damp to the touch. Vince sighed and heard Kairu weeping in his sleep. He thought of Masumi, and his head hung low. He'd never thanked her for everything she'd done for Suako's birthday, which now seemed like a distant dream.

Vince wondered what day is was, and how long he'd slept while he'd been transported all the way to Torusan. His arm was sore in the crease of his elbow. He squinted at it and could see a faint puncture wound where an needle had been. The cell was uncomfortable, and he wondered about how Suako dealt with it for all of her years here. Then a thought came: *If we're in the same cells, are we all guinea pigs for the C.D.F.P.?* He shuttered and prayed his imagination was just being cruel.

The problem was, it was all too possible. *Why else are we still alive?* Suako was being kept too far away for him to question her about her time here in private. Lying awake for hours he stewed in his thoughts, and they became muddled until he couldn't separate them. It was then that he noticed his clothing, it was different. He felt it, it was a cheap cotton weave that wasn't very soft. Vince had been too preoccupied up until now to notice.

He wondered where his clothes were, it was cold. Then it hit him that his journal was in his jacket pocket. He prayed it was safe. *Cold...* Begrudgingly he grabbed the filthy sheet and crawled into a corner wrapping himself up in it.

Vince thought then about Masumi, he could imagine her in his mind, lying there in the hull of the ship, caged like an animal, unable to speak and every breath a torture within itself. Like inhaling nails and broken glass, slowly drawing them in, unable to stop. She was another piece of cargo on the ship. No one came to check, and if they had, no one would have cared, *would* they? Vince watched her, in his mind, dying there like an animal. Prolonging her pain with an IV keeping her from dehydration and starvation.

Vince tried to erase the image he'd created, but it wouldn't leave. Masumi lay helplessly there in his mind looking for help. Searching for mercy on her poor soul. It had come, but not soon enough from what Kairu described. Self-pity felt greedy. Trying to shut off his mind, he sat there trying to sleep. Just as death took it's time gracing Masumi, sleep did the same to Vince, it took a painstakingly long time reaching him...

Ching- Ch... C... Ching! A weird tingling noise woke Vince from a nightmare he had been having about Masumi. Like chimes the jingling continued. Disoriented by the dream, and waking up in the dark, he didn't know what to make of it at first. It stopped. Then a smack against his door and the jingling commenced once again.

They were keys unlocking his cell. His eyes widened and he felt himself pushing against the floor and at the wall, as if to try and go through it. His heart sped; true terror had announced itself within him.

The key sounded as if it were caught in the lock. Vince looked around, but there was no way out, and there was no where to hide. He thought he might try and get past the guards at the door, but he thought twice about it. They'd likely be armed, and then he'd be killed or wounded. Options were running low. Adrenaline began to stream threw his circulatory system, he couldn't think, the door was opening...

Run! No, you can't! They'll kill you... what do they want? Oh, Suako how did you deal with this? I'm a fucking rat in a trap... Shit! ... "Vince!" Adamu came into his cell. Vince looked on at him dumbfounded. Vince stood there in the light looking, frightened, depleted and dirty. "A, Adamu?" Vince looked at him standing there with a wrinkle in his brow. "It's alright. We're here to help. Common, I'll explain later," Adamu then went onto the next cell to open it. A moment later Vince saw Seresuto walk past his cell door with a bundle in her arms. Walking with steps of caution, he went to the door, and then stepped into the hall. Vince wondered if he was dreaming. *Whamp!* Seresuto threw his clothes at him, and his journal whacked his square in the chest. He stumbled backward on unsubstantial legs. "Get dressed!" She beckoned.

Vince didn't need a second request. He dropped his rags to the floor and pulled on his clothing that now fit a size too big. He pulled free his journal of his suit and kissed it, then placed it back into the protective pocket of his camouflage coat. He came out the door, where the others were starting to merge in oversized clothing. He saw Suako and ran to her, and they held each other tearfully.

Lastly Kairu walked out of his cell to join the others. His eyes were puffy and swollen from crying, he looked like a broken man. "We're sorry Kairu," Mei said and attempted to embrace him, but he refused her. "Let's just get these fucking bastards," his voice was wrathful. "There's an empty room not too far from here where we put all of your weapons. We can hide in there for a little while. There's food too. Common!" Seresuto told them and than ran off to lead them.

"What happened?" Adamu asked Kato as they scuffled threw the dark corridor. "After we left you n' Kukotan we met a girl. 'Er name was Masumi. Her parents had been killed in some civil war the Imperial Continent 's in. She was going wit' us to da' end. Then she got sick on t' way back here. Kairu an' her were close," Kato explained, trying to cut his emotions off. "So, that was who that was. Well I'm sorry," was all Adamu could think of to say. "Yeah... me too," Kato nodded.

They ducked into a hidden crevasse, which had a ladder leading upwards. "This way. It's unused by the C.D.F.P., they all use the elevator," Seresuto explained. One by one they went up. The rusty ladder creaked and shook with every step. The metal rungs jumped into the body and like a virus, spreading a freeze that went bitterly down to the bone. They were travelling up a vent shaft that blew old air, which reeked of decay. The fowl stench turned their stomachs upside down.

Coming up to the next floor there was an actual floor, not just firm soil. Blue tinted sterile lights started to get brighter. Crawling out of the sealed of vent shaft the light hit them hard, scolding the eyes. Suako felt uneasy as her head came up from the shaft to see the room, she remembered the first time she stepped onto this floor when she was escaping. Random flashes of her past kept confusing Suako with reality.

Out of no where the earth started to rumble, and Suako's body was thrown harshly against the metal siding. She cried out but no one could hear her amongst the grumbling earth. Her foot slipped off the metal ladder rung, and Suako hung from one hand. Reaching up with the other she supported herself, violently breathing. She clung onto the old ladder, but its old rusted structure couldn't handle it.

Pealing free of the wall it was bolted to, the top of the ladder hit against the wall behind her. Suako dangled there in mid air. The tremors finally toned down, and eventually stopped. "Suako are you ok?" Yu-Lee called from above. "Peachy!" Suako yelled sarcastically. She climbed through the rungs and came out the top, badly bruised on her arm and ribs. Minor scratches drew tiny droplets of blood, and in the shock of it all she'd accidentally bit her lip as well. Suako mumbled curses beneath her breath. The quakes had reached Torusan in very little time; decay was finally coming to its originator.

Mei came up last, behind Suako. Through the rungs she pulled herself up, then squirmed herself free of the shaft and placed her feet down on the floor. Her eyes strained to see, it was so bright that it burned. Her dry eyes wished to produce tears but they would not come. "Over here!" Seresuto called Mei in a harsh whisper. They swept into a vacant room blindly. Last to leave the room, Adamu shut the shaft behind them, and scuttled into the other room.

Surrounded by the noise of the vent, it was obvious why this room was out of use. The sound was overpowering and all around them, it was trapping and induced a swarming feeling of claustrophobia. There were no windows in this room either. They were still deep beneath the earth's surface. As they got used to, again, another change in the light dynamics, Adamu lit up a burner. They were in an old cafeteria type room. "We managed to salvage most of your stuff. Here're your maps Jenko..." Adamu began dispersing their personal belongings to them.

The small trip left everyone quite fatigued, their bodies hadn't moved much in a long while. "What happened?" Mack asked taking a seat on a stool. Adamu warmed water at the stove for tea. As he turned to face everyone, the glow of the flame from the stove lit his face. It was badly scarred where the glass had penetrated when their ship had crashed. Many inch-long lines of scar tissue designed his face. "A lot..." Adamu replied, his voice serious.

"We stayed in the city after you left, but none of the residents ever came back to it. Seresuto healed slowly, but she recovered. We stayed in that house you left us at. We were waited for you to come back. There was nothing to do but wait with the ship sunk. About a month and a half later we wake up one morning and there's a commotion in the town. We thought it might be you. Then we saw a massive ship in the harbour, and some people in uniforms came scouring through the city. They were collecting provisions, probably for a trip across the ocean, we thought. We weren't sure if you'd be coming back, so we thought it best to hitch a ride back across the ocean while we could."

"When we were going through the streets to get to their ship we nearly were caught by two officers. That's when we heard them talking. They were going on about some prisoners they'd caught in the Capitol City. I *knew* it was you. Just before they left we snuck on board. We hide ourselves in some empty boxes. The seamen put some heavy crates on top of the boxes we were in so we were trapped inside, but I could see you guys through a peephole."

"I saw that girl you were with, Masumi was it? ... She was soaking wet. She had woken up and been screaming at one of the soldiers. He threw a bucket of seawater on her... When she still wouldn't pipe down he went in and, and... and it was bloody awful. After that, the girl got pretty sick. I thought she'd get better but... she got worse and worse... I couldn't even get out to help her. I had to sit there and watch... she just laid there. When I woke up the on third day I thought she was dead. She wasn't moving. Then I heard her breathing. It was coarse and ghastly. It sent a chill up my spine. She sounded like she was in so much pain... Well after five days of lying there she finally stopped breathing... I'm sorry Kairu, I heard you screaming. *Sigh.* After they knocked Kairu out for freaking out, nothing else happened, which I thanked god for..."

"We were only at sea for *seven* days and we were back at the East Green Continent. I couldn't believe it. While they were distracted unloading the hull, Seresuto and I snuck out. When we saw you being put onto a truck we got in too. It was a couple day's drive and we came to Torusan. We only got to see the city for a second when we were going between the truck and this building. It's massive here..."

"Anyway, we couldn't stay with you. After they took you away we had to search all over this damn place to find you. We accidentally stumbled upon this basement area. It's creepy as hell. We got into an elevator shaft, planning to climb up, but then we saw it going down. We thought we were on the bottom floor as it was. We must be at least *five* floors beneath the earth. It was so weird. We heard some screaming coming from somewhere. We checked out every floor on the way. Finally, we found your stuff, so we figured you were close. Then we found the air duct and went down. We weren't sure if there'd be anything but there you were. We've been waiting for an opportunity to get you out. Phew! Well here we are. So, what happened with you?" Adamu asked as he passed out the tea. Shivering hands received it thankfully; the room was an icebox.

"Well..." Mack began. He gave them the low down. From the discovery of the new civil war outbreak, to the ice cavern, twisters, and finally their attempt in Tomakomai, they heard it all. It was quite a story. Mack went up to the warm flames of the stove and showed them the loss of his eye. Many things had happened, and the world's brutality had taken a toll on them.

They ate from the kitchen stores. Canned sardines were all that had been available, and the scent was sickly strong. Their bodies revolted the food at first, then rumbled for more. The alien substance gave them much energy that they were craving. "So, what now?" Seresuto questioned looking down at the sorry looking bunch. "*What now?* Hmmp!" Mack sighed and turned away from her. "Yeah! *What now?*" Seresuto's fire hand been fanned, and now it flared, "... You can't tell me you're giving up! Not after you've come so far!" she insisted. Mack stood revered in silence. "I won't stop," Mei said, bitterly protesting the idea, "I'd die first." "I feel da' same," Kato agreed. "I have to fulfil Masumi's last request. It's my duty to fight for her, as well as for Yokutan. And... I have to save Okichi," Kairu said. "Those bastards stole me from my home, from my family, I grew up a fucking science project to them! No damn way I'm letting them go free," Suako hissed. "I'm not giving up," Vince conquered. Yu-Lee gave a nod, "For a planet once rich with life, I serve her fully." "No way I'm jumping deck now," Jenko spoke up.

Still Mack said nothing. "Mack, you were always the smart one. You were never the one to hesitate. You always knew what had to be done..." Came the voice of a mysterious invisible guest. Everyone drew their weapons and aimed in the direction of the voice. An arrow soared threw Mack's heart when he heard the voice. *It can't be...* "Kazuo!" he exclaimed as he spun around. As sure as his assumption the shadowy figure came free from the corner of the room, and Kazuo walked towards them. Mack just stood there in stunned silence.

"We found him in the cell block you were in," Adamu said. Mack's head turned to Adamu. Slowly he felt his eyelid come down, and as if the world had drastically slowed time he looked back to Kazuo. Adamu's words sunk in, but did not feel real. *A dream? Am I dreaming? He's really alive... How?* Thoughts came and went faster than answers could reach them.

Kazuo reached the light, and Mack could see that his friend's once thick black hair grew thin, his face was gaunt, and his body withered from malnutrition. Eyes that had seen too many things looked at Mack. Only his voice spoke with any reminisce of a past long left behind. Feebly, Kazuo stood there. Mouth to the floor, Mack's eye started to tear with happiness; all those years of searching, hoping, and never giving up had finally paid off. Standing there, they both just stared at each other. Mack looked upon the remnants of a once strong and peace-desiring soldier. He had been a man of stature and great cause. Kazuo had once been a muscular man, with perfect posture, lively eyes, and glorious hair. Now the balding man was only recognisable by his handsome voice, which had surprisingly not changed at all. Reversibly, Kazuo looked upon his old childhood friend, to see that Mack had become strong. The once never defiant man now a renegade justice fighter. Inner strength that once had only shown itself occasionally shone brightly. An eye lost to cause, his path decided. Mack overwhelmed with swelling emotion hurried to embrace a friend he had thought to be long dead. "I knew you'd find me. I knew it..." Kazuo whispered.

Everyone introduced his or herself. Adamu reminded them that guard checks would be soon. Time was precious. They needed to figure out what they were doing, and quickly. It was time to get down to business, to finish what they'd started once and for all.

"Kazuo, the documents?" Mack had to ask. "Finally, I can tell you what they tried to shut up in me..." Kazuo started. Then his eyes clouded over, he was deep in thought as memories flooded his mind. He began to pant. As if another person had come take over him, Kazuo morphed, his personality switched. The strong confident man twisted into a frightened soul. He blanked out.

"Kazuo?" Mack interrupted. *Snap!* He was back and, "Oh... uh, sorry. What was it again? ... Oh yes, the documents. I memorised them. All the years they held me. I never forgot. I rehearsed them again and again. Bastards! I'd never forget that. That one document. I couldn't believe it. Nope. Couldn't believe it..." again Kazuo fell into a cavern of memories. Psychologically Kazuo was unstable when he referred to the documents or his entrapment. Forever it would haunt him. Other subjects he spoke normally without disturbance of mind, as they later found; digging deep into the painful instalment of this stretch of time in his life brought about incoherent speech the rest of his life.

"Umm, Kazuo?" Mack said again. Like he never stopped speaking, Kazuo picked up where he left off, "What was written was disgusting. So, I confronted them. Then they took me. They would have killed me but I hid the document. They needed me to tell them where it was. So, they kept me alive. They took me all over. The back... back of the truck, so dark... bumpy..." *Pause.* "Everywhere... where did I go? I went... they took me..." *Pause.* His head jerked and his face changed.

"Horrible, horrible words... on purpose... signed by Genjo Anami... the C.D.F.P. leader. Ngh..." Kazuo began a sway, "One of them stated the proposal to sway the Company to use filters. Cut down on carbon emissions. A reply with the word *'terminate'* at the top responded... I memorised it: As the new Chairman of the C.D.F.P. after my late father, I, Genjo Anami, refuse the proposed. It is not my will to cut back on the emissions. The people not living under air domes who defy us must suffer their decided fate. Both this and the emission deposit report are to be destroyed. No more mention of this shall be done without severe consequence..." Kazuo trailed off in tears. Mack hurried to comfort the broken man.

Kazuo's parents couldn't afford to live in a domed area at that time. He wanted to confront Genjo, which resulted in imprisonment, that would have been murder had he not hidden the incriminating documents. Although the C.D.F.P. was strong, it still was under Imperial Rule. The Empire would not stand for it. That alone saved Kazuo's life.

Mack rubbed Kazuo's back, "Just let it all out. It's all right." Kazuo just cried for some time. No one said anything. Suako's hand squeezed Vince's firmly, and Mei feel back into Kato's arms. The need for comfort and escaping, and the feeling of abandonment was empathetically spreading.

"Kazuo," Mack spoke softly. "You're safe now. They can't hurt you anymore. Where are the documents?" he asked, holding his friend paternally. "Here..." Kazuo mumbled. A bubble of gel-like spit muffled the word. Kazuo pulled away from the nurturing embrace of his friend. He went to the wall and took Mei's dagger, which had lain freely on the counter. The walls were concrete blocks. He counted several times over from the corner of the room. After satisfying himself that he'd found the right block, he commenced to chisel at one.

Mack, and some of the others, found themselves ruffling their brows. Kazuo, how he'd spoken, seemed almost senile. Jenko was about to speak up when he saw the wall flaking apart. It was plaster and crumbled away. Kazuo had to stop though. He took a break, fatigued, his body weak. Mack offered to help but Kazuo was determined to be the one to free them.

Once most of the plaster had gone, Kazuo reached his hand back into the dark space. Pulling back something crinkled against the back of the wall. He struggled in a kind of tug-o-war with it until he finally brought it through the dark hole. A dust-covered tan colored folder was in his hand. The original color of the folder, and the once white paper inside, had been augmented by its surroundings. He blew on it and a cloud of dust and plaster bits flew off into a rolling cloud. "Here... I hid it here," Kazuo had regained his former composure.

"I remember so well... I got a stone cutter and cut out a block. I stashed the files away and sealed the hole. Then I blocked off the room so no one would come in. I made a non-lethal chemical blend, you smell that? Well it's released every so-often to make it seem like a gas leek. They'd never be able to find it, I put it behind the wall... I figured they'd just stop using this room, keeping these babies safe. There are more correspondences in here about other terrible activities that would ruin Genjo, murder, and that kind of thing. There was also something about some human experiments," Kazuo said. "I can vouch for that," Suako said squeezing Vince's hand even harder. Her nails clawed his skin unknowingly, and sympathetically Vince glanced her way.

"So, we finally have proof," Jenko said bobbing his head, "we need to get this to Keiji Kane, the sooner the better. Once he finds out what's going on he'll be on our side..." "But Jenko, we can't leave things like this now. Those quakes are already here! In Torusan! They spread across the continent in just a few months. By the time we get *all* the way back to Tomakomai and *then* get them to come here, there'll be nothing left to save!" Vince enthusiastically protested. "I agree," Mei said. All of them knew it to be true. "Fuck..." Jenko sighed. He took a moment, then crossed his arms, "So, what is our game plan?"

A second chance. The last chance.

Chapter 26: The Plan

"It's this way! Common Kato, stop dragging your ass!" Mei teased. "Oh yea, like you just flew up 'ere," Kato grunted in a sort of half laugh, as he pulled himself up an elevator cable. His biceps bulged, and burned, with every strenuous pull. The leather gloves on his hands barely felt as if they'd prevent the wire from splintering into his skin. When he reached the doors, Mei pulled him into the hall; it was empty. They were still in the sub-levels of the building.

It had to have been the wee hours of the morning Mei thought. Next to no lights were on, no busy workers were using the hall, it was too quiet. Still her guard was up, they'd failed once, and now it was time to take the chance they were given and complete their mission. The droning blue lights glowed off Kato's eyes like mirrors. More elevator doors were on the opposite side of the hall, with the triangular *up* and *down* buttons, which shone in a clear crisp yellow. The bluish tile floor was hard and polar, numbing raw flesh.

"Kazuo said it was this way," Mei said point with her right arm, and helping Kato in with the other. He looked to the direction in which she pointed as he hauled his lower body in, "Right... Heh, this is gonna be some show, eh?" "One no one will soon forget," Mei concurred. Kato stood up with Mei, and they swiftly swept down the hall.

"Hurry Vince! ... *Phew*! We sure got loaded with the brunt of this, hmm? Haha!" Suako hadn't been more joyful since anytime she could remember. Finally, the day came for revenge. It was bittersweet. "We're making good time. Damn this is heavy though!" Vince remarked as he jogged along side her. His breath was running short. *Heave! Pant!* "You're not kidding. This is gonna be great... I hope the others are safe," she replied.

Footsteps rung into the chamber of the hallway. They were back on the bottom floor, only barbaric torches lit up the cell area. Clouds of dust rose from beneath their feet as they persevered forward. At a four-way intersection of the halls they stopped. "I'm going this way. We'll meet back here as soon as we're done. Be quick... be careful," Vince kissed Suako on the forehead and then dashed off into an engulfing darkness. On her lonesome Suako went in the opposite direction. Disappearing into the shadows...

"Do you think they'll make it Mack?" Jenko asked, hope in his voice, as they ran down the hall. Yu-Lee and Kairu followed up the rear. "We can only hope. Adamu is the only one who can navigate a ship, and Seresuto's strong willed, so I'm sure they will. We can only hope that they get there quickly. Those boats they have now... If we're lucky they'll be there and back in two weeks. Right now, let's focus on our job Jenko," Mack said pragmatically. "Right," Jenko nodded. Mack's boots slide on the floor as he halted; they had reached an elevator door.

"All of these elevators are monitored. We can't just get in and go up. Any ideas?" Mack asked. His small dispatch neglected an immediate response from Jenko, the concentration of their minds, while on the edge, was poorly managed. "I know!" Yu-Lee suddenly exclaimed. Mack and Jenko flinched fearfully, startled by her exuberance. "Oh sorry. Listen to this. I used to do a thing called *'Glamour Magick'*. I can use it for us now..." she began to explain. "'*Glamour magick'*?" Kairu asked, without a clue, his innate curiosity present, showing a glimpse of his leadership skills.

"Yes. I can use the 'Life Force' to manipulate our appearances temporarily. Other people won't be able to recognise us. We won't be able to see any differences ourselves, and anyone who knows us, like Yoshida, won't see the guise either. It'll hide us from the guards though. What do you think?" Yu-Lee suggested. Everyone excluding Mack gave a sign of approval. Mack took a step toward her with a blank face and reached his hands to her head. Nervously, in the confusion of his sudden and strange action, Yu-Lee hadn't any idea what to think. Then Mack leaned forward and planted a kiss on each of her cheeks. Pulling away he looked at her with a goofy happy smile, "You're a genius," he declared. She laughed bashfully. "Let's do it!" Mack approved.

"It reeks down here... Yuck..." Seresuto complained as Adamu lowed her down a manhole. "It's the only safe way out of here. These documents mean the survival of, well... everyone! So just grin and bare it will ya?" Adamu barked. Seresuto stood knee deep in the cities water run off, looking dumbfounded; Adamu had never talked back to her. The seriousness of the situation was really hitting home. She bit her tongue from there on in, feeling guilty for her selfishness, "Adamu you're right. I'm sorry. Let's do this!"

"Everything went alright?" Suako asked when Vince re-emerged from the tunnel. "Yea. You?" Vince nodded. "No problems," Suako confirmed. "Let's take this one together, then onto the next floor. We need to speed this up. Mack need us to..." Vince said. "I know, I know, let's go..." Suako agreed.

"Is this it?" Mei asked. "Dunno. I can't see shi' in here its so dark," Kato sighed. "Well at least help me try and figure it out... It feels like it could be... Oh, this is so stupid. I don't hear anyone. Just turn on the lights for a minute," Mei complained. "No Mei, too risky. I'll help..."

Kato said. There was a long pause as they worked their way around the room. Only lit up button lights prevented the total opaqueness of the darkness.

It was frustrating and stressful; everything needed to be relatively timed to the plan Mack had drawn up. Like invalids they navigated the room, touch allowed their imaginations too much room to play. Mei's patience was running thin. Turning to go across the room, she kicked her foot on a hard something, which sent Mei spinning around, but she caught herself on some sort of desk. Her hand hit something on the way down which grabbed her attention.

Mei's eyes flew open. "Kato! Come here, please tell me this is what I think it is," Mei excitedly called him. He made his way over in the vision crippling room. "What?" he asked. "Here!" Mei took his hand and planted it down. The object was a mix of plastic and metal. It stretched long horizontally, like a stapler, it pressed down and made a *click* noise.

Kato reached his hands back, and like a blind man he began to identify his surroundings with his fingertips. Trying to envision the object in his head, he closed his eyes to block out the distracting lit up knobs that his peripheral sight caught. At first nothing logical would present itself. He scrunched his face as he thought. *What the hell is this? Smells like copper. It feels like...! It can't be!* "Morse code?" Kato said opening his eyes. "I thought so too! Do you know any?" Mei asked excitedly. "Yea I do," he said. "Listen, I have an idea. ..." Mei continued.

Ding! The elevator door slid open; it was empty, they stepped in. Cloaked by a shield they could not confirm to be working, they faithfully trusted it. In military garb they fit in as soldiers. *Ding!* The shifting door closed, and up the vertical column they climbed. The hum of the lights above sounded like a colony of bees working away in their nest.

A few floors up the elevator stopped, and a few employees stepped in. There were no questions asked, the employees just carried on the conversation they'd had going before. "...So, then the generators in Atani have been low in production?" one asked. "Yes. We haven't received conformation on why yet. I'm having some of the soldiers look into it," a second replied. "Koto won't be pleased. He's been getting tired of these setbacks. If *he* ends up going out there to check it out, well... I can just see my pay check dropping a few notches," a third said. "Don't worry about it so much. Koto has been keeping busy with some of our other departments. He'll probably dismiss it, or just send someone else to go check it out," the first one said. *Ding!* "I hope you're right. Now what about..." Their voices faded as they stepped out and the door closed. Again, they went up.

"Who's 'Koto'?" Kairu asked. "He's the chairman's son. He's just as dirty as his old man," Kazuo replied. "Koto..." Yu-Lee said beneath her breath in thought. It didn't go unnoticed by Jenko, "What is it, Yu-Lee?" Her head slowly rose to look at him, "That name... sounds familiar. I don't like it. I just... No, never mind," she suddenly shut off her will to prattle on. "Yu-Lee?" Jenko worried about her sudden discretion. "It's all right. Really, I'm fine. Don't worry about it," she tried to reassure him. "Are you sure?" he touched her arm. "Yes," she met his eyes, "I'm positive."

Onward they ascended. The hum of the light became soothing the longer they were in the elevator. Over exerting hearts lessened their pace. The counting ticker above the doors accumulated. There were many swirling notions in their overactive brains, and it induced silence among them. So many questions, and nothing but time coming to pass could cure their devouring power. Ticker read: **38**

"Vince? ... Vince!?" Suako ran around. She called for him fretfully. Behind her, a door creaked open, and he appeared. "Vince!" she exclaimed, and flew into his arms. "I was thinking. This is going to take too long. We've already planted on the first two bottom floors, we should just do every other floor for the rest of the way up. ... Vince? Vince, what is it?" Suako asked. He stood there looking dazed, "It's..." was all he could muster to say. Like a zombie his body gave out, and he fell back to lean against the wall behind him, and slide against it to the floor. His head sunk and he balanced his forehead on his hand. Suako crouched next to him, trying to make sense of his babble, but her efforts failed.

The door from where he'd came stood open an inch. Looking closer she saw the faded sign on the door: **Authorised Personnel Only**. Suako pushed herself up with her leg, feeling the muscles work as she did. Something was pulling her in, something was in there; there was no doubt about it, she *had* to go in. Some cosmic force was drawing her internally, and the rest of the world lost any attention she had been granting it. Suako had tunnel vision for this task.

Suako felt her pulse race as she pressed her fingertips against the door, it was cold to the touch, and incredibly heavy. The tendons on her arm stood out. She applied pressure to the door, and her fingers went white from red as she pushed. Gradually the door opened, the hinges squealed like a dying boar as it did. The light in the laboratory was sterile, the incandescent blue cast a hue over everything.

Despite the urge to run, Suako couldn't turn back. Nervously she stepped forward, crossing one leg over the other. She shook, like leaves on trees on a rough windy autumn day, but she did not turn back. No one was inside the lab, no scientists prowled around this hellish room, which she had so long ago condemned. The smells remained the same, that of flesh and chemicals. The sickly strong scent of bleach was nearly overwhelming.

Some instruments were scattered across the floor, a scalpel, some scissors, and a few needles, beneath an out of place tray, were among the clutter. The compression of an air pump periodically hissed, as it performed its objective duty. *Beep!... Beep!* The most distracting device in use sounded constantly, it was the vitals monitor, and it tracked a heart rate.

Mortified Suako still couldn't go back; her legs walked forward without her permission. She could not deny them. Suako heard herself breathing, heavy and brisk. Vince had come in behind her but she did not hear him. One step closer, closer, closer...

A chair, all to familiar to her, showed its back to her. *Step...* Cords from the monitor swept down towards it. *Step...* That chair she vowed never to go into again, so close to her now. *Step...* Breathing... *Step...* Someone was in that chair now. *Step...* Their hair-raising breaths persisted in constant intervals. *Step...* Each one a struggle. *Step...* A will to survive. *Step...* Or lack of courage to die. *Step... Who is it? Step, step, step...*

Suako gasped and feel to her knees, shock gripped her, and then she burst into an outpouring of uncontrollable tears. She felt like she couldn't breathe, and started to struggle for air, like a fish out of water. Her right knee had landed on a sharp prodding tool, which had pierced her skin. She was bleeding, but ignored it. Her left hand clasped over her mouth. Between short exhumed breaths she managed out, "No! No! No! ..." continuously said, with no distinct sound to them.

Struggling on her knee's, the object digging further into her skin, Suako squirmed. A limp arm, bruised and scabbed, rested over the armrest of the chair. Suako took the hand in hers, it was frigid. Hoisted up she looked at the weak depleted leftovers of the woman resting in the chair. Half clad, and left alone to starve and suffer in the pits of this imitated hell. Remorsefully Suako spoke out to the scarred creature, which lay before her. Her voice was flat and weak. Suako looked on at her sister, and choked as she spoke her name through warbling lips, "...Renee..."

Floor: **64** *Be ready. Be prepared. Don't forget to breathe, don't forget to breathe...*

"Hey Mei, what 'bout dis'?" Kato asked as he groped a cylinder-shaped object in his hands. "Hmm? Let me feel. ... It's hard to tell. There's a panel over there, but I can't read it. What do you say we just trash it all?" Mei suggested mischievously. Kato's big arm swept around her waist and drew her near. He kissed her affectionately, "Oh babe, I love ya'..." he had a dopey grin as he leaned over her. Mei giggled. "Let's do this!" Her eyes burned, and pierced like a feline's. Up she lifted a massive wrench.

"Wait..." Kato put his hand on her upraised arm. "What?" she asked impatiently. "Let's do this right," he told her and lowered the wrench down. Mei looked upon Kato curiously. He closed his eyes and then took a long, deep, soothing breath. Again, a deep inhale. Mei now understood and joined him. After a moment of relaxing, solitary being Kato spoke, "For Jake..." Mei opened her eyes and turned to look at Kato, "For Nayu..." Both of them now jointly prepared the wrench, brandishing it high above their heads, "Lights out!" ...

There was a rumble to the ground, and Seresuto lost her balance and fell face first into the disgusting dirty water. It wasn't an earthquake this time. The constant electrical hum that had never ceased now stopped. It gave one last belch, which faded low until it dissipated. It rung in their ears for a while. Adamu helped Seresuto back onto her feet. Looking up he spoke softly, with true sincerity, "Good luck you guys."

The elevator came to a screeching halt. They had slid down the shaft, but only by about a floor before the emergency brakes has stopped them. When it stopped gravity caught up to them, and they felt themselves being jostled around harshly. They had been alone in the elevator when it happed, and the light went out. An emergency backup, from a small generator attached to the elevator had kicked in, which had engaged the brakes that keep them from falling to untimely deaths. A red bulb lit up in the elevator, just as one had in the train to Tomakomai.

"Is everyone alright?" Mack asked, as the world stopped spinning. "I'm fine," Yu-Lee replied, pressed tight against the rear wall next to Jenko. "Same here. Hit my head, but I'll live" Jenko said. Kazuo and Kairu checked in, rattle, but alright too. "Anyone catch the last floor we were at?" Mack questioned, his eye gazing up at the deadened ticker. "It was at 71," Kairu answered. "So, we're around 70, you think?" Jenko asked aloud. "Probably. Let's get these doors open..." Mack skimmed his hand across the surface to find the dividing break.

Kairu and Jenko went to help. Yu-Lee and Kazuo stood like bystanders in the back, watching and waiting anxiously. Using brut force, and synchronisation, they pried the stiff doors open. "Yu-Lee! The pins!" Mack grunted in spurts. "Oh! Sorry!" she pulled them free of the backpack she'd found in the room they met Kazuo in. She quickly went over to the door, dropped onto her knees, and carefully she inserted the pins. The small metal holders somehow kept the doors from shutting.

Between floors, the moonlight threw windows shone in from above. The top of the elevator entrance was at the bottom of the flor they'd stopped at, giving them only two feet at the top of the elevator door to get out. Mack looked around and saw a plaque posted by the stairwell entrance read: **Floor 70**. They were where they predicted to have stopped; the brakes had worked incredibly well.

Everyone tossed their things up out the elevator door, onto the floor above. Then Jenko and Kairu formed a stair with their interlocked arms for Yu-Lee the climb up on. Partially up, her bust laying against the cool marble floor, she pulled herself out. The floor was so clean that it reflected her image to her back to her like a mirror. With the strength of her arms she managed to wiggle the rest of her body up. The hall was empty, though she heard a few footsteps above her head, and murmurs from a vent linking to the floor below. The voices complained of the power outage.

The C.D.F.P. building was one big electronic machine. Without electricity the run it, none of the mechanisms could function. The employees had heavy reliance on there technology to work, so the disturbance worked just as planned. They had completely lucked out that this floor had no one up and about, Yu-Lee thought as she stood up in the empty hallway. "The coast is clear, come on out," she told the others, and offered Kazuo a hand up.

Once they were all happily out of the elevator, they gathered the few things that they had brought along. "Hey! What's that?" Kairu's keen youthful ears perked up. The others silenced themselves to listen, and after a moment, could hear the stomping of feet was drawing in. "Shit! C.D.F.P. soldiers? Probably following up on the power outage. We've got to hide," Mack insisted, searching for an escape or hiding place. "Over here!" Jenko called twisting a door handle. The door swung into a dark office, and they scurried in. The same emergency red lighting was on inside the office.

Jenko began to tug the door shut, but Kairu ran out. "What are you doing?" Jenko harshly scolded, in frightened bewilderment. "The pins! If the doors are open they'll know something's up..." Kairu replied as he ran. He had taken Mack's shotgun and used the nozzle to flick away the pins. They clinked around as they flew away, and the doors closed. The hasty group was getting closer. "Kairu!" Jenko waved him back demandingly to get in the office room. Kairu flew in like a breeze, in just enough time, Jenko closed the door behind them. The gentle penetrating latch slid into its slot as Jenko let the door handle slide back through his fingers.

Noiselessly they stood holding their breaths. The pattering footsteps grew and then passed right by them, but two soldiers stopped dead cold near the stairs. Someone told them to stay there and keep watch for 'suspicious activity'. For now, they were stuck; it was too early to start a commotion.

A translucent respirator tube had been inserted down Renee's throat. Emotionally distraught, Suako forced herself to gather her wits. "R... Renee? It's me, Suako... h...honey, I'm gonna pull, pull this tube out... OK?" Suako's skin folded between her eyebrows as she looked mournfully at her sister. With her right hand she lovingly stroked her fingers through Renee's hair. At first, Renee flinched when she was touched. It was instinctual, since as long as she could remember, human contact had been only done to torment, and she couldn't help but be wary. The small reaction alone flooded Suako with guilt.

Renee just barely tilted her head as if to answer 'yes'. Drawing her mothering hand away, Suako pinched the tube between her fingers. Vacillating, Suako reluctantly extracted the tube. As she did Renee looked to be gagging on in. Sticky, dripping and bubbled saliva coated the exterior of the tube. When it came free Renee gulped for air and then meekly heaved. Suako hugged her sister, releasing the tube, it plunged to the ground.

"Suako?" Renee seemed to have forgotten. "Y, yes... I'm your sister. Remember me?" Suako's glossy eyes held back forceful tears. Vince stood back just watching the scene unfold. The image of the sickly creature gave him a new knowledge, for no words could have painted this picture in his mind. Vince was at a loss for what to do with himself.

"Suako..." Renee's next to non-existent voice dimmed, and her eyes dulled. "I'm so sorry I left you Renee... I'm so sorry. I thought you were dead..." Suako barely constructed understandable sentences, her voice rose and fell in drastic measures. Suako's mouth drew back in a painfully straining upside-down smile. Wrinkles of skin formed around her cheeks. Her face was blotched with red spots, and her eyes were strained, and looking like jelly. Shamefully she dropped her head and sunk down weeping.

As if someone had come behind her and startled her, Renee sucked in a gasp of air, "I remember you... you said we... we'd get away... someday..." Her poor body was weak. Renee's frail voice was clear and pure. She was still the child she'd been that had been abducted from her home with her sister so long ago. Her soul was as tattered and torn as her body. The vulnerable girl lay there unmoving besides her breathing.

"Will des' stairs ever end... Holy shi'... S, stop. I ne' to catch my breath..." Kato nearly collapsed on the stairs. Perspiration drenched his shirt. Mei slowed to a stop, undeniably she needed to stop and catch her breath as well. Sitting down on the steps they rested, and Blood surged through their twittered veins. Like inhaling fire, they pulled in the razor blades of oxygen. Painful injections aerated overextended lunges, as their chests expanded brutally. The energy flow still soared through unmoving legs.

Stomp! Stomp! Stomp! A parade of marching feet, climbing upwards, sounded from below. They knew was too early in this final campaign to give themselves away with gunfire. With critiquing ears, the distinction of simply three or four people coming up, presented itself. The metal clang of feet hitting the stairs was amplified in the chamber pillar. Deceiving legs refused to run; Mei and Kato were simply to exhausted. They pulled out their knife and dagger, and awaited to ambush their opponents...

They hadn't moved, but Mack could only halt their attack so long. Soon the building would be lively, and, if not already, their empty cells would be discovered. The decision was a challenging one. "Mack?" Kairu whispered, "what are we going to do?" "I'm not sure yet," Mack replied, lost in those questions himself.

Mack stared blankly at the door, which was barely taking shape under the minute red light. The light clicking of heels on the hard floor came down the hallway. It was brisk, and almost angry. It paused at the area where the soldiers had stopped walking earlier. Some non-retrievable words impacted the guards, and they left a moment later. Then the clicking left the stationed post.

Mack backed away from the door, holding his breath. It didn't work. The harassing clicks just grew in a bellowing way. Right before the door the clicking stopped, and the door handle shook. It twisted and opened, and the moonlight poured into the reddish room from around the slender silhouette of Tamiko. Before any of them could make a move, an uplifted head produced raven like eyes, which met Yu-Lee's eyes dead on. "Hello Tamiko," Yu-Lee said blankly. Straight through Yu-Lee's guise, Tamiko could clearly see her porcelain face that had been seamless to the effects of age. All Tamiko could utter was, "Mother?" …

Suako found herself unravelling, she scrambled to her feet and hurried to the sink to vomit. Violently her body convulsed. Renee kept her eyes on Suako, whenever she could hold them open. "So sorry…" Suako tried to speak between hurling. Like an out of body experience, Vince watched himself walk over to Renee's side and look down at her. Time had slowed. The battered girl lay before him like a nightmare from a twisted mind, it was so bizarre that it didn't feel real. Prodded into her body numerous tubes and needles stuck her.

Renee's eyes reached up to meet his, a certain vagueness hazed within them. They were eyes that had seen many awful things. He didn't want to know what she had seen, what she had been through; he did not even want to imagine it. Renee's shaky hand touched his. Somehow, he refrained from jumping back. He clasped it in his. She was asking for help, it was a silent plea. Sorrowfully, he returned her look with compassionate eyes.

Suako returned to Renee, and angrily pulled off the wires that were monitoring Renee like a science project. Since the power died the monitors had gone blank anyway. "I'm getting you out of here," Suako said as she worked with urgency. Suako was working in high-speed, her fingers tripped over each other as she freed her sister's body of the intruding tubes and needles.

"Vince," Suako said between wiping away a waterfall of tears. "I need you to do me, *sniff*... a favour. I need you to get Renee out of here," Suako began to explain. "Suako," he attempted to protest the concerning their situation. Suako grabbed his arm firmly, "Just listen! Please?" her eyes pleaded. Her look was intense, and Vince could do nothing but comply with her wishes, so he nodded in agreement. "Thank you. Here's what I want you to do," she began.

"I want you to get her out of this place. As fast as you can. Don't worry about our set up, I'll take care of it. I'm the explosives expert anyway, and I can do it quickly. It won't be a problem, so don't worry! Once you're out, get her somewhere safe. Then, well... I guess we'll see you when it's all gone down," she blinked and then put on a half smile. "But, but... what about all of the pick-up points? You know where to collect on the floors?" Vince struggled for excuses. "Vince trust me, please! Mei and I used to do this for all of the reactors. I know where to go," she reassured him. Vince closed his eyes, he had no choice but to give in. "Alright, Suako... I'll do it. Just be careful," he pulled her close and held her tight. "I love you..." he whispered in her ear. "Go now, Suako. Hurry. Don't worry about us."

Reluctantly Suako drew away. She took her time viewing Vince, she took him into her soul, burning his image into her heart. "Thank you," she said, and used her lips to soundlessly say '*I love you too...*' as she released his hand. She took his pack and slung it on top of the one she already had. The weight was strenuous to carry, but it was the last thought in her mind. With one last look and a kiss to her sister's cheek she then ran off out the door.

Like a younger version of Yu-Lee, Tamiko stood stunned in the doorway. Kairu held off on his original plan of using his jujitsu skills to disable the intrusive person from taking them on. Tamiko's sharp face looked over the crew. Tamiko stood there with her hair back in its usual tight bun, wearing a bland grey suit, white blouse, and plaid grey and white pumps with black straps.

Finally, after a long silence she spoke. "What is going on?" she inquisitively asked. Her focus dropped on Yu-Lee. "A lot has happened Tamiko. Maybe had you not left, and continued your studies you could have foreseen..." Yu-Lee started but was cut off. "Quiet!" Tamiko bit back, "I left because I didn't want to die there. I wanted a life *I* could enjoy. We lived in the middle of nowhere, scrounging for food, and starving for oxygen. Don't you *dare* say a word about my leaving." Yu-Lee did not respond. She looked away from her daughter, unable to begrudge her.

"Tamiko you chose your path. That was *your* choice. That's fine, but it was the easy road out. It was a selfish thing to do. You basically took up arms against the rest of the human race, no, not just us, of all earthly life. Instead of destroying the problems of your life, you joined them. Evil begets evil. Just so you know Tamiko, whether you believe this or not, your *easy road* is coming to an end. It was going to be ending soon regardless of us too. Those earthquakes you're having here now are going to get worse. Okagwa was swallowed whole into the earth. Genjo is fully aware..." again Yu-Lee was cut off. "Mother, you can save your breath. I know that too," Tamiko said, unwavering, and unmoved by her mother's plight.

Yu-Lee took Tamiko's words like a slap in the face, "Tamiko!? He's doing it intentionally to spite the people, and you don't care?" "I was informed. We're safe from it here," Tamiko said, firm in her belief. "No Tamiko you're not! The entire planet is going to implode!" Yu-Lee said, desperation in her voice. "Save your wild stories mother. I grow weary of them," Tamiko replied. "Tamiko... How you've changed," Yu-Lee fought backs from weeping. There was no talking to the daughter she once knew. She was stubborn and had grown into a different person. Tamiko refused to deviate from her path, but Yu-Lee struggled to come to terms with it.

"Well then," Mack had a hard-core expression on his face. Having had been conned into wanting the life Tamiko had, he had given her sympathy at first. Now he was close to loathing her, knowing that she *knew* what she did. "It's a good thing your co-operation is mandatory," he said tapping his riffle. "Fine. What do you want?" Tamiko asked in frustration, her voice venomous. "What exactly *is* your job?" he asked. Tamiko sighed impatiently, "I'm the head of the Dome and Generator accounting and maintenance. Why?" Her snarky snapping was testing Mack's patience. "Watch it!" he warned, raising his gun.

Fuck! Goddamn these stupid wires! Why the hell do they always come loose…? I don't have time for this. Shit. … Ugh! Come out… son… of… a… "Ouff!" *Geese… Finally! OK now get this little thing in there… OK done! Next one…* Suako jumped up to her feet. Stabilising for a moment she got her balance. Her mind was razor sharp; she was on a mission. All other thoughts she numbed for the time being. Then like a bolt of lightning, she took off towards her next target.

"What the hell were they? Trainees?" Mei asked in almost a confused laugh as she wiped her bloody nose. "No shi'. Dropped like flies," Kato agreed in the same kind of distorted speech. The few soldiers lay unconscious on the stairs. They'd gone down without much effort at all. "We'd better get going. Someone's gonna notice that they're missing sooner or later," Mei commented. "Yeah… stairs again. Great," Kato sighed. Mei let out a hardy laugh. Up the spiralling tower of stairs they mounted.

It became like an endless stretch of climbing stairs. The quivering metal vibrated beneath their feet with every step. The steps looked like cheese graters with their tiny oval holes. Through the net like staircase, they could see down to what was beneath them, which now, so high up, disappeared into a sea of black. It was dizzying the higher they got. Onward they pressed, despite refuting legs that made their protesting clear. The pain had to be ignored. Sheer will drove them forward, up and up and up...

"... So, you're saying that the domes actually don't cost anything to generate, except their initial construction, and to keep energy going to their projectors?" Kairu asked bewildered. "Yes. There was a dome around the continent put in place, just like the one over the whole Imperial continent, but it never turned on. Genjo isn't willing to give air to those unwilling to pay for it, just like his father. It was his father who had approved the construction of domes over cities to control taxation," Tamiko explained under interrogation. "It's virtually one hundred percent profit despite the minimal up-front costs," Kazuo shook his head. "Tamiko, why isn't giving everyone a good life like you always wanted good enough? I don't understand your decision," Jenko couldn't comprehend it. "Genjo is a powerful man. I wouldn't defy him, or Koto," she replied.

Again, Tamiko was relentless, deflecting their futile logical portraits. "So, how do we activate the oxygen dome?" Mack asked. "It's a manual process. You'd need to go to every projector and turn them on. They each have their own individual four-digit numerical activation codes. All you have to do is enter the code to each of them and they will start the filtration process," Tamiko explained.

"You have those codes?" Mack asked, nearly as a statement. Tamiko sighed, "Yes I do." "Good. We'd like them, now," Mack commanded. Tamiko's eyes rolled, and

Mack just grinned. "Alright. They're kept downstairs in one of the filing rooms. I'll go get them," she conceded. Mack's grin widened, "Jenko will escort you. We'll be waiting," he took pleasure in messing with Tamiko. "Let's go," Jenko said standing up.

Vince carried Renee's immobile body on his back. She was extremely light, her protruding ribs and hipbones dug into his skin, through his jacket. Before he'd taken her out of the laboratory, he'd found some water to douse her dry throat with. She took a sip that seemed like nothing. After a few more attempts she got a decent few gulps down, and then felt ill to have something in her shrunken stomach. He decided then that it had been time to leave.

Now, on the lowest floor, Vince torpedoed though maze like hallways. It was disorienting. The crackling of the torches kept him paranoid. *Out... Out... Where the hell is out!?* He screamed within the confines of his head. He searched desperately. Forward, looking around the corner, then running back, he went without a definite pattern. Everything looked the same, and the stagnant air was giving him a headache...

"Explain it to me please," Jenko insisted. "What's to tell?" Tamiko replied, annoyed. Jenko and Tamiko stood in the middle of the empty file room. The door was labelled **Documents A-G** in big block letters. Tamiko slipped paper after paper threw her fingers as she searched for the codes. "You said you left home because you were tired of a hard life. You can have it without working for these people now. They're murderers. I just... It *doesn't* make sense to me. I know you don't have to answer, but... I can't grasp it," Jenko said. Tamiko sighed and tensed her neck as she took in a long deep soothing drink of air, "Alright, I'll tell you."

Tamiko ceased what she was doing, curved her neck, twisted round to face him. Her violet eyes, just like her mother's, met his without fear. Jenko found himself surprised by her confidence. Placing her hand on her hip she spoke with pride, "Have you ever had a dream fulfilled? After you have it, what's left? When we get what we want, we crave for something else. It's human instinct. Now that I have my perfect life I want *the vision*. I listen to Genjo speak with his resolve and I believe in him. Think what you will of it," She swept a loose hair back behind her ear. "The *vision?*" Jenko curiously wanted to hear more.

"Genjo wants the world. It has been so long since his ancestors had removed themselves from the Imperial continent that it seems their extending rule over here is foolish. Genjo is a charismatic man. If he wants something, he *will* get it... I've worked my way up from the *pits* of this company. I laboured for next to no money, but I moved up in the world. I'm high on the food chain here. When Genjo manifests his wishes, I will be sure to collect my share of the bounty," she explained. "How do you know that you'd get *anything* from a man willing to step on anyone in order to get his way?" Jenko asked unsatisfied.

The pre-spoken response was enough to raise the hairs on Jenko's arms. Tamiko saw something in her eyes that made them glint. Her head lowered slightly, and her lip piqued up to the right. She looked like a predator on the prowl. "I know because..." she spoke slowly in a reassured, and somewhat cocky manner. Tamiko seemed to have an underlying evil way to her flowing words, "I'm with his son." Back to the documents she went searching in her anal way as she previously had been. Obviously, she didn't see her mother and her entourage as a threat to her ambitious goals. Jenko asked no more from her.

"Wha'... wha' floor are we be on?" Kato wheezed. "I dunno... Uhh... forty-six," Mei huffed as she read a sign next to an exiting door. "H... How, how many are der'?" Kato gasped. "Too many!" Mei snorted back. Kato groaned. His leaden legs were starting to lose sensation. Numbly he climbed behind Mei. Mei kept up a good pace, which seemed impossible to Kato for any human maintain. The endless stairs just kept coming. One after the other...

"Yu-Lee, why didn't you ever say anything about her?" Mack sympathetically asked Yu-Lee, who had closed up like a clam. He leaned next to the desk by which Yu-Lee had been standing. "I couldn't. I... I know life was cruel trying to survive there but... I never thought she'd do *this*. When she was a teenager she bore such hatred toward me for not excepting an air dome from the C.D.F.P. It was foolish I thought... such a small thing. But I refused to support the Company. I suppose my reasons were not clear enough to her..."

"It's not your fault Yu-Lee. Everyone has there own free will. You know this better then any of us. She's another piece of the Life Energy, right?" Kairu attempted to pull Yu-Lee free from her trance-like thought state. "You're right," she said out of feelings of obligation. She gave a nervous type of giggle that was the only thing she could produce from a muddled mind. Her inevitable awkward feelings kept her shyly secluding herself. "Yu-Lee?" Kairu attempted to reach out again. Mack shook his head at him. "I just... Just give me some time," she said, composure still somehow intact. She sat behind the clean desk to think.

What's that? Oh shit... Oh shit! It's coming, coming... where? Where the hell am I gonna hide? Sh, shit, shit! There's no where to go... Suako had crouched down behind a furnace. The hissing of gas had made the approaching janitor soundless until it was too late for Suako to get away. Suako ingested the fumes, which gave her a nasty headache.

The man was quite old. His grey hair was on the verge of white, and his moustache was rather quaint. He had a weathered face with many wrinkles. He wore a faded blue pair of overalls, and gold rimmed pair of spectacles, and hummed a gentle tune as he went about his daily tasks. Suako prayed he wouldn't see her, while simultaneously contemplating the actual result of it happening. He was one of those citizens who travelled from the lower class in to Grid One to work all day, just to go home with little more to fill their pockets and feed their families.

The heat radiating from the furnace started to burn Suako. She felt sweat dripping off her face like a water fall, trickling down her neck, and creating a river on her arms. Her scalp began to tingle, and then her nerves started to scream as the intensity of the heat increased. Her supporting arms quivered and she prayed for the strength the wait it out.

Just as he had come, the man left, taking a mop and pail with him. As soon as she heard the slam of the door twang she dropped her bottom to the floor and quickly crawled away. Suako let out a extravagant squawk, then coughed and exorbitantly sucked in clean air, away from the dizzying gas line. For a moment she let her body relax. Her shoulders dropped, and ribs cage collapsed. *Close call...*

The following hours consisted of many tasks being taken care of. Mei and Kato had met up with Mack, as they by chance caught sight of Kairu peering out the door to check the floor. They waited for Jenko and Tamiko to return. Vince had made his way threw the same drainpipe Adamu and Seresuto had earlier that day, and escaped from Grid One with Renee. Suako continued to drop off her special "presents", planting them around the building. Seresuto and Adam had reached the city outskirts and snuck out beyond the dome. They were almost ready...

Final Preparations… This is it… Please, oh please let this work! … And please, let everyone be safe…

Chapter 27: The Final Showdown

It was nearing one O'clock in the afternoon, and all electrical systems were still malfunctioning. The mess downstairs was irreversible, there was no fixing it, it required replacement. Nervous tension was peaking in Tamiko's office. The light of day was the only comfort; the sun was bright against the crystal clear blue sky. It twinkled and made rainbows through glass that projected around the room.

Human traffic had remained fairly light, with the power outage, the building wasn't filled to the brim with employees. Turned away at the door, Mack had figured. It was exactly what he had wanted, the less bodies the better. Detoured civilians were preferable to a mass of wandering eyes with questioning brains.

Every so often the vents would flare up in a distracting way, sending warm air into the little room to ward off the airy chill of late winter. Out the windows, the city streets doled farewell to the melting snow. The red light had automatically shut off at daybreak. It was almost *too* clean in Tamiko's office; everything was in its place, even her random work piles seemed to be neat and tidy. Pens were arranged by size, books alphabetised on the shelves, color coded files, and on top of it all, not a speck of dust.

Yu-Lee had reverted to being quite reserved, so they left her alone. While they waited, they snooped threw Tamiko's documents and file folders. It was time to explore all they could while they were still able. Most of what was pulled had no great importance, many financial figures and profit graphs; they were making money from providing virtually nothing.

As time ticked on, the more the pile of overviewed data sheets accumulated. It was dry to read, and their boredom levels increased. The energetic vibe was practically null and void at this point. Kairu dropped the binder he'd been looking at, he grew weary of the accounting section. He ventured over to the **Maintenance** headed section and grabbed a random folder. Kairu's eyes skimmed over another droll looking sheet. Moments later his head jolted back and eyes widened, and his lip parted slightly, lifting to a smile. "Mack, I found something," he crawled over the mounds of piled bundles of information. "Take a look," he said handing Mack the papers.

Mack took the document in his hand. Everyone else put down their reading material to inspect what was being reviewed. Mack took in the eyeful. The same daft response Kairu had given had been repeated through Mack. He chuckled, "This is great," he spoke to the page. "Listen up everyone," Mack addressed them, "Kairu found a list of *every* reactor location. Now we can take them *all* out. Kudos Kairu," Mack said without lifting his eye from the page. A round of praise followed Mack's lead.

A breeze blew up from the south. It carried with it the essence from the ocean. It was soothing, yet gave warning of a turning tide. The gravel crunched beneath the weight of the tires. The smell faded away, as did the roar of the engine as Vince turned it off. He left the keys in the ignition. His door handle clicked as he pulled it to release its closed hold to the body of the vehicle. He hopped out onto the ground and slammed the door shut, and then circled the pickup truck, and opened the passenger door. Cat-like Renee stirred from her sleep. "We're here," Vince told her, waking her up.

Vince scooped her up off of the seat, and hit the door, to close it, with his foot. It swung in and made a faint noise to indicate a secure closed hold. The gravel rustled under his feet as he walked. Renee squinted her eyes in pain, it hadn't been since her first few years alive that she'd seen the sun. Renee couldn't remember it, and It attacked her eyes like a plague. "What is it?" she groaned in a child-like whine. "The sun. You'll get used to it," he tried to comfort her.

Up the path of the junkyard, Vince made his way to the great big doors of their hideout. He sat Renee down as he hauled the massive doors open. Within everything had been just as it was when they'd left so many months ago. The table and out-slid stools still rested in the middle of the immensely wide space. Hidden around the corner, to the right, Vince could visualise the shower with it's fire-hydrant red shower curtain, and the blue patch in the center of it that's seams were loosening. It felt safe to him here; the was the best place to go. Vince lifted Renee back up, and she wrapped her scrawny arms back around his neck to support herself. Vince took her to the far back of the building and laid her down on a mattress. He attended to her with some blankets. Although they were old and worn they were warm. The journey had exhausted Renee, and she drifted in and out of consciousness.

Vince fetched her some water and some jarred applesauce he remembered they'd had stored there. Vince stroked the side of her face until she jolted awake. Renee screamed and then saw her surroundings and calmed down. Vince's warm face helped to relax her neurotic nature. He lifted her head with his hand, and held the glass of water up to her cracked dry lips. As best she could, she drank it down. Some droplets dribbled down her chin, she pulled away and Vince set he back down.

Renee's eyes asked him '*why?*' again and again. He couldn't find an answer to verbalise. They did not break eye contact for several minutes, as he ran his fingers through what was left of her depleting hair. Her eyes closed gradually and she wept. A recollection of her sister stroking her in the same loving way, as they lay in their dank cell, cropped up in her mind. Renee was drifting to sleep. Before she completely left the waking world, Vince leaned forward to whisper in her ear, "I'm going back for Suako. You'll be all right here. I promise I'll come back for you. Nothing bad will happen to you like that ever again." More tears sprouted from her eyes. She rocked her head minutely to acknowledge his words, but was now a little too distracted to sleep. Vince cradled her in his arms and recited a poem to her to help relax her.

"Soft breezes,
Off of the Aquarius sea,
Rustle through leaves,
Which speak to me.
Dancing stars,
Twinkle on the velvet cloth of night,
As fireflies glow,
Above flowers in a green meadow..."

Vince had reiterated the poem in a flowing rhythm. The simplistic juvenile poem appealed to the child Renee never had a chance to grow up from. She nodded off, and he lay her down gently. He parted her side with a kiss to her forehead.

Though the building population had significantly decreased, the maintenance crews, and the soldier patrol, were working in high gear. It was tricky to move down the hallways, and took a timed strategy that included dodging in and out of the rooms along the way. Suako's ears listened as sharply as a bat's. It was taking a frustratingly long time to move from place to place, and time was running out...

The poison of the real world struck immediately. Seresuto and Adamu felt near the point of respiratory failure after crossing through into the vast outstretched lands outside of Torusan. Seresuto nearly collapsed from the drastic shock she endured. Adamu, not much stronger, helped her to walk. They stumbled with fuzzy vision across the southern badlands toward the beach shore. Adamu had tunnel vision for the dock where they'd come in.

By mid afternoon Tamiko and Jenko returned to Tamiko's office where everyone else had been waiting. Kato and Mei had gathered the story from Kazuo and Mack about Yu-Lee's strained relationship with her. When they first saw the young dominatrix looking woman they were thrown aback by her resemblance to her mother. Tamiko was the spitting image of Yu-Lee, only slightly more youthful, and with much different fashion taste. Tamiko's sour expression had not varied in the least. "How did it go?" Kazuo asked looking at the fatigued Jenko. "Good. It was just hard to find. There was so much down there. Tamiko found it quickly considering..." he shrugged, "No one questioned us either." "Good," Mack was relieved. Jenko pulled the file free from the innards of his coat. He passed it off to Mack, who in turn gave it to Kairu.

"What?" Kairu said taking it. "I want you to take that. It's *your* responsibility to keep that safe, and get it out of here," Mack told him. Mack needed Kairu to have a reason to regard his life after his distress for Masumi.

"Why me?" Kairu asked baffled. "Because, your highness, you are the most vital person to get out of here now. You have a rule to overtake. We have to watch your back anyway, and this keeps thing simple. The fewer worries the better," Mack replied tightening his leather finger free gloves around his hands. Kairu starred at the papers, and after giving it some thought, Kairu responsibly accepted, "Right."

Mack clipped on an extra ammunition belt, and clicked the safety off on his riffle, as well as his holstered gun. Mei fastened on an emergency blade, binding it to her ankle. Yu-Lee borrowed a handgun from Kato, and tried to clear her mind. Each fixed them self up in their own way for battle. Once Mack was ready, he stepped up to the impatient looking Tamiko, looking fearlessly into her eyes and said with a grin, "Now, Tamiko, we'd like to see Genjo."

They had Tamiko set up everything under their guiding influence. She'd used a device that connected the building, called a "telecommunication system" which worked regardless of the power outage. It allowed voice waves to travel along a wire and be heard at the other end of the wire just as if someone was speaking right next to you. Kairu remembered seeing the same thing in Tomakomai. Tamiko used it to arrange the meeting with Genjo.

All that was left to do was wait; the meeting was set for 1700h. It left just enough time for a brief discussion to prepare a plan of attack. They had thirty minutes before the meeting to get their strategy ready.

Kairu practised some of his offensive moves, which Mei paid close attention to. Yu-Lee had Kato show her the best way to aim, and how to deal with the recoil of her gun. The others simply sat around waiting, focusing their minds.

"I'm glad you're alive Kazuo," Mack told his long-lost friend. "I knew you'd find me. It's all I held onto all those years... You really saved me. Thank you, Mack," Kazuo held out his hand to shake Mack's. "Kazuo... I... it took so long..." Despite Mack's excuses Kazuo simply shook his head and kept his arm extended. Mack gave in and took Kazuo's hand. Kazuo shook and then pulled Mack in for a hug. "Thank you, my friend," Kazuo said from the bottom of his heart. Mack could barely keep his composure.

Just enough for one more floor... I'm so tired... Suako rested her pounding head in her hands. She slid down the wall she leaned against to the floor. She had worked non-stop for the entire day, and the strain was catching up to her. Her stomach was protesting from not being fed, and her dry throat scratched her as she breathed. *I need to finish...* Suako tried to stand back up. Her legs had turned into jelly and would not comply.

Suako sat there on the floor of a storage closet. There were no windows, but the door was cracked open just slightly, letting in light. Every so often some booted feet stomped on by. Her chest caved in with every exasperated breath. Suako felt her eyelids getting heavy, and she rested them closed. Suako's arms fell limply to her sides, motionless she rested on the hard-ceramic floor.

Renee… Why didn't I get you when I left? What happened? I can't remember… Wait! I do remember. I did look for you… I had been running. That stupid, stupid doctor… I was covered in his blood, it was dripping from my hair, and it stained my skin… I left the sword, but kept the gun... The halls were so dark, so long, and I was so tired… Somehow, I was running, the callus on my feet cracked. My muscles screamed in agony. So much pain… The scar… the laser wound was still burning…

For a moment Suako hushed her brain. Her thoughts dwelled solely about her mutilated stomach. Suako rubbed her hand over her belly, her fingers groping over the rise and fall of sloping scar tissue between patches of unaffected flesh. Her hand began to quiver as she touched the squiggly laser inflicted scar.

I found the lab you were in… I looked in and they were working on you… You weren't moving. I couldn't see you breathing… but that wasn't enough for me. I went to go in, but… then I saw that it… you're monitor didn't show a heart rate… It was flat… but… you really weren't dead. I'm so, so sorry… Renee…

Now on his own, Vince made excellent time. He'd crossed the terrain, heading back towards grid one, speedily in the truck. After burning rubber, he left the truck, and ducked back into the storm drains. He hurried through the tunnels back the way he'd come earlier. The water was freezing, and the foul odour was sickening. A mix of melted snow, dirt, garbage and random undiscernible things, were carried in off the streets, which made up this soup of filth he trudged through. Ignoring it, he waded his way through the cylinder tube of flowing drainage.

"It's time," Tamiko announced, looking up from her watch. "Good," Mack rubbed his fists together. Like a military accompaniment, they flocked around Tamiko as she went down the hall. Some random soldier had passed by them without a word. They dipped into the stairwell, and Mei and Kato winced upon the very first step, their hamstring pain came back to life all too quickly.

Just two stories up they went, and as they did Yu-Lee dashed up to Mack's side and whispered to him, "Please, don't harm Tamiko." "Don't worry. She'll be fine," he took Yu-Lee's hand, "I promise." Back out into the polished looking halls, they stepped out of the stairwell. Two adjoining thick wooden doors awaited them at the very end of the hall, and they seemed to grow larger with every step forward. Kazuo felt the heat of the sun through the floor to ceiling windows lining this hallway. He'd not felt such glorious radiant heat in years, and missed the simple pleasure terribly. The thought of that alone injected him with the courage to enter the conference room ahead.

Mei and Kato interlocked fingers, and kissed each other while walking; both pulsating with a burning passion for revenge that was preparing to erupt. What had been awaited so long to achieve was now but a few footsteps away. They treaded lightly on the floor, with a feeling of divine inner peace. The past soon could be kept in the past, and old ghosts laid to rest.

Jenko walked alongside Mack, he supported his long-term friend to the bitter end. He had found himself feeling a new sense of commitment. No longer was he simply tagging along for the journey, Jenko felt an obligation to his planet. Yu-Lee attended Jenko's other side, and she was ready to fight for that which she had dedicated all of her existence to: *Life*.

The ever unyielding and unwavering appeal of Mack kept up its appearance. His will was as strong as iron, and he was ready to make his assault. This would be the icing on the cake. The Company had made its mistake by bringing them here, something they would not have been able to do on their own. They only invisible way to sneak into grid one was threw the drainpipes, which, can only be unlocked and opened from the grid one side. Now they could bring down the C.D.F.P. at its core, and as well, prevent its reconstruction. *Justice... Sweet, sweet justice.*

Every piece of the walk down that last stretch of their journey inscribed itself forever within them. The smell was of a waxed floor drying, coffee in the air, and Tamiko's rose perfume. The granite floors shimmered in the daylight. Maroon curtains were drawn back from the eyes of windows by gold tasselled ropes. Every set of doors was of a dark walnut wood, and the wallpaper was rich yellow-orange, with deep brown trim that matched the wood of the doors. It was peacefully quiet less for their footsteps. The doors came...

Uhn... Where am I?... What's that beeping? Ugh... stop... Oh no! Suako sprang awake. "Fuck! What time is it?" she smacked her head getting up too fast in the dark. Dumping everything back into her satchel, Suako threw it over her shoulder, struggling with the strap for her other arm. To the door she went and peeked out the crack. The coast was clear, and it was still light out. She breathed a relieving sigh. *You're lucky... damn lucky girl...*

"Hello," Mack announced their entry in a cocky tone, confident, and filled with bitter anger. Tamiko ran in and over to Koto who stood by his father. The windowless room was constructed all out of wood from the swamps of Quan. Portraits of past C.D.F.P. chairmen filled the wood panel divots. A mahogany boarder, carved uniquely for each individual leader, framed each portrait. Genjo sat beneath his father's picture at the far end of the room, at the head of the conference table.

Around a polished black glass table, Genjo had been waiting. The podgy man reached for his glasses without any sense of haste. Yoshida sat to the right of Genjo, and his jaw had nearly hit the table when her saw Mack and his entourage stroll in. Yoshida went to stand up, but the rise of Mack's hand had him lower himself back into his seat. Mei and Kato took sentry at the flank, and closed the doors. They slammed as if to make the statement, *You're trapped!*

Mack took a seat directly opposite of Genjo. Kazuo, Yu-Lee, and Kairu swarmed his sides and took their seats. Simply being there in bigger numbers, a sensation of power came authoritatively to Mack, and feeling that commanding power, Mack took a new lease on the situation. Originally, he'd planned to come in and destroy the source from which the veil spawned. Now he'd decided on a much better fate...

"Who are you?" Genjo asked adjusting his glasses on his face. "Mack Yamamoto," he replied from across the way. An obvious bell of recognition was ringing in Genjo's head. He noticed Kazuo next to Mack, and then finally realised that Mack was the man that had once confronted him many years ago. Yu-Lee's striking resemblance to Tamiko also got some wheels turning. "You're dead?" Genjo was confused, remembering an accident report that mentioned Mack's untimely death. "You should have listened to Yoshida," Mack smugly replied.

Genjo took a moment to gather his thoughts. Yoshida looked to be on the brink of exploding, fidgeting while trying not to speak. Koto just stood there nonplussed, with Tamiko near him, his arms crossed. "So, what is this?" Genjo asked raising his head. Mack was ecstatic that he finally asked. Calmly leaning forward with his elbows on the table, Mack took his time to speak, "The end of the C.D.F.P." Mack felt a sense of relief after the words had been verbalised. Genjo couldn't retain his laughter, but it soon faded when he saw that Mack had not flinched. No one else had laughed either.

"You can't possibly think a hand full of people can destroy this company!" Genjo angrily spat. "Oh, but I have," Mack's casual response just made Genjo ever angrier. The man slammed his hand down against the table. "How?!" he growled. So, Mack explained, "It was all a matter of time. After we learned of the documentation that finds you guilty of having full knowledge of the toxins your company produces, and still continuing production, we just had to find them. You hid Kazuo, the only man who knew where these were. But we found him, and he gave us the documents. They'll be in the Empires hands in short order. Your organization is finished." Glowing smiles appeared on everyone surrounding Mack.

Genjo clenched his fists, and he looked like a spoiled child in a toy store whose parents would not buy him a toy he wanted. "You can't possibly think we believe you," Yoshida stood up and towered over the table. "Believe it or not, *you're ruined,*" Mack articulated his last words slowly. "How the hell did you get out of your cells?" Yoshida demanded. He was still in disbelief of his opponent's resurrection to the playing field. "You're not the only one with friends," Mack replied.

Vince grabbed onto the ladder and crawled up through the doors he'd left open for himself, after having unlocked it to enter the drain earlier. He pushed up a grate, and crawled out into the cave like hallway of the C.D.F.P.'s very bottom floor. Vince was wet with filth up to his knees, and as he came up on the floor dry dirt stuck to his wet pant legs, and damp hands. He ignored the grit and got up onto his feet.

Over to a torch he hurried, and he checked his timer. "Fifty-three minutes…" he muttered to himself as he caught his breath. One arm extended, dirty palm pressed against the dirt rock wall, he rested, briefly. Breathing in and out, slowly he tried to lower the pace of his racing heart. *Common Vince... no time to rest, it's time to go.* He pep-talked himself.

"Well then," Mack pushed his chair back and stood up. "You're all under arrest," they were silent in acceptance. Genjo maintained a spiteful glare as everyone on Mack's side circled around the table toward Yoshida to attain them as prisoners. Mack drew a pair of cuffs, which he'd gathered from the lower level's supply room. Mack walked to Yoshida to take him down himself. *Click!* "Like hell!" Yoshida raged, pulling out his revolver, and pointing his gun at Mack. Mack froze in pose. He'd left his shotgun over on his chair, so he couldn't counter.

Mei and Kato ran from the doors, weapons drawn to reclaim the situation. Unexpectedly, Mack impetuously knocked Yoshida's gun to the floor with a roundhouse kick. A round was fired, damaging one of the founders' pictures. They brawled, their deep hatred, seeded from long ago, finally released. Malice and detestation fanned the flames of this dog-eyed fight.

Genjo dove for the dropped revolver, and Mei saw him from the corner of her eye. She jumped up onto the table, and then ran over to the escape oriented man below. Her knees impacted his back as she dropped on him, causing him to sprawl out on the floor beneath her. He screamed, but then reached for the gun. A cold metal blade crept up against his neck. "Just try it!" Mei screamed, only wishing for him to keep going so she could watch him bleed out like a stuck pig. Her eyes strained open, a near insanity glazed over them; Genjo stopped cold turkey.

A flurry of flying fists came down in smacking blows, while legs flailed, and voices raged. Battle cries and wails of inflicted pain merged into one loud blur. Yoshida had Mack on the ground, his hands squeezed tightly about Mack's neck, which was turning purple. Mack swung at the air, but Yoshida was out of his reach. Mack squirmed for air. *POW!*

Mack's face was showered in bright red blood and brain matter, as Yoshida toppled over, dead, onto the floor. Like a fountain, blood leaked out into a puddle on the floor, it oozed out sticky and vibrantly shinning. Mack lifted himself up onto his elbows, and looked down at the accumulating sanguine fluid, which, in its purity, reflected his face as clearly as a mirror would. It was beautiful in its own morbid way, and it mesmerised Mack temporarily. He didn't even hear Tamiko shriek.

Mack turned his head to see Kazuo, chest heaving, with the smoking gun still aimed in his hands. He had an amazing look of satisfaction on his face, as if a great weight had finally been lifted. There were no signs of remorse. Yoshida lay there slumped over with his eyes wide open, his face had released its tension, yet kept the intense expression it last held. Eerily he looked to still be alive.

In the hysteria of it all Genjo tried again for the gun, and his fingers tickled the tip. He wriggled it into his hand. "Mei!" Kato screamed. She looked down to see Genjo swinging the barrel up at her, and instinct took over at once. Like cutting through butter the blade sliced through soft neck tissues. Warm blood gushed out over Mei hand like water from a pipe. Genjo dropped the gun and held his neck as he choked to death on his own blood.

Tamiko stood there looking on at the horror scene, frozen in place. The reality of the situation was hitting home. Her head swayed just noticeably back and forth, and every exhumed bit of air made a subtle sound. The bloodbath before her was the crashing of all she'd been working for. "Eh, everyone!" Kato suddenly interjected. "Where di' Koto go?" Eyes looked around the room. Jenko saw past Kato's head and to the open unblocked doors. Mack's shotgun was gone. "Oh no..." Mack uttered.

"We need to get out of here now," Mack said. Kairu pointed his gun at Tamiko, "Where's Okichi?!" he yelled. "I, I, I'll take you to here!" Tamiko replied, terrified.

Suako had finally finished the last placement, she left the bag she'd been carrying, and got up to leave. Stepping out of the office and into the hall, the coast was clear. She was only on the twentieth floor. Looking at her timer she still had forty-one minutes; more than enough time to clear the premises.

Suako jogged toward the other side of the floor to get to the stairs, when suddenly, there was a loud *bang!* Then like a swish of air near her ear, she heard a blowing noise. Right in front of her line of vision, a bullet intercepted the wall, exploding plaster and chalk onto the floor. Immediately she dove into the nearest room. *Holy shit!*

Gathering her wits, Suako crouched low to the floor. Her heart was pumping double time from the sudden scare. Fumbling for her pistol, Suako pulled it free of her belt holster. She trembled as a fretful shiver quivered up her spine from the thought of the close call in the hall. Taking in a deep cleansing breath, she attempted to bring herself down to a more focused state. Now ready, she listened for the approaching footsteps. With her target in her mind's eye, she prepared herself.

Out the door she hung, pistol aimed at her enemy. She pulled the trigger. *Tick!* Nothing happened. Again. *Tick!* Suako pulled back. *Shit! What the hell... Oh common! Not now, you can't be... jammed? ... Fuck!* Suako tossed the useless mechanism aside, and pulled out her second gun. Suako checked the chamber of the handgun, it held only two bullets. She had no extra ammunition for this specific gun either. Again, Suako prepared herself, with one long exhalation...

POW! POW! Two simultaneous shots brought down the unsuspecting officer, both bullets planted themselves directly between his eyes. Suako sunk back into the office. Now useless by itself, Suako discarded her handgun. She took a moment to gather herself, when she heard a bunch of footsteps coming the same way the officer had. Sticking her head back out to take a peek, she saw several approaching soldiers. She pulled her head back before any of them could see her.

Desperation became Suako's predominant feeling. Frustrated with her situation, Suako was just about ready to cry; the stress was taking its toll. Between her teeth she bit down on her bottom lip, in an attempt to focus, but her concentration was scattered. Though the footsteps had stopped around the distance back where the officer she'd shot down, Suako *knew* that they'd be coming toward her sooner of later.

Step! Step! Someone was coming. *Kairu... I hope you taught me right...* She listened intently to place her enemy's location. For simplicity of movement, Suako slipped her jacked off, shimmying it silently down her arms, then tossed it aside. Closing her eyes, she clasped her hands together. *Spirits please watch over me...* she shook in her skin. Opening her eyes, she separated her hands and curled them into white-knuckled fists. Hopping up onto her feet, she waited with her ear by the edge of the door.

The man came up almost beside her when he entered the room. Suako could hear him breathing lightly; she could tell he was trying to be quiet, but she was wise to that game. With a courageous leap of faith, Suako jumped out from her hideaway. The soldier was taken aback by the surprise appearance, and she took advantage of it. Without pausing, Suako kicked free his howitzer, which flew away and thwacked against the adjacent wall. Scared frozen the soldier just stood there, cowering. Just as Kairu had showed her before, she used her middle and index fingers to jab at his neck. She hit the body point dead on, and the soldier dropped instantaneously upon contact to the floor unconscious.

"Get her!" yelled one of the men still surrounding the fallen officer, who had seen the incident. He pointed at Suako as if she were some sort of animal. Three soldiers, two men and a woman who looked just as masculine as the actual men, sprinted forward past the man pointing at Suako threateningly. Each searched for their piece with their hands as they ran at her. Suako brought her guard up and, and swallowing her fear ran at them. She knew had to engage them in a fight before they could get a chance to shoot her.

Suako could see their eyes as plain as anything else, and they came at her with an empty fury. They fought because of orders. Only one of the men showed any true depth of hatred toward her for the murder they'd stumbled upon. Like a tiger he showed his teeth, and Suako worried he just might growl and then tear her to pieces. And they came...

Ten minutes they were still at it. The original three on one battle had morphed down to two on one. Suako had got in a good kick to one man's temple with her steel toed boots, and the impact killed him instantly. Then the C.D.F.P. replenished itself when the rear man, who had scared Suako with his war cry to attack her earlier, took the third man's place. Suako had managed to disarm all of them as soon as they came within her reach. Then she'd managed to keep them busy enough so that they wouldn't have the time to retrieve their lost weapons.

Exhaustion was wearing down on Suako. Tension had built up at the base of her neck, and her sides had taken the brunt force of the beating. Suako bled from newly inflicted cuts of her arms, legs and torso. Brutally, the feline-like woman jumped at Suako and dug her nails deep within Suako's back, and dragged them downward, tearing away her skin. Suako arched her back and screamed in agony. Saliva flew from her mouth. Suako leaned forward and balanced on one leg as she lifted the other, and pounded it back down on the woman's chest. The female soldier flew back and hit her head on a doorframe, falling down, she didn't get back up.

Every extending limb cried out, Suako burned throughout her entire body. Each time she punched out a stinging sensation buzzed where her arm folded at the elbow. Red skin poured out perspiration, and called for oxygen. Tuffs of hair had loosened themselves from her ponytail. Suako panted heavily. The world seemed to be spinning at the pace of the battle. *Duck! Weave! Block! Hit! Kick! Duck! Jump! Duck! Punch! Parry! Kick, kick! Trip! Block! Throw!* Signals to react released from her brain without anytime to consider.

What time is it! Shit! STOP ATTACKING ME! FUCK OFF! Ugh... "Oww!" *I can't keep this up... What am I going to do? ... Ouff!* "Ouff!" *Son of a bitch... It hurts...* Panic was setting in. As Suako became more distracted she also became more of a punching bag. A final boot to the gut brought down Suako to her hands and knees. Now infuriated, Suako scowled at them. A second foot was coming at her head, but Suako swerved out of the way and then tripped the angered man onto the floor.

The other guy had used the time to run and grab one of the lost guns off of the floor. Suako scurried to her feet, and kicked it from him before he could shoot. It spiralled round and round then landed in Suako's hands. *POW!* She shot the soldier down dead. Spinning around she shot the one behind her as well. Her bushy ponytail came following around, sticking to her damp skin as it stung her, hitting her like a whip.

Standing, there breathing heavily, Suako's mind was running to catch up to her actions. Once it had processed everything she lowed the gun. She looked at the pile of bodies lying ahead of her. Suako's pulse continued at the pace of a racehorse as she stood in stillness. Hot sweat now chilled her. Like a striking bolt of lightening, Suako remembered the time. Suako spun back around to get to the stairwell. Then without warning it came... *POW!*

Suako lay sprawled out on the floor. One arm lay over her midsection, the other curved about her head on the floor. Suako's eyes darkened, and a ridge formed between her eyebrows. The nauseating raw taste of salty fleshy goo dominated her mouth. Blood trickled down from her lips. A wide gaping hole in her stomach bleed out profusely and gathered in a growing pool beneath her awkwardly displayed body.

Time seemed to have been suspended for Suako. She didn't stir from where she lay. Self pity deteriorated relatively quickly as the expanse of endless time weaned away. The morbid situation she took into acceptance, as the confusion faded to dust. Unexpectedly it seemed that fate had dropped by to pay its respects; it was like a veil lifting itself up, uncloaking her clouded vision. It was spectacular enlightenment. As slow as ever her heart took a beat, and the throb echoed in the chasm of her expanded rib cage, making its way through her entire body, and causing stress on her wound.

Seconds later Vince came up the last few stairs as skidded into the corridor. He had heard the enormous shot that followed the two prior ones. Just too late, he'd seen Koto come down the stairs from above and swivel into the hallway before him. He went to examine the situation and then he saw her; his beloved splayed out on the floor bleeding horribly. She was battered and bruised, her amber hair sticking together in a mix of her own sweat and velvet-like gore.

An uncontrollable rage came over Vince. Like an animal, Vince jumped on Koto and brought him to the floor. In the shock of the back-attack, Koto dropped the shotgun. Koto struggled over onto his back to see who was on him. Vince pounded down on Koto with heavy unrelenting fists. When Koto tried to block his face from the furious beating, Vince came down even harder and broke his arm. Koto shrieked like a suffering animal at the crippling blow.

Vince felt as if he was sitting back and watching it all happen, like some sort of movie. He watched as Koto's handsome face as it migrated into a bloody, disfigured, and unrecognisable pulp. Each stroke evoked a new squealing cry. Koto had a few good swings in, but Vince had been so enraged that his body felt numb to the hits. In desperation Koto remembered a he'd had a pen in his pocked. Reaching down he pulled it out, and with substantial, force he drove it into Vince's right arm. Vince didn't even flinch.

Now intoxicated with passionate ferocity Vince took Koto's head in his hands and slammed it down repeatedly against the floor. Just three crashes down and Koto stopped moving. A rattling pair of keys slid out from Koto's pocket onto the floor from the jostling. Vince pocketed them, then checked, and Koto's neck, and he could feel that he still had a pulse. Regardless it was time to go, and with difficulty, Vince dragged himself away. His fists were a royal mess, already badly swollen.

Vince's body wobbled as the energy he'd invoked left him. He pulled free the pen that had been awkwardly injected into his arm, and now that the adrenaline was fading, he felt the pain acutely. By Suako's side, he dropped down to the ground. His eyes consumed the scene; Suako stared up at the ceiling, a water glaze covered her eyes. "S... Suako?" he whispered weakly, holding back a floodgate of tears. "Vince..." her voice was serene. Vince pulled off his jacket and placed it on the stomach wound. He put her hand on top of it to hold it down.

Remorsefully, Vince looked down on his sweet Suako, and caressed her face with his trembling fingers. Vince looked down to his watch, *Still, sixteen* minutes...

they had time. "I'm getting you out of here!" carefully he swept up Suako into his arms. He could hear the trickling of blood drop from her sopping tank top onto the puddle on the floor.

Fast on his feet, Vince scuttled down the stairs. Suako's eyes began to roll back. "No, no, no! Suako, stay with me... Stay with me Suako..." he cried as they plummeted down the wall-hugging spiralling stair case. Talking to Suako constantly as they went, to keep her conscious, he prayed for her to stay awake and alive. The twenty floors seemed to vanish in a blink of the eye.

Running out through the lobby, Vince tried to glimpse the time on his watch once more, but the bounce of his step as he ran blurred his sight too badly to read the numbers though. The suction release of the door sounded as Vince kicked it open. Out into the parking lot, they left the C.D.F.P. headquarters. Most of the lot was empty, but ten feet ahead Koto's black sports car was parked. Vince thought the boy had looked high enough up on the food chain for it to be his, so he checked the keys in the door, and sure enough, it opened.

Laying Suako carefully down in passenger seat, Vince secured her safely. Now scuttling over to the driver's side, he hopped in and put the key in the ignition. The engine growled loudly as it was revved up. Vince burned rubber as he screeched free of the parking spot, and the tire treads imprinted themselves into the asphalt. Through the parking lot they sped at full speed. Pulling into the lamp lit city streets, Vince continued to speed away. He squeezed the steering wheel between his puffy fingers, while dodging the regular city traffic. He peered over at Suako worrisomely from time to time, her color was draining away and she was turning a pasty white. Honking horns screamed at his fly-by driving.

Moments later, Mack and the others had escaped out of the building with Okichi in tow, and they trudged to the back of the C.D.F.P. parking lot by foot, before taking cover behind a stone carved company sign. There they waited for Vince and Suako to regroup with them, as planned. They also were on the lookout for Koto. Tamiko had come with them; Yu-Lee had forcefully dragged her along. Behind the company sign they watched and waited, as the seconds counted down...

In a straight arrow they went to the edge of grid one, where Vince bulldozed through the barrier fence. The front tire was impaled on a piece of rebar, so after busting through, the car spun and looped around in the dirty garbage yard they'd emerged into. Vince put the car in park, and then got out of the car and ran around to Suako's doors. He pulled her out and cradled her in his arms as he sunk down to the muddy terrace. He gently and lovingly rocked her back and forth in his arms.

They sat facing the C.D.F.P. building, and it looked dim in the early evening sky. Vince looked down at his timer, there was only thirty seconds left on the count down. Suako rested her eyes closed, her energy clearly gone. "Suako? Suako open your eyes... You have to see the show sweety..." he told her in desperate hope. Nervously, he entangled his fingers in his long hair. Suako moaned, opening her darkened eyes, she looked out into the world, and right away she fixated her vision on Vince. He smiled, fighting back the welling build-up of misery from expression. "Look!" he said pointing over to The Company headquarters. Suako's eyes lowered down to see it.

Seconds later it began; great waves of bursting flames exploded, shattering windows into millions of tiny shards. They tinkled like the clinging of the Champaign glasses in Tomakomai on Suako's birthday. The lower part of the building was writhed in flames of bright brilliant orange shades. It lit up the surrounding area with it's bright emitting light. The life-filled flames searched for escape from the chamber of the building, and it pillared upwards.

Next came the sound, like the thunder following lightening, the explosion finally caught up to them. Suako's planted bombs had all gone off simultaneously, erupting to create one massive fireworks show. For several seconds the building just stood their, never looking as good as it did with whisking flames to wisp about the shaking structure.

The otherwise quiet night air was disrupted by the chaotic demise of a fortress of evil. Moments later began to collapse in on itself, and the rumble of the falling building shook the ground. The tremors could be felt from miles away, and it had been deeply satisfying. The gratification of a life's devotion turned into success was indescribable. Black and grey smoke climbed, billowing into the plush pink of the early evening sky, up from the rubble of a fallen empire.

Vince shed tears of joy and of despair, his heart fearful for Suako. Suako was mesmerized with the sight of the destruction. Her nightmare was finally over, her soul could rest, and she took from it a sense of closure. Vince's heart guided his eyes back to Suako. In her own time, she pulled her eyes away and looked upon her lover's face. "Vince…" she smiled. "I'm here," he fought the lump in the back of his throat. "We did it…" a tear streamlined down her ghostly white cheek. Vince swept up her hand in his. She squeezed it with what little strength she had retained, "Yeah… We did…" Sorrow afflicted his very soul. "Vince, I'm sorry…" she tried to apologize, but Vince hushed her. "Suako don't. You didn't do anything wrong…" His voice cracked. Vince pressed his lips against her bloody hand to kiss her reassuringly. Suako once again smiled, the blood in the corner of her mouth twinkled in the light. They sat solemnly, just being with each other. There was so much to say that nothing could come out. A sudden worry broke Suako's silence. "…Renee?" she wondered what happened. "Don't worry. She's safe. I took her to the hideout," each word was a struggle to produce.

"Vince, I need," Suako coughed, choking on her own blood. She pushed through it bitterly, "I need you… you to do me a favour…" Her hand now squeezed his with some strength. "Anything," Vince wept. "Tell Mack, thanks… thanks for everything…" she said. Vince gasped, not wanting to admit to the morbid truth of reality. "Suako," he shook his head fearfully. Suako simply nodded with pleading eyes. For a minute Vince had to stop, he wanted time to stop, but it refused to comply. He nodded his head for her to continue.

"Tell Mei, and, and Kato... Be strong..." she paused. "Vince... remember in Yokutan... We bought Mei the pendant?" he nodded. "... I've carried it with me since... It's in my pocket... Make sure she gets it..." Vince nodded vigorously. "...Let Kairu know he'll be... he'll be a great, great chief... Tell Jenko to keep travelling..." she coughed again. The blood bath she lay it was growing. "Yu-Lee... tell her I'm sorry... so sorry I couldn't study magick with her... and take care of Renee..." Suako started to shiver, her body was going into severe shock. Her hand had gone cold. "Suako no..." Vince was losing his voice.

"Vince, I... I love you so much... I'm sorry we can't be together... I wanted so much for that..." her voice wheezed out. "No, Suako... no..." Vince's voice cracked up. He couldn't bare the thought of loosing her. "I'm so... so cold... Please... Vince... s, sing for me like you used to..." Suako was getting drowsy, her time left was short.

To the best he was able, Vince tried to fulfill Suako's request. His voice was shattered, but with all of his strength he tried to hold it together:

"Come my love,
Let's fly away,
Into a never-ending day,
Where I'll be yours,

And you'll be mine,
There we'll stay,
For all of time..."

  Vince couldn't continue, his voice fell flat, and tears overcame him. "Thank you..." she looked up gratefully to him. Vince pulled her close and kissed her salty lips one last time. He wished this moment would stretch on into eternity. He could barely breath. The pain in his heart was so great it felt as if it would kill him inside. He dreaded to pull away, but desired to look upon her gorgeous face.

  Their eyes locked, staring into each other's souls, Vince came to accept her coming earthly departure. Suako's eyelids came down slowly, and when they reopened they twinkled, and saw past Vince to the horizon. "Wow... Look at that sunset..." she said dreamily. Vince turned to see it, the sky was a dusty rose above followed a pale yellow. A pillar of rising black smoke dissipated into the blue of the darkening sky, where the first stars of the night had come out to shine. The top rim of the sun was just dipping beneath the horizon line, making the few tiny tufts of cloud in the sky glow like threaded gold; it was a heavenly sight. Vince's eyes welled up with tears, he looked back at Suako, and felt his heart skip a beat.

  Like an angel she lay in his arms. Closing her eyes, she let out one final breath, and her body became heavy in his arms. Suako's grasp on his hand went limp, and her ribs collapsed. As her last breath swept across Vince's body, he swore he could feel her spirit pass right through him. A rupturing pain, horrendous, worse than any physical wounding, burst inside of his being. A piece of his soul was dying.

Vince began hyperventilating, and started to gasp for air, as if it were being denied to his very being. Mournfully he wailed, as the excruciating anguish inside him searched for a release. Vince held Suako tight and rocked back and forth, and the motion helped to soothe his broken soul. He kissed her forehead and stroked her head. She was still warm to the touch. Incoherently he whispered to Suako, "...I love you... Don't go... I didn't get a chance... Oh god, please, god, no! ..." Up to his heart he lifted Suako's cold dead fingers and pressed them against his chest. Suako looked like a porcelain doll.

Sitting there alone, but for Suako's lifeless body, Vince stayed with her for what seemed to be forever. He didn't want to let her go. Nothing else in life mattered to him now. Suako, his beloved Suako, was lost to the wind. He grieved late into the night. When Vince finally lay her down, he wiped away the blood from her mouth. He could still taste it in his mouth. Respectively he folded her arms across her stomach, and there he stayed, by her side, until the morning light.

In the parking lot of the C.D.F.P. building, watching the building explode and burn was much more intense. The shattering glass was ear piercing, and the heat from the blasts were tangible. Mack had watched in awe as the building burst into flames. Tamiko watched it all in horror, her life, her dreams, shattering to pieces just the building. Yu-Lee watched with a sense of justice, and peace, and the balance of the planet was one step closer to being restored. Jenko walked up behind Yu-Lee and put his arms around her, and they watched together.

Long supressed pain in Mei and Kato welt up at the culmination of their plan. Tears ran unrelenting, it was a cleanse for their tortured souls. Kazuo fell to his knees, as he watched his long-time prison burn, his soul was finally liberated. Kairu stood, ever the warrior, looking at the burning building as it collapsed. No one heard him whisper, "...for you, Masumi..."

Long into the night the building burned, and they watched it go in silence. Each worried as the hours went by and there had been no sign of Vince or Suako. They continued to hold out hope, waiting for their friends to show up. Tamiko noticed Koto's car missing from the parking lot, and held out hope he'd escaped alive. None of them slept that night.

When the sun peeked back up the next morning, and there had still been no sign of Suako or Vince, Mack decided that it was time to go looking for them. As they approached the building to search the rubble, they noticed some tire tread imprints. They hotwired one of the cars in the parking lot, and followed the trail to the Grid One boarder, and out into the disposal yard. There they stumble upon the mortifying scene, and after some time, Vince told them all that had happened...

And so, they fell...

Chapter 28: Freedom

"Dear Journal,

It is March 29th. It was exactly one year ago today that the C.D.F.P. fell to ruin, and it has been a long year since. After the decimation of the Company Headquarters, Torusan was in disarray. The poor citizens rejoiced, while the rich wondered and worried about their livelihood. Mei and Kato had apparently sent a message, in old Morse code, to Kairu's father, Mu-Kai, in Yokutan. He brought a platoon of soldiers to help assist with the city. They calmed the city down, restored order, and monitored it.

Luck it seemed had been on our side. Not two days later did Seresuto and Adamu return to Torusan with Keiji Kane. Our journey across the ocean had not been in vain. Keiji had had his suspicions about the C.D.F.P. prior to our arrival, and Aater our plea, he decided to see for himself. When Yoshida had shipped us back to Torusan, Mr. Kane had followed in a ship from behind.

As soon as Keiji had the documents for proof, his authoritative reproach changed the East Green Continent forever. He declared the C.D.F.P. would never rise again, and he had his troops hunt down and capture anyone who had lived that had been voluntarily involved with the company. The planetary cleansing had thus begun.

Next, Keiji had appointed Mack to govern over the affairs of the entire East Green Continent, as reward for his contributions in bringing down the Imperial criminals. Kazuo was made his second in command. Mack's first order of business was to activate the continent-wide oxygen dome. The four co-dependent devices were located at the cardinal points of the continent. After he had found them all, and input the codes in each, breathable air was provided for all. Within a month of the C.D.F.P.'s ruin the whole continent had air. Following that, Mack had set out to destroy all of the remaining generators.

When summer came, we mutually we agreed to destroy Torusan and then rebuild it from scratch. It had become nothing more then a junk heap. So together, we disposed of it. We had it all embedded with high-explosives, and by the end of it, the city was nothing more than a pile of dust. Immediately clean up and the rebuilding proceeded.

The earth has seemed to be responding well. The massive earthquakes and turbulent weather have rapidly decreased, and some new plant life has emerged. Slowly but surely it has been accumulating. As well, we have brought animals over from the Imperial Continent to repopulate, and they have been giving off abundant offspring here.

Yu-Lee had a temple built in Quan, where she now resides with Tamiko. As I mentioned in my previous entries, we had discovered she had been being brainwashed. She is doing much better now. They live a happy life and teach the children of Quan about life energy and magick.

Mei and Kato have been journeying at Mack's command, bringing down all of the generators this past year. They are planning to cross the waters and go to Sheikarah when their work is done here. They want to bring air dome technology to the desert continent. They are leaving next week. Mei is expecting their child in May. They hope to return here in time for the birth. Mack has set up his offices in Torusan where he works. He is finally able to relax. I spoke to him about it just last night, and he has told me he is now able to sleep at night. He and Kazuo are inseparable. They have been working together to unify the Continent. Most days they can be found fishing at a nearby lake.

Jenko has set up a home base back in Torusan. He frequents Quan for it's delectable fish whenever the chance arises, and to visit Yu-Lee. Now that he has mapped both the East green and the Imperial continents he plans to go to the desert continent to map it next. He is travelling over with Mei and Kato next week.

As for me, with Renee, I have kept my promise to Suako to watch over her. She seems to do a little better every day. I watch over her like I know Suako would have wanted me to. As she experiences life, I can see the troubled pieces of her past fade away. She reminds me so much of her sister...

I've spent much of this past year recounting our journey. We cannot let history repeat itself. I'm finishing up the last details on the book, and will get it into mass printing by summer. No one should forget the horrible things that have been done, or the people who sacrificed themselves to save everyone...

Suako's body rests at the bottom of the sea with Masumi. We found Masumi's remains and took them both out into the ocean a year ago. Kairu released Masumi into the water. She submerged and sunk down to the seabed. Then I placed Suako in the still waters where she drifted away from me. Darkness engulfed her and she faded from my sight forever... I think of her daily. Mei never takes off the pendant we got her that day. Suako and her were like sisters themselves.

I find myself going to the shorelines whenever I can find the time. The waves breaking on the coastal cove make me feel like Suako is trying to speak to me. When the tide brushes in up over my feet I feel like I can touch her soul. I talk to her there. I know she can hear me. I only wish she could be there with me to see what her sacrifice helped to do...

As for Kairu, he has become Chief of Old Ryoko. He is greatly respected there. He reads through his ancestors' scriptures daily. The city is blooming as it once had before the Imperial invasion so long ago. Seresuto and Adamu have returned there where they live a simple life.

Today we're all here in Quan together. It's Kairu's wedding day. He and Okichi are to be wed by Otojiro later today. I can hear the children playing. Spring is early this year. Already greenery and budding blossoms are showing themselves. The festivities will be starting shortly. Mack as well deemed today to be one of commemoration. Anyone who has ever died due to the C.D.F.P. is remembered on this day..."

"Vince?" Renee ran into his tent. Her gauze dress swished about as she did. Her hair was held back in the same way Suako used to hold hers. "Vince, common! They'll be starting soon!" Renee called to him. Her cheeks were rosy, and eyes brightened by her sprint inside. "I'll be right there," he replied turning from his journal. She nodded, smiled, and then ran off.

"It is time for me to go and join in on the festivities. The salmon is beginning to tease my nose.

Sincerely,
Vince"

Vince placed his pen down on the open book's page, and went outside. White material draped over nearly everything decoratively. There were tables and tables of delectable food laid out, and the delectable aroma's rose up into the air. The sky was as crystal clear as it had been a year ago. The sun was warm, and the snow vanished. People were laughing and dancing as music played.

Birds were chirping merrily around the marshes and in the bushes. Children were running around with spring blossoms in their hair, playing with streamers. Around the bonfire friends awaited Vince with cold sweet ale. Renee went and took his hand playfully, and led him over to the others. Vince peered over to the pond and thought he saw Suako's reflection in its murky waves. He blinked and she was gone. He smiled and sat down with his friends to celebrate. Life was decadent.

"Suako you will live on forever inside of me..."

We have a new world to start over with. We have another chance for all life to start over. We are no longer prisoners. We have...

Freedom.

Acknowledgements

This book was an incredible undertaking, and I am truly grateful for all the support and feedback I have received over the years. It has helped me to fine tune this novel so it can be best enjoyed.

A big thank you to my mother, Deborah Rose, who went through the manuscript to help me start editing.

Thank you to my husband, Daniel McCutcheon, who when we'd just started dating read this book, despite not being much of a reader, and encouraged me to keep going. In addition to supporting me, I'm beyond words grateful for the incredible book cover he's designed for me.

Thank you to Kayln Jones, Benjamin Isreal, and Andrew Fantasia, my wonderful friends, who read the raw script and gave me critical feedback that helped me sculpt the end result into what it is today. I appreciate you help beyond words.

Lastly, thank you, for reading this book, and embarking on this fantastical journey with me. It's my greatest joy to share this story; this is all for you.

ABOUT THE AUTHOR

Amanda Rose, author of Manifesting on Purpose, is an avid reader and storyteller. Working in a variety of mediums and genres, communicating new ways of thinking is her passion.

Amanda works as an online Health and Fitness coach, Law of Attraction Coach, Actor, Model, and Writer. Residing in Kingston, Ontario, with her husband and 3 cats, Amanda is currently working on her next novel. Get in touch with Amanda by visiting her website, www.AmandaRoseFitness.com

Made in the USA
Middletown, DE
16 February 2019